IN PASSION'S GRIP

Serena began sobbing, and then jumped in surprise when Fairborough suddenly embraced her from behind.

"Let go of me!" she cried as she thrashed violently in his grasp. Faith, but he felt as strong and solid as a fortress. His arms were thick and firm as they wrapped around her, and for a fleeting moment she thought she might turn into liquid as her knees buckled beneath her. She felt as if he were squeezing all the rage out of her, all the grief, and she tightened her entire body, as if by doing so she could keep that rage and grief from escaping. She didn't want to lose them. She wanted to keep them. She wanted to stay furious with him.

But she also wanted to remain in his embrace forever.

TRUE PRETENSES

KAREN LINGEFELT

LEISURE BOOKS   NEW YORK CITY

LEISURE BOOKS ®

November 2003

Published by

Dorchester Publishing Co., Inc.
200 Madison Avenue
New York, NY 10016

If you purchased this book without a cover you should be aware that this book is stolen property. It was reported as "unsold and destroyed" to the publisher and neither the author nor the publisher has received any payment for this "stripped book."

Copyright © 2003 by Karen Lingefelt

All rights reserved. No part of this book may be reproduced or transmitted in any form or by any electronic or mechanical means, including photocopying, recording or by any information storage and retrieval system, without the written permission of the publisher, except where permitted by law.

ISBN 0-8439-5292-X

The name "Leisure Books" and the stylized "L" with design are trademarks of Dorchester Publishing Co., Inc.

Printed in the United States of America.

Visit us on the web at www.dorchesterpub.com.

DEDICATION

*In loving memory of my two favorite heroines:
My paternal grandmother, Estene Fletcher, and
my only daughter, Fiona Lingefelt, a little girl forever.
Two courageous souls, two beautiful angels,
and always the two ladies I love the most.*

TRUE PRETENSES

Chapter One

Hampstead Heath, England, June 1813

The first time Christopher "Kit" James Alexander Woodard, the eleventh Duke of Fairborough, saw his betrothed another man was peering up her skirt.

Standing on the threshold of the Langley House library with his mouth agape at this appalling sight, Kit only knew the lady perched high on the ladder against the bookcase was his prospective bride because the man who stood directly beneath her called her by her first name.

Could that young buck be the reason Miss Serena Langley refused to even meet Kit, let alone marry him?

She tightly clutched the topmost rung as she swayed precariously on the ladder. "Stop it, Warren, before I drop the whole Domesday Book on you!"

"If you don't want me peering up your skirt, Serena, you shouldn't climb ladders."

She shot him an outraged expression. "Are you

foxed? I scaled this ladder to search for a book, not so you could enjoy the view."

With a loud grunt she jabbed her heel into her tormentor's face, then shrieked as the ladder tilted backward a few inches, only to slam against the bookcase again. Undeterred, the young man howled a curse and grabbed her ankles.

As Kit lunged across the library to bring a halt to the ridiculous antics, the inevitable finally happened.

The ladder pitched back again—this time too far back—and Serena slipped off the rungs.

Kit tried to catch her, but instead he merely broke her fall as she threw him off balance, and together they tumbled to the floor. He landed on his side while she sprawled on top of him, knocking the wind out of him.

Feminine shrieks and masculine grunts abruptly gave way to stunned silence. Memories of his last visit to the Langley House assailed him. He waited for her mother to storm in and scream bloody murder over their compromising position—just as she had nine years ago, only now he was with the woman's own daughter instead of her sister. Not that it mattered, since according to his father's will, Kit would have to marry Serena anyway. At least this time he wouldn't be banished to India.

As the air seeped back into his lungs, he became acutely aware of the tantalizing warmth that covered him, with lilac-scented curls tickling his face, soft breasts pressed against his thundering heart, and a silk-clad leg lodged too intimately against his suddenly throbbing groin. He brushed her silky ringlets from his face, listening to her ragged breath as it ebbed to a normal, steady rhythm.

He was about to ask if she was all right when she bolted upright and slapped him hard across the face.

Kit grunted. He had his answer.

"You miserable cur—you could have broken both our necks!" She scrambled to her feet, shaking golden-brown curls from her face as she stared down at him with wide, silvery blue eyes. "Oh, dear heavens! Who are you?"

He slowly sat up, rubbing his sore cheek. He was so dazed that he started to reveal his true identity, "I'm Fai—" *No, you fool,* he berated himself. If he told her the truth, she'd probably hit him again. No, he had to stick to his plan—for now. He heaved himself to his feet and with a bow said, "Alfred Gibson, at your service. I'm here to see about the coachman's position."

Serena gaped at the prospective coachman, who was dressed in very plain, ill-fitting clothes, save for a pair of rather fine boots. He was the tallest man she'd ever seen, with dark chestnut hair and warm brown eyes to match. He even had a dimple in his chin. How in the world could she ever have mistaken such a man for her cousin Warren?

"I am so sorry." She'd never been in such close contact with a man before. She still felt the heat of his body on her own, and she pressed her hands to her cheeks as if to hide the fact. "I thought you were Lord Winslow."

Gibson gestured toward the desk. "Is that Lord Winslow?"

Turning to see her cousin slumped against the mahogany desk, Serena fought the urge to kick him. "Yes, I'm afraid it is. He must have hit his head on the desk, or perhaps the ladder hit him. I suppose it's too much to hope either one has knocked any sense into him."

With a twinge of disgust—for she couldn't bear the idea of touching Warren, even when he might be hurt—she ruffled his straw-colored hair and found a bump the size of his brain—which she'd long since learned was not much bigger than a walnut. She stepped back as he groaned and muttered a curse.

"Well, 'tis not as if he hasn't been in such a state before, though usually when he's drunk—which is frequently, I might add. You're aware that our last coachman was forced to leave after he injured his back trying to carry Lord Winslow into the house, because he was too deep in his cups to even stand up straight, let alone walk?"

Gibson lifted the ladder, which had fallen across the desk, and replaced it against the bookcase. "I was told only that the position was open, Miss Langley."

She knit her brow. "How did you know my name?"

"I, uh, heard Lord Winslow address you by your Christian name, and I already knew from my previous employer that there was a lady here by that name, so I just assumed . . ."

"Who was your previous employer?"

"The Duke of Colfax."

"Ahh." Then Gibson came with good references. She swept behind the desk to the sparkling array of crystal decanters on the credenza. She selected one at random and tugged on the stopper. It was stuck. "Excuse me, but could you assist me with opening this? I seem to be having a bit of trouble."

He looked as if she'd offered to pour him a glass of hemlock. "Surely you don't tipple?"

"Don't I? Lord Winslow could drive a nun to drink."

Gibson frowned in obvious disapproval. So he was going to be one of *those* servants, thought Serena, as she concentrated on pretending the decanter was Warren and the stopper his head. The sort of servant who was even haughtier than his employers.

"Oh, don't look so reproachful," she chided him, as she finally ripped Warren's wretched head from his fool neck. "Especially when you don't even have the position yet. This isn't for me, it's for Lord Winslow." She aimed the mouth of the decanter at her cousin and gave it a single thrust, splattering him with just enough liquor to make him reek.

She glanced up as she heard someone in the hallway, calling her name. "I'm in here."

Miriam entered the library, her gaze immediately locking on Gibson. "What's going on? And who's this?"

"Miriam, this is Mr. Alfred Gibson, who hopes to be our new coachman. Mr. Gibson, this is Miss Miriam Evans, my abigail."

Coachman and abigail exchanged nods. "Lord Paxton is on his way down, as he wants to interview the new coachman himself," Miriam said.

"A pity he couldn't have been here five minutes ago—not to impugn your chivalry, Gibson. After all, it's not as if Lord Paxton could have broken my fall as well as you did." Serena favored him with an admiring glance, and to her surprise he smiled, revealing even white teeth and a dimple in his left cheek, which still showed a faintly pink handprint.

Miriam clucked. "Did you fall off the ladder again? Why didn't you ask Crosby—"

"Crosby was evidently busy admitting applicants for the coachman's position." Serena crooked her index finger. "Come here, and I'll show you why I fell off the ladder this time."

Miriam bustled over, casting frequent glances at Gibson till she spotted Warren slumped against the side of the desk. "Oh no. Not again. Don't tell me—"

"Very well, I won't—but the coachman arrived just in time."

Miriam gaped at Gibson. "Did you knock him out?"

Before he could respond, Serena said, "As usual, Lord Winslow knocked himself out. By the by, Gibson, you might wish to wait for the earl out in the hallway.

It might be best if His Lordship thinks you've been there all this time."

"I understand, Miss Langley. I was out there originally, but came in when it sounded as if you needed assistance."

"For which I'm very grateful to you." She picked up a stack of books from the corner of the desk.

"Could I help you with those?"

"Thank you, but I've got them, and I have a fairly long way to go with them." She led the way out of the library. Gibson followed the two women out the door, which he closed behind them.

"It was very nice to meet you," Miriam told him with what Serena thought was just a little too much eagerness. "I hope you get the position."

Judging from her tone of voice, Miriam was probably praying for it. Come to think of it, so was Serena. The Langleys desperately needed a new coachman, and after weeks without one, a candidate more ideal than Gibson didn't seem likely to materialize. She flashed him a pleasant smile. "Good luck."

"Thank you, ladies."

Proceeding down the hallway, Serena swore she could feel his eyes on her, burning into her back till they seemed to touch her very core. Just as she reached the turn at the end of the hallway, she couldn't resist. She had to look back.

And just as she suspected, he was gazing at her, his expression serious and intent. The burning sensation spread to her face and set her heart racing.

As she and Miriam turned the corner and headed for the French doors leading to the garden, the burning subsided along with her pounding heart.

Once they were headed down the garden path toward the cottage, Miriam said, "That Gibson is so charming, and terribly handsome. Did you see the way he smiled?"

"Yes." Serena glanced the other way so Miriam couldn't see the way *she* smiled at the memory. "But surely you don't expect me to fall at his feet."

"Who said anything about you falling at his feet? He's only a coachman."

No one had said anything, but for some baffling reason, Serena had been thinking it. "Well, I'm certainly not so high in the instep that I'd let his being a mere coachman keep me from falling at his feet. You know me better than that."

"Indeed I do. Enough to know you'd refrain from falling at any man's feet simply because he's a man."

Annoyance jabbed Serena and she nearly dropped her stack of books. "That's not true. I only refrain from falling at the feet of cousin Warren and the Duke of Fairborough."

Miriam reached for some of the books, relieving Serena of nearly half the load. "Let me carry some of those. I'm good for other things aside from lecturing you. Now which duke of Fairborough do you refer to? The late tenth, or the new eleventh, whom you haven't even met yet?"

"The new eleventh, whom I shall *never* meet." Serena quickened her step on the graveled path, as if to flee the sudden, unpleasant turn in their conversation.

"But for all you know, he's nothing like the tenth."

"I do know. He's worse."

"How so? Simply because he waited a month after returning from India before making any effort to see you? That's more than you can say for his older brother, who *never* made any effort to see you. The new duke had to call soon enough—certainly before the end of summer, so it's not as if he waited till the last minute. After all, he turns thirty in September, and you know what'll happen if he isn't married by then."

"Miriam, I should like to think I'm a better person than one who would refuse to see him because he waited a month before sending his card. It wouldn't have mattered if he'd appeared on our doorstep the minute he returned to England. I have no desire to ever see him, let alone marry him."

In her mind's eye, Serena read again the note Fairborough had sent to Langley House last week, politely if dispassionately requesting permission to call on her in the next few days so they might discuss their forthcoming marriage. Serena had shot back a very scathing reply that let His Grace know in no uncertain terms that she had no intention of marrying him now or ever. Fortunately, cousin Harriet—the countess—had been in Town that morning. Had Harriet been at home, she'd surely have intercepted the duke's missive and insisted he come immediately.

Miriam broke into Serena's reverie. "There are sixty thousand pounds at stake. He has to marry a daughter from the Langley family to claim that trust fund."

"And all because of his father's guilty conscience. If Fairborough has to marry a Langley daughter, then let Jemma marry him." Now that Serena thought about it, maybe she should have gone ahead and invited the duke to call, then pushed Jemma at him—not that it would have been necessary, since Harriet would have been there to throw her daughter at his feet.

"But you're older than Jemma, so I'm afraid you're first in line to be his bride. And you're already four and twenty. Think of what you could do for Felice with that money!"

Serena stopped to glare at her abigail. "All I can think of is what the new duke could do to my sister if I married him and brought her into his household."

Miriam narrowed her eyes. "Are you referring to that

incident with your aunt Leah? That was nine years ago and you weren't even there that night. You were away at school."

"But I know what happened. The dowager duchess herself told me. He knew Leah couldn't scream for help."

"And you think the same thing would happen to Felice simply because—because—"

"Because she's Felice," Serena supplied, as they resumed their stroll down the garden path amid yellow roses in full bloom. "He's obviously no better than his wastrel of an older brother, who took our farmhouse in exchange for Grandfather's markers and turned it into a—"

"Don't say it!" Miriam interjected. "I know what he turned it into. It's bad enough you have to know."

"I was actually grateful Simon ignored me. Yet just when I thought I was free, along comes his younger brother with a reputation of his own. Even if Kit Woodard left Felice alone, the fact remains that he attacked my aunt, who couldn't even cry for help, let alone fight him off. Why would I want to spend the rest of my life with someone like that?"

Miriam sighed. "I know I wouldn't mind spending the rest of my life with that coachman."

"You scarcely know him. Besides, whatever happened to Mr. Jennings?"

"Master Philip's tutor?" Miriam let out a little snort. "He barely knows I exist. I'm quite ready to give up on him. Mr. Gibson's willingness to help you just now speaks well of him, regardless of his station."

Serena couldn't suppress a smile, thinking of Gibson's quick and very timely intervention in the library. "True enough. But don't you think he's a little young? I mean for you? He doesn't look as if he could be more than thirty."

Miriam feigned a pout. "Oh, very well, but if I were ten years younger, I'd definitely set my cap for him!"

Serena laughed. "You'd still be older, if only by a few years."

As they approached the cottage nestled at the edge of the garden, Serena continued smiling as she recalled that fleeting moment when she'd been sprawled on top of the coachman. A strange surge of warmth coursed through her. *How* could she ever have mistaken such a man for a weasel like Warren?

Now that she thought about it, it would be all too easy to fall at the feet of a man like Alfred Gibson. Coachman or not.

Kit paced the hall outside the library, his head swimming. So *that* was the chit who'd fired back the missive with venom dripping off the page! The one who despised him for reasons she refused to disclose. Who wouldn't even meet with him, writing that she'd rather wed the devil than the Duke of Fairborough.

When he'd first learned of their arranged betrothal, he'd been resigned to wedding a woman he'd never seen. After learning that his fiancée meant to fight him every last step to the altar, however, his resignation had given way to a determination equal to her own. Winning her would be worth this ridiculous charade. At least he knew she wasn't interested in his title or fortune, which was unusual considering her straitened circumstances.

His thoughts darted back to the trust fund his father had laid in the trap as bait to wed Serena. Established a year after Kit had departed for India, his father had placed ten thousand pounds per annum in the trust until his death two years ago. It now totaled sixty thousand pounds. "The ninth Duke of Fairborough has decreed that the next Duchess of Fairborough must be descended from the Earls of Paxton," Kit's solicitor had dryly informed him, "and that the bridegroom must take her to wife before his thirtieth birthday or forfeit the trust fund, which shall subsequently pass to Calvin Granger," Kit's cousin and son of his father's sister.

Calvin was master of the biggest and wealthiest plantation in the West Indies—made big and wealthy from the blood and sweat of slaves. Kit was not about to let so much money go to the acquisition of more land—and more slaves to work it. En route to India nine years ago, his ship had stopped at an African port where he'd seen hordes of shackled, naked Negroes—some of them with their children and even infants—awaiting transport to the island where Calvin reigned as lord. The very sight had sickened Kit.

It was obvious, however, that Kit's father had wanted to atone—on his eldest son's behalf—for the loss of the Langleys' farm in Kent by making the Langley daughter a duchess. But she didn't want to be a duchess, and God alone knew why, unless it had something to do with that debacle nine years ago in this very house—only Kit had done nothing wrong that night!

In his mind he'd relived that night a thousand times. His true intentions had been to help the woman. Where was she now? After all, she was the key to proving his innocence. He'd said as much when his father, only days after the incident, had coldly announced he'd just purchased for his younger son a commission in India, and that Kit would be leaving immediately. There had been no opportunity for him to find the woman—who seemed to have vanished into thin air—and thus prove his innocence.

If not for the trust fund, Kit might have been perfectly happy to release Serena from her obligations, leaving him free to seek a more willing bride elsewhere.

But he couldn't let his cousin get his greedy, blood-stained hands on so much money. So wed Serena he must—before the end of this summer.

Heavy footsteps approached. A well-dressed, rotund man appeared, addressing Kit with a Northumberland accent similar to that of his former commander in India.

"I'm Lord Paxton. Here for the coachman's position?"

"Yes—my lord." Kit sketched a quick bow, nearly forgetting the proper courtesies. He was going to have to remember that while the Duke of Fairborough outranked every member of the Langley family, every member of the Langley family outranked Alfred Gibson.

Paxton peered upward at Kit, who stood nearly a full head taller. "You look like a strong man. Good."

He led Kit into the library. Halfway to his desk, Paxton stopped short and mumbled a curse under his breath as he spotted Lord Winslow, who was still slumped on the floor against the desk, groaning and rubbing the back of his head.

Paxton gave a loud, suspicious sniff. "Bloody hell, not again," he muttered, stepping over Winslow to the chair behind the desk. He glanced at Kit. "One of your duties will be to carry my firstborn here from the steps of his club in Town to the carriage, and from the carriage to the doorstep here." He held out his hand. "References?"

Kit pulled a paper from his pocket and gave it to Paxton, who loudly cleared his throat as he sat, donning a pair of spectacles before reading the reference. Another groan rose like a noxious vapor from the floor next to the desk.

Paxton did not look up. "So your previous employer was the Duke of Colfax? Why did you not remain in his employ?"

TRUE PRETENSES

Kit recited his carefully rehearsed speech. "I was coachman at his ancestral home in Kent. But I preferred to be near London so I could be closer to my frail grandmother, and His Grace already had a coachman in Town."

Paxton nodded absently, flicking his eyes to the young sot who finally struggled to his feet, gawking dazedly at his father as he continued rubbing the back of his head. "What happened?"

Paxton sniffed again, then briefly turned to the array of decanters behind him. "What happened is the London clubs evidently don't provide enough liquor for your needs, so you felt compelled to help yourself to my own supply. Here's the man who'll be carrying you home from now on." He glanced down at the reference, then back at Kit. "Alfred Gibson. Well, we do need a driver posthaste and I don't know when a driver as big and robust as you is likely to come along again, so the position is yours. Your wages will be fifteen shillings a month, and you will be quartered in the carriage house, where you may go now to become familiar with the horses and equipment. Any questions?"

Yes. How can any human being live on fifteen shillings a month? Kit made a mental note to check on the wages of the staff he himself had inherited. If they were anything close to what Lord Paxton was paying, then the Woodard family retainers were in for a substantial pay raise. "No, my lord."

"Then that will be all for now, Gibson."

But instead of heading for the carriage house, Kit returned to a copse down the road from Langley House, where a carriage awaited him. Upon seeing him, both driver and footman climbed down from the carriage.

"You may tell the Duke of Colfax I won't be returning

to Town today," Kit told them. "But I'll see him tonight when he comes here to dine."

"Yes, Your Grace," the footman replied.

Kit shook his head, thinking it was probably a good thing he wasn't yet accustomed to being a duke. "Until further notice, you may call me 'Mr. Gibson.'"

Chapter Two

"Listen well, young lady: We did not come all the way to London from Northumberland just so you could set your cap for a—a—" Poor cousin Harriet couldn't even voice the word, as if it were too vulgar for a lady to speak aloud.

"A Scot?" Serena dared to interject, fully expecting Harriet to shriek in horror. Surprisingly she didn't.

"But he's heir to an earldom, Mama," Jemma protested.

"You've met some perfectly eligible, *English* heirs to earldoms this season, not to mention a few marquesses and even dukes. In fact, we have one coming to dinner tonight. Try to show some interest in him."

Serena stiffened. "It's not Fairborough, is it, cousin?"

"You will address me as *my—lady*," Harriet said icily.

Serena closed her eyes. It was the only way to keep them from rolling.

15

"But who is the duke?" asked Jemma.

"Colfax," Harriet replied, as she marched out of her daughter's bedchamber.

Serena heaved a sigh of relief. She'd been living in fear of dukes calling at Langley House for the past month now, ever since receiving word of the eleventh Duke of Fairborough's return from India. Colfax, on the other hand, she could endure. After all, her grandfather hadn't struck a marriage deal with *his* father.

She was about to follow Harriet out of the room but stopped short, remembering that even Jemma outranked her now. She smiled at her younger cousin, short and just a bit plump at eighteen, with hair of strawberry blond and freckles lightly sprinkled across a slightly pugged nose. "Perhaps you'd better go first—*my*—*lady*."

"Please don't call me that, Serena—you don't have to when Mama's not around. I actually miss being plain Miss Jemma Langley, when it wouldn't have mattered who I married, as long as I married someone."

"Someone who wasn't a Scot," Serena dryly amended, as she followed Jemma out the door.

"If only she and Papa would consent to meet Hamish, they—"

"Ah, we're on a first-name basis already, are we?"

Jemma lowered her voice. "He doesn't care for stuffy titles any more than I do. But if only they'd agree to meet him, they'd find him no different than any of the Englishmen they wish for me. Hamish can even speak like an Englishman when he wants. He studied at Oxford. He only reverts to his Scottish brogue to annoy people like my mother."

Serena laughed as they approached the head of the staircase. "I like him already. But unfortunately, annoying your mother didn't exactly advance his cause where you're concerned."

Jemma sighed wistfully. "I know, and he knows it, too. He said it was before he realized I was the one he wanted to wed. Whatever will we do?"

"Well, there's always Gretna Green," Serena said, as they descended the staircase. "I'm rather surprised he hasn't considered that, being a—" she cleared her throat and lowered her voice to a whisper "—a Scot."

Reaching the foot of the staircase, they heard cousin Archie bellowing in the nearby drawing room.

"What do you mean, Lord Winslow won't be here for dinner? I told him the Duke of Colfax was coming. Where is he?"

The butler's voice: "I believe Lord Winslow said something about going to his club in Town, my lord."

"Again? He didn't take the new coachman, did he?"

"No, my lord, he took the dappled gray, just as he's been doing since the previous coachman was forced to leave."

Cousin Archie spewed a string of extremely impolite words, which Harriet didn't seem to hear. Serena wondered what might have happened had Jemma's father thrown in the word *Scot* amongst all the references to the Savior, divine condemnation, and a certain place that was much hotter than England.

"That will be all, Crosby," Archie said, after finishing his colorful tirade.

Thank heavens Warren was in Town again. Serena wouldn't have to sit next to him at dinner and constantly kick him every time he tried toying with her foot and furtively slipping his hand into her lap.

The dinner guest arrived moments later. It nearly ruined Serena's appetite to watch Harriet gushing over Nicholas Maxwell, the Duke of Colfax. He was already betrothed to an heiress in America who was separated from him because of the war between their two countries. But Harriet obviously saw no harm in trying to switch his affections to her own daughter.

Serena had known Nicholas since childhood, as his ancestral home had been adjacent to her father's farm. He'd been the older brother she'd never had. He had brownish black hair and ice-blue eyes, and he was charming and full of fun. He enjoyed pranks, and Serena would have loved to see him pull one on her cousins, but unfortunately he chose to behave himself this evening.

Archie and Harriet reigned at either end of the cherry-wood dining table, with Nicholas on Harriet's right. Jemma, of course, sat next to him, but was too busy pining over Hamish to pay much attention to their dinner guest.

Not that Serena was a mind reader, but Jemma couldn't possibly be concentrating on anything else. Otherwise she would already have died of embarrassment from Harriet's monologue, consisting mainly of what a marvelous duchess Jemma would make for some lucky duke. As it was, Serena was already embarrassed for her—and for Nicholas, too.

Yet she could barely suppress a smile as she peered at him over the fruit-laden epergne. Certainly he gave Harriet his full attention, but his eyes were glazed with the desperation of a man fervently wishing this woman would just shut up and let him eat in peace. At one point he swallowed hard on a bite of beef, looking as if he hoped to choke on it if for no other reason than to put himself out of his misery. Serena had to hold a napkin to her mouth to stifle a giggle.

At dinner's end, the three ladies rose to leave Nicholas and Archie to their brandy and cigars.

"Oh, but before you ladies depart, I have something for Miss Langley." Nicholas thrust a hand into his coat pocket. "Fairborough asked me to give this to you. It's a letter."

Serena sighed. Not another one. And to make matters worse, there would be no hiding this one from her cousins.

Harriet snatched the letter from him and tore it open.

"Fairborough mentioned it was personal, Lady Paxton."

"Yes, but we are still responsible for Miss Langley, Your Grace, so we have every right to read her correspondence."

He cast an apologetic look at Serena. "But they're engaged."

"Ha! You'd never know it to listen to her. She's made it quite clear she has no intention of ever wedding him." Harriet now concentrated on the contents of the letter. "What's this? He's written her before and we never knew it?" She frowned at her husband. "My lord, it seems the Duke of Fairborough wrote to your cousin last week, requesting permission to call, and she denied his request." She fired her blazing eyes at Serena. "Why weren't we told of this?"

"As you said a few moments ago, cousin—"

"*My—lady,*" Harriet harshly corrected her.

"As you said yourself a few moments ago, *my—lady*, I've made it quite clear I have no intention of ever wedding Fairborough."

Harriet glanced at her husband. "My lord, say something!"

Archie swiped his napkin across both his lips, then both his chins. "Why not leave us to our brandy and cigars, ladies?"

"Ar—my lord!"

"*Go!*" The candles on the table flickered as if cowering in fear, and Serena noticed that even Nicholas blanched.

She braced herself for the next cannonade as she followed Harriet and Jemma down the hall to the drawing room.

Once there, Harriet aimed her glare at Serena and commenced firing. "How dare you speak that way in front of His Grace?"

"You mean truthfully?" She dodged out of the way just as Harriet raised her hand.

Harriet chased her around the pianoforte. "Come here, you insolent henwit!"

"So you can strike me? Do you think I'm daft?" Serena twirled gracefully around the pianoforte, while Harriet's hip struck the sharp corner, jolting the instrument.

She yowled like a cat whose tail had been pulled, clutching her hip as she glowered at Serena. "You're daft enough to turn down Fairborough. Marriage to him means sixty thousand pounds!"

"For him—not for you."

"But he'll have obligations to his wife's family." Harriet crept around the pianoforte, still rubbing her hip. "We have the title, this house, and nothing more."

"You're forgetting Paxton Hall," Serena reminded her.

"Which is all the way up in Yorkshire. We may as well have remained in Northumberland. And there's no money to keep it up though sixty thousand pounds would certainly help. We don't even have that farm in Kent to provide us with additional revenue, because it was never entailed—no thanks to your grandfather."

"That's because Grandfather bought it for my parents as a wedding present. But he held the deed, which Lord Linden later took in exchange for Grandfather's vowels."

TRUE PRETENSES

"And who holds it now? Linden's brother—your betrothed! If you marry him, you'll have your childhood home back."

"But I don't want it back." Serena turned for the doors. "Now good night, *my—lady*."

"Where do you think you're going? His Lordship and His Grace will soon be joi—"

"Give them my regrets." Serena threw open the doors and stormed down the hall. Since Nicholas was like a brother to her, she wasn't too worried about offending him.

She had no intention of marrying Fairborough so he could collect sixty thousand pounds, only to redistribute it to her relatives. It wasn't his responsibility to restore her ancestral home. She'd never even been to Paxton Hall, and she had no fond memories of the small farm in Kent where she'd grown up.

Her father had been happy there, despite his complaints about having only daughters, one of whom was "a little dolt," as he'd called Felice. Their mother, meanwhile, had pined for the glitter of London. Serena scarcely remembered her mother, for she was always off to Town, visiting Papa's dashing cousin Marcus. When she was very young, Serena had thought Mama was playing a childish game of "horsey" with cousin Marcus, because Papa always called Mama a horse when referring to her games with Marcus. Now that Serena was older and knew more than she sometimes wished, she realized her father was actually calling her mother a name that only sounded similar to "horse."

After Grandfather lost the farm, Papa was forced to move his daughters to the family estate in Hampstead Heath. A year later, Papa and Marcus had fought a duel over Mama. Papa was killed, while Marcus was forced to flee the country.

And Mama left her daughters to go with him, never

to be heard from again. Serena had been only fifteen, Felice ten.

The farmhouse burned down last year, killing the tenth Duke of Fairborough. Though Serena had longed to be released from her betrothal to Simon, she certainly hadn't wanted it to end *that* way. His were the only remains recovered from the charred ruins, identified only by his signet ring. The authorities who investigated the smoldering site opined he must have knocked over a candelabrum while in a drunken stupor. This had surprised no one since Simon had been a notorious drinker. Serena could scarcely bring herself to mourn the rakehell fiancé she'd barely known; she could only deplore the tragic waste of a human life.

At such times, she considered Felice's mysterious condition a blessing in disguise. Thankfully, her sister had never noticed her father's scathing remarks, and after so many years, she still didn't realize that both her parents were gone; she'd simply plodded on in her own little world as if nothing had happened.

But Serena wasn't so blessed. With a sigh she pulled herself back to the present and headed for the kitchen, where most of the servants would be gathered. Whether at Langley House or at the farm in Kent, the servants had always been more of a family to Serena and Felice than their own flesh and blood.

So it hardly surprised Serena that the new coachman could charm her so easily, when she knew she ought to be accepting the suit of a duke.

Kit stood beneath an arbor in the garden behind Langley House, shivering despite his coat. Even though it was June and the weather was mild for England, after nine years in sweltering India the midnight air seemed almost arctic to him. He heard footsteps approaching and peered into the darkness, spotting a silhouette vaguely shaped like Nicholas.

"Fairborough?"

He emerged from the arbor. "Right here, Colfax. Did you deliver the letter?"

Nicholas pulled the crumpled missive from his pocket and handed it to Kit. "I tried, but Lady Paxton intercepted it. Your intended is now deep in the suds because her cousins never knew of your previous efforts to call on her."

"Didn't she even see it?"

Nicholas took out two cheroots, offering one to Kit. "I'm afraid not. Incidentally, the new earl and countess do have a daughter of their own, though she's much younger than Serena. I believe she only came out this year."

Kit accepted the light that followed the cheroot. "According to my father's will, I could just as easily marry this daughter if I choose. Did you meet her?"

"Oh, Lady Paxton more than called my attention to her. Her name is Jemma. She doesn't have much to say for herself, because Lady Paxton says it all for her."

"In that case, never mind. I'm afraid a domineering mother doesn't make Jemma a very tempting prospect."

"Incidentally," Nicholas said, with a smile that warned Kit he was about to be either amused or appalled, "do you know who Paxton was before he inherited the earldom?"

"I can't imagine, but I'm afraid you're going to enjoy telling me."

"He was Lord Gorham's estate manager in Northumberland."

Kit decided he was amused. "I thought he might be from the north. And my stepmother is Gorham's daughter. She'd probably have an apoplectic fit if I married the daughter of her father's former estate manager."

Nicholas grinned. "Makes Jemma all the more tempting, eh?"

"Not as tempting as Serena." Or as challenging. What sort of female was she, to vehemently refuse marriage to a wealthy duke?

A female definitely worth pursuing.

"Did you finally get to meet her?" Nicholas asked.

"Yes, and oddly enough, she seemed quite taken with me, even though I'm only her coachman. I'm hoping that will make it easier to learn why she wants nothing to do with me as Fairborough."

"I'm sure it's either because of Simon or that alleged incident with you and her aunt Leah."

"But there was *nothing* about me and her aunt Leah! Doesn't anyone know where she is?"

"She disappeared about the same time you went to India. But that may not even be the reason Serena won't see you. After all, she was a schoolgirl at the time of the alleged scandal, so it was probably kept secret from her—especially if, as you say, Serena's father was the real culprit."

Kit inhaled deeply on his cheroot. "So maybe it's because of my brother that she won't marry me."

"Well, he did take her childhood home and turn it into a bucolic brothel for gentlemen of the ton. You do realize you own what's left of that farm now?"

"Now that you mention it, yes. When I learned of my brother's demise, I'm afraid it never occurred to me that I'd inherited the remains of the farm where he surely coughed and choked his last." He felt a melancholy shudder deep inside himself. He and his brother had never been close, despite the mere thirteen-month gap in their ages. But their many differences hadn't stopped Kit from frequently agonizing this past year over how much Simon must have suffered in his last moments. To perish in a fire was a horrible, terrifying way to die, and Kit could only hope that his brother had gone quickly.

"I'm sorry, Kit. Perhaps it's just as well he and Serena never had a tendresse for each other. I apologize for saying so, but I can't say as I blame Serena, since you know he was only interested in one kind of woman. Remember his three *D*s?"

"Yes, and you needn't apologize for speaking the truth." Expelled from half a dozen schools and sent down from Oxford after only one term, Simon had been a self-professed disciple of what he smugly called the three *D*s—dice, drinking, and doxies. While no one in the family understood why he was such a hellion, everyone else authoritatively blamed his profligate ways on his French mother. Never mind that no one in the ton had ever had the chance to know her—she'd spent her two brief years in England pregnant and confined to Fairborough Castle, only to die giving birth to Kit. But everyone instantly assumed that simply because she was French, she was reckless and amoral—so Simon must have taken after her. Why Kit didn't turn out the same way, no one ever bothered to contemplate.

Until that night here at Langley House, nine years ago, when just like that, he suddenly became his French mother's son.

He glanced up at his friend. "To think I was sent abroad for something I didn't even do, while Simon remained in England to continue his pursuit of the three *D*s. Father said it was because Simon, at least, had the good sense to confine himself to whores, while I was accused of scandalizing the family by forcing myself on a lady I couldn't wed."

"I agree it's not fair, and I know you're innocent, Kit.

Karen Lingefelt

You were set up, plain and simple. Your problem now is convincing Serena of that."

Kit grunted churlishly. "A fine state of affairs when a duke must pose as a coachman just to meet his betrothed."

Nicholas chuckled. "Think of it as a lark. When was the last time you had a lark?"

"I've never had a lark—at least not like this one—"

"Then you're long overdue." Nicholas slapped him on the back. " 'Twill be good for you, take some of the starch out of your neckcloth."

"I still can't believe you came up with this harebrained scheme—*and* that I let you talk me into it!"

"That's because you want a lark but you just don't realize it. I notice you've changed your accent to fit the part. You sound very bourgeois."

"I picked it up from my fellow soldiers while in India. If anyone asks, my father was your tutor before you went to Eton. I love driving horses too much to follow in his footsteps. I'm content to waste my life as a mere coachman."

Nicholas grinned. "So my letter of recommendation was sufficient?"

"More than sufficient, though I'm surprised Paxton didn't want to see how I handled his horses and carriage. I'm top-sawyer, or I wouldn't be doing this. Let's just hope the real Alfred Gibson doesn't show up in the meantime wanting my job."

Nicholas tossed down his cheroot. "The real one disappeared about a year ago—I think he ran off with one of our kitchen maids. My mother says—"

"Who's there?" called out a brisk, feminine voice.

Kit coughed on his own cheroot and dropped it, grinding it out with his boot as Nicholas raised his voice. "Miss Langley, is that you? It's just me, Colfax, and your new coachman."

What was Serena doing out here? Kit wondered, as she materialized before the arbor like an apparition in the faint moonlight, wearing a pale blue gown that displayed more than a hint of her modestly sized bosom, despite the shawl draped haphazardly around her shoulders. She carried a large covered basket in her arms. Wasn't it a little late for a picnic?

"What are you doing in the garden at this hour?" Nicholas's thoughts obviously ran along the same lines as Kit's.

She shifted the basket in her arms. "I might ask the same of you. Are you meeting someone?"

"I'm meeting him now. I'm just having a word with your new coachman before I return to Mayfair. Did you know his father was my tutor before I went to Eton?"

"No, but it certainly explains why he speaks so well. I met him this morning, so I'm aware he was also once your coachman."

Kit stepped from the shadows of the arbor. "How do you do, Miss Langley? A bit late for a picnic, isn't it?"

"Now I know why I wasn't sorry to see you go, Gibson." Nicholas slapped Kit on the arm with his gloves. "You always had a vexing tendency to address your betters without waiting for them to address you first."

Annoyed, Kit wanted to snatch the gloves from Nicholas and slap him across the face with them. But he knew his friend was right. He'd have to watch himself every minute now, and remember that for the time being he was no longer a duke, but a mere coachman. He brushed against Nicholas as he stuffed the letter back into his friend's pocket.

"Aside from his propensity for sometimes overstepping his bounds, I think you'll find Gibson quite pleasant and reliable," Nicholas told Serena.

"That probably won't matter much, since I prefer to drive my own phaeton."

"You drive your own phaeton?" Kit rightly felt like an idiot as soon as the words spilled out of his mouth. *Isn't that what she said, you blithering idiot?*

"Of course. It's not that far."

"What do you mean? To where, Miss Langley?"

"That's none of your affair," Nicholas put in, with another smack of the gloves.

The hell it wasn't, Kit thought angrily, silently bristling at the confines of his charade.

"It's all right, Your Grace." She glanced from Nicholas to Kit. "I only drive into Town, and I always take Miriam."

Into Town? Not anymore, Kit told himself grimly. He wasn't about to waste time driving all the other Langleys to wherever they wished, while his fiancée traipsed back and forth between Hampstead Heath and London in her own phaeton. That was not why he was subjecting himself to this ignominy.

Making a mental note to fix her little phaeton before morning, he furtively batted his hand against Nick's pocket, and Nick pulled out the letter.

"Oh, and, Miss Langley, I'm sure you'd like to have this. I'm sorry about what happened this evening. Had I known Lady Paxton was going to behave the way she did, I would have been much more discreet about passing Fairborough's letter to you."

"Thank you, but I don't want it."

Kit felt as if she'd punched him in the stomach. "But it's from your betrothed."

Nicholas slapped him with the gloves again. "I'll remind you only once more, Gibson, to remember your place."

Kit fought to suppress a growl, as Serena leveled her piercing gaze on him. "I know who Fairborough is, Gibson. And I have no desire to read his letter."

"Why not?" Nicholas demanded.

"Because I don't want to marry him! And I don't see that it's any concern of yours."

"I agree, but he asked me to pass it on to you, since—"

"Then kindly inform him that you're not his messenger. Heavens, you're a duke, yet you let everyone walk all over you. Fairborough has only just attained his title and here you are doing his bidding. At dinner you surrendered the letter to Lady Paxton with scarcely a protest. You'd probably even let Gibson give you orders."

Kit clamped a hand over his mouth as he made a coughing noise to conceal his mirth.

"Not to mention your dear mother," she added.

"Ouch," Nicholas said.

"Oh, and let's not forget me," she amended, as she continued down the path. "You can't even use your God-given position to force that letter on me."

Nicholas looked askance at Kit as she vanished from sight. He spoke in a whisper. "And you want to marry her?"

Kit snickered. "I must admit, I'm starting to really like her. Go on—give her the letter!"

Nicholas raised his voice. "Miss Langley, what should I do with this letter?"

"I told you. Take it back to Fairborough and tell him you're a duke, not a messenger boy."

"Where is she going with that basket at this ghastly hour?" Kit whispered. "Ask her—it may not be Gibson's business, but it's certainly mine."

"Where are you going with that basket at this ghastly hour?" Nicholas called after her.

"Good night," came her voice from the shadows.

"Is she meeting someone for a midnight picnic?" Kit whispered. "Is that why she won't marry me—because she has her cap set for someone else?"

Karen Lingefelt

"How should I know if she's meeting someone?"

"No, I want you to ask her—quick, before she disappears!"

"Are you meeting someone for a midnight picnic?" shouted Nicholas into the shadows.

"Ask her if that's why she won't marry me," Kit prompted.

"Is that why you won't marry me?" Nicholas called out.

"*You?*" Kit exclaimed in a hoarse whisper.

"Why, Your Grace, I don't recall you offering for me," Serena called back sweetly.

Kit punched him in the arm. Nicholas yelped and clutched his bicep.

"I meant Fairborough," he ground out. "Why won't you marry Fairborough, Serena?"

"I'm not going to stand out here in the dark shouting with you about this."

Kit gave Nicholas a hard shove. "Go after her!"

Nicholas glared at him, still rubbing his arm. "Damnation, Kit—hitting me, pushing me—"

"You slapped me twice—no, *three* times with your bloody gloves!"

"That's because you kept overstepping your bounds, *Gibson!*"

He grabbed Nick's sleeve and dragged him down the path. "Come on, let's go after her—"

"You can't go after her," Nicholas growled. "You're only the coachman, for the hundredth time—and a bloody presumptuous one at that."

"I'll hide in the bushes while you talk to her—just find out if she's—"

"Your Grace, who are you talking to?" Serena's voice sounded fainter now. "Is the coachman still with you?"

"I'm just leaving, Miss Langley—good night," Kit shouted.

Whap! went Nick's gloves on Kit's arm. *Whap* again, then *whap, whap*—he finally tore the gloves from Nick's grasp and hurled them into the shrubbery.

"Damn and blast, Kit, those are new gloves!"

"After her!" he exclaimed in a whisper, as they nearly stumbled over each other on their way down the path.

Serena was nowhere to be seen in the cool darkness now, but as they rounded a bend in the path, Kit spotted a faint light glowing warmly in the distance. "What's that over there? Is it a carriage lamp?"

"No, it's from a cottage. There's a cottage on the grounds of Langley House, or didn't you know?"

"No, I didn't. I've only been to Langley House once before, and that was nine very long years ago. I'm afraid I had no opportunity to explore the grounds, since I was too busy immersing myself in a scandal."

"Well, it's a cottage. But I don't know what it's used for, or if anyone even lives there."

Kit looked hard at his friend. "Oh, I can think of a use for it, and so can you. How about a midnight tryst?"

"Do you really believe Serena has a lover hidden away in that cottage?"

"Why else would she come out here at this hour?"

"Mm, good question." They stealthily approached the cottage. "What are you planning to do?"

"I don't know yet, but I'm open to suggestions."

Nicholas seized Kit's shoulders. "Then I suggest you turn around and return to the carriage house, Coachman Gibson."

"I'll do that as soon as you find out what's going on in there." Nicholas opened his mouth to protest, but before he could yell *Me!* Kit hastily added, "You are representing my interests—not Gibson's, but Fairborough's. Until I agree to let her cry off the betrothal—"

"You mean you might *not marry her?*" Nicholas removed his hands from Kit's shoulders, staring at him in disbelief. "I have just three words for you, Kit: sixty thousand pounds."

"I have the right to know why she refuses to marry me. You could emphasize to her that I might be persuaded to release her from the betrothal, given sufficient grounds to do so."

"I believe you'd be much happier if you found some way to marry her."

"And I will, even though I'm starting to think I'd be much happier back in India." Kit rapped briskly on the cottage door.

"What the bloody hell are you doing?"

"I just told you." Kit ducked into the shadows to wait.

Nicholas gawked stupidly at the door. "Her lover will probably answer, pistol in hand, and blow my head clean off my shoulders."

"You have my word, Colfax, I will avenge your death," Kit said stoutly, thinking his next voyage would be to Australia.

Chapter Three

"Don't answer it, Mrs. Kaye," Serena said. "It's Colfax."

"You mean the duke?" Miriam opened the large basket Serena had set on the table. "Did he follow you out here?"

"Yes, and what he was doing out in the garden when he should have been on his way back to Town, I can only imagine." Just having a word with his former coachman—ha! She thought Nicholas knew her better than that—that he deemed her smarter than one of his silly sisters. He'd obviously been planning to ambush Serena in hopes of pressing Fairborough's unwanted letter on her. Only how could he have known she'd be passing through the garden so late at night? Her cousins wouldn't have told him. Like her grandfather and parents, they preferred to keep quiet about her sister's existence. Even though they'd been neighbors as children, Nicholas had never known about Felice, who was born about the same time he'd gone away to Eton.

The rapping had thankfully ceased, and she was just

about to heave a sigh of relief when it suddenly resumed, more persistent than ever.

Again Felice's nurse stepped to the door, and Serena said, "*No*, Mrs. Kaye. Just let him knock till his knuckles are raw. It'll teach him a lesson."

"But he's apt to wake Felice sooner or later. And that kind of knocking—which is getting to be more like pounding—well, I needn't tell you—"

"Miss Langley!" bellowed a voice through the door.

Miriam stopped what she was doing to peer at Serena. "That doesn't sound like the Duke of Colfax."

Serena's heart tripped. "That's because it's the coachman."

"You mean that handsome Mr. Gibson?"

"What about Mr. Jennings?"

"Is the new coachman really handsome?" Mrs. Kaye asked.

"Oh, much more than the tutor," said Miriam.

Serena hurried to the door. "I'd think twice if I were you. At the moment I can assure you that Mr. Jennings at least stands a better chance than Mr. Gibson of remaining steadily employed." She opened the door, ready to give the new coachman an enormous piece of her mind—something she'd never done to any servant in all of her four and twenty years. Yet just the very sight of him standing on the threshold stopped her— no, not cold. Suddenly she didn't feel the least bit cold. She was still overly warm from her trek through the garden, toting the heavy basket full of leftover food for Felice and Mrs. Kaye.

In the light from the kitchen behind her, she could see Gibson much better now than she had in the garden, and for the second time today, she was struck dumb and inert by the very sight of him. Why did the most handsome man she'd ever seen have to be a coachman?

TRUE PRETENSES

Words gushed out of him in a torrent. "I'm terribly sorry to disturb you, Miss Langley, but the Duke of Colfax threatened to go to Lord Paxton and have me sacked without a reference if I didn't do his bidding." He pulled a crumpled paper out of his pocket. Serena rolled her eyes as she recognized that blasted letter. "He insists you take this, and he says if you don't, he'll have me sacked—but I need this position."

"Why do you no longer have a position with the duke?"

"Because I needed a position in London. I was his coachman in Kent and he already had a driver here, one who only drives him around Town, and he wasn't willing to swap."

"Why don't you let him in—come in, Gibson!" Miriam lunged forward and hauled Gibson inside the cottage as if he were an errant child about to get his ears boxed for having too good a time in the mud. "I take it you have family in London? Do sit down. Miss Langley has just brought back some delicious—"

"Miriam, I did not bring this basket for the coachman in case he might come for a midnight visit. He should already have had his evening meal, and if he considered himself too good to sup with the rest of the staff in the servants' hall, then he'll have to return to his quarters with an empty stomach." She turned to Gibson, who'd been eyeing the modest bounty that would feed Felice and her nurse tomorrow. "The housekeeper said you did not come to supper tonight, and that you sent the groom to fetch something for you, because you refused to sup in the servants' hall. Maybe they do things a little differently down at Colfax Park, but here at Langley House, you will take your meals with the rest of the staff. If you go to bed hungry tonight, then I hope you've learned a valuable lesson."

"I beg your pardon, Miss Langley, but I was too busy

acquainting myself with the horses and carriages to come to the house for supper. You can be sure I've learned my lesson, and it won't happen again."

His explanation was certainly plausible, even if it wasn't what she'd heard when she collected the basket tonight. The housekeeper, in fact, went so far as to say that the new coachman was almost as high in the instep as Lady Paxton. Almost.

"Now give me the letter," Serena said, and Gibson heaved a visible sigh of relief as he passed it to her.

Miriam said, "Couldn't he at least stay for—"

"It's midnight," said Serena, "and I'd like to retire."

Gibson knit his brow. "Do you sleep in this cottage, Miss Langley?"

"Not that it's any affair of yours, but yes, I do."

When she tossed the letter into the fireplace, the coachman was indignant. "Miss Langley, you're not going to burn that letter?"

"I most certainly am." She grabbed the poker and stabbed the offending missive into the glowing orange embers.

"But the duke will have me sacked if you don't read it!"

Serena offered him a sweetly reassuring smile. "Well, the duke isn't here, is he? Why can't you just tell him that I read it? How will he know if I haven't?"

His gaze darted desperately around the room, as if he could find the answer in one of the many watercolor paintings that papered the four walls, all products of Serena's artistically prolific sister. "He'll know because—because—"

"Because he bade you to bring him some sort of receipt from Miss Langley?" Miriam suggested.

Gibson's eyes lit up again. "Yes, that's it exactly!"

Annoyance burned through Serena as she thrust the poker into the grate, the smoldering letter impaled on its tip. "No, that's not it. Miriam, would you kindly not provide him with answers to the questions I ask?"

He rushed around the table to the fireplace. "But that is the answer, Miss Langley, truly." He wrenched the poker out of the grate and held it up as if he'd just freed Excalibur. "His Grace said that—that—"

Serena glanced swiftly and sharply at her abigail, who looked ready to burst with another helpful suggestion. "No, Miriam, you let him answer on his own."

He plucked the partially blackened letter from the poker tip. "His Grace said that he, uh, wanted you to scribble some sort of response on the letter—something that would prove you'd actually read it."

Serena eyed him askance. "And he's waiting outside for a response? He wouldn't even come here himself."

"He stated that as you said, Miss Langley, he's a duke, not a messenger boy, but someone like me could double as one quite nicely."

She went to the door and threw it open, but Nicholas was nowhere in sight. "Your Grace? Come out from wherever you're hiding and show yourself!"

There was no response from the dark, chilly silence outside the cottage, where the moon now lurked behind thick clouds. She ventured out a few steps, shivering as she glanced around at the shadows and inky splotches of trees and shrubs, listening for any kind of rustling or footsteps, but she heard nothing.

Except Miriam's voice inside the cottage, as she interrogated the hapless coachman. "As I was saying before, Gibson, I take it you have family in London, and that's why you sought a situation so close?"

"Er, uh—yes, that's so." Did he suffer from a stutter, or wasn't he sure why he wanted to be closer to London? So he had a family. Did that mean he was married?

Why did Serena even care?

But Miriam cared, and Serena caught a hint of anxiety in her voice as she asked, "Oh, so there's a Mrs. Gibson?"

Another long pause, as if he had to think about whether or not he had a wife. Serena wondered if the new coachman had something to conceal. She'd have to ask Nicholas—if he ever bothered to step out from his hiding place.

"Colfax!" She immediately berated herself as she realized that she'd drowned out Gibson's response to Miriam's question. *Only why do I even care?*

"—sleep all the way out here when she has that big house?" she heard him ask.

How dare he! Serena didn't care if he'd broken her fall off the library ladder this morning, that did not give him leave to gossip about her with her own abigail. Nor did he need to know about Felice. If the ton weren't supposed to know about her, then why should anyone else, least of all the new coachman?

"Surely that incident in the library should be sufficient explanation," said Miriam.

"She obviously needs the protection of a husband." Why, the coachman actually sounded as if he considered himself just the man for the job!

Serena stormed back into the cottage, at once resigned to the fact that Nicholas had decamped back to Mayfair where he belonged, and determined to bring an end to servants' gossip. "I can protect myself, thank you very much!"

"I was only explaining to Gibson why you spend your nights out here with—with me and Mrs. Kaye," said Miriam. "You know, it's the only place you feel safe from Lord Winslow."

"If you don't mind my saying so, Miss Langley, you could scarcely protect yourself this morning," Gibson said.

TRUE PRETENSES

"If not for Gibson, you might have broken your neck," Miriam inserted.

"I only fell off a ladder, I wasn't thrown from a horse." Serena cast her eyes on the coachman, who still clutched that cursed letter. "It seems the Duke of Colfax decided not to wait for you to return with evidence that I read the letter, so would you please return it to me now?"

He hesitated, much to her annoyance. "But you will read it—that is, what's left of it?"

She snatched it from his fingers. "For the last time, no!" Thinking she should have done this in the first place, she ripped the letter in half, then into quarters, and finally into eighths before flinging the torn pieces into the fireplace.

"Why not?" he boldly demanded. "If you married the Duke of Fairborough, then you wouldn't have to spend your nights in this dreary little cottage. And you wouldn't have to worry about that—about Winslow anymore."

She glared at him. "Really, you're the most forward and presumptuous—"

"Servant you've ever met?" he glibly supplied. "That may be, Miss Langley, but you can't say I'm wrong about marriage to Fairborough."

"Oh, yes, I can." She pointed to the open doorway. "Colfax was certainly right about you. Now good night, Gibson, and in the future remember your place."

He bowed. "Good night then, ladies."

As soon as he closed the door behind him, Serena heaved such a sigh of exasperation that it nearly came out as a shriek. "I vow, the next time I see the Duke of Colfax, I'm going to have a few words with him about that coachman. So he quit his position at Colfax Park to be closer to London? Why, if I could set foot in White's, I'd wager every penny of Fairborough's trust fund that Colfax discharged him for his—" Oh, how she longed to use some of those colorful adjectives, like the ones cousin Archie had hurled at Crosby this evening upon learning that Warren was off to his club again. They were practically dancing on the tip of her tongue, but her breeding wouldn't permit her to sputter any of them. She had to content herself with "—absolutely downright insolent behavior!"

"I'd prefer to say he's just a plain-speaking man," Mrs. Kaye piped up. "You must admit there's a lot of common sense in what he says."

"Concerning what?"

"Why, your marrying Fairborough, of course. Lord Winslow certainly wouldn't cause you any more trouble."

"No, but Fairborough could cause Felice plenty of trouble. I can fend off Winslow quite nicely, but how much of a wedge could I put between Fairborough and Felice? You and Miriam know I don't spend my nights out here to be safe from Lord Winslow. It's because I'd rather be with my sister."

"I didn't want to tell him about Felice," said Miriam. "Not that I think she's someone to be ashamed of—but you know how people are, and that's why I said you slept out here to be safe from your cousin."

"I know that—then again, you didn't have to tell him anything at all," Serena said sharply. "You were gossiping about me while I was outside looking for Colfax!"

Miriam stuck out her lower lip, as if to pout. "Well, you obviously heard every word, so it's not as if we were gossiping behind your back."

Serena crossed her arms over her chest. "As a matter of fact, I didn't hear every word. I didn't catch his reply when you asked if there was a Mrs. Gibson."

A hint of a smile twitched at the corner of Miriam's

mouth as she cocked her head to one side. "Now who's gossiping, miss?"

Serena smiled back. "There's no harm in discussing the coachman's marital status, is there?"

"Why do you even wish to know? You're ready to have him discharged as it is, and he's scarcely been here a day. And when will you ever have need of his services? Don't you always insist on driving yourself to Town? What difference should it—"

"Just tell me if there's a Mrs. Gibson!"

Miriam lifted her chin. "As a matter of fact, there is."

Serena was baffled by the sudden, heavy sensation in her breast. "Indeed? For someone who's quite taken with him, you don't seem too vexed about it. Could it be you're going to remain faithful to the obstinate Mr. Jennings?"

"I daresay Mr. Jennings had his chance," Miriam said with a sniff. "No, the Mrs. Gibson in question is his grandmother."

Serena's heart lightened. "So there's no wife?"

"As you might expect, coachmen don't make very good husbands. Always away from home, transporting the ton from one townhouse or grand estate to another."

"Rather like sailors in the Royal Navy," Mrs. Kaye chimed in. "Only with coachmen, a girl at every posting house."

"But at least they're not as prone to scurvy," Miriam added. "No, all he has for family is a frail grandmother who lives somewhere in London, which is why he needs to be so near."

This certainly cast the forward, presumptuous, and absolutely downright insolent coachman in a different light. Deep concern for his frail grandmother softened Serena's heart, which in the past few moments had been reluctantly hardening against him. She smiled at Miriam.

"So what were you saying a few moments ago about coachmen not making very good husbands?"

Miriam stiffened. "Well, I should think they don't."

"But you still intend to set your cap for this one?"

"Why not? I can always change him," Miriam said with great feminine conviction.

Strident female voices jolted Kit from his sleep.

He could have sworn he'd just closed his eyes, but no, the sun was already glaring through threadbare curtains into the tiny room over the carriage house. These austere quarters—not much worse than what he'd had in India, really—would be his abode until he charmed the recalcitrant Serena Langley to her senses.

And it sounded as if his obdurate bride was one of the females who had just torn him from a very hot, but much too fleeting dream about a naked woman with tawny brown hair, redolent of lilacs, lying on top of him pressing against his throbbing loins.

"Calm down, Serena," he heard Miriam saying. "You're acting as if Gibson himself might have broken that wheel!"

The commotion outside his door quickly dissipated the sultry clouds in his befogged mind. Obviously Serena had wasted no time discovering her disabled phaeton.

Only it had to be so damned early in the morning! Where had he ever gotten the foolish notion that ladies liked to sleep in late each morning—the higher their rank, the later? A duchess, for instance, seldom rose before noon.

Then again, Serena wasn't a duchess—yet. She was

still a mere honorable—the earliest riser of all ladies in the ton, damn his rotten luck.

"Gibson, open the door," she called out. "I need your services immediately."

He sat up on the creaking bed, rubbing his eyes.

More pounding on the door. "Gibson, are you awake?"

"Evidently not," Miriam said. "Serena, no—"

The door flew open with a bang. Kit flinched as he saw Serena standing in the doorway with her mouth hanging open. Both she and the abigail gasped audibly.

He suddenly realized why: He wore nothing but his breeches. He pulled the blanket to his chin and then dropped it, realizing how silly he looked covering himself like a lady caught in her hip bath. Let the two women be shocked; it would serve them right for crashing in on him before he scarcely had the chance to open his eyes.

But he thoroughly enjoyed the look on Serena's face—as if she were starving and had just stumbled upon a sumptuous feast. It was the same look he'd worn while gawping at that basket of food last night, and his empty stomach rumbled at the memory. "If you ladies will excuse me so I might get dressed . . ."

Miriam grabbed her charge and pulled her out of sight. Kit couldn't help thinking she did so not to protect Serena's innocence, but so the abigail herself could enjoy a better view of his manly attributes.

She continued ogling his chest. "Miss Langley likes to get an early start when she goes to Town—the road isn't so crowded. But then we discovered the wheel on her phaeton is broken! You wouldn't know what happened to it?"

Kit rose to his full height, holding the blanket in front of himself. He figured Miriam had seen more than enough for one day, plus his breeches were still bulging from that fiendishly erotic dream. "Now how would I know anything about that, since I've been here less than twenty-four hours?"

She looked rather put out, though he wasn't sure whether it was from his words or the fact she could no longer feast her gaze on his chest. "Didn't you say you missed supper last night because you were busy familiarizing yourself with the vehicles? You must have noticed the phaeton."

"I paid no mind to it, as it's not the sort of vehicle I might be called upon to drive."

"Well, you'll have to drive me and Miss Langley in the open carriage then."

"That's my job. Now if you'll excuse me."

He donned his most intimidating glare, the one which, at Fairborough, he usually reserved for indolent servants and, when he was in India, derelict soldiers subordinate to him. With a little huff she ducked out of sight and he closed the door.

His stomach growled persistently as he quickly made himself presentable, and he cursed himself. Because of his own snobbish refusal to eat at the same table as the rest of the staff last night, he'd unwittingly cheated himself out of supper. And now, thanks to Serena's demands for his services—and at such a ghastly hour, too—he would have to miss breakfast.

But that was also his own fault, wasn't it? If he hadn't had the brilliant foresight to vandalize her phaeton last night, thus forcing her to seek those services at said ghastly hour, then he could still be enjoying his deliciously erotic dream.

If only he could blame Nick. After all, this entire charade had been Nick's less than splendid idea. But Kit had been stupid enough to take his dare! A lark, indeed.

Washed, shaved, and dressed in dark green livery that was too short on him, but fortunately wide enough for his broad shoulders (his predecessor had been quite portly), he finally made his way downstairs.

"Good morning, Miss Langley, and where would you like to go today?" he asked as he reached the foot of the steps.

"To Town, of course." She stood next to her disabled phaeton as if she couldn't bring herself to leave it behind. Now that he was a little more alert, he noted how fetching she looked in her sunny yellow spencer and matching sprigged dress, her golden brown curls peeking out from a straw bonnet tied under her chin with bright yellow streamers. She was just above medium height and while she wasn't pretty, she was interesting to look at. Her silvery blue eyes were set close together, and her nose was rather prominent, but Kit thought it gave her an air of intelligence, which he'd already learned she had in abundance. Had she been as cork-brained as most females of his acquaintance, he might not still be putting himself to all this trouble.

She gifted him with a brilliant smile, quite a change from last night when she'd all but spat nails at him, but he remained on his guard. He suspected if he confessed here and now who he really was, the smile would vanish and she'd cosh him over the head with the reticule she clutched in both hands, as if it held everything she owned in the world aside from that damned phaeton.

Guilt stabbed him for having crippled her obviously beloved phaeton, but it was for her own good—not to mention his. He turned to the larger carriage, surprised to see the horses already hitched to it. "Well, I see you managed to rouse the groom before me."

"He's busy sleeping off his ale," Miriam said sourly. "Miss Langley and I hitched up ourselves."

"You ladies shouldn't have done that. I could have done it." Kit felt another twinge of annoyance at the groom, who he'd already learned was useless. When he'd sent him to the house for supper last night, the groom hadn't returned with any food, but he had brought with him a couple of flasks, no doubt purloined from Lord Paxton's supply in the library. Kit's stomach grumbled again.

"It was no trouble," said Serena. "I always hitch up the phaeton myself. It gave us something to do while we were waiting for you."

He tried to find a hint of reproach in those words, but found none. Nevertheless, "I'm sorry to have kept you waiting, but as you're aware, I did have to get dressed."

"Oh, we're more than aware of that." Miriam shot him an arch smile while Serena lowered her eyes, pursing her lips as if to hide a smile of her own. Ah, so she too liked what she'd seen. And with a little luck, he thought, she'd get to see it again one day very soon.

He helped them into the open carriage. "Where in Town do you wish to go, Miss Langley?"

She gave him a very familiar direction in Park Lane.

He didn't realize how stunned he must have looked until she leaned forward to peer at him, saying, "Don't you know where that is, Gibson?"

He quickly composed himself and turned to mount the driver's box. "Of course, Miss Langley."

And well he should. She wanted to visit his family's town house!

Was she hoping to see *him?* Was she finally coming around to her senses? Perhaps by nightfall he wouldn't have to masquerade as a coachman any longer. Perhaps tonight he'd get to sleep in his own bed.

He hadn't even been to the town house since his return from India—he'd been staying with Nicholas while in Town—but he knew his stepmother, whose idea of hell was anyplace outside of London, was very likely in residence there.

He flicked the reins, and the horses slowly pulled the carriage into the early morning sunshine. He figured it would take about an hour to reach the town house, if that long, since it was still quite early. Would Daphne even be awake by the time they arrived? She was, after all, a duchess.

And oh, how she enjoyed being a duchess!

Kit's father had been gone for two years now, so he didn't think Daphne was still in mourning—if she'd ever been in mourning at all. According to the letter he'd received from his grandmother, Daphne had been in London when Father had passed away at the ancestral home in Devon. If there'd been one thing Kit and Simon had shared in common besides the same parents, it was the conviction that their stepmother had married their father only for his title and vast fortune.

Which reminded Kit of his last encounter with her, only moments after learning his father had bought him military exile to India. Storming out of the study at their London town house, he'd flung open the door to find Daphne bent nearly in half, head level with the keyhole. With surprise heaped on top of his already boiling rage at Father, he'd said something foolishly thoughtless about her being little more than a common piece of baggage who'd only married his father for his title and fortune. Daphne had fallen into one of her swoons, Father had bellowed some more, Kit had bellowed back, and on and on and round and round till it was almost a relief to leave England.

He felt a painful tremor in his heart at the memory. He hadn't left England on good terms with anyone save his grandmother. Kit had always gotten along very well with his father, much better than Simon ever had—until that calamitous night at Langley House. How could Father have doubted Kit's innocence while believing the damning lies of others? It was the only time in his life Kit had gotten into trouble—damn it, from childhood he'd been a paragon compared to Simon—didn't that count for anything? Father's sudden, inexplicable loss of trust had driven a sharp wedge between them, which seven years and thousands of miles between England and India could not dislodge.

And now Father and Simon were gone.

For now he had to concentrate on his driving. If he started brooding over family breaches that could no longer be healed, he'd land his prospective bride and her abigail in a ditch.

But as he guided the horses onto the main road leading to Town, he couldn't help listening to the conversation behind him. Instead of discussing their reasons for visiting the Woodard family's London residence, his passengers chatted about Lady Jemma's tendresse for a certain Lord Dunbar. Kit remembered a Hamish Dunbar at Oxford, though the Scot was a couple of years his junior.

"As much as I'd like Jemma to be happy, I'd almost prefer that she marry Fairborough instead," said Serena.

Well, it certainly didn't sound as though Serena was visiting his family's town house to see him. Perhaps she wasn't planning to call on Kit, but Daphne. Only what sort of business would his reluctant betrothed have with his stepmother?

Now that he thought about it, he'd bet every penny of that wretched trust fund that Daphne played a very big part in setting Serena against him. Daphne, he knew, would never forgive him for his parting words to

TRUE PRETENSES

her nine years ago. What better way to get revenge?

He tightened his grip on the reins as he realized what he had to do now. Once they arrived at the town house, he would act the coachman until Serena was inside.

Then he would confront them both, and end this ridiculous charade—and whatever outrageous misunderstanding Serena had about him—today!

Chapter Four

In all her years of living at Langley House, Serena had never noticed the dark hunter green of the servants' livery, till she saw it stretched across the back of the new coachman as he sat in front of her and Miriam on the carriage box. Like a pair of twining arms, her thoughts slid around Gibson from his back to the broad, muscular chest she'd seen this morning. She stole a guilty glance at Miriam, worried that she might read her thoughts and berate her for them.

Gibson finally brought the grays to a halt in front of Woodard House. He jumped down from the box and opened the carriage door, all the while gazing across the street through the trees that dappled Hyde Park, where a few riders could be seen enjoying the rare morning sunshine.

"See anyone you know in the park, Gibson?" asked Miriam.

He snapped his gaze to his passengers and swiftly

held out his hand. "No. Forgive me, I must have been woolgathering."

Serena picked up the two long scrolls, one tied with a blue ribbon and the other with a red one, from where they had been resting on the opposite seat.

"Could I hold those for you, Miss Langley?" asked Gibson.

"That's all right, I've got them. And I just now realized something—you haven't eaten since midday yesterday, have you?"

He helped her out of the carriage as gracefully as any lord. "No, Miss Langley."

She favored him with her brightest smile. He smiled back, revealing that dimple in his left cheek, identical to the one that was always in his chin regardless. "I'm sorry about last night, Gibson. Why don't you take the carriage around back and charm Her Grace's cook into something to break your fast? You should have no trouble, and we should be no more than an hour."

"Thank you, Miss Langley." He bowed and climbed aboard the driver's box, urging the horses forward.

"You took the words right out of my mouth," said Miriam. "Only I'd say he could charm an entire feast out of the cook."

"He's too young for you," said Serena, as they ascended the front steps of the imposing Palladian house.

"And too low for you. Might I remind you that he's merely a coachman, while you're the granddaughter of an earl, and the betrothed of a duke!"

"Who could just as easily marry Jemma," retorted Serena, still thinking of the coachman's dimples. Strange, she'd never noticed if any of the other servants had dimples—not that she'd ever thought to look. Whatever had possessed her to seek such features now—and on Gibson of all people?

"What about her Scotsman?"

Serena plied the heavy brass knocker. "What gives you the idea he's from Scotland? Certainly not his speech, which I must say is almost too fine for a coachman. Of course, Colfax told me Gibson's father was a tutor, so he obviously managed to get some education, and I think that's a good thing for—"

She broke off her words as Miriam, standing next to her, suddenly leaned forward and turned her head to give Serena a long, hard look.

Serena gazed back at her, nonplussed. "What's wrong? Do I have a crumb of toast stuck on my front tooth again?"

"Not at all. What's wrong is that I'm now talking about one man while you're still dwelling on another."

"I'm not dwelling on him!"

"Then why didn't you realize I'm talking about Lady Jemma's Scot?"

Heat flashed in Serena's cheeks as she repeatedly banged the knocker, silently praying for the butler's swift deliverance. "What about her Scot?"

"I thought you wished her well with him."

"I also wish Napoleon might direct his energies toward the other side of the Atlantic. What was he thinking, practically giving Louisiana to Mr. Jefferson? He could have taken over every acre of it and populated it with as many people as he squandered in Russia last year. Such a foo—"

"You're evading my question," Miriam said crisply.

"No, you're missing my point. Just because I wish for something, doesn't mean it will come true. I wish for Jemma to marry her Scotsman and be happy—but I also wish to avoid marriage to Fair—"

Thank heavens the butler finally opened the door.

TRUE PRETENSES

He ushered them into the study, where they waited for nearly half an hour before Daphne, the Dowager Duchess of Fairborough, made her entrance.

"Good morning, Serena."

"Good morning, Your Grace." Serena brandished the two long scrolls. "I have another delivery."

"Excellent. Let's see what miracle she's wrought this time." Daphne gestured to a large table in front of the window looking out on Hyde Park. Serena handed the scroll with the red ribbon to Daphne, then untied the blue ribbon from the other and unfurled it across the table.

Daphne drew a sharp breath before asking the same question she always asked whenever Serena made one of these deliveries: "Now which one is this?"

Serena lifted the upper left corner to reveal the small, smudgy initials FCL scrawled in charcoal.

"You're looking at the copy." She disliked the word *forgery*, and besides, it wasn't really a forgery, because Daphne had repeatedly assured her that those who eventually acquired these canvases knew they were buying copies, and were grateful to have them. Not everyone could afford an original, but many people were content to own a copy if it was a good one. And Felice made very good copies.

This particular painting was a basic hunting scene, which at first glance was like any other of men astride their horses, surrounded by dogs as they galloped over sloping fields in pursuit of an elusive fox. But only when the copy was compared to the original, which Daphne was now unrolling, could one appreciate all the little nuances: the varied splotches of color on each individual beagle, the different facial features of the men, the capricious shape of the clouds, and the horses! Serena couldn't draw anything even remotely resembling a horse. But Felice did it so effortlessly, or so it seemed when Serena watched her, and every minute detail in the copy was totally faithful to the same detail in the original.

Daphne turned to Miriam, who was just as admiring. "She doesn't need a chaperone right now, Evans. She'll be perfectly safe with me."

Miriam frowned at Daphne's condescending tone, but she knew a dismissal when she heard one. Serena tried to sweeten things by adding, "Perhaps you could join Gibson for a cup of tea."

"I could at that." Miriam brightened as she hastened out of the study, and Serena could not help chuckling.

"Who is Gibson?" asked Daphne, furling the original and tucking it under her arm.

"Our new coachman." Serena deftly tied the red ribbon around the original to secure it, as Daphne released it from under her arm. "He's very handsome."

"My stepson wouldn't like to hear you discussing another man that way," said Daphne, though she scarcely sounded disapproving. "Has Fairborough called on you yet?"

Serena sighed. "He's tried, but I can't bring myself to receive him. I don't even know what he looks like—or does he resemble his brother?"

Daphne glided over to the large desk. "As I recall, Kit is actually taller than his older brother, and he has dark hair and brown eyes. Simon had his father's fair hair and blue eyes, but Kit resembles his mother, or so my husband always said. She was from France, but no one ever got a good look at her. She spent little more than two years in England, every moment of it in confinement at Fairborough. I haven't even seen Kit since he returned from India, though I've heard he's been staying with friends while in Town."

"He's staying with the Duke of Colfax, who came to

dinner last night and brought me a letter from him. Of course I refused to read it."

Daphne opened a drawer and pulled out a ten-pound note, which she gave to Serena. "Kit behaved very badly toward me the last time I saw him, so I understand only too well your reluctance toward him."

Daphne'd mentioned this before, though she'd never elaborated. Since Daphne was very beautiful, Serena could only imagine what had happened, in light of what had transpired between Kit and Aunt Leah. Daphne had always been considered a diamond of the first water, with her glistening golden hair, skin like smooth porcelain, a mouth that looked as soft and pink as a rosebud, and a curvaceous bosom that always seemed on the verge of spilling out of her low-cut gowns.

Whenever Serena looked at someone like Daphne, and then looked at her own reflection in the mirror, she couldn't help thinking the new Duke of Fairborough might find her just a bit too drab for his taste. His predecessor certainly had. Serena's hair couldn't seem to make up its mind whether to be brown or blond, while her eyes couldn't settle on blue or gray. Not to mention that her nose was entirely too big for her face, while her own bosom—well, it was certainly nothing like Daphne's. She had Kit's older brother to thank for pointing out the latter two flaws. She frowned at the thought that she looked more like one of the horses in the painting.

She tucked the ten-pound note into her reticule. "If only I could thank the man who sells Felice's copies for me. Why don't you let me take that canvas to him, just this once?"

Daphne swiftly stepped in front of the copied painting, as if to prevent Serena from snatching it up. "Oh no, not today!"

"Why not?"

Daphne smiled tremulously, and Serena thought she saw something akin to fear flickering in her china-blue eyes. "Perhaps next time. I don't have his direction at hand, and my coachman—who would know precisely how to get there—is off today. But rest assured Mr. Plumlee knows you're grateful for his patronage. Now tell me about your handsome new coachman."

Serena couldn't help feeling that Daphne had some other, less innocuous reason for not allowing her to meet Mr. Plumlee, and her sudden eagerness to change the subject only reinforced that suspicion. Like most aristocrats, Daphne had never been the sort to take an interest in servants, beyond what they could do for her, but Serena was only too happy to discuss Gibson, and she couldn't help smiling. "He came to work for us just yesterday. He's tall, with chestnut hair and brown eyes."

"You've noticed that much about him?"

"I daresay it's not much of a description, Your Grace."

"Enough of one. You said his hair is chestnut, as opposed to merely brown, and you smiled when you said it."

"Well, it is chestnut," Serena said defensively. "And I smile to be pleasant."

Daphne tugged on the bellpull. "So what color is my butler's hair?"

Serena pondered. "Brown, I think. I've never given it much thought."

"You've known my butler for months, yet you've only known your coachman since yesterday, and look at how much thought you've given him already."

Flustered, Serena toyed with her reticule. First Miriam, and now Daphne had remarked on her interest in the new coachman. Just how interested was she in a man who, according to society's rigid rules, should have been far beneath her touch?

The butler appeared in the doorway. "Yes, Your Grace?"

"Come here, Hollings, over by the window so we can see you better." The bemused butler obeyed. "Brown hair, you say?"

"Hm, maybe with some gray streaks." Serena studied the butler's thinning hair. "All that matters is that it's brown."

"Well, isn't that all that matters with your coachman? That will be all, Hollings."

He bowed and quit the study.

"I think I'd like to see this coachman," said Daphne. "Tall men with brown hair and eyes are like coals in Newcastle—didn't I just tell you that Kit is tall with hair and eyes of brown? But a man with hair of chestnut must be extraordinary indeed."

Serena fought to suppress another self-betraying smile. "He's in your kitchen at present, if you'd care to take a peek."

Daphne looked taken aback, as if Serena had just suggested an outing to the stews. "Surely you're not serious?"

"I sent him there."

"That's not what I mean. This handsome manservant with chestnut hair seems to have charmed not only your abigail—but you, too."

Serena felt her cheeks flush hot again, dismayed at the thought that Daphne might very well be right.

Mrs. Bannen gasped at the sight of him in the kitchen doorway.

"Master Kit, is it really ye?" The Scottish cook, who had been more of a mother to him than Daphne, nearly crushed him in her arms, which were almost as strong and thick as his own. "What are ye doin', comin' into yer own house this way? Why, ye be the duke himself now!"

"Not quite. For now I'm coachman to the lady they say I'm supposed to wed before my next birthday."

"Less 'n three months away. And what do ye mean, bein' your bride's coachman? Dinna tell me ye've been pressed into yet another one o' Master Nicky's pranks?"

Kit roared with laughter, and Mrs. Bannen dropped her hands against her apron with an emphatic slap as her mouth dropped open. "Ye have! And Master Nicky a duke now, too! Why dinna either o' ye grow up already?"

"Before I tell you what trouble he's gotten me into this time, how about some breakfast? I'm famished."

"I'm not surprised. Ye bein' a coachman, ye're not apt to eat as well as a toff."

Kit sat at the kitchen table. She poured him a cup of piping-hot tea, and as she whipped up breakfast for him, he told her the whole ludicrous story about the stipulation in his father's will, Serena's refusal to even receive him, and the night less than a week ago when over brandy—a *lot* of brandy, Kit sheepishly admitted under Mrs. Bannen's reproving glare—Nicholas had mentioned hearing that the Langleys were in desperate need of a new coachman, and had half-jokingly suggested that Kit apply for the position as there seemed no other way for him to meet his betrothed.

Mrs. Bannen set in front of him a huge plate of ham and eggs, cooked just the way he liked them. "Well, have ye met her?"

"I drove her here this morning."

"And she doesna suspect a thing?"

"Not yet." He shoveled a huge forkful into his mouth. "Delicious, Mrs. Bannen."

" 'Tis pleased I am to cook some sort o' breakfast for someone. Her Grace scarcely eats more 'n toast 'n' chocolate. What sort o' alias do ye have? I mean, should I call ye 'Yer Grace' or 'Coachman' or what?"

"Colfax suggested I use the name of his former coachman, one Alfred Gibson, who abandoned his position about a year ago."

Mrs. Bannen refilled his teacup. "Aye, I remember hearin' somethin' aboot that. Ran off with the Maxwells' kitchen maid. Some say the two o' them eloped to me bonny homeland. Others claim he joined the army to fight Boney, while she became one o' Master Simon's Cyprians at . . ." Her words trailed off as she realized who she was addressing.

"At the Langley farm down in Kent?" Kit calmly supplied. "It's all right, Mrs. Bannen, I know what my brother was up to at the time of his death. Remember, he took it from Miss Langley's grandfather before I was even sent to India. The old earl owed my brother enough money from the gaming tables to have financed for Napoleon a campaign all the way to Peking, and until Moscow it wouldn't have surprised me. I don't doubt Simon poached some of his Cyprians from among the ton's maidservants."

"Still, I didna mean for it to slip oot like that."

"But that brings up something else. What do you know of Miss Langley's refusal to marry me?"

She knit her brow. "Now how would I ken o' that?"

"Because it's long been my experience that servants know their master's business better than their master—and they invariably share that knowledge with the servants of other masters—or mistresses, as the case may be."

"I've heard nothing, and that's God's truth. Ye could

go up and show yerself to her now, what's to stop ye?"

"This breakfast." He shoveled another forkful into his mouth. "Does she call on my stepmother very often?"

"Mm, aboot once a month or so. They have some sort o' business arrangement."

He stiffened as he gulped down the food. "What do you mean?"

"Miss Langley enjoys dabblin' in watercolors like any fine lass. She sells her pictures to Her Grace."

"Why? Are her straits that dire?"

"So it seems, which is why I dinna understand why she doesna wish to marry ye."

"What does my stepmother do with the watercolors? Are they gracing the walls of Woodard House even as we speak?"

"Her Grace takes them to a Mr. Plumlee just off Piccadilly, who sells them."

Kit fell silent, contemplating the cook's words as he finished his breakfast. He recalled the two long scrolls Serena had with her this morning, and then he remembered all the unframed watercolors he'd seen tacked on the walls of her cottage last night. His fiancée was quite the little Michelangelo. Of course he had no objections to that, but he certainly objected to everything else he was hearing.

Something wasn't right. It went without saying that Plumlee collected a commission, at least 10 percent, and that was assuming quite liberally that he was scrupulous. But Daphne didn't seem constitutionally capable of doing business with scrupulous people. And what was *she* getting out of all of this? She had to be getting something, certainly more than what Serena was getting. Daphne had never been one to do anything for nothing. No, every little move his stepmother made was carefully calculated to benefit only

TRUE PRETENSES

her and no one else, not even Rosalind, Kit's sixteen-year-old half sister. Just how badly was Serena being cheated?

He scraped his plate, drained his teacup, then slammed it into the saucer with a discordant clink. "This will not do. I'm going to end all of this, right now."

Mrs. Bannen furrowed her brow. "What d'ye mean?"

He pushed back his chair with a piercing screech on the flagstone floor. "I will not allow my future wife or my stepmother to conduct themselves in this manner. And now is as good a time as any to let Miss Langley know that I am the Duke of Fairborough and *she* will be my wife."

He marched over to the kitchen door and threw it open. He leapt back in surprise as Miriam nearly tumbled head over heels into the kitchen.

"What the deuce—" He helped the flustered abigail to her feet. "And just how long have you been crouching outside this door eavesdropping, Evans?"

She brushed herself off with as much dignity as she could muster before she glared at him. "How dare you accuse me of such a thing!"

"I dare," he shot back. "The last time I opened a door on an eavesdropper, she tumbled to my feet like one of those acrobats at Vauxhall Gardens—exactly as you just did. How much of our conversation did you hear?"

Miriam cowered before him. "Oh dear, it's really you, isn't it? How did you, why are you—oh, please, Your Grace, please don't look at me that way. God forgive me, at this moment I do believe you could have done it."

"Done what?" Kit roared.

She started swaying and fluttering her eyes, as if she were about to faint, but she quickly stiffened as Kit took her firmly by the shoulders.

"Never mind." He guided her to the table and pulled

out a chair for her. "You will stay here and say nothing for the time being. Mrs. Bannen, some tea for Miss Langley's abigail, if you please."

He stormed out of the kitchen and up the dark, narrow stairwell. He'd get a special license today and bring an end to this whole travesty once and for all.

Tonight he'd sleep in his own bed—and by God, Serena would be next to him! But only after he had her beneath him, and—oh! Kit felt the familiar tightening in his groin as he remembered his erotic dream this morning, and the way she'd sprawled over him yesterday on the library floor—perhaps she could spend some time on top of him, too!

But first things first.

He emerged from the servants' quarters into the familiar first-floor hallway. Now where would Daphne and Serena be scheming over their teacups? The drawing room, of course. It was toward the front of the house, opposite the study.

He swaggered down the hallway, and was halfway to his intended destination when someone who could only be the butler stepped out of nowhere and firmly planted himself right in front of Kit. He was obviously a new butler—that is, one retained since Kit went to India, since he didn't recognize him.

"Who the bloody hell are you?" asked the butler.

"I'll tell you who the bloody hell I am," Kit retorted. "Though I do so hate doing this. I am the eleventh Duke of Fairborough."

The butler flicked his understandably disbelieving gaze over Kit's dubious attire.

Kit grasped the lapels of his dark green livery. "Oh, I realize it's not one of Mr. Weston's superfine creations, and my boots may not be genuine Hessians, but—"

TRUE PRETENSES

"If you're Duke of Fairborough, then I'm Prince of Wales," growled the butler.

"Well, I don't blame you for not believing me, especially since I don't believe you either. But why don't we humor each other, just this once? Have I your permission to speak with Miss Langley, Your Royal Highness? As you may have heard, she is my betrothed, and I understand she's with my dear stepmother, the dowager duchess."

He stepped around the butler, who clawed fruitlessly at his coat. "Now see here, whoever you are, you'd best get out of here before I summon the watch. Stop!"

The butler sped past Kit, hurtling not into the drawing room but into the study, slamming the door behind him.

Kit reached the threshold of the drawing room, only to find it vacant.

But he did hear excited feminine voices across the hall. In the study. Where the door was firmly closed.

Two long strides placed Kit at the study door, where he yanked on the gilt door handle. Closed and locked.

He put his ear to the door as he recalled that this was where he'd last seen Daphne—eavesdropping, just like Miriam.

"Calm down, Hollings, what do you mean there's an intruder roaming the house?" his stepmother demanded.

"He's out in the hallway, Your Grace—that's why I locked the doors. He could be very dangerous. He demanded to see Miss Langley!"

"Oh dear, no." Serena's voice, sounding decidedly forlorn. "Don't tell me it's Fairborough. How did he know I would be here at precisely this hour?"

"Oh, he's scarcely the duke, though he said as

much, Miss Langley. He clearly belongs in Bedlam. He thought I was the prince regent!"

"Well, don't just stand there, Hollings, do something about him," Daphne said. "He could be ransacking this house even as we speak. Miss Langley and I will keep ourselves safely locked in here. Now go on, go!"

Kit stood back as the butler unlocked the door. It slowly swung inward, and Kit pushed his entire weight against it, knocking the butler to one side.

"It's the intruder!" Hollings exclaimed, as Daphne and Serena gaped at Kit in astonishment.

Serena was the first to recover. "Oh, goodness me, Hollings, it's only my coachman." She scowled at Kit. "Just what do you think you're doing now, Gibson?"

But Kit ignored her, fixing his gaze on the trembling, ashen Daphne, her wide blue eyes flecked with fear as she clutched the pearls at her throat.

"Hello, Daphne," he said, flashing a triumphant smile from his stepmother to his betrothed, who only stared at him in shock.

Chapter Five

Scarcely able to contain her outrage, Serena glared back at the coachman, who looked unbearably smug. "What do you think you're doing? How dare you address the duchess that way!" She turned to Daphne, who, not surprisingly, looked even more affronted. "Your Grace, I'm so dreadfully sorry—Gibson previously worked for Colfax, who warned me that he was very—"

She broke off her sentence as Daphne slumped to the floor.

"Oh my God!" the butler burst out. "I mean, pardon me, Miss Langley, but—"

"Never mind, Hollings, go and blaspheme no more." Serena crouched down next to the duchess. "She's only fainted. Have one of the maids bring smelling salts."

Hollings whirled on Gibson, pointing his finger at the coachman as if it were a loaded pistol. "This is all your fault, you blackguard. I'll see you in Newgate for this!"

"You can see him in Newgate after you fetch a hartshorn." Serena glowered up at Gibson. "Perhaps you wouldn't mind explaining your presence in this part of the house?"

He knelt on the other side of Daphne, clearly chagrined now. "I'm terribly sorry, Miss Langley. I do have a very good reason for behaving so familiarly toward the duchess."

"What reason could you possi—oh, never mind, I don't want to know!" Horror crept over Serena at the thought of what such familiarity might mean. She'd heard of married ladies in the ton who, having provided their husbands with the requisite heir, sometimes took other men—such as footmen, gardeners, and yea, even coachmen—as illicit lovers.

But the notion that Daphne might have enjoyed such a dalliance with Gibson of all people was enough to make Serena feel . . . envious. Why couldn't she feel sick with repugnance instead?

Suddenly she resented the duchess for whatever she might have shared with Gibson. "Just tell me if that's why you came in here—did you wish to speak with Her Grace?"

"No, I meant to speak with you."

"Concerning what?" She raised her eyes to his. Despite her simmering fury, she couldn't help thinking how much he looked like a puppy who had just been caught soiling the parlor rug. It had to be those brown eyes of his.

"This may not be the right moment to explain, Miss Langley, since the duchess is unconscious and—"

"In other words, you don't have an answer because Miriam isn't here to provide you with one?"

His face brightened, and now the puppy looked as if

he were eager to play fetch-the-stick. "Oh, but—but it was she who sent me here."

"Why did she not come herself?"

"Because—because—" Oh dear, he was stammering again. Apparently this was a penchant of his. She rubbed Daphne's wrists as she patiently waited for the coachman to get his words in order.

"Miss Evans sent me to tell you that—that she was feeling faint," he finally said.

That was nothing unusual. Miriam, after all, was nearing that age when, if she didn't feel faint, then she experienced moments of scalding heat. She'd complained of just such a moment the other day.

Serena glanced back at Gibson. He looked not only relieved to have told her, but quite pleased with himself, as if proud that he was able to come up with a plausible explanation without any help from Miriam.

"So why did you call the butler the prince regent and yourself the Duke of Fairborough? Hollings looks nothing like the prince, and even if you were the duke, why would you wander the halls of your own house dressed as a coachman?"

Now the puppy dropped the stick and soiled the rug again.

"Never mind, Gibson, it's not important. I suppose pretending to be the duke was the only way you could get past the butler to bring me Miriam's message." The coachman, she noted with amusement, looked quite put out at her words, as if his reasons for briefly impersonating a duke were far loftier than that, but Serena saw no point in pursuing such a trivial matter any further. She rose to her feet. "Perhaps you could place her on that sofa near the fireplace?"

Gibson gingerly picked up Daphne and carried her over to the sofa, where he carefully laid her down.

"I think she'll be all right," he said, as Daphne began shifting and moaning.

"I think you should step back now." With all her strength, Serena pushed him away from the sofa. "If she should open her eyes to see you standing over her, she's likely to have a relapse. I tend to think she doesn't want to see you again." At least Serena hoped not.

"Oh, I know she doesn't."

"That will do, Gibson." She scowled at him, and again he looked like the puppy who couldn't tell the difference between an Aubusson and the *Times*. That imaginary rug was ruined by now.

Hollings reappeared with a maid, who had a hartshorn for Daphne. "Should I summon a doctor, Miss Langley?"

"I don't think that's necessary. As soon as she comes around, she should be quite all right. Gibson was only trying to bring me a message from my abigail, who is suddenly unwell." She returned to the table where Felice's painting lay. "But I know of one thing you could do for me, Hollings. Do you know the direction of Mr. Plumlee's establishment?"

"It's somewhere off Piccadilly," the coachman piped up.

That was quick. "You seem familiar with it, Gibson."

"I've only heard of it, Miss Langley."

She swiftly rolled up the canvas, casting her eyes on the butler. "Her Grace told me that her coachman had the direction but he was off today, and I was wondering, Hollings—knowing how you servants like to gossip about the affairs of your masters and mistresses—if perhaps you might—" She noticed Gibson looked ready to explode with laughter. "What is so amusing, Gibson?"

TRUE PRETENSES

"Nothing, Miss Langley, except I'd be happy to take you to Plumlee's, provided I have the direction."

She concentrated on retying the blue ribbon around the canvas. "I haven't said yet that I wish to go there, but that is what I had in mind. I'm afraid Her Grace won't be well enough to go out for a while, and the least I can do for her after this unpleasant incident is to take this painting to Mr. Plumlee myself. Hollings, see that Gibson gets the direction, and also find out what you can about Miss Evans." She returned to the sofa as Daphne groaned again. "Your Grace?"

The coachman leaned over to peer at the duchess, and again Serena pushed him away. "As I said before, Gibson, it might be best if she didn't see you again. Go with Hollings and see about that direction."

"Yes, Miss Langley." He looked decidedly crestfallen as he followed the butler out of the study.

Daphne's eyelids fluttered. "Oh, dear me, what happened?"

"You fainted." Serena saw no need to add that the appearance of her coachman had been the trigger. "I think you'll be all right now. But don't fret about getting the canvas to Mr. Plumlee. I'll take care of it."

Daphne struggled to sit up. "No, Serena, you mustn't."

She headed for the door. "I must."

"No!" Daphne gasped.

Serena glanced at the maid. "Don't let her get up. She needs to rest."

Serena left before Daphne could protest any further. Why didn't she want her to visit Plumlee?

Half an hour later, as the horses cantered down Piccadilly Street, Kit tightly clenched the reins, wishing he could use the crop. Not on the horses, but on Miss Miriam Evans.

He couldn't help listening to the conversation behind him. Miriam spoke just loud enough for him to hear—because she *wanted* him to hear.

"Have you noticed, Serena, what a noble mien Gibson has?"

"A noble what?"

"Mien. You know, he looks and carries himself like an aristocrat. And the cook at Woodard House says he looks like Fairborough—that is, the present one known as Kit."

"I've never seen him, so I wouldn't know," Serena replied.

"Oh, Gibson," Miriam called out. "Do you perchance have French blood?"

That sounded like a pistol, loaded and primed, Kit thought. He did not turn around, as Piccadilly was a very congested street requiring constant attention to other carriages, horsemen, meandering pedestrians, and muddy ruts. He called back over his shoulder, "Why do you ask?"

"Think about it. The duke's mother was French, correct? Now consider the Revolution. She must have left scores of relatives behind in France, most of whom would have lost their heads."

From what Kit had learned in his youth, all of them had. Now that he thought about it, he was all that remained of his mother's family.

Miriam continued, "Suppose not all of them lost their heads. Perhaps one of them—the duke's aunt, for example—had an infant she managed to pass to her faithful maid, who then smuggled him out of Paris and into the hands of friends, who would have seen to his safe passage across the Channel. You're too young to remember, Serena, but many refugees of the French Revolution found safe haven in England. The previous

Duke of Colfax took in quite a few, since his ancestral home is near Dover."

"And you're saying our new coachman may be that infant. That would make him younger than I am, and I'm afraid he looks older. I was a babe myself when they stormed the Bastille. Those infamous round-the-clock beheadings, I believe, came a few years later. Though if he's my age or younger, then perhaps he only looks older because his life has been harder than mine."

"Miss Langley, I assure you I am just old enough to remember the French Revolution," Kit declared. "For all you know, I'm the long-lost dauphin."

Serena burst into laughter. "Now there's a notion I do find intriguing. It would certainly explain a lot about you."

He smiled as he carefully guided the horses into the narrow, appointed street just off Piccadilly.

"Oh, let's not go that far," Miriam scoffed. "We're not talking about the dauphin, but someone from the family of Fairborough's mother. Instead of an infant, perhaps the faithful maid smuggled a child out of Paris."

Kit had had enough. "No maid, faithful or otherwise, did any such thing. I was born in England and by God's grace I'll die in England."

"Spoken like a true Englishman, though I understand your subterfuge. Nowadays it would be too easy for someone to use your French blood against you."

"They've already—" He saw the trap just in time, and like the trap he quickly clamped his jaws shut. He'd been about to blurt out, *They've already done that.* It was one of the reasons people had found it so easy to believe he'd attacked Serena's aunt.

"What were you about to say?" Miriam prodded.

He tightened his jaw. "I said, after this they probably

will, since we're shouting about it in the middle of London."

"Aha! So you do admit to having French blood!"

"I don't admit to anything. My point is that even without French blood, all of London would assume otherwise just from this conversation. Yet they can't possibly hear the whole story, only bits and pieces, from which they construct a totally wrong assumption. And that's the problem with people. Too often they make wrong assumptions about others without bothering to garner all the facts."

He turned to fix his glare not on Miriam but on Serena, who looked thoroughly fed up.

"Well, if you *were* the duke," she said, "I'd tell you to save such rants for when the House of Lords is in session."

Oh, she would, would she? thought Kit with a mind-boggling twinge of irritated amusement, as he turned back to his driving.

"But since you're the *coachman*, I'll thank you to hold your tongue and watch where you're going. Miriam, please don't vex him. You know how presumptuous he is, and all of this taradiddle about dukes and long-lost dauphins only encourages him."

Miriam fell silent. Kit released his grip on the crop.

The street grew darker and narrower the farther the carriage traveled. Kit hoped another conveyance would not approach from the other direction. The street was not wide enough to accommodate two vehicles abreast.

"Whoa!" he barked as they nearly passed a small sign bearing Plumlee's name. The establishment was scarcely wider than its front door. "Here we are, Miss Langley."

"Do you think you'll be all right going in there by yourself?" asked Miriam, as Kit jumped down from the box. "We're scarcely in a seedy neighborhood, and Mr. Plumlee is surely a nice man if Her Grace deals with him."

Seeing the apprehensive look on Serena's face, Kit said, "I don't think that's a good idea."

Miriam scowled at him. "Oh, who asked you? Help her down."

That nearly knocked him to the ground in astonishment. So much for the coy, middle-aged coquette, now that she was on to him. A pity, too. Until her tumble into the kitchen, he'd found Miriam's silly infatuation with him harmlessly amusing, even a bit flattering.

Her sudden change of character wasn't lost on Serena. "Miriam, are you having another one of your . . ." She glanced uncomfortably at Kit, who obligingly looked the other way, as if that magically rendered him deaf to her delicate query. ". . . spells?"

"I am," Miriam said hastily. "If I could just sit in the carriage for a bit to collect myself, perhaps I could join you momentarily. Surely you'll be all right for a few minutes."

"Very well." Serena took Kit's hand, which he'd been holding out all this time. "Gibson can keep an eye on you."

"Perhaps I should go in with you, Miss Langley." He didn't like all this havey-cavey business concerning his stepmother and Serena's paintings and this Plumlee character. He had to give Serena credit for her apprehension.

"Nonsense," she scoffed, and he promptly withdrew his credit. "What could possibly happen with you and Miriam right outside? Mr. Plumlee is an art dealer, not a—a—well, whatever he could otherwise be."

Clutching the rolled-up painting, she strutted into Plumlee's shop, whereupon Kit pinned Miriam with his most thunderous look. "Just what do you think you're up to? You're not having any spells."

"No, I just wanted to get you alone for a few moments." She leaned forward, inspecting him as if he were a horse at Tattersall's. "You really are Duke of Fairborough, aren't you?"

He crossed his arms over his chest. "Yes. Now tell me why Miss Langley won't have anything to do with me."

Miriam sat back on the squabs. "Her aunt Leah, of course."

His heart plummeted. Of all the reasons Serena might have had for not wanting to marry him, it had to be the worst one of all—the one that wasn't even true. The one most difficult, if not impossible, to disprove and overcome.

He dropped his arms to his sides. "I feared as much. But I'm not the one who attacked her."

"You were found in a compromising position with her."

"I concede that, but I never *attacked* her. I was set up. Do you know who really attacked her? The previous Viscount Winslow, Miss Langley's father."

Miriam tilted her head to one side. "And how do you expect her to believe that?"

"That's the problem. Do *you* believe it?"

She gazed at him for a long moment, her expression growing wistful. "If you're anything like the man you've been pretending to be since yesterday, then I wish more than anything to believe it. All I know is the rumors I've heard—the same ones that Miss Langley has heard. The *on-dit* is that Lady Winslow entered her boudoir to find you in a compromising position with her mute sister."

With a dejected sigh, Kit glanced down as he idly

kicked the toe of his boot against one of the cobbles, as if trying to dislodge it.

"Why do you say Miss Langley's father did it?"

He looked up. "Because I *saw* him. I was on holiday from Oxford and was invited to a party at Langley House, at which Prinny was a guest. I went upstairs to answer a certain call of nature, got lost, and stumbled into Lady Winslow's bedchamber. At first I thought I'd found both Winslows performing their marital duties, despite all their guests downstairs, but then I realized the viscount was struggling to have his way with a woman other than the viscountess. Do stop blushing, Evans. You saw me without my shirt this morning, and you certainly weren't blushing then. You looked as if you could have devoured me whole, complete with sugar and cream."

He didn't add that Serena had looked the same. Miriam only turned redder and glanced away.

Kit continued: "The woman, while silent, didn't look as if she wanted Winslow's attentions. I pulled him away from her and offered him a taste of my knuckles. He must have knocked me out cold defending himself, for the next thing I remember is opening my eyes to find myself lying on top of the woman, with Lady Winslow standing over us screaming for all of Britain to come and behold. That's when I learned they were sisters.

"Because Lady Winslow's sister was more than a decade older than I and had an affliction, neither her family nor mine wanted to force a marriage. Winslow was her closest male relative—and only by marriage, at that—but he knew better than to call me out since he, not I, was the guilty party. Though nothing might have pleased me more than to meet him over pistols at dawn, if only to defend my own honor."

"Then why didn't you?"

"Because I wasn't about to deprive a young girl of her father. Miss Langley was still in school then."

Miriam's eyes widened. "You went to India so she would not lose her father."

Kit nodded. "Much good it did, since his cousin Marcus killed him in a duel about a year later."

Miriam studied the reticule in her lap. Clearly she was weighing his words, yearning to give him the benefit of the doubt. Why didn't people believe him? Until that night, he'd never given anyone reason to believe he was capable of such vile behavior.

But neither had Serena's father. He had always seemed fairly content to work his farm and hadn't had a reputation with the ladies. While his wife carried on with his cousin Marcus, had he tried unsuccessfully to seek solace with Leah? Or perhaps he had mistaken his mute sister-in-law for his wife? Kit thought it might be possible if he'd been foxed that night.

"Did you ever know Miss Langley's father?" he asked.

Miriam shook her head. "I didn't join their household till after she lost her parents. So I never knew him, but I do know you. And I believe now that you're innocent."

Kit sighed in relief. "I appreciate that. Perhaps you could plead my case to Miss Langley?"

"Why didn't you unmask yourself to her at Woodard House, when you had the chance?"

"I was about to, but then my stepmother fainted. It didn't seem a good time to reveal my true identity to Miss Langley."

Miriam smiled. "Especially when she already has a tendresse for Alfred Gibson."

"Don't toy with me. She couldn't. He's just the coachman."

"Come, I know you lords have—shall we say, an *eye*

TRUE PRETENSES

for the women beneath you? What makes you think your ladies don't have an eye for the men beneath them?"

"Are you saying Miss Langley is wont to dally with a servant?"

"Not any servant, just you," Miriam said airily. "Why the ruffled feathers, Your Grace? Coachman or duke, the fact remains that Serena is already growing fond of *you*. And now that I think about it, I don't believe you should tell her the truth about yourself just yet."

"Why not?"

Miriam narrowed her eyes. "Do you really think she's going to believe that you, the Duke of Fairborough, have been masquerading as a coachman all this time just to—why have you been doing it?"

"Why do you think? You know she won't have anything to do with me—she won't even read my letters. This is the only way I can get near her, and now you're saying it's the only way I can court her."

Miriam smiled brightly. "It seems quite the amusing lark."

"You and Colfax. Why wouldn't she believe the charade? You obviously believe it."

"Only because I overheard your conversation with the cook."

Frustration gripped him. "So how can I change her mind about me, if she won't believe I'm really Fairborough in disguise?"

"You don't. I propose that for the time being, you continue being your charming self to her, but as Alfred Gibson. She's desperate for a way out of marriage to Fairborough. One certain way out of it would be for the coachman to seduce her."

"To *seduce* her!" The very idea stunned him as much as the fact that Serena's own abigail had dared to even advise such a thing. "Are you suggesting that Gibson—"

"It won't be Gibson, it'll be *you!* Once she's been compromised by you—as Gibson—she'll think that you—as Fairborough—won't want a soiled dove for a bride."

"Why would she expect me to condemn her for taking a lover, if she believes I ravished her aunt?"

"Because we women know you men have harsh double standards. You may have all the fun you want with whatever filly you choose, whether she's some other duke's wife or one of the scullery maids, but you gentlemen expect your own wives to be lily-white paragons of chastity."

Kit was silent because she was right.

"Once she considers herself a soiled dove in the eyes of Fairborough, she'll think her cousin will have to marry him instead," Miriam continued. "Safely off the hook, she'll join the rest of the ton at Fairborough Castle to celebrate Lady Jemma's marriage to the duke. When Miss Langley realizes that the bridegroom is really her dashing, beloved coachman in disguise—well, I daresay true love will prevail."

Kit gazed at Miriam for a long moment, digesting all of this.

She smiled. "So what do you think of my proposal?"

"I see two things wrong with it. In the first place, the scenario you described would leave Lady Jemma the laughingstock of the ton. Under no circumstances will I embarrass an innocent party, having once been an innocent party embarrassed myself."

"She'll survive. She has her Scotsman."

"So I've heard. She also has her parents who strongly disapprove of said Scotsman."

"Who has surely heard of a convenient place just over the northern border called Gretna Green. Now what else do you find wrong?"

Kit stroked the withers of the horse nearest the curb.

TRUE PRETENSES

"It still doesn't solve the problem of what Miss Langley believes about me and her aunt Leah."

Miriam tossed her hand up. "Pah! By then she'll be so besotted with you that she'll believe you're innocent."

"That's a pretty notion, but I'd prefer to find Leah—even if it means hiring a Bow Street Runner—and prove my innocence once and for all, instead of relying on Miss Langley's infatuation to exonerate me. I think she has more sense than to let an attraction blind her to my alleged faults, especially this one."

"Very well, Your Grace, but for her to fall in love with you at all, she must first fall in love with Gibson."

He rested his head against the mare's flank, breathing in the equine aroma of straw, oats, and horse sweat. "There must be a better way."

"There is no *other* way, Your Grace. You paid your penny to step into this quagmire, now you must pay a pound to get out of it."

He couldn't help laughing as he lifted his head. "Then I'll pay it. I want Serena."

He'd continue impersonating the coachman if that's what it took to win Serena's heart. He was already fond of her. In fact, he'd felt drawn to her immediately. An image of her delectable figure perched on the library ladder flashed in his head. It wasn't just her appearance that appealed to him either. He liked a woman who was intelligent and well read, as opposed to one who didn't know anything beyond what was the most fashionable color this season. Serena was bright and lively, which would suit Kit perfectly.

Miriam smiled. "So you'll follow my plan?"

He nodded, stroking the horse's mane. "You'll encourage her to dally with the coachman?"

"Of course, Your Grace."

"And that's another thing. You might want to forget

about My Grace until we're ready for the final stage of your scheme. You don't want to blurt it out in front of Serena or anyone else in the meantime. For now I'm still Coachman Gibson."

"Very well, though I'm going to miss flirting with you," she said with an affected little pout.

Kit returned to the side of the carriage. "Now, for our next order of business." His eyes bored into hers, and she looked very much as if she dreaded what was coming next. "What is the story behind my stepmother selling Miss Langley's watercolors to this Plumlee character?"

"Watercolors? Those aren't—oh dear, I nearly forgot about her!" Miriam leaped from the carriage.

"I hope you're not evading my question. I expect to learn the whole story eventually. I have a right to know."

She threw him a scathing look as she opened Plumlee's door. "I think not, Gibson. Don't forget, you're just the coachman."

He cursed under his breath, throwing his hat into the carriage as she went inside the shop. For tuppence he'd follow her. Why not? There was no one around. The horses seemed content to stand and rest. He would be just inside the door. Before he could act on his impulse though, a panic-stricken Miriam reappeared.

"Come quickly! Serena needs you!"

Chapter Six

The shop was small, so crammed with statuary, urns, busts, vases, figurines, and glassware that Serena could barely move. The walls were covered from floor to ceiling with paintings, and she recognized one of Felice's previous "copies" mounted high on the wall, waiting for a buyer. Serena felt a warm frisson of pride for her little sister.

"Be with you in a moment," shouted a male voice from somewhere in the back. "Feel free to look, but do be careful not to break anything."

There was much to survey. Most of the human figures were naked or nearly so. The male forms were especially intriguing. Serena found herself comparing them to what she'd seen in the carriage house this morning. Unfortunately, all she could compare were the chests, none of which measured up to Gibson's. For one thing, none of them boasted hair.

That could only mean nothing else on the male figures measured up to anything beneath the coachman's livery. And Gibson was a large man, tall with long legs, long arms . . . no doubt everything about him was very long.

Had Miriam accompanied her in here, she would have yanked Serena right back outside. She doubted her abigail was even having one of her spells. Most likely Miriam just wanted to flirt some more with Gibson.

Serena could scarcely blame her.

She craned her neck to peer out the front window of the shop. Gibson stood next to the carriage pontificating about something to a solemn and attentive Miriam, who looked as if she were listening to a sermon in church.

"May I help you, miss?"

Serena turned to see a short, balding man in a dark doorway at the back of the shop, rubbing his spectacles with a handkerchief.

"Are you Mr. Plumlee?"

"I am." He donned his spectacles along with that ingratiating smile peculiar to those aspiring to make a substantial sale. "Is there something you wish to buy?"

She brandished the rolled-up canvas. "Actually, I have something I wish to sell."

A skeptical frown frosted over the smile. "I'm sorry, but I'm not interested in—"

"But I'm delivering this on behalf of the Duchess of Fairborough." She gingerly inched her way through the maze of exotic clutter to the counter, where Plumlee stood with the air of a judge watching a defendant approach the bench to receive sentence. She untied the blue ribbon and spread the canvas across the counter. A corner of it curled over, revealing her sister's initials.

Plumlee jabbed a stubby finger at the charcoal marking. "What's this?"

"The initials of the person who made this copy," Serena replied. "They're on the backs of all the paintings Her Grace has sold to you, to tell them apart from the originals. Surely she explained to you that—"

"Are you telling me this is only a copy?"

Serena was taken aback. There had to be some sort of misunderstanding here. Still, she didn't like the look on Plumlee's face. Or his stance. He stood with one hand—no, his *fist*—on the canvas, with the other fist planted on his hip—in practically the very place where a man might conceal a weapon.

She clutched her reticule—unfortunately, the deadliest weapon on her own person. "But they've always been copies. Every painting Her Grace has brought to you is a copy of an original."

He shook his head. "I don't know who you are or how you know the Duchess of Fairborough, but she has never sold me a *copy* of any painting. Nor would she. Perhaps you think because my shop is so very modest, and I'm not situated in Oxford or Bond Street, that you can stroll in here and try to foist a forgery on me. Well, I run a respectable establishment, and no—"

"Mr. Plumlee, please." She pointed to the painting on the wall. "Did the duchess not bring you that picture up there?"

"So what if she did? I assure you it's an original."

Serena smiled, though she felt anything but pleasant. "Why don't you check the back of the canvas? I think you'll find the initials FCL in the upper left corner."

He picked up a stool as he stepped around the counter, nimbly slithering over to Felice's painting. "If those initials were on the backs of every painting Her Grace has sold to me, then I would have noticed them. But I never have."

Serena watched as he set the stool beneath the picture in question, a pastoral scene from half a century ago portraying lords and ladies frolicking on a picnic. "She assured me that you're buying the pictures with the knowledge that they're copies, and that your own buyers are also aware of that fact."

He stood on the stool to reach the painting. "Are you certain we're discussing the same duchess?"

"The younger dowager Duchess of Fairborough? Yes."

He removed the pastoral from the wall and jumped down from the stool. "She's always brought me the paintings herself. Why would she send someone else to bring me one that is clearly—and by that person's own admission, no less—a forgery?"

"I never said it was a forgery, I said it was a *copy*," Serena declared, as he returned to the counter. "A forgery is a fake that one tries to pass off as genuine. At no time since I set foot in your shop, Mr. Plumlee, have I tried to present the canvas I brought as a genuine work of the original artist whose signature appears in the lower right corner."

He laid the picture facedown on the counter. "Who really sent you here?"

"No one. The duchess was unwell, and couldn't bring the canvas herself. I thought I would do her a favor."

Plumlee carefully extricated the pastoral scene from the frame. Much to her dismay, Serena saw that the entire back of the canvas was blank. She knit her brow as she studied the upper left corner, thinking that perhaps somebody might have managed to erase Felice's charcoal initials. But no, that corner, like the rest of the back, was pristine white.

He sneered at her. "An original. What do you have to say for yourself?"

Serena knew her mouth was hanging open, but she

couldn't seem to close it. And she certainly didn't know what to say for herself at this point.

She felt a stinging sense of betrayal. Her earlier suspicions had been right on target. No wonder Daphne hadn't wanted her to meet Plumlee!

The dowager duchess had been playing Serena—and Felice—for fools all this time.

Horrible realization swept over Serena in a huge, sickening wave. All this time, she'd been led to believe that Daphne was helping her and Felice. All this time, she thought Daphne had been loaning them paintings from the Fairborough estate for Felice to copy to her heart's content, only to return the originals to their proper place while the copies were sold. Daphne had given Serena no more than ten pounds a painting. It was a meager supplement to the hundred pounds a year Serena had inherited from her grandmother, which was just enough to keep her and Felice comfortable, and also provide Felice with the art supplies she needed to indulge her wonderful passion.

Daphne was selling the Woodard family's art collection, piece by piece, and all Serena and Felice got out of it was . . . ten paltry pounds.

And what, pray tell, was Daphne doing with the copies Felice made? Surely they weren't mounted on the walls of Fairborough Castle, with no one save Daphne the wiser?

"I think you should leave now," Plumlee said icily, placing the pastoral and its frame to one side.

"I'm sorry if I've caused you any trouble," Serena quavered. "But it seems I've been deceived."

"*You've* been deceived!" he growled. "You're the one who came in here attempting to gull me into buying a forgery!"

Serena saw no point in trying a second time to chase that annoying bee out of his bonnet. "We've both been deceived, Mr. Plumlee. If you please, I'll take this copied canvas and be on my way."

Before she could even touch it, he quickly swept it behind the counter. "I've decided to keep it."

She gaped at him in disbelief. "But you don't want it. It's only a copy."

He smirked. "Yes, but I think I'm entitled to it anyway, for all the trouble you've caused me today."

"What trouble? How have you been inconvenienced since I came in here—with the best of intentions, I might add?"

He snorted derisively, and as he spoke he slowly stalked around the counter to where she stood, unwilling to budge until she could retrieve Felice's painting. "First you led me to believe you had something of value for me. It was most disappointing to learn otherwise. Secondly, you exhorted me to go to all that trouble to remove this pastoral from the wall and then its frame. Now I'm going to have to go to even more trouble just to replace it in the frame and mount it on the wall again. Have you any idea how much work that is? Thirdly, the fact that you deemed me foolish enough to buy an obvious forgery is nothing short of a barefaced insult not only to my honor, but also to my professional expertise. If you were a man, I'd call you out and demand satisfaction." As he came to a halt in front of her, she saw the cold, menacing glint in his eyes, and she knew it wasn't from the dim lamplight hitting his spectacles. "But since you're nothing but a silly female, I'll simply have to demand satisfaction of a different sort."

Serena threw a glance at the front of the shop, trying to catch a glimpse of Miriam or Gibson through the window, but all the priceless urns and statuary blocked her view. Even if she tried to flee without Felice's painting, there was no way she could make a hasty exit without upsetting and likely shattering at least a dozen different objects from as many ancient dynasties and empires. Then she'd have no choice but to marry Daphne's stepson, because she'd need the money from that trust fund just to pay for all the damage.

She yelped as Plumlee wrapped his arms around her and pressed her to him. Her own arms were trapped against her sides.

"You may as well dispense with the ladylike airs. I know you're nothing but a—"

Serena screamed, and Plumlee leaped back as if thrown by the force of her shrill voice. She turned and dashed around to the other side of the counter to retrieve Felice's painting. She bent to pick it up from the floor just as Plumlee crashed into her and sent her sprawling to the floor.

She howled in pain. Surely Miriam or Gibson could hear her screaming and howling? What on earth were they doing out there? Did Miriam faint again, after all? Of all the times when she wasn't with her . . .

To her everlasting relief, Serena heard the front door open, but Plumlee heard it too, for he promptly clamped a hand over her mouth as he used his weight to flatten her against the floor. Serena felt herself suffocating.

"Hello?" Miriam's voice. "Miss Langley, where are you?"

Plumlee sprang to his feet, and Serena took a huge gulp of air. "She's back here. She fainted!"

Serena scrambled to her feet, scurrying to the other side of the counter. "I didn't faint, Miriam. I'm all right, but fetch Gibson at once."

Miriam dashed back out the door, and Serena glared at Plumlee in disgust. "Return my painting."

"Come back here and get it," Plumlee answered.

Gibson entered the shop, followed by Miriam. Serena had a sudden urge to run into his arms, and told herself it was only from relief that help had arrived.

"Is everything all right, Miss Langley?" he asked.

"I'm fine. I was only trying to retrieve the painting, which Mr. Plumlee has refused to buy but also refuses to return to me."

Gibson swiftly—and, she thought, gracefully—threaded around the many breakables to the counter. As he came abreast of her, she felt his hand on her back, but for only a heartbeat, as if he'd suddenly recognized the impropriety. He glowered at Plumlee. "Return the painting to this lady at once."

Plumlee swept his disdainful gaze over the coachman's dark green livery. "Who are you to give me orders?"

Gibson didn't pause for a moment. "I am the Duke of Fairborough, and the lady happens to be my betrothed!"

Miriam gasped and gaped at Serena, who merely gaped back at Gibson. Far be it from her to contradict him under the circumstances! A bubble of laughter welled up inside her as she clamped a hand over her mouth. This would be the second time today her coachman pretended to be her unwanted betrothed. Well, it got him results the first time; now all she could do was pray his charade would succeed again.

Plumlee's eyes narrowed. "What do you mean, you're the Duke of Fairborough? Then why do you look like a servant?"

Serena threw Miriam a pleading look. *Now* would be a good time for Miriam to suggest answers to awkward questions, but no, she just stood there like Lot's wife, staring at Gibson as if for once she expected *him* to come up with a good Banbury tale.

TRUE PRETENSES

To Serena's astonishment, he did. "Our marriage was arranged before we even met. But she's so reluctant to wed someone she believes to be a rake that she's refused to even meet with me—so the only way I could meet her and convince her that I'm not a rake was to take a position in her household—as the coachman." He beamed a broad smile at Serena. "Yes, it's true, Miss Langley—I am actually your fiancé, the Duke of Fairborough."

An outrageous and utterly audacious ruse, thought Serena as she gazed at him incredulously. She was quite sure the real Fairborough could never conceive something so daring. For a duke to pose as a servant was simply unthinkable.

Still smiling, he widened his shining brown eyes, as if entreating her to believe it. She smiled back, feeling a flush of—this was the only word she could think of—*enchantment*.

Plumlee broke the spell. "That's the most absurd thing I've ever heard."

Gibson turned to scowl at him. "I don't care what you think, Plumlee. All that matters is what Miss Langley thinks."

Plumlee picked up the pastoral. "Very well, if you're Duke of Fairborough, then perhaps you can tell me where this painting came from—or for that matter, this one." He bent down to pick up the hunting scene, holding it aloft for Gibson's perusal.

Gibson glanced from one to the other. He'd missed his calling, Serena thought. He should have been an actor, for he looked exactly like the real duke might: He looked as if he recognized both paintings.

"These aren't watercolors," he muttered, half to himself.

"Whoever said they were?" Plumlee snapped back.

Who indeed? Serena wondered, though it didn't stop

her from marveling at Gibson's brilliant performance. She stole a glance at Miriam, who was still staring at Gibson as if he embodied the destruction of Sodom and Gomorrah.

"These are both from the Fairborough estate," he said authoritatively.

"Are you certain they're *both* from the Fairborough estate?" Plumlee flipped over the hunting scene to show Gibson the telltale initials. "Behold the signature of a very clever forger, sir."

Gibson directed his gaze at Serena, sweeping his hand over the paintings. "What is going on here?"

Now he was overplaying his part, and overstepping his bounds again. "I don't believe that's any of your concern."

"Oh, but it is. These paintings belong to my family, and you're going to be my wife before summer's end," he said a little too convincingly. "I have the right to some answers."

She supposed it might be wise to continue playing along with his charade, so she forced her sweetest smile on him, though her words were seasoned with vinegar. "Shouldn't we discuss this privately . . . Your Grace?"

He smiled back. "Indeed we should, my dear. And I shall look forward to it."

She continued smiling. "Now won't you please indulge your betrothed and insist that Mr. Plumlee return the hunting scene? That one's rightfully mine."

Gibson shifted his gaze to Plumlee. "You heard the lady. Surely you want nothing to do with a forgery?"

Plumlee carelessly rolled up the canvas and thrust it at the coachman. "You might warn FCL that a forgery like that could earn him passage on the next transport to Botany Bay."

"Could we please be on our way?" Serena snatched

the canvas from Gibson and held it out to Miriam, who still stood there like a pillar of salt. "Miriam . . . ?"

Miriam started, gaping at the furled canvas for a moment before taking it. Serena hoped the abigail wasn't having another one of her spells.

"You ladies go ahead," Gibson said. "I'd like to have a private word with Plumlee."

No doubt he wanted to give the man a piece of his mind, or more likely a piece of his fist for attacking Serena. While it gave her a warm feeling to think of him defending her honor, she decided there'd been enough trouble already. "It's very good of you, Gibson, but I'd prefer we just go."

Plumlee quirked a brow. "Don't you mean 'Your Grace'?"

Serena's patience had been stretched too thin, and it finally snapped. She tore her reticule from her wrist and began swinging it like a medieval warrior wielding a mace.

"Oh, would you stop, you horrid man!" She whapped him repeatedly with her reticule as he held his arms over his head. "Till just a few"—*whap*—"minutes ago he made me"—*whap*—"think he was the"—*whap*—"coachman"—*whap*—"so I'm still not"—*whap*—"accustomed to addressing him"—*whap*—"by his real"—*whap*—"name! Don't forget what you tried to do before he came in here." To Gibson, who looked very impressed, "I hereby retract what I told you a moment ago. By all means feel free to avenge my honor."

She grabbed the empty frame that had held the pastoral and brought it down over Plumlee's head. It was just big enough to slide over his shoulders and lock his arms to his sides.

"What the—" He glanced from Serena to Gibson. "Well, fine! Go ahead and do your worst, coachman or duke or whoever you are! I'll have the satisfaction of seeing you brought to justice the day you marry *her*, and when you do, may God have mercy on your soul."

Miriam tugged Serena's sleeve. "Come, let's wait outside."

Once out the door, they stood in front of the shop for several moments, both glancing aghast up and down the narrow, shadowy street. Miriam was the first to finally ask:

"Where are the horses and the carriage?"

Chapter Seven

Kit had only enough time to free Plumlee from the frame, toss a gold guinea onto the counter, and learn that for the past year, Daphne had been selling his family's vast art collection, piece by piece, before Miriam and Serena crashed back into the shop, both shrieking and babbling excitedly.

"Stop and be quiet!" he roared, and they froze in shock before they could knock anything over. He was damned if he was going to pay for any of the rubbish Plumlee peddled, particularly if it was broken. He advanced to the front of the shop. "What is the trouble, ladies?"

Both cackled at once, gesturing wildly outside, and he still didn't understand a word. Miriam took his left arm while Serena took his right, and they dragged him out to an empty street.

"What happened?" he asked, even though it was quite obvious what had happened.

"Someone took our horses and carriage!" Serena began scurrying in the direction of Piccadilly.

"Where are you going?" he asked.

She whirled around. "Maybe we can spot them and catch up to them. If they're on Piccadilly, then they can't have gone far for all the traffic."

"They couldn't have gone back to Piccadilly, because there's no room here for them to turn around." Kit stood in the very middle of the street, stretching his arms to his sides. Had his arms been just a foot longer, he might have been able to touch the buildings on both sides of the street. "This must be the narrowest street in Mayfair, it's scarcely more than an alley. They would have had to go all the way to the other end. Why don't you ladies go back to Piccadilly, while I go the other way to find the carriage and horses?"

"If you don't, you'll be looking for a new position by the end of the day," Serena warned. "And if Lord Paxton has his way, you'll likely find it in the Fleet."

Kit's heart dropped. After his confession in Plumlee's shop—which had left Serena with such a look of enchantment on her face that he'd actually believed that he—as Fairborough—had won her over, heart and all, she *still* thought of him as merely the coachman.

"I can see by your countenance that you definitely don't want to end up in the Fleet," she said not too perceptively. "So you'd best find them. But I want you to know that I thought you played your part as the duke very well."

Now his heart bobbed upward. "Did I? I say, don't you ladies think I'd make a fine duke? Miss Evans did say on our way here that I—"

"That will do, Gibson," Serena said sharply. "Though maybe you would make a finer duke than a coachman, since we're missing the horses and carriage, which are your responsibility!"

Anger blazed within him. "Pardon me, Miss Langley,

but it just so happens I had no choice but to be irresponsible about the horses and carriage, lest you suffer some dire fate at the hands of Plumlee. And, might I remind you, it was only the second time since yesterday that I've had to rescue you from the clutches of some scoundrel."

"And I do appreciate that, but I don't need you to help me out of every little scrape I get into."

"No, you need me to *keep* you from getting into all these little scrapes in the first place!"

Sparks shot from her silvery blue eyes. "Who are you to assume the role of my protector?"

Kit knew that as Gibson, he was not only sticking his neck out—he was thrusting the axe right into her hands. But he didn't care now.

"Why not me? You don't trust any other man."

His words seemed to douse the sparks in her eyes.

"I admire a lady who tries to look after herself when there's no man to do it for her," Kit confessed. "But that doesn't make the world a less dangerous place for her. I know you'd rather get out of scrapes on your own, Miss Langley, but if those scrapes involve unsavory men, I'm not about to stand back and let you get out of them on your own. It's not that I doubt you could, it's just that I'd never forgive myself if I turned away, and for some reason you couldn't. I'd be just as much a blackguard as your tormentor."

Serena was speechless, and appeared to be on the verge of tears. Kit ached to take her into his arms and comfort her, assure her that everything would be all right, that she'd have nothing to fear as long as she entrusted her heart to him.

But he was in no position to do it at the moment.

"Now if you ladies will excuse me, I have a carriage and a pair of horses to track down," he said. "Perhaps I'll meet you at the Piccadilly end of this street?"

Karen Lingefelt

He blew out a huge breath as he sprinted down the narrow street in the opposite direction. If only he could have made that speech as Fairborough instead of Gibson. Serena saw only what she wanted to see—and she definitely didn't want to see the duke! It was hardly surprising, since she likewise believed only what she wanted to believe—that he, and not her father, had attacked her aunt Leah. Kit could scarcely blame her for taking her father's part, but the fact remained that her father was the guilty party. How was he ever going to convince her of the truth without making her despise him even more?

Maybe Miriam was right. Maybe the only way to charm Serena was for Kit to go on being Alfred Gibson, coachman, presumptuous oaf, and sometime orator. Once she fell in love with Gibson—and ultimately Fairborough—then Kit could worry about the pain he'd have to inflict on her by breaking the dreadful truth about her father to her.

With any luck, maybe he'd never have to. Maybe she'd love him enough to forgive him for the crime he'd never committed against her aunt.

And on top of that was this coil involving his family's art collection. Kit hadn't been at his ancestral home for more than a fortnight since returning from India, so he hadn't taken much time to reacquaint himself with the surroundings. He hadn't noticed anything amiss, probably because it had been nine long years and he hadn't thought to look. But he did recall now having seen that pastoral in his grandmother's boudoir when he was a young boy. Strange how he'd never even noticed the absence of the hunting scene—which he now realized should have been in the library—till Plumlee showed it to him a short while ago.

Only it wasn't the same one. It was a very clever forgery painted by a brazen, highly skilled artist boasting the initials FCL. Whom did he know whose last name began with L?

Langley.

But Serena's name didn't start with F, and she couldn't have painted that forgery! Like all ladies, she only did watercolors—or did she? Mrs. Bannen said it was Serena's watercolors that Daphne was selling to Plumlee, but it was obvious the cook didn't know much more than Kit. And he'd already deduced that Miss Serena Langley wasn't like all ladies. Much to his increasing bewilderment, that fact alone was proving to be a more powerful lure to him than the sixty thousand pounds.

He was simply going to have to wring the truth out of his conniving stepmother. The trick would be finding a moment went he wasn't busy playing the coachman, he thought as he continued his search for the Langleys' horses and carriage. Where exactly *did* this this street end?

Serena continued trembling inside as she accompanied Miriam up the narrow street toward Piccadilly. She knew Gibson was right. She couldn't always look out for herself and Felice. His words had shaken her to her very core. She'd nearly burst into tears, and had ached to rush over to him and beg him to hold her close—somehow she'd felt that he alone could have comforted her and allayed all her fears. But she couldn't cry in front of servants, and certainly not in public. And it surely wouldn't be appropriate for her to run into the arms of one of those servants!

"He's right, you know," Miriam said, once again reading her thoughts. "I know you don't trust men, dear, but you have to trust at least one. Why not let it be Gibson?"

"Even though he's a servant?" Serena asked in disbelief, still battling her raging emotions.

"If you're so determined to never marry, then you may as well, and hang the proprieties. Just be discreet."

Serena halted in her tracks to stare at the abigail. "Goodness, Miriam, you're practically suggesting that I—I—" Do what? Have with Gibson the sort of arrangement he probably once had with Daphne?

"You wouldn't be the first lady in the ton to do it," Miriam reassured her. "And with any luck, it would end for good the threat of marriage to Fairborough."

"Miriam, I scarcely believe you're suggesting such a thing!"

"Are you shocked by the notion, or merely shocked that I'm the one advising it?"

Serena had to think about that for a moment. She had to admit she was envious of whatever Daphne had enjoyed with Gibson. The very idea of such a dalliance sent a strange, warm thrill coursing through her veins, quickening her heart and throwing her senses into a reel more forbidden than a waltz.

Oh yes, the idea was tempting. She just couldn't reconcile herself to the fact that Miriam—the person charged with keeping her within the bounds of propriety—was the one proposing it!

"Your mother had an abigail, too," Miriam reminded her. "Do you think she constantly exhorted your mother to stay away from your cousin Marcus? No, I've heard she actually aided and abetted your mother every step of the way."

"But I don't want to be like my mother. You know, unfaithful to my marriage vows; indiscreet, not caring who knows about my behavior." And worst of all, not even caring about her two daughters, driving them to seek affection from the servants.

TRUE PRETENSES

"Ah, but you don't ever intend to marry, do you? And who will ever have to know, as long you're discreet? Indiscretion, dear girl, is not something that happens by chance. You can be as discreet as you like, simply by deciding to do so."

Serena sighed wistfully. A pity Gibson wasn't really the Duke of Fairborough. The coachman, oddly enough, seemed precisely her cup of tea. Certainly he enjoyed impersonating a duke, which was scarcely surprising given his presumptuous nature. Miriam was right about one thing—he certainly carried himself like a member of the ton. Somehow that made her proposal less sordid—and even more tempting.

And dallying with him might get Serena out of marriage to Fairborough once and for all. How could it be any less scandalous than what her own mother had done?

They emerged onto Piccadilly. Serena glanced up and down the busy street, then settled her gaze directly forward. "Why, it's Colfax's carriage right in front of us—almost as if he were waiting for us." Sure enough, the carriage door swung open as Serena approached. "Nick! What luck to find you right here!"

He tipped his hat. "My dear Serena, what are you doing here? Do you need a ride anywhere?"

"I'm afraid we've lost our carriage and horses. Gibson's gone looking for them."

Nicholas reared his head back and blinked. Serena thought that looked just a little too affected. "Now how did that ever happen? Gibson would never be that irresponsible."

"It's a long story, but suffice it to say he had to leave them unattended for a few moments, and that's when they disappeared."

"Why don't I take you back to my town house? My mother and youngest sister just came up from Colfax Park yesterday, and I'm sure they would love to see you. Lucy's dying to show some other spinster the ring she got from Lord Humphries last week."

"Oh yes, I saw the announcement in the *Times* the other day." Serena might have felt sorry for Humphries if only he weren't as much of a ninnyhammer as Lady Lucinda Maxwell. They clearly deserved each other.

"Your family should be getting invitations to the party my mother is giving this Friday to celebrate," said Nicholas.

"Very well, but I don't know how we're going to get there if Gibson doesn't return with our transportation. You wouldn't happen to know where this little street ends?"

She caught the mischievous twinkle in his ice-blue eyes. "I wouldn't fret too much if I were you. That little street ends very near the mews adjacent to my house in Curzon Street. He's bound to show up on my doorstep sooner or later, so you may as well come back with me."

He held out his hand to her, but Serena only stood there with her eyes narrowed suspiciously. "Nick, why do I have the feeling you know more about what's going on than I do?"

He feigned—yes, that was the word—he clearly *feigned* incomprehension. "What are you talking about? Whatever do you imagine is going on?"

Her gaze swept over his carriage, a very stately affair trimmed in gold with lamps held aloft by half-naked gilt cherubs, the Colfax crest emblazoned on the door, and a coachman clad in livery so fine the prince regent himself might be proud to wear it for his coronation, if the day ever came. Why, the only thing missing from this splendid array was a footman.

She settled her gaze on the center of this magnificent little universe drawn by a pair of sleek black Arabians. "I don't think I'm imagining anything. But I do think you had your footman steal my carriage."

He still held out his hand. "Now, Serena, it was only to teach Gibson a lesson."

"I don't need you to teach him anything. He doesn't work for you anymore, not in any capacity. He doesn't drive you anywhere, and he doesn't deliver messages for you from Fairborough—which reminds me, he's not going to be at your sister's betrothal party, is he?"

"Not as a guest, but he'll have to drive you and your dear cousins there."

"I'm not talking about Gibson. I mean Fairborough."

"He won't be there, I promise."

"How do I know you won't trick me?"

"Serena, when have I ever behaved in so unseemly a fashion?"

"Just now, when you sent your footman to steal my carriage. And last night, when you tried to use poor Gibson to force Fairborough's letter on me. . . ."

"Poor Gibson?" Nicholas looked ready to explode with laughter as she finally took his hand and entered the carriage.

She settled herself into the plush velvet squabs as he helped Miriam aboard. "Just take me to your town house, and pray that Gibson returns with my carriage." She still needed to purchase more art supplies for Felice.

Only Serena didn't think Felice would be doing any more paintings for Daphne.

As the carriage lurched into motion, she gazed out the window at Piccadilly Street without really seeing it. All she saw now was the day seven years ago when the ninth Duke of Fairborough, along with his wife, Daphne, and eldest son, the Marquess of Linden, had called at Langley House. The duke and duchess had sat at one end of the drawing room while Serena's grandfather sat at the other. Halfway between them

Serena had shared a settee with Simon, a thin, pallid young man with fair hair and sallow eyes. It was the day she learned she was to be the next Duchess of Fairborough.

Serena had nothing but an annuity of a hundred pounds from her late grandmother. Her grandfather, an inveterate gambler, hadn't the money for her dowry, and there would be nothing for her when he died, since anything he hadn't squandered at the gaming tables was entailed on some distant cousin. The ninth duke wanted Serena as a daughter-in-law in exchange for keeping Grandfather solvent and out of debtor's prison.

She should have been thrilled by the prospect of becoming Marchioness of Linden and then, one day, Duchess of Fairborough. Instead she felt as if Grandfather had gambled her away to the Ninth just as he'd gambled away Papa's farm to Simon.

Grandfather presented Serena's portrait to Simon, who remained totally indifferent. Daphne asked who the artist was, so she herself might commission a portrait from him. Grandfather told her the name; then Serena said no, he was wrong.

"What do you mean?" Grandfather barked. "He came out here every day for a month to do that portrait of you."

"Yes, and then Felice copied it. If you look on the back of the canvas, you'll find her initials."

"Felice! Why, that little dolt can barely speak a coherent sentence, let alone draw a straight line."

"That's what you think."

"How dare you speak to me that way! And right after I've practically made you a duchess! Where's the original of this painting, you impertinent ingrate?"

"I beg your pardon, but who is Felice?" queried Daphne.

"My sister," replied Serena.

"I didn't know you had a sister."

"That's because she's little more than a lunatic," Grandfather said curtly. "She's not even worth mentioning."

"I don't want any lunatics in our family," Simon snapped.

"Ha! It's far too late for that sentiment, my boy," chortled the ninth. "I sometimes wonder if our entire family shouldn't be locked away in Bedlam, myself included. You'll marry this gel before you turn thirty if you want the money in that trust fund."

Grandfather quickly changed the subject to the matter of that trust fund, and no more was said of Felice.

Simon never said a word to Serena that afternoon, unlike his father, who was very charming to her. She liked the ninth duke immensely, and wondered how such an amiable man could have sired a pair of ne'er-do-wells like Simon and Kit.

When it came time for the Woodards to depart, she remained in the foyer while Grandfather accompanied them out the front door. As they emerged onto the portico, she overheard Daphne asking her stepson, "So what do you think of your betrothed, Simon?"

"She reminds me of a Roman statue. Cold, hard, and with a big nose. Why couldn't she have big breasts, instead?"

"I think she's a very bright young woman," said the Ninth.

Grandfather snorted. "Too bright for her own good."

"I don't want bright, I want beautiful," said Simon, like a spoiled, petulant child. Serena took silent umbrage at the way they spoke of her. She'd never thought about the size of her nose or her breasts till that day, and she'd been self-conscious about them ever since.

Afterward Grandfather had rung a mighty peal over Serena's head for mentioning Felice. "Did you hear what the marquess said about lunatics, you foolish chit? Thank God his father countermanded him. You nearly ruined everything! You could have sent me to debtor's prison with that traitorous tongue of yours!" As if his gambling debts were all Serena's fault. He added that she was as worthless as her failure of a father, her whore of a mother . . . and her dolt of a sister. His hateful words only fueled Serena's resentment of the betrothal.

The original of her portrait was now buried somewhere in the attic at Langley House, while the copy went to Fairborough Castle. Then last year at Simon's funeral, Daphne had approached Serena and offered to loan her paintings from Fairborough for Felice to copy. Daphne understood that Serena had very little money of her own, and she sympathized with Serena's reluctance to wed Daphne's stepson. Hence the odd business arrangement which had come to an abrupt end today.

A sudden roar of laughter from Nicholas startled her out of her pensive reverie.

"Forgive me for being so rude, but I'm afraid I wasn't attending and evidently missed something," said Serena.

"It doesn't sound to me as if you've missed much at all," he said, his bubbling voice ready to boil over with more laughter. "I understand you met your betrothed today."

She knit her brow. "What do you mean my—" Suddenly it hit her. "Oh, you mean Gibson!"

Miriam dabbed her eyes with a handkerchief. "I'm afraid I told His Grace about the coachman's charade at Plumlee's."

"Well, that was quite a performance he put on, that's

all I can say," Serena said dryly. "He almost had *me* convinced."

Nicholas chuckled. "What would you say if he really were Fairborough?"

"But he's not. What duke in his right mind would leave the comforts of his position to pose as someone's coachman?"

"A duke who wants to meet you very badly, and can't seem to do so any other way."

"That's nonsense. If I were the only female descendant of the earls of Paxton, I might believe it, but thanks to Lady Paxton, he can always meet Jemma any time he wants. Though I must warn you, she's not interested in being his bride, either. She's in love with a Scottish viscount."

"And who are you in love with?"

A picture of Gibson flashed into her mind at Nick's query, but she quickly erased it. That wasn't possible.

"Not Fairborough," she muttered, glancing out the window. By now they were off Piccadilly.

"I didn't ask who you *aren't* in love with."

"I don't think it's any of your concern." Serena shot him a cold glare. "Honestly, you're as inquisitive as Gibson. Oh, and that reminds me. Are you sure you didn't discharge him for his constant arrogance?"

"I considered it a number of times, but he was so good at handling the horses I endured him. I'm afraid he's the one who gave notice. I think he wanted to be near his grandmother."

Serena smiled. "Then he couldn't be Fairborough, could he?"

"You never know. Maybe Fairborough would like to be near *his* grandmother."

"Then he couldn't be in London, because I know she's down in Devon. Besides, would *you* do something so ludicrous as pretend to be a coachman?"

"With sixty thousand pounds at stake?" Nicholas furrowed his brow and tapped his chin with his finger, as he made an exaggerated show of mulling over that. Then he widened his eyes at her, as if she'd asked an appallingly inane question. "Why, yes, Serena, I do believe I would."

She eyed him askance. "I suspect your belief would be easier to profess than to practice. If Gibson really were Fairborough, don't you think he would have mentioned it by now?"

"He mentioned it in Plumlee's, didn't he?"

"He was helping her out of a bind the only way he knew how, Your Grace," Miriam offered. "He learned earlier at Woodard House that he could get away with posing as the duke, and you know how presumptuous he is. No doubt he'll seize any opportunity to play Fairborough now. Heaven help us all should he aspire to play the regent."

"Besides, Nick, Gibson was your coachman before he became ours," added Serena. "Why would Fairborough pose as *your* coachman?"

"Well, it couldn't have been because it was the only way he could meet Lucinda." Nicholas grinned sheepishly. "Speaking of which, here we are—oh, and I see Humphries is here, too. That looks like his curricle."

Serena prayed that Gibson had already found the mews—with their carriage and horses. She didn't want to spend any more time than necessary with Lucinda and her betrothed.

She much preferred the company of her coachman—and not just because he might be the key out of her unwanted betrothal.

Chapter Eight

For the second time that day, Kit stormed from the kitchen into the part of the house generally off-limits to coachmen. The groom at the mews had told him that Nicholas planned to bring Serena and her abigail here to the Maxwells' town house.

A footman sped past him. Kit knew he'd only have to follow the servant, who was surely on his way to alert the duke of Colfax about the mad coachman rampaging through the house. He broke into a run, and in no time he stumbled into the drawing room quite literally on the heels of the hapless footman.

Before Kit had the chance to assess who was in the drawing room and sitting where, he heard Serena say, "Why am I not surprised to see my coachman here?"

Nicholas set down his cup and saucer with a discordant clink. "What do you think you're doing here, Gibson?"

"That's not our former coachman, is it, Nick?" asked

a young woman seated on the sofa next to Serena. "I thought he—"

Nicholas cut her off. "You thought wrong, as usual."

Kit peered intently at the buxom young woman. Wasn't that Nick's youngest sister, Lucinda? He was fairly sure it was. Last time he'd seen her, almost ten years ago, she'd been a child. A vexing child who, with her two older sisters, had followed him around during a house party at Colfax Park, thinking they could flirt with him and get his attention by constantly calling out "Here, Kitty, Kitty, Kitty."

She might recognize him, but Kit guessed there was a good chance she wouldn't. The Lucinda he remembered would never guess a duke might pose as a coachman. She simply didn't possess that much imagination.

Serena set down her cup and saucer as she rose to her feet. "Never mind, the important thing is that he found me and now I can return home. Though maybe he's here to retaliate for your foul trick, and if so, he has my permission to do so."

Nicholas stood up, and a second man whom Kit didn't recognize followed suit. "Oh, come now, Serena, how many times do I have to apologize to you?"

"Maybe for once you should apologize to my coachman." She glanced at Kit. "Gibson, it's not your fault if you lost the horses and carriage. It seems His Grace—"

"Surely you can't mean that, Serena," said Lucinda. "One simply doesn't apologize to servants, now matter how badly they've been wronged."

"Never mind. Let's go, Gibson."

"If I may, I think I'd like to have a word with him first," said Nicholas.

"You're not going to apologize to him?" asked Lucinda.

"I'm going to have a word with him, and it doesn't concern you," he answered. "In my study, Gibson. You know the way."

"Please don't be too long with him," Serena said. "I need to get back before one of my cousins requires his services."

"Strange, but I don't recall our former coachman looked like that," Lucinda mused. "I thought he was much shorter."

Nicholas glared at his sister. "Since when did you ever notice any of the servants?"

She stiffened on the sofa. "Never, of course," she said hastily, as if noticing the servants was as bad as allowing a young man to take liberties with her.

"There you go. Come, Gibson."

Kit's heart somersaulted as Lucinda added, "Do you know who he reminds me of, now that I think of it?"

Nicholas glanced at Kit, who managed to remain expressionless.

"He reminds me of Kit Woodard," she said, tilting her head to one side as she surveyed him. "Isn't he the new Duke of Fairborough? Why, he's your betrothed, isn't he, Serena?"

"Yes, but I've never seen him, so I wouldn't know if there's a resemblance to my coachman."

"Well, I haven't seen him in quite a few years myself," Lucinda said. "He's been in India all this time, but of course you know that. Either way, one doesn't forget a gentleman as handsome as Kit Woodard."

The other man, who'd been standing there like an unlit street lamp all this time—Kit didn't think he looked as if there was sufficient oil in his bowl to make any light—cleared his throat in the manner of one trying to get someone's attention.

Lucinda giggled and flapped her hand at him. "Oh, Humphries, I scarcely remember him!" she flip-flopped. "Really, your jealousy flatters me."

With all his strength, Nicholas pushed Kit back into the hallway. "We'll only be a moment, Serena."

"As long as you're only a moment," she called after him, sounding very anxious to leave. Kit could scarcely blame her. If his father had wanted to punish him for his supposed behavior with Leah, then a few minutes in the company of any of Nick's sisters would have been far crueler than nine years in India.

He followed Nicholas to the study, doffing his gloves and stuffing them into his pocket. "Are you sure you want to be alone with me after what you did this morning?"

"I don't need witnesses," Nicholas replied, as they entered the study. "They'll know you were the last person to see me alive, and that you have a motive."

No sooner did he close the door than Kit got right to the point. "What did you hope to accomplish by stealing my horses and carriage?"

Nicholas quirked a brow. "*Your* horses and carriage?"

He yelped as Kit grabbed him by the neckcloth and jerked him forward. "Don't try my patience any further, Colfax. I'm dizzy from having to act the duke pretending to be a coachman pretending to be a duke. I'm not even sure who I'm supposed to be at this moment—"

"At this moment, you're the duke."

"Thank you. I'm exhausted from running through half of Mayfair tracking down the horses and carriage you so thoughtfully stole. My stepmother is selling off pieces of my family's art collection and replacing them with forgeries. My fiancée with the heart of Pharaoh wants nothing to do with me because of a crime I never committed—"

"Ah, so it is about Leah." Nicholas twisted around in

a vain attempt to wrench his neckcloth out of Kit's grasp.

"—and I just now saw your sister. Suffice it to say, Colfax, this has not been one of the better days of my life. Now kindly state your business so I can drive Serena back home. She doesn't want to be in your sister's company any more than I do."

"I have some forwarded mail for you that came in just this morning, if you would only desist from strangling me."

Kit desisted. Nicholas stumbled to the other side of the desk and opened a drawer. He withdrew a small bundle of letters and handed them to Kit. "There's one from your grandmother, probably asking when you're bringing Serena down to Devon."

Kit tore it open and scanned the contents. "You're right. In fact, she's sending out invitations. She plans to throw a house party next month to officially announce our engagement."

"Do you think you can win Serena by then?"

"If I can't, Gibson will."

"What do you mean?"

Kit momentarily ignored his friend's question as he opened the next letter. "How nice, a letter from my former commanding officer in Calcutta. It seems he returned to England shortly after I did. I promised him an invitation to Fairborough whenever he returned. He can join the house party." He tore into the next envelope. "By the by, the abigail—Evans—knows who I am."

He told Nicholas about his conversation with Miriam and her scandalous proposal, as he continued opening his mail, most of it invitations from various members of the ton, who'd heard he was back in England and were eager to court the new duke.

"So you're going to make Serena fall in love with the coachman?"

Kit smiled back. "You said I needed a lark. Incidentally, do you know a Hamish Dunbar?"

"Taller than either of us, with hair the color of hell?"

"That sounds close enough. I understand he and Lady Jemma Langley have been dangling after each other."

"That would explain a few things. Her mother did seem more interested in me last night than Jemma did."

Kit handed the sheaf of letters back to Nicholas. "If you'll allow me to borrow your desk, I would like to write a letter to my grandmother, and ask her to add Lord Dunbar and Colonel Logue to the guest list."

"Why Dunbar?" asked Nicholas, as Kit sat behind the desk and helped himself to a blank sheet of vellum.

He reached for a quill and dipped it in the silver inkpot. "To bring him together with Jemma. They want to marry, against her mother's wishes, of course. Perhaps if they eloped from Fairborough during the marriage celebrations? Serena might have no choice but to marry me then, but by that time I should hope she'll want to."

"Why don't I ask Mother to invite them this Friday evening? She's having a party to celebrate Lucy's betrothal to Lord Humphries."

Kit did not look up from his writing. "You mean that dull-looking gentleman I saw in your drawing room a short while ago?"

Nicholas sighed. "I know, Mother was holding out for someone much grander—such as a duke. She actually wanted you for a son-in-law, but there's that stipulation in your father's will, and Lucy's not willing to hedge her bets even this close to your birthday. After all, she just turned twenty and she already feels as if she's far back on the shelf, hidden behind the fresher eighteen- and nineteen-year-olds."

Kit let out a sigh of feigned dejection, for the first time deeply grateful to his father for that troublesome stipulation. "Alas, she just couldn't wait for me. I might have been a free man after September. Will my stepmother perchance be invited?"

"Almost certainly. Why?"

"Perhaps I'll presume to invite myself. My evening coat, I believe, is still in one of your guest rooms upstairs."

"Kit, I promised Serena you wouldn't be here Friday."

"I only want to see Daphne. I won't even bother Serena."

"But if she sees you—"

"At a Town crush? In this house, where the ballroom can barely hold four hundred? But if I know your mother—and I do—she'll try to pack in at least twice that many, even if she has to bring in gentry from Ireland to do it. Just try and lure Daphne into the garden sometime that evening. I won't even have to come indoors, except to retrieve the proper attire, and I can do that without being seen. I'll use the servants' backstairs."

"But won't you be . . . working for the Langleys?"

Kit continued writing. "I'll only be driving them to and from. I'll need something to do in between." And that something was finding out what Daphne was up to, selling off his family's art collection. "Do me a favor, would you? Two favors, in fact. See what you can find out before that party about Daphne's finances—debts, that sort of thing."

"Consider it done."

"And hire a Bow Street Runner to find Serena's aunt Leah."

"I'm surprised you haven't done that already, but I know just the man. I'll visit him this afternoon." Nicholas sat on the edge of the desk. "Even if for some reason you're not married to Serena by your birthday, and you lose the trust fund—would you still want to try to win her and ultimately wed her?"

Kit stopped writing in midsentence as he pondered his friend's words, and suddenly realized he didn't even have to consider himself betrothed to Serena at this point. It was everyone else, from his grandmother all the way down to Lucinda, who took it for granted that Kit and Serena had been officially engaged since Simon's death.

Kit could still court and even marry whomever he pleased—but only if he was willing to forfeit that trust fund.

Was it worth sixty thousand pounds to search the marriage mart for a bride more willing than Serena?

Was it worth sixty thousand pounds to continue the fight to win her heart—even if he had to do it as a lowly coachman?

Granted, Kit didn't need the money. But then that horrible picture flashed into his mind: all of those African men, women, and children—especially the children—naked and in chains, being herded aboard a ship bound for the island that his cousin Calvin practically owned. That Britain had outlawed the slave trade six years earlier didn't matter. Laws were for the law-abiding, and it was no secret the slave trade continued to flourish at the behest of those who weren't. From what Kit knew about his cousin, he'd wager Calvin was not the law-abiding sort, and certainly not concerned with his slaves' welfare.

Calvin was ten years older than Kit, who remembered him mostly for his love of torturing dogs, cats, or any other creatures smaller and weaker than he.

TRUE PRETENSES

That included little boys a decade his junior. Kit still shuddered at the memory of his cousin holding him upside down by the ankles over a well at the Fairborough estate. "It goes all the way through the earth to China," Calvin had told the terrified four-year-old, "and if you survive the fall, the Chinese will sell you as food in the Shanghai market!" Only the sudden, fortuitous appearance of some estate workers had stopped Calvin from dropping him down the well, so he'd dropped him to the ground instead.

Kit had fled the scene, and very wisely made it his business to never again be alone with Calvin. Later that evening, a servant reported hearing dogs howling from the bottom of the well, and indeed, at least two dogs were discovered missing from the duke's kennel. By dawn the howling had subsided. Everyone had been distraught over this except for Calvin, and for some strange, maddening reason, young Kit had been the only one to notice. But no one had wanted to believe the accusations of a highly imaginative four-year-old against his much older cousin.

No, he couldn't—he *wouldn't* allow Calvin to collect that money.

"Hello?" He jumped at Nick's voice, and splattered a few dots of ink on the vellum. "You didn't answer my question."

Kit scratched the quill against the vellum, but no ink appeared. "What was the question?"

"I said, even if you lose the sixty thousand pounds, would you continue trying to win Serena's hand?"

"Of course. I've been out of England for so many years, she's the only eligible lady I know. I haven't even met her cousin Jemma. Be a good fellow and hand me the letters from Dunbar and Colonel Logue. I need their directions to give to Grandmother."

Nicholas riffled through the stack of letters and

pulled out the two Kit had requested. "So you have no intention of searching the marriage mart?"

"Why should I, if I can marry Serena?"

Still sitting on the edge of the desk, Nicholas leaned back to peer at Kit, grinning broadly. "You've already grown quite fond of her, haven't you?"

Kit dunked the quill into the inkpot, then resumed writing. "What if I have? So much the better, don't you think?"

He couldn't deny it any longer. Scarcely twenty-four hours had passed, and already he was falling for her. So far it was a dizzying drop. He couldn't imagine finding another bride who could outshine her, not even those so-called diamonds of the first water, admired mainly for their beauty. Serena reminded him more of an opal than a diamond, seemingly dull at first glance, but the more he looked and considered it—her—the more he realized she could show incandescent flashes of unexpected fire and iridescence. Even her eyes were the color of opals.

Diamonds were pretty, but unlike opals, they often had too many facets to contend with—and sometimes those facets were flawed. Besides, weren't diamonds the hardest substance known to man?

Nicholas broke into his reverie. "Ah, who says there is no such thing as love at first sight? But if it turns out you can't win her before your birthday, will you hold the loss of the trust fund against her?"

"That's not going to happen," Kit said firmly. "She is going to marry me before then, even if she has to marry me as Alfred Gibson."

Nicholas chuckled. "Do you think at this point she's as fond of you—as Gibson—as you are of her?"

Kit felt a light flip in his chest as he remembered the look on her face at Plumlee's, when he thought he'd revealed his true identity to her. Serena wasn't enchanted by the fact that the coachman was really the Duke of Fairborough in disguise. She was simply enchanted by the coachman.

Could she just as easily be enchanted by plain Kit Woodard?

"Kit . . . ?"

"Do you mind terribly if I finish this letter before you continue your inquisition?"

A staccato rap at the door. "Nick?"

It was Serena. Kit paused in his writing for only the length of a heartbeat, then continued as quickly as he could.

Her muffled voice came through the door. "Nick, are you done making amends with my coachman yet?"

"Just one more minute," he called out, turning to Kit. "You are almost finished, aren't you?"

"Finis," Kit said, signing his full first name, Christopher, with a flourish. It was probably the shortest letter he'd ever written to his grandmother, no thanks to Nick's constant interruptions, but at least all the pertinent facts were there. Yes, he would be at Fairborough Castle next month to celebrate his marriage to Serena. He asked Grandmother to issue invitations to Dunbar and Colonel Logue, and included their directions in London. He'd probably get another letter from her, asking for a complete genealogy of both men going all the way back to the Conquest, but he'd deal with that later. If necessary, he'd issue the two invitations personally.

He had until the weekend of that celebration to make Serena fall in love with him. His dearest hope was that she would fall not for the coachman, and not even for the duke—but for plain, old Kit Woodard.

He stepped from behind the desk as Nicholas finally went to open the study door.

* * *

Serena glanced anxiously down the hallway, worried that Lucinda and her mother would catch up to her before she could leave. She couldn't stand another minute in Lucinda's company, and she was in no mood to encounter the formidable Dowager Duchess of Colfax. She'd made her escape as soon as Lucinda went to see why her mother was taking so long in coming downstairs.

What was Nicholas doing in there with Gibson? Gibson no longer worked for him. She pounded on the door again. "Come on, Nick, he's my servant, not yours. You'd better not be giving him more letters from Fairborough."

The door finally opened. "Sorry to keep you waiting."

She glanced over Nick's shoulder at Gibson, who looked oddly amused. "No letters from Fairborough, Miss Langley."

"Give my regrets to your mother, Nick, but I'm afraid I couldn't stay to exchange pleasantries with her." Desperate to leave before Lucinda showed up with the duchess in tow, Serena grabbed Gibson by the arm and yanked him into the hallway. He looked thoroughly taken aback as she practically dragged him into the front hall.

"Miss Langley, shouldn't I fetch the carriage first? And what about Miss Evans?"

"I already sent a footman to see to both. I just want to leave."

"Oh, Serena!" Lucinda's call pierced Serena's ears like a cobbler's awl, and she surmised it had the same effect on Gibson, for she could have sworn she saw him cringe at the sound of Lucinda's voice. "What do you think you're doing with your coachman, and where are you going? My mother will be down in just a few moments."

Serena realized she was still holding the coachman's

arm—not that it had been proper for her to grab it in the first place, but she'd been in a hurry. She promptly unhanded him and turned to address Lucinda, who stood halfway up the staircase. "I told you, I'm leaving. My carriage is being brought around front."

"But shouldn't your coachman go out through the rear?"

Serena glanced at the front door half a dozen paces away, where the butler stood scowling disapprovingly, then back to Lucinda. "Since my carriage awaits me out front, I see no reason to send the coachman all the way to the other end of the house."

"But it just isn't done to let him out the front door! There's a service passage right beneath this staircase that will take him back to where he belongs."

"For now he belongs with me." Serena approached the double doors, where the butler made no move to open them. Apparently he sided with Lucinda.

Gibson stepped forward. "Do allow me, Miss Langley."

"Oh, my goodness, no!" Lucinda cried.

"Oh, come, Lucinda," said Serena, as Gibson swung the door open. "I promise you the house will not collapse into rubble if the coachman goes out the front door. Just watch—or turn away if you fear the sight will be too ghastly."

As she stepped over the threshold, she grabbed the coachman again, pulling him out of doors just as she heard the voice of Lucinda's mother, calling her name.

Much to Serena's relief, Gibson swiftly closed the door behind them. The great house did not so much as shudder in protest at having been so scandalously violated.

She gazed at the street in front of her. Nick's carriage had long since moved on, though Humphries's curricle remained.

"Where is our carriage? They've had ample time to bring it. Let's go find it."

"Miss Langley, I'm sure it will show up shortly."

She hastened down the front steps. "We are not going to stand here and wait, Gibson. I want to get away from this place before I lose my mind."

"I understand perfectly. We might wish to go this way—the carriage is more likely to come around from this direction."

"What do you mean, you understand perfectly?"

He looked straight ahead as they strolled down the street. "I did work for them at one time."

So he did, she recalled, peering at him intently as they ambled down the street. She noticed he was missing his hat. It allowed her to get a better look at him, especially his dark chestnut hair. It was thick and slightly wavy, and looked unusually clean.

He was one of the handsomest men she'd ever seen. Lucinda had thought he looked like Serena's fiancé. That was very odd since according to Miriam, the cook at Woodard House had likewise mentioned a resemblance; then twice today he'd pretended to be Fairborough—and in both instances, gotten away with it. The resemblance must be very striking, she thought.

He stole a glance at her and she quickly turned away, feeling a rush of heat in her face as she realized she'd been staring at him all this time.

Staring—and admiring.

"Is something the matter, Miss Langley?"

"I was just thinking . . . Lady Lucinda thought you looked like the Duke of Fairborough. And Mrs. Bannen made a similar observation. I suppose that's where you got the idea to pose as Fairborough to get past the butler and then fool Mr. Plumlee."

She glanced back at Gibson, who was now studying her intently. Studying—and admiring?

TRUE PRETENSES

"Why would you be so interested in knowing if I resemble your betrothed?" he inquired. "Could it be you're changing your mind about him?"

"What makes you think I would change my mind about him if he happens to resemble you?"

"Because he looks like me, and perhaps you have feelings for me, Miss Langley."

She froze in her tracks, and her heart flipped as she gaped at him. "What on earth do you mean?"

He looked not a whit abashed. "Or perhaps you don't have feelings for me. After all, I'm just a coachman."

"That's not—what I mean is—" She nervously wound the strings of her reticule around her wrist. "I have feelings for all the servants, in the sense that I care for their well-being—you know, that they're not ill, they have warm blankets at night, enough to eat, that sort of thing."

His velvety brown eyes bored into hers. "Yes, but you couldn't possibly have any—*romantic* feelings for them."

Serena knew she was supposed to say something to indicate she agreed with that statement, but she only stood there in stupefied silence. Again she looked down as she struggled to untangle the reticule strings from her wrist.

"Could you?" he prodded. Oh dear, why did he have to press the issue? Why didn't she just agree with him?

And why couldn't she remind him to remember his place?

"Certainly I'm not supposed to have such feelings," she sputtered, her tongue as tangled as the reticule strings.

"No, but if I might be so bold as to use Lady Jemma Langley as an example. I understand she's not supposed to have romantic feelings for a certain Scotsman. But does that mean it isn't possible for her to have such feelings?"

Serena's thoughts were as snarled as her tongue, her reticule strings, and everything else that had happened since she fell off the library ladder scarcely twenty-four hours ago.

Flustered, she scurried ahead of the coachman, tugging desperately at the reticule strings that were now hopelessly knotted around her wrist. If she could only free the reticule, then perhaps she could think clearly, speak articulately—

"Have I offended you, Miss Langley?" asked Gibson, as he swiftly caught up to her.

"No, of course not." Even though she knew she ought to be. "You've raised an excellent point. I suppose it's possible for me to have romantic feelings for you, I'm just not supposed to."

Again she stopped in her tracks. Dear Lord, what did she just say?

"I mean, while it's possible for me to have romantic feelings for *servants*—"

"And I'm a servant." He stepped in front of her, blocking her path. "So while you're not supposed to, it's possible for you to have romantic feelings for me. Just as I could have them for you—although I'm not supposed to."

She stared at him, scarcely able to breathe. She knew she should tell him their conversation was highly improper. Yet she couldn't help what slipped out of her mouth next: "You mean you could?"

He gazed back at her, expressionless—but even his blank countenance turned her legs to jelly. "I'm not supposed to, Miss Langley. *We* are not supposed to. But of course I could. Just as you could."

She concentrated on untangling the stubborn strings of her reticule, not daring to look at him now.

TRUE PRETENSES

She felt as if he, like Miriam, could read her thoughts. She swore those thoughts were tangible, hanging in the air between them as obvious as frosted breath on a cold winter day.

"Could I help you with that, Miss Langley?"

"I seem to be having a dreadful time with it." She held out her hand with the reticule dangling from her wrist like a traitor swinging from a gibbet.

She watched his fingers as he nimbly untangled the strings. His were scarcely the hands of a working man, but she knew a coachman usually wore gloves, just as he usually wore a hat. Gibson's hands were clean and uncallused, his nails neatly trimmed with no unsightly black dirt beneath them. His smooth fingertips burned through her thin kid gloves to her skin beneath, sending a wonderfully warm sensation through her body.

"Perhaps if I removed the glove," she said. "One of the strings seems to be wound around the button."

"Allow me." He deftly released the tiny button, then slowly tugged on the glove till it slid free of her fingers. With a strange tingle of longing in the very tips of her breasts, Serena caught her breath as the coachman's fingers brushed over hers.

"Now we only have to worry about separating the reticule from your glove." He clutched the glove and reticule in his right hand while her bare hand nestled in the warmth of his left. With the pad of his thumb he tentatively stroked the tiny, pulsating mound of flesh on her wrist.

"You're very much alive," he said. "Your pulse is racing."

"It's not supposed to race," she whispered. "But it does."

Though she knew she should, she made no move to pull her hand away. Let all of London see her and be scandalized! She raised her eyes to meet the coachman's. His were liquid brown and simmering, like hot chocolate ready to bubble over and scald her. She knew her mouth was open, but she couldn't close it, for she longed to taste whatever he offered her, even if she burned her tongue in the process.

A smile quirked at the corner of his mouth as he lowered his head to her palm.

Serena had once read in one of the thick tomes from the Langley House library that the ancient Egyptians believed a vein ran from the ring finger to the heart. She herself must have one branching out from her entire hand to her lips, the very tips of her breasts, and one other place that was threatening to melt her into a puddle at the coachman's feet.

He lifted her hand. "I know I'm not supposed to, Miss Langley, but is it possible?"

"It is," she whispered.

He turned her hand palm down, then lightly brushed his lips across the back of it. She felt a moist warmth penetrating her skin; then all too quickly it evaporated as he abruptly stiffened and dropped her hand.

That was when she heard the approaching *clip-clop* of horses. She glanced over his shoulder as the carriage came into view, driven by a footman in Colfax livery. Miriam sat within.

As Gibson hastily untangled the strings of her reticule from her glove, she said, "Before we return home, I still need to visit a certain shop on Piccadilly where they sell oils and canvases and such. I need to buy more for—" She abruptly broke her words off as she realized she'd been about to mention Felice.

He finally separated the reticule from her glove. "Do you paint with oils, Miss Langley?"

"Not I." She grabbed the glove and quickly donned it, certain if Miriam saw the back of her hand, she'd know the coachman had had his lips there. She felt as if she'd been branded. "Someday I'll tell you who does."

He held out the reticule, which dangled from his index finger. "Why can't you tell me now?"

She berated herself as she relieved him of the reticule. Why did Felice have to be a forbidden topic, especially when Serena had just allowed something infinitely more wicked than mentioning her sister's existence?

"Please, Gibson," she quavered, "one transgression at a time."

Chapter Nine

No sooner did the Langleys arrive at the Maxwells' party the following Friday evening than Serena rushed up the ballroom staircase to an Italianate loggia that embraced the cavernous room. It provided the perfect place to study the press of people below. She posted herself just to the left of the staircase, where she had the clearest possible view of everyone present.

She wasn't concerned with meeting her fiancé, since Nicholas had given his word that her betrothed would not be present this evening. But she was very interested in seeking out Fairborough's duplicitous stepmother.

She idly listened to the two matrons on the other side of the gilded column where she stood, exclaiming to each other over the shockingly low décolletage of a certain duchess below. Everything, according to the two matrons, was exposed. Their comments made it easier for Serena to spot Daphne.

Her heart sank at the realization that she would

TRUE PRETENSES

have to descend into the ballroom if she ever hoped to confront Daphne, but she knew once she reached the foot of the staircase, she would lose sight of her quarry, and heaven only knew if she'd able to find her again this evening. Her only alternative was to wait here all night, and hope that sooner or later Daphne would have to come upstairs and avail herself of the ladies' retiring room.

Daphne's décolletage was certainly the lowest in the ballroom, but she only appeared bare-breasted if observed from the loggia. Every gentleman who came near her gifted her with a brilliant smile, and with good reason, Serena thought. They'd probably smile even more widely if they could see Daphne from the loggia.

Serena's heart skipped a beat as she recognized one of Daphne's admirers. Nicholas must have been the only duke among those grouped around the duchess, as he was the only one to whom Daphne offered her hand. Serena watched in disgust as Daphne tilted her head this way and that, fluttered her fan, then tapped it on his chest. He said something in response, holding out his arm to her—he scarcely had room to do so in that crowd—and she eagerly took it, pressing too close to him as they slowly made their way toward the French doors at the other end of the ballroom. So they were headed for the garden.

Fortunately the Maxwells' London garden wasn't too big, certainly no bigger than this ballroom. And there probably wouldn't be many people out there tonight, since it had been raining throughout the day. Serena simply dreaded the prospect of having to descend the staircase at one end of the ballroom, and fight her way to the French doors at the other end. But do it she must, if she intended to seek justice for her sister.

She was about to move away from the balustrade just as a man's voice behind her boomed, "Why, Lord

Christopher—oh, dash it, I mean Fairborough—I forgot you're now the duke! I say, did you get lost? I didn't think this house was that big. That looks like the servants' stairs you're coming out of."

So the fiancé she'd never met—and still didn't want to—*was* here this evening—and evidently only a few paces behind her!

She thought her heart would explode from her chest, and she pressed against the nearby column as if she hoped to become a part of it. She dared not turn and look, as much as she wanted to, if for no other reason than to see how much he looked like her new coachman. Blast Nick! He'd promised her Fairborough wouldn't be here tonight!

She listened intently to see if she could pick out the duke's voice. The man who had addressed him continued bantering: "Or were you flirting with one of the Maxwells' maids, perhaps? They do have some pretty ones hidden away."

"Well, I never!" burst out one of the matrons from the other side of the column. "Have you no decency, sir, no regard for ladies in hearing?"

The column felt cold against Serena's cheek, and was clammy from her own perspiration. She dared not breathe, afraid the sound of her inhaling and exhaling might draw Fairborough's unwanted attention.

"I think you owe an apology to the ladies as well as myself," spoke the voice of what could only be Serena's dreaded betrothed. She cringed at his unbearably stiff, arch, aristocratic accent, which she herself had never bothered to master. Harriet practiced it constantly, but still sounded like a Northumbrian trying to imitate the highest-born aristocrat in the kingdom while suffering from a bad cold. Fairborough, however, spoke like a true noble, and Serena shuddered. She couldn't live the rest of her life with a man who spoke like that, not without screaming every time he opened his mouth. Without even turning to look, she could tell just from his diction that his nose was in the air.

"I beg your pardon, ladies, Your Grace," said the now chastened man.

Serena heard no more from either of the men, but she remained frozen against the column. They must have gone their separate ways, for she heard the offended matron mutter to her companion, "You don't suppose Fairborough really was dallying with a maidservant?"

"So what if he was?" replied the other woman. "He's a duke, and frightfully wealthy. I can't understand why Miss Serena Langley is so loath to marry him."

"Nor can I. But the *on-dit* is that Lady Paxton is hoping he'll offer for her daughter instead."

Had they forgotten the scandal that had ruined her family and sent Fairborough to India in disgrace nine years ago? Serena wondered what would happen if she stepped away from the column and revealed herself to the gossiping geese, but decided it would be more interesting to try to catch a glimpse of her unwanted betrothed from a safe distance.

Her heart fluttered as a tall man with dark brown hair descended the staircase. Though his back was to her, Serena was certain he was Fairborough. Daphne had said that he was tall and had dark brown hair.

Lucinda appeared at the foot of the staircase, looking up at him as she called out, "Here, Kitty, Kitty, Kitty!"

Serena cringed at the bizarre greeting, though it confirmed his identity as Christopher "Kit" Woodard. He also flinched. As he neared the bottom of the staircase, Lucinda held her hand up and out toward him like a Roman centurion saluting Caesar.

He took her hand and gave the air just above it a

hasty brush of his lips, as if he wanted to get the gesture over with as quickly as possible. It was a stark contrast to the other day when Gibson had slowly brought Serena's hand to his own lips, as if he'd wanted to prolong and savor the forbidden moment.

Giggling and fluttering, Lucinda slapped Fairborough on the arm, then wagged her finger at him. He tried to squeeze by her into the crowd, but she grabbed his arm and leaned close to him, as if confiding something. He burst into laughter, shaking his head as if she'd imparted something absurd. Coming from Lucinda, it no doubt was.

She elbowed at least two people as she set her arms akimbo and stamped her foot. "It's true!" she cried, loud enough for even Serena to hear. Fairborough continued shaking his head.

Lucinda suddenly spotted Serena at the top of the staircase, and she waved. "Serena, your betrothed is here!" She slapped him on the arm again. "Look, Kit, it's Serena—now's your chance to see her! Behind you, up there on the loggia!"

But he resolutely kept his back to Serena, as if he had no interest in seeing his elusive fiancée now.

Could he have given up on her?

Why did she feel so dismayed? Wasn't this what she'd always wanted? Why did his refusal to acknowledge her rankle her so—especially when she'd been refusing to acknowledge him since his return from India, and been much more overt about it?

She saw Harriet fighting her way toward the staircase, dragging Jemma behind her. Apparently someone had alerted them to the Duke of Fairborough's descent into the ballroom.

Obviously eager to recommend an alternative to Serena, Harriet nearly shoved Jemma into the duke while elbowing Lucinda to one side. Lucinda returned to her fiancé's side, flashing her betrothal ring at anyone who glanced her way.

Serena watched as Fairborough said something to Harriet, who smiled and nodded vigorously in response before melting back into the crowd. Evidently he wished a moment alone—whatever that meant in a crush like this—with Jemma, and Harriet was only too eager to consent. He was, after all, a duke.

To Serena's surprise, he and Jemma seemed to have an instant rapport. His back was still to Serena, but she could ascertain he was doing all the talking, and Jemma looked absolutely enraptured by whatever he was saying.

It was obvious now that he'd switched his suit to her young cousin. Just like that! Serena only wondered if he would be able to charm Jemma away from Hamish.

She waited till a group of women, fresh from the retiring room, began descending the stairs; then she positioned herself behind them. Even if Fairborough had given up on her, she still didn't want to draw his attention. As she moved closer, she hoped to get a better view of him—she was still wondering how much he resembled Gibson—but by the time she reached the foot of the staircase, he was lost in the sea of people.

She slowly made her way across the ballroom to the garden. At least a dozen people greeted her on the journey. Each prided him- or herself in the misguided belief that he or she was the first person to apprise Serena of Fairborough's presence in the same room. The females, being inherently more inquisitive than the males, all wanted to know if the engagement was still on, or if Fairborough planned to wed her cousin instead. Serena patiently referred all inquiries to Lady Paxton.

She was nearly suffocating by the time she reached the French doors. Even though they were wide open, she still couldn't catch any fresh air till she actually crossed the threshold onto the shadowy terrace.

"Good evening, Miss Langley," said a nearby voice.

She turned to see a tall, lanky man hovering near the doors. Even in the shadows, she saw that he had blazing red hair.

"Lord Dunbar?"

"Yes. I assume Lady Jemma has mentioned me?"

"Indeed she has. How do you do, my lord? Have you seen her yet this evening?"

"No, but I know she's here. The Duke of Colfax said he would arrange for her to meet me out here. I understand you're sympathetic to her and me."

"Yes." Though Serena now wondered if Jemma would spurn Dunbar before evening's end. She had no idea if her cousin was the fickle sort.

"Trouble is, I thought Colfax would bring Jemma to me," said Dunbar. "Instead I saw him walk right by me a short while ago with—well, he wasn't alone."

Serena nodded. "Do you know which way they went?"

"I believe they went to the conservatory."

"Thank you. I need to catch up with Colfax. If I see Jemma later in the evening I will direct her this way." She stepped onto the path leading to the conservatory, which was separate from the town house. She'd been here before and knew exactly where it was.

As she scurried down the path, she felt a few raindrops plopping on her face and the back of her neck. The ground was soft and sticky beneath her slippered feet. Perfect! Not only would she have muddy feet the rest of the evening, but her slippers were probably ruined. They were the only pair she had that was suitable for formal evening affairs.

"Oh, bother," she muttered, as she stepped into the deepest part of a cold puddle. She stormed over to the conservatory, where the door was ajar. She paused on the threshold and listened carefully.

They weren't here. At least she didn't think they were, since the conservatory was pitch-dark, the only light coming from the moon half hidden behind thick clouds. It wasn't enough to reveal anything. Nor could she hear anything, save for the occasional plop of a raindrop on the glass above.

She was about to leave, thinking Nicholas and Daphne must have gone to another part of the garden, when she realized the raindrops were falling quicker and closer together. She turned back to the open doorway. If she tried to return to the house now, she would be soaked.

A sudden voice from the other side of the conservatory startled her. "Is that rain?"

So they *were* here. She recognized Daphne's voice, realizing the duchess had the same haughty, nose-in-the-air accent as her stepson. Why had Serena never noticed it before?

"No, my dear," Nicholas answered smoothly. "What you hear is the applause of our guests at the sight of your lovely breasts. Surely you've noticed we're surrounded completely by glass, so anyone can see us?"

"Not when it's so dark and the windows are so wet," Daphne replied. "But rest assured they're not quite as wet as I am."

Fortunately for Nicholas and Daphne, the steady beating of rain on the glass roof drowned out Serena's gasp of shock. While she wasn't certain what Daphne meant by that last remark, she couldn't help thinking it had nothing to do with having been in the rain, and everything to do with indecent behavior. She was trapped in this glass cage with them. Should she confront them, or let them continue with whatever it was they were doing?

"Now that you mention it, I do find the notion of everyone seeing me like this rather exciting," Daphne said. "I feel like one of those nymphs painted on my bedroom ceiling."

"You look like them. After all, you are sitting here naked to the waist."

Daphne made an odd noise that sent an equally odd shudder through Serena—the same shudder she'd felt the other day when Gibson had removed her glove and kissed her hand. Even now, she still felt the burning spot where his lips had touched her. She crossed her arms over her breasts as she felt her nipples puckering, and told herself it was from the cold rain. But why did she feel so warm?

She closed her eyes as she tried not to listen to Nicholas and Daphne, but she couldn't help it any more than she could wipe the image of herself with Gibson from her turbulent mind. She wasn't supposed to think of the coachman that way, just as she wasn't supposed to feel this way about him. But she did.

Then she remembered that Gibson had once been very close to Daphne—close enough that he had addressed her by her first name the other day. Had he ever been with her the way Nicholas was with her now? Serena shivered, whether from that dreadful idea or from the cool, wet draft that wafted through the open doorway, she didn't know.

The steady drumming of rain on the glass panes was almost a relief, for it washed away the forbidden noises on the other side of the conservatory. But it couldn't drown out the slosh of heavy footsteps rapidly approaching the door from outside. Serena stepped back among the potted plants as she saw the silhouette of a tall man burst into the conservatory. He didn't even pause, but headed straight for Nicholas and Daphne, as if he knew exactly where he was going and whom he expected to meet.

"What is this?" thundered a strangely familiar baritone.

"Oh my God, it's Kit!" Daphne cried.

Indignantly, Nick said, "Now see here, Fairborough—"

"Don't you 'now see here' me," he retorted with that imperious accent Serena had heard on the loggia. "For God's sake, Colfax, she's old enough to be your mother!"

Serena nearly sputtered with laughter.

"How dare you!" Daphne snarled. She couldn't have been more than a dozen years older than either of the dukes.

"Sheathe your claws, woman," Fairborough growled. "And your bosoms, while you're at it. Have you no shame? And it's not even two years since my father's demise."

"If you insist, I'll procure a special license from the bishop on the morrow," said Nicholas.

"And what about your American betrothed?" said Fairborough. "You'd better hope the war with America lasts longer than the one with France. The only thing I insist on is that you leave us."

"No, Nick, he can't make you do that!" Daphne protested. "This is *your* conservatory."

"Believe me, Daphne, Fairborough can make me do anything he wants. Do pardon me, but I'm afraid I must go back to the house and see to my guests."

"Coward!" she screamed, as he rushed through the maze of potted plants and out the door, into the rain that by now was pouring onto the glass roof with a continuous, thundering rumble that only made the atmosphere inside the conservatory all the more ominous.

"Now that he's gone," said Fairborough, more calmly, "perhaps you and I could have a word or two."

"I don't answer to you. I'll take a lover if I please. I don't have to remain faithful to your father once he's dead."

He burst into laughter. "As if you were faithful to him when he was alive. I don't care about that, Daphne. But what I do care about is my family's art collection, and how you're having pieces of it copied before selling off the originals."

A long pause followed. Serena gingerly moved closer, wanting to hear more. So her fiancé wanted to confront Daphne for the same reason she did. Only how did he know about it?

"I don't know what you're talking about," Daphne said, in a tone of voice that clearly indicated she knew exactly what he was talking about.

"Does the name Plumlee mean anything to you?" he asked, and Serena's heart tripped.

"Of course not," Daphne answered.

"Are you sure?"

"I don't know who he is," she rapped out.

"That's odd. He knows you. He's trying to sell a pastoral that once hung in my grandmother's boudoir. He says you delivered it to him personally, *and* that for the past year you've been bringing him other paintings, one by one. He described some of them to me. Who outside our family, do you suppose, would wish to own a portrait painted by Holbein of the first Duke of Fairborough?"

"No one, of course. That would be my first reason for not selling it."

"Ah, but you did, stepmother mine. Plumlee found a buyer for it in the person of Lord Brinkley, a known collector of portraits of exceptionally handsome men. It might explain why there's never been a Lady Brinkley, for all that he's sixty years old now. Who do you think will buy my fiancée's portrait, which I saw on my recent visit to Fairborough Castle?"

"What *are* you blathering about, Kit?"

"You may as well stop dissembling, Daphne, forasmuch as you're not very good at it. You have been taking paintings from Fairborough Castle, one at a time, and handing them over to my fiancée, who has them copied by an extremely skilled forger. You send the copies to Fairborough as substitutes for the originals, which you pass on to Plumlee to sell for you."

"Serena sent you here, didn't she? I suppose she told you everything, the lying chit! All this time she's been saying she has no intention of ever marrying you, yet—"

"Leave Serena out of this. Just tell me who's copying the paintings."

"She didn't tell you *that?*"

"Obviously not, or I wouldn't be asking," he said testily. "Who is this man with the initials FCL?"

Serena's heart pounded in almost perfect rhythm with the beating of the rain on the glass roof.

"It's not a man, it's a woman," Daphne replied. "She's Serena's idiot sister."

Serena pressed her lips together and squeezed her eyes shut as Daphne's words slashed through her heart.

"She has a sister?" he asked incredulously.

"An *idiot* sister. She's kept hidden from the rest of the world because she's so monstrous."

Serena flexed her cold fingers, longing to dig them into Daphne's jeweled throat and strangle her.

"No idiot or monster could do that sort of work," he scoffed. "I've seen some of it."

"Where?"

"Out at Fairborough, where do you think? That's

where you're sending the copies after passing the originals to Plumlee."

"Do you mean to tell me that you examined the back of every painting out there to see if it was a forgery?"

"How else would I know?" he said sarcastically. "Ah, the life of an idle aristocrat who has nothing better to do with his time."

"Then you know that most of the original paintings are still out there."

"And they're going to stay out there. How are you doing this without my grandmother's knowledge?"

"She's spent most of the past year either at Bath or visiting other people's estates. I suppose she's been lonely. She only returned to Fairborough Castle when you did."

"And how much are you paying the Langley sisters for their part in your little scheme?"

"Ten pounds for each painting."

"Yet Plumlee is selling the originals, and you collect most of the profit while he nets just enough to pay his bills. Daphne, I've been to the family solicitor since returning from India, so I've seen my father's will. He left twenty thousand pounds to you, and settled another twenty thousand on Rosalind, which—unfortunately for you—remains in my control until her marriage or twenty-first birthday, whichever comes first. Moreover, you're residing in Woodard House strictly at my pleasure, since it is entailed to me. Where has all your money gone?"

She suddenly burst out sobbing.

"I've made a few inquiries. You have no gambling debts. As a matter of fact, you have no debts anywhere. You're not starving and you're exceedingly well dressed—at least partially. What are you doing with the money from the paintings, Daphne? Is someone blackmailing you?"

With a gasp, she abruptly stopped sobbing. "Why would anyone blackmail me?"

"Because you have something in your past that you don't want anyone in the ton to know about. But a certain acquaintance of yours knows about it, and he happens to need money. That's usually how blackmail works, but it can work in other ways, too—for instance, the solicitor has informed me that I must marry the Honorable Serena Langley before I turn thirty, or my cousin, Mr. Calvin Granger, will become the instant beneficiary of a very large trust fund. I believe you know why Miss Langley refuses to marry me. My dear Daphne, what could you possibly have in your past that's worse than in mine?"

So he didn't deny his scurrilous past, thought Serena. He didn't even seem contrite about it. She didn't know much about Fairborough's cousin, except he lived in the West Indies.

"I remember after Father remarried, hearing the servants whispering among themselves that my new stepmother was nothing but a side-slip of the Earl of Gorham," Fairborough recalled. "Twenty years ago I believed them because I wanted to. Should I believe them now because it *is* true, Daphne?"

She said nothing, but only burst into fresh sobs.

"I shall take that as an affirmative response," he said flatly, seemingly unmoved by his stepmother's tears.

Serena felt only the slightest trace of pity for Daphne. She might have felt more if not for the fact that Daphne had taken advantage of her and her sister and said awful things about Felice—not to mention the fact that she had probably once enjoyed the favors of a certain coachman. Heavens, why did she resent Daphne for that?

But an even more disturbing thought stabbed her: Could cousin Archie be the blackmailer? After all,

Grandfather had left very little aside from entailed property. And Archie had been Lord Gorham's estate manager before he inherited the earldom of Paxton. It made perfect sense. The very notion, however, appalled her—almost as much as what Fairborough said next:

"Who is your blackmailer? It wouldn't be Lord Paxton, would it? I happen to know he was once your father's estate manager, so he might be in a position to know more about you than other people would. And he could certainly use the money."

Serena was stunned by how closely Fairborough's thoughts ran to hers.

"It isn't Paxton," Daphne gasped. "I can't tell you who it is, or the blackmailer will hire a footpad to kill me."

"What were you planning to do for money after all the paintings were copied and sold?"

"I'm hoping that soon the blackmailer will have enough and just leave me alone."

"No blackmailer ever has enough to leave his chosen victim alone. Have you considered hiring a footpad yourself to eliminate him?"

He suggested that so dispassionately, as if he were asking Daphne if she'd ever considered rearranging the furniture in her drawing room. Serena felt sick, but was scarcely surprised considering everything else she knew about her fiancé.

"I've thought about it," Daphne conceded, as nonchalantly as her stepson. What sort of people made up this family? "I just don't know how to find one without getting one of my servants involved. Would you happen to know—"

"No, and I wouldn't do it if I were you. Just because I inquired about it doesn't mean I condone it. Does Serena know why you're paying her for every painting her sister copies?"

"Of course not. She thinks I'm only doing a kindness to her and her idiot sister."

Something finally snapped inside Serena. "Stop calling my sister an idiot!" She rushed through a tunnel of plants, brushing them aside and knocking over at least one. Long, sharp leaves stabbed into her bare arms as she stumbled through the dark conservatory to the two silhouettes, one of whom still sat on the bench.

"Serena!" Daphne gasped. "How long have you been here?"

She glared at the form sitting on the bench. "Long enough to know you're wetter than the windows. How dare you refer to my sister that way!"

"Oh, come, I'm not the only one. Your grandfather called her as much, and so did your mother. Your sister embarrassed her, just as your aunt did. If Felice isn't mad, then why has she never taken her proper place in society?"

"She isn't mad!"

"What precisely is wrong with her?" Fairborough inquired.

She whirled on the hulking form behind her, but in the dark she couldn't make out any of his features. "There's nothing wrong with her, Your Grace, which you should know if you've seen her paintings as you've claimed. She just doesn't understand certain things." Tears began streaming down her cheeks, as thickly as the rivulets of rain pouring down the glass panes of the conservatory. "You would take advantage of her the way you did my aunt Leah, and that's why I won't marry you! I won't let you near my sister, and I won't let you put her in Bedlam!"

"I never attacked your aunt, and I would never, ever

do anything to hurt your sister," he said fiercely.

"And why should I believe you?" she sputtered, her voice breaking. "How can you prove you didn't attack my aunt?"

"I can't. You'll just have to trust me."

"I won't! I'm not a fool! I won't let anyone, especially you, hurt my sister. It's bad enough she's already been hurt by your stepmother."

In the dark she felt him reaching out to her, but she smacked him away with a swift chopping motion of her arm.

"I've never even met your sister!" said Daphne.

"You didn't have to. You've used her talents to your own benefit, just as others would take advantage of her in far less savory ways given the opportunity."

"If she's the paragon you say she is, then why has no one ever seen her? Why is she kept hidden away from the rest of the world, as if she's a monster?"

With all her strength, Serena pushed a shrieking Daphne backward off the bench. "You're the monster! Both of you are monsters, and I want nothing to do with either of you!"

Sobs wracked her shoulders and she squealed in surprise when Fairborough suddenly embraced her from behind.

"Let go of me!" she cried, as she thrashed violently in his grasp. Faith, but he felt as strong and solid as a fortress—but not as cold. His arms were thick and firm as they wrapped around her, and for a fleeting moment she thought she might turn into liquid as her knees buckled beneath her. She felt as if he were squeezing all the rage out of her, all the grief, and she tightened her entire body, as if by doing so she could keep that rage and grief from escaping. She didn't want to lose them. She wanted to keep them. She wanted to stay furious with him as well as Daphne; she wanted to continue crying over the cruel injustices constantly dealt to her innocent sister.

But she also wanted to remain in his embrace forever.

Good heavens, how could she feel that way about him? This was the same man who, only moments ago, had coldly reduced Daphne to tears after ruthlessly confronting her with a terrible secret from her past. The same man who spoke of hiring a footpad as he would of hiring a hackney for the evening. This same man had attacked Serena's defenseless aunt at Langley House nine years ago, and would certainly attack Felice if only Serena gave him the opportunity—which she would if she married him.

Never. With that thought, she redoubled her efforts to break free of him, but the baffling sense of security she felt in his embrace was strangely more powerful than his physical hold.

"Scream, Serena," said Daphne. "That's where you have the advantage over your aunt Leah. She couldn't scream at all the night Kit attacked *her.*"

Fairborough abruptly released Serena as if she'd suddenly gone up in flames.

Daphne laughed wickedly. "Of course, all the screaming in the world won't save you from Kit on your wedding night. I only wonder what's going to save your sister from him."

"Blast you, Daphne!" the duke exploded. Serena struggled upright, then made a dash for the conservatory door, knocking over more plants in the dark. She had no desire to watch him vent his fury on Daphne. She already knew he was capable of committing any atrocity.

It seemed to be a Woodard family trait.

Chapter Ten

Despite the torrential rain Serena didn't return indoors. Instead she sought the shelter of her family's carriage.

Finding it wasn't easy. She splashed through myriad puddles alongside a seemingly endless parade of carriages lined up around the Maxwells' town house. She saw that many of the coachmen, footmen, and grooms actually dared to take shelter in their masters' conveyances. On a night like this, she certainly wouldn't object to finding Gibson inside the Paxton coach. And not just because of the rain. She needed the sort of consolation he'd offered her outside Plumlee's the other day.

All the carriages seemed identical in the rainy darkness; she had to squint through the cold downpour at the various crests emblazoned on the doors. If there were a hundred carriages, then hers must have been the ninety-eighth in line. And it would have held that position regardless of which end she started from.

TRUE PRETENSES

She finally found the carriage with the Paxton crest. The groom was on the box, but the coachman was nowhere in sight. Was the presumptuous Gibson truly taking shelter inside the carriage? She fumbled with the latch on the door, but it was stuck. She banged on the door, but there was no response from within. Was he asleep?

The groom, however, did respond by falling off the box into the mud. Serena caught a whiff of the same spirits she'd splattered on Warren the other day in the library.

"Where's the coachman?" she shouted through the rain.

The groom stood up and swayed, grabbing the latch to keep his balance. "D'know, m'lady," he slurred, pitching forward into the mud again as the latch gave way under his hand and the door flew open.

Serena only shook her head as she ducked inside the carriage and swung the door closed. Shivering, she curled up on the far corner of the seat and let the tears flow.

She felt a fresh stab of pain in her heart every time she thought of what Daphne had said in the conservatory about Felice . . . *idiot* . . . *monster* . . . *mad.* An embarrassment to her own mother and grandfather, someone scorned and ridiculed by the world because she didn't seem to have any feelings. True, Felice appeared oblivious of the world around her. She seemed not to have noticed when her father was killed, or when her mother disappeared. Her own world consisted of her art, and it was only when she was drawing or painting that she showed even a flicker of emotion. But that did not give anyone the right to attack her, verbally or otherwise.

Whatever pain Felice did not feel, Serena felt for her. And oh, how she felt it at this moment!

Rain pounded on the carriage roof as she wept over Daphne's betrayal and the memory of her first encounter with her fiancé—if he still was her fiancé. She hoped not. All that encouraged her was the possibility that he wouldn't want to marry her after tonight, knowing she had a sister he thought too mad to be the gifted artist she was. Serena would never forget his disbelieving response when Daphne had told him about Felice's gift: "No idiot or monster could do that sort of work."

If not for his belief that Felice was mad, then perhaps the knowledge that Serena had been a conspirator in Daphne's scheme—albeit an unwitting one—might be sufficient cause for him to switch his affections, such as they were, to Jemma. But did Jemma deserve a scoundrel like Fairborough, either?

What a coil! Why did either Serena or Jemma have to be held hostage for the rest of her life, simply to prevent that odious man's cousin from collecting sixty thousand pounds? A cousin who needed it more than the wealthy duke? Serena couldn't imagine life was easy on a tiny tropical island.

Then again, it certainly didn't seem easy on a large, rainy, northern island.

Kit should have known the night was destined for disaster the moment he made a wrong turn in the servants' staircase, and emerged not in the garden, but on the loggia in full evening dress, prompting bystanders to assume he'd been dallying with the domestics. Simon had been notorious for such behavior, but Kit was not his brother.

Upon being presented to Lady Jemma Langley and sending her mother out of earshot, he'd wasted no time in offering to bring her together with Hamish Dunbar. Nicholas had mentioned earlier that he'd told Jemma her heart's desire was waiting for her out in the garden, if ever she could manage to break free of her mother. The original plan had been for Kit to speak only to Dunbar, but when he found himself forced into the ballroom and face-to-face with Jemma, he decided he might as well make lemonade out of this evening's rapidly growing pile of lemons, and take her to the garden to meet her Dunbar. Since Lady Paxton was eager to have a duke for a son-in-law, separating daughter from mother had been joyously simple.

After taking Jemma to Dunbar, Kit had continued to the conservatory, where everything otherwise proceeded as planned.

Until Serena had materialized out of nowhere!

Having changed back into his coachman's livery, Kit raced alongside the line of carriages, clutching an umbrella. He finally reached the Paxton carriage where the groom, draped in an oilskin cape splattered with mud, was struggling to climb onto the box. He looked as if he'd fallen off several times already, which wouldn't have surprised Kit in the least. The man was more soaked with liquor than rain.

Kit had seen other coachmen taking shelter in their masters' conveyances—apparently Alfred Gibson wasn't the only presumptuous one—and thus decided he would do the same. He threw the coach door open, and nearly stumbled backward into the mud as he saw Serena curled up on the seat within.

He felt just as astonished as she looked. "Miss Langley! Pardon me, but I thought you were still at the party."

She shook her head as she shivered. "Please come in."

Kit did not have to be told twice. He offered the umbrella to the groom, then climbed inside. The exterior carriage lamps provided scant light, but it was enough for him to notice that Serena's peach gown was plastered to her damp skin, leaving only the best parts to his imagination. She folded her arms across her breasts as she hugged herself, shivering against a chill, while her knees were drawn up nearly to her chin. At least he knew she had very shapely legs.

"May I offer you my coat, Miss Langley?" He quickly doffed his hat and gloves, and then the coat as he sat on the seat across from her. "It's relatively dry because I had an umbrella. I'm very afraid you'll catch your death of cold."

"Perhaps it would be better if I did," she said morosely, her teeth chattering as she leaned forward to accept the coat he draped around her quivering shoulders.

"You can't mean that. Who else will constantly remind me of my place?"

She burst into tears as she rested her head against his chest. "Right now I don't care what your place is."

He wrapped his arms around her and held her close against him, reveling in the scent of lilacs that clung to her.

He scarcely blamed her for being so distraught, as he recalled his conversation with Daphne and how Serena had confronted him in the dark. Dear God, he would never attack her sister any more than he had attacked her aunt! He wished he knew exactly what was wrong with her sister, and if there was anything that could be done for her. Daphne had known very little.

While in the conservatory, Serena had fought him as fiercely as the tiger he'd once hunted while in India—and just like the tiger, she'd managed to escape him. He didn't regret losing the tiger. But Serena was too beautiful a creature to ever let go. She didn't fight him now. No, from Gibson she sought comfort.

TRUE PRETENSES

Her hands snaked around his waist to his back as she wept into his shirt. She babbled incoherently about what had happened tonight, beginning with her own intentions to confront Daphne with her betrayal.

"How did Fairborough even know about the paintings?" Serena cried. "Where did he get the notion to check the canvases at his ancestral home to see if they were copies?"

That was obviously a rhetorical question for Coachman Gibson, so Kit did not respond. But he'd correctly figured out Daphne's scheme, and only fabricated the part about checking the backs of the canvases to avoid telling his stepmother the true story of how he found out—by masquerading as Serena's coachman.

Damn! Had he done so, then Serena, lurking nearby in the dark conservatory, would have learned his true identity.

"And then Fairborough grabbed me from behind!" she exclaimed. "I thought he was going to—to—"

"Perhaps he only wanted to console you because he saw how distraught you were, the way I'm doing with you now."

"No, I just know he had improper intentions. The duchess has been telling me for years what sort of rake he is, so he couldn't have been doing anything other than—than doing what he always seems to do with ladies who don't have coachmen like you at hand to rescue them."

He abruptly broke the embrace. At least he had the self-control not to angrily push her away, much as he wanted to.

She gaped at him, clearly nonplussed. "What's wrong? You told me the other day outside Plumlee's that I needed someone like you to protect me from unsavory men. And I needed you in that conservatory tonight!"

Kit longed to tell her that he *had* been there for her tonight, if only she'd given him a chance.

He gazed into her swollen, silvery blue eyes. "After what the duchess has done to you and your sister, how can you believe anything she says about your fiancé?"

"Because it's true. Did you know he was in the servants' backstairs this evening, doing heaven knows what with some innocent maid?"

He fought to conceal his mounting fury. "I can't say as I did. How did you happen to know?"

"I was only a few feet away when he emerged from the servants' staircase."

And he never saw her? he thought in shock. Then again, at the time he'd been so dismayed by his unexpected, ignominious entrance that he hadn't even considered Serena. On the ballroom floor Lucinda had tried in vain to point her out to him (after telling him how much he resembled the Langleys' new coachman), but he hadn't realized they'd just missed colliding with each other on the loggia. Serena had obviously seen him, though—so why didn't she realize by now that he and Gibson were the same person?

"So I'm not gossiping," she went on. "I know why he was sent to India, and he only came back because he'd inherited the dukedom. Why do you suppose he's kept himself hidden away since returning to England, till tonight? I daresay his reclusion is proof of his guilt."

"Well, he obviously wasn't reclusive tonight, if he came to this party. So he must be innocent."

Serena shook her head vehemently. "Perhaps he suddenly realized his past crimes mean nothing now, forasmuch as he's become a duke and one of the richest, most powerful men in England. Indeed, not one person in that ballroom gave him the cut direct. Quite the contrary, in fact."

Kit slumped back on the squabs as he fought to conceal his exasperation. She certainly had everything figured out entirely to his disadvantage.

He tried to assume a conversational tone. "So you saw the Duke of Fairborough come out of the servants' stairwell and—"

"No, I didn't actually see that. I was standing nearby with my back to the duke, and I overheard someone remarking on his rather scandalous entrance. I even heard the duke himself speak—but I didn't turn around for fear he might recognize me. I only saw him from a distance, so I never got close enough to determine if he might resemble you." She pulled his coat closer around her trembling shoulders. "Though I noticed he seemed to get along very well with my cousin Jemma."

"Then why worry? Perhaps he'll marry her instead." And perhaps the flames of hell would freeze into glaciers.

"I'm sure she was just being cordial to fool her mother. I wish neither of us had to marry him. But at least she has her Scotsman to help her avoid marrying the duke. I have no weapons against him."

Those words were manna from heaven, and Kit briefly cast his eyes upward to thank the Almighty. He glanced back at Serena, and tentatively reached for her gloved hands, taking them into his own.

"You do have a weapon, Miss Langley. Did I not tell you the other day that I would protect you from the Fairboroughs and Winslows and Plumlees of this world?"

In the wan lamplight, he saw fresh tears shining in her eyes. "You did," she said. "And I do want you to protect me, Gibson, only—only what happened between you and the duchess?"

Kit felt totally at sea. "What are you talking about?"

"The other day, at Woodard House, you asked if I

wanted to know why you were so familiar with her. I didn't want to know then, but I'm afraid I must know now."

Oh, *that!* Kit had forgotten all about that episode. He seemed to have one too many juggling acts in his mind these days. Come to think of it, Daphne seemed to have forgotten it, too, since she didn't mention it this evening, but that wasn't surprising since she'd promptly fainted upon seeing him that day. Also, she most likely had been distracted by his accusations of blackmail.

"Why did you address her by her Christian name?" asked Serena. "What were you up to? Have you ever kissed her?"

He smiled. "A true man of honor never tells such tales."

"So you *have* kissed her!"

He should have known by now that she believed whatever she wanted. "Miss Langley, you've accused me often enough of not knowing my proper place. So why should it surprise you that I called her by her Christian name?"

"Because you've never called me by my Christian name. Nor have you ever kissed me."

Kit had enough experience to recognize an invitation when it was offered. He moved swiftly across the carriage to the seat next to her. "Would you like me to do those things?"

She smiled thinly. "Would you?"

Before he could even move to grant her irresistible request, she slid her hands over his shoulders, touching her silken cheek to his slightly rougher one.

"Serena." He laced his fingers through her damp hair, entwining them in the sodden ringlets that seemed to go limp at his touch, even as he felt a certain part of himself hardening at hers. He wrapped his arms around her, reveling in all of her many wonders: her rain-kissed warmth, her soft breasts, tipped with hardened nipples protruding through the thin, wet silk of her gown; her fingers brushing the nape of his neck; and at last the smoothness of her cheek sliding against the roughness of his as her mouth found his . . . or did he find hers?

By now he was too mindless with desire to care. The important thing was that he was finally kissing the woman who he was still determined, now more than ever, to make his duchess.

As his open mouth covered her soft lips, they parted in warm welcome with a gentle purr deep in her throat. Kit slowly slid his tongue around hers and nearly groaned as he tasted a hint of strawberry. Her arms tightened around his shoulders as he deepened the kiss, drawing her tongue into his own mouth as he carefully slid his coat from her shoulders and pulled her closer against him, stroking his hands over the damp silk on the back of her gown. How he longed to take her right now, right inside this carriage, while the rain pelted down all around them!

Serena felt comfortable and secure in Gibson's embrace, ready to melt into a hot, strangely pulsating liquid as his tongue languidly caressed hers. From the moment he'd taken her into his arms, she'd felt all the fury and fear that had raged within her at the conservatory melt away; no longer did she want to hang on to them. She'd felt those same turbulent emotions trying to ebb away from her while Kit had held her, but she'd had to cling tenaciously to them. It was as if Kit, by taking her into his arms, had wielded the same power over her that Gibson did now.

But how could that be, if she didn't want Kit? Would she fall prey to that same power if just any man—for instance, Nicholas or Warren—took her into his arms?

Could it be she was willing to surrender to any man, whether he was a coachman or a duke—*a true gentleman or an immoral cad?* Then why had she never surrendered to Warren? Well, because he was her cousin and a revolting beast. But why had she felt earlier that she could just as easily surrender to Kit as to Gibson, when she knew Kit was just as revolting a beast as Warren? Why had she been forced to consciously fight the power Kit had seemed to wield over her—the same power Gibson was wielding now?

Her confusing thoughts warred with her burgeoning desire, as Gibson's hand slid around and cupped one of her breasts. A moan escaped her throat and slithered into his mouth as his thumb teased the hardened nub poking through her damp bodice. Now she understood even more clearly what Nicholas and Daphne had been up to in the conservatory this evening. Serena ached to pull her dress down to her waist, exposing her breasts to Gibson's heated touch. His finger slid along the edge of her bodice, as if he was thinking of doing the same. Briefly she couldn't help wondering if Daphne had lowered her own dress this evening, or if Nicholas had done it for her. Or if Serena were wanton enough to allow any man—Nicholas or even Kit, let alone the coachman—to pull her dress down.

Perhaps she shouldn't allow even Gibson such a liberty, lest she end up like Daphne—or even her own mother.

But if they were caught, she probably wouldn't have to marry Fairborough.

Torn between wanting to avoid her arranged marriage and not wishing to emulate her mother, Serena forced herself to break away from the coachman altogether.

"It's all right, don't be afraid," he whispered, gently

stroking her cheek and running his fingers under her chin, lifting it delicately. "I would never do anything to hurt you."

Serena touched her lips that still burned with the heat from his, just as she still felt that spot on the back of her hand where he'd kissed her the other day. "I've never been kissed before. I've never done anything like what happened just now—because I'm not like the dowager duchess, and I'm not like my mother! I don't want to be like them."

"I don't believe you're anything like them. You've done nothing wrong."

She sighed as she sat back, feeling suddenly weak. "I only wonder if Fairborough would agree. Lud, but he was so cold and pompous in the conservatory this evening."

Gibson smiled, and even in the feeble lamplight from outside, Serena could see the dimple in his left cheek. "Believe me, if he's as cold and pompous as you say, then the fact that we've only kissed should be sufficient for him to demand you cry off."

She smiled back. "You do have a point. Many people would consider a mere kiss as bad as—as—"

"And how wrong they are. There's nothing bad about a kiss, but I can assure you that 'as—as' is even better." He took her hand into his as a rumbling sound thundered from the box outside. "All we have to do is be caught by the proper authorites, and if that sound is any indication, then I believe we'll be caught very shortly."

"Oh dear." She felt her resolve wavering and almost pulled her hand away, but he grasped it firmly.

"Courage, my dear." He smiled as he sat next to her with his back to the door.

Serena gazed at him as if she could draw strength from the sight of him, squeezing his hand and bracing for the oncoming explosion, as she heard the groom fumbling with the latch. Already she could hear Harriet's strident voice approaching, asking the groom the whereabouts of that blasted coachman.

The door finally swung open, and a gust of cold, wet air rushed in. " 'E's in 'ere with Miss Langley, yer ladyship."

"What do you mean, he's—" Harriet's scowling face appeared in the doorway. "Well! I might have known. Is this why you've been resisting marriage to Fairborough all this time, Serena—because of your regard for a mere servant?"

"Perhaps." Serena's heart thumped rapidly as she glanced back at Gibson, who looked terribly amused.

"You, coachman!" Harriet barked. "You're discharged—as soon as you drive us back to Hampstead."

She climbed into the carriage as Gibson grabbed his coat and snatched up his hat and gloves, swiftly exiting through the other side without a word or backward glance. Serena quickly moved to the opposite seat to make room for her cousins.

Jemma entered the carriage behind her mother. "But, Mama, couldn't you see for yourself that Hamish is just as—"

"You're marrying Fairborough and that's final! Especially since it's patently obvious your cousin here has been acquitting herself quite shamelessly with the coachman." Harriet glared at Serena. "I only hope you're pleased with yourself. Fairborough wouldn't dream of wedding you now."

"Then why should he dream of wedding me after the way I acquitted myself with Hamish?" asked Jemma.

"Just hold your tongue!" Harriet did not appreciate having the contradictions in her logic pointed out to her.

"But, Mama, he's the one who took me to Hamish tonight!"

"Fairborough would never have done any such thing! Why would he, when he knows he must wed a descendant of the earls of Paxton to inherit that sixty thousand pounds?"

Harriet did have a point, and Serena had seen for herself that Fairborough and Jemma seemed to have gotten along very well, so why would he hand her over to Hamish? Jemma was clearly grasping at straws, not that Serena could blame her.

"I shall write a letter to Fairborough first thing in the morning, informing him of Serena's scandalous behavior so he'll marry you instead," Harriet added. "Thank heavens he didn't see what I saw you doing with that—that—"

"Scotsman?" Serena couldn't help supplying.

"Not another word out of you!" Harriet snapped. "You both behaved like a pair of common tavern wenches tonight!"

The carriage began slowly moving, easing its way out of the line of other conveyances along Curzon Street.

"Mother, what about Papa and Warren?" Jemma queried. "Shan't we wait for them?"

"They have their clubs," Harriet said sourly. "And I should think you wouldn't want to see either of them any time soon. Just wait until your father hears of your despicable behavior this evening!"

Serena wondered just how despicably her hapless young cousin had behaved with Dunbar. Did they do more than what Serena had done with Gibson? Did they go as far as Nicholas seemed to have gone with Daphne in the conservatory?

But what difference did it make now? Serena felt only relief at the realization that thanks to the letter Harriet was threatening to write, she would not have to marry Fairborough, after all. The nightmare of dread, which had stretched on for seven years, was finally behind her. She knew she should feel bad for Jemma, but she also knew that one of them, sooner or later, would have to make the supreme sacrifice for those sixty thousand pieces of silver.

So she would not have to compromise herself any further with Gibson—not that she'd be able to after tonight. After all, Harriet had just given him notice.

Fresh tears attacked Serena's cheeks as she realized, with a breaking heart, the beginning of a whole new nightmare.

Chapter Eleven

Serena could only describe Miriam's reaction to her long, plaintive account of this evening as "cheerily indifferent."

"Haven't you heard a word I've said since coming home?" Serena said in exasperation, as the abigail helped her get ready for bed. She was spending the night in Langley House since it was too late and rainy to venture out to the cottage.

"I've heard every word," Miriam said briskly, holding out Serena's night rail. "Fairborough knows all about Felice and those paintings. You finally met him but still don't know how much he resembles Gibson. Then Lady Paxton, after finding her daughter in a compromising position with Lord Dunbar, found you in a compromising position with Gibson and gave him notice. I must say, for someone whose very existence would seem synonymous with the word *stubborn*, you certainly didn't waste any time heeding my advice."

Karen Lingefelt

"And look at what's happened!" Serena pulled her night rail over her head.

"Yes. You're finally free of Fairborough."

"But Gibson is gone."

Miriam threw back the counterpane and punched the pillow. "Servants come and servants go. Anyway, you were right that he was too young for me. I'm resuming my pursuit of Mr. Jennings."

"You're missing my point. Don't you realize that Gibson—that he and I—"

"I haven't missed a thing." Miriam straightened up, arms akimbo. "All you wanted was to be free of Fairborough. And thanks to the coachman, your wish has been granted. Whatever is the trouble? He only kissed you, did he not?"

Yes, he *only* kissed Serena. Only a kiss, and nothing more. There would be nothing else between them.

She plopped onto the edge of the bed. "Just a few days ago, you were exhorting me to—to do so much more with him!"

"And isn't it a relief to know you won't have to submit to that, after all?"

What could Serena possibly say? That she'd actually *wanted* to submit to *that* with Gibson—a mere coachman?

Only to Serena, he wasn't a mere coachman, any more than Miriam was a mere abigail. Miriam was one person, but to Serena she represented so many different people—mother, nurse, maid, friend, and confidante. In the space of just a few days, Serena realized that Gibson could easily fill just as many roles—some of them roles Miriam could never play.

Like lover.

Miriam looked hard at her. "Good heavens, do you mean to tell me that you've fallen in love with Gibson?"

TRUE PRETENSES

Still too astounded by the notion to admit it, she only said, "Isn't that what you wanted?"

"I only wanted what you wanted, which was to avoid marriage to Fairborough. I only meant you should trust Gibson to help you achieve your heart's desire. And he obviously did that tonight, without having to take your virtue, which might have been necessary had your cousins not found you when they did—and all things considered, perhaps that's just as well."

Serena slumped back on her pillow. "But, Miriam, I learned tonight that strange as it sounds, the coachman may well be my heart's desire. And now he's gone. If you ask me, my cousins found us far too soon."

"I have the feeling everything will work out in the end. Perhaps there is something better in store for you."

Serena pulled up the counterpane. "Better than what?"

"Just better. Now try to get some sleep."

The rain abated by late morning, when she awoke to the distant clamor of her cousins' quarreling voices.

Serena dressed herself, and as she came downstairs the belligerent voices grew louder, flying from the dining room amid the angry clatter of silver and china. Halfway down she froze as she heard the word *coachman*.

"Henceforth, Harriet, I will discharge any servants when appropriate," Archie said.

"But, my lord, I thought that was *my* duty."

"Then where were you when Gibson first came here for the coachman's position the other day? Why, you were abed."

"But, my lord, I couldn't possibly rise before noon!"

"Then why are you here now, when it's scarcely past eleven? And try not to preface your reply with 'but, my lord.' "

"I wanted to write that letter to Fairborough and explain to you about the coachman as soon as you came home. By the by, where is Winslow?"

"Who?"

"Our firstborn, my lord."

"He left the party to visit his club with a Lord Dunbar."

Serena continued down the staircase as Jemma suddenly wailed.

"Dry your tears, gel," Harriet snapped. "You should be overjoyed. You're going to be a duchess."

"If it makes you feel any better, puss, I don't especially want to be an earl," Archie told his daughter. "I was quite content as Lord Gorham's estate manager. Never wanted to be on equal footing with him."

"But, my lord, once our daughter weds Fairborough and he collects that trust fund, you'll be an even wealthier earl than Gorham," said Harriet. "And don't you find it wonderfully ironic that Jemma's intended is the stepson of Gorham's daughter?"

Gorham's *illegitimate* daughter, thought Serena, cringing as she stepped on a creak in the next tread down. It had to be true, if someone was successfully blackmailing Daphne with such information. Only who could it be, if it wasn't Archie?

She slipped past the dining room, heading for the French doors to the garden. She stopped short as they suddenly swung open to reveal Warren, who sported a black eye, a pair of discolored cheeks, a nose that had recently bled, and a cut, swollen lip.

Someone had obviously given Warren the thrashing of his life: the thrashing he deserved. Serena wisely held her tongue, stepping aside to let him pass. He didn't look as if he was in any condition to make trouble for her.

TRUE PRETENSES

"Where are you off to, Serena?" he asked with a slight lisp, as if he had a loose tooth.

"The cottage. Are you all right?"

He gave her a half smile; his lip would probably start bleeding again if he smiled fully. "Do I look all right to you? Are you as blind as your aunt was dumb?"

"I'm sorry. Were you set upon by footpads?"

"No, I was planting facers on Dunbar. There's one Scot who won't be flaunting his sporran around here ever again."

"It looks as if he planted as many facers on you."

"Right, so I need some nursing." He lowered his gaze to her bosom. Shouldn't he have been in too much pain for that sort of thing? "You're very good at taking care of others, Serena. Why don't you take care of me? Wouldn't you like to see where Dunbar kicked me?"

"No, since he obviously didn't kick you hard enough." She tried to step past him, but he turned and grabbed her arm. He spun her around till her back was to the French doors and his to the hallway. In the light streaming through the glass doors, she saw even more clearly the livid bruises and jagged, blood-encrusted cuts on his face.

"At least give me a kiss to make me feel better."

"I'll do no such thing," she hissed. "Now let me go."

"What's this, my son isn't good enough for you?" Serena glanced over Warren's shoulder to see his mother standing at the other end of the hallway outside the dining room. "Oh, dear me, I forgot," Harriet continued snidely, "he is a viscount, after all, which makes him *too* good for you. Unhand her, Warren. She's already been soiled by the coachman."

He grinned lasciviously at Serena. "So glad to hear that," he murmured, releasing his grip on her arm. "That should make things easier in the future."

Dread surged through her at those ominous words.

He finally turned to face his mother, who instantly shrieked.

"Warren! What on earth happened to you?"

Archie emerged from the dining room, followed by Jemma. "Now what? I thought you went to your club with Dunbar."

"So I did," Warren replied. "Then he took me to see the sights on the docks."

"Dear me!" Harriet put a hand to her bosom. "I don't believe you should say another word in front of us ladies."

" 'Tis nothing no one here has heard of before," said Warren. "We only ran afoul of a press gang."

"What!" Archie burst out.

"You told me Dunbar did this to you," Serena said.

"And so he did. He took me all the way down to the docks; then wouldn't you know it, he tried to rob me for the blunt he needed to enjoy himself. You know how parsimonious the Scots are. He wasn't about to spend his own if he had any. Luckily those sailors came along—and even luckier they all hate Scots. They might have pressed me, too, had I lingered any longer than I did. They were having too much sport with Dunbar."

"But what happened to him?" Jemma cried fearfully.

Warren shrugged. "No doubt he's swabbing the decks aboard one of His Majesty's frigates."

"But for how long?"

"Till Wellington chases Boney back to Corsica with his tail between his little legs," Archie put in. "And that could take donkey's years at the rate things are going."

Jemma burst into a fresh spate of sobs. Serena felt a horrible ache in her heart for her hapless cousin, who made a sudden dash upstairs.

"Ha! Did I not say time and again he was nothing but a bounder?" Harriet crowed.

TRUE PRETENSES

"It seems to me you said time and again he was nothing but a Scot," said Serena. "Though heaven knows you could scarcely bring yourself to say even that."

"Not another word out of you!" Harriet snarled. "Not only is he a—a Scot—but he's obviously a rake and a thief. Because of him, our son could have suffered the same fate Dunbar most deservedly did." She scurried down the hallway to her son. "Come, dear boy, let's tend to your wounds."

"That's all right, Mother, Serena has already offered to nurse me."

Before Serena could even open her mouth to protest, Harriet, shooting her a scathing look, said, "You're not up to that sort of nursing. Now come along and we'll summon the housekeeper."

Pity the poor housekeeper, thought Serena, as she opened the French doors and fled into the gardens. Her heart squeezed painfully at the thought of what had happened to Hamish Dunbar. She couldn't help wondering if instead it hadn't been Warren's idea to visit the docks, as a means of getting Jemma's true love out of the way. It seemed like the sort of thing Harriet might have put her son up to. Serena had never been to that part of London, but she knew it was an area rife with footpads and press gangs. It would not have been difficult for the two men to encounter the sort of trouble they did. What a shame the sailors hadn't pressed Warren, too—or rather, instead!

A feeble sun struggled to shine through leaden clouds still swollen and heavy with the threat of more rain. The yellow roses glittered with last night's raindrops as if sprinkled by tiny diamonds. Serena stepped gingerly over the wet graveled path, not wishing to ruin another pair of slippers.

After this latest unpleasant encounter with Warren, she now understood the wisdom of Gibson's words the other day outside Plumlee's shop. He'd agreed it was no bad thing for her to be independent and able to resist the advances of cads like Warren. But wouldn't it be nice to have someone who could step in and help her, in case she couldn't fight him off by herself?

If only Aunt Leah had had someone like that the night Kit Woodard had attacked her! Because of her affliction, no man had wanted Leah—and because of that, she'd been forced to fend for herself as best she could. Serena had always admired that. But her independence, such as it was, had cost Leah dearly—so dearly that she'd fled London, never to be heard from anyone again. Serena didn't even know if her aunt was still alive.

Leah had had little choice but to remain a spinster. Serena, on the other hand, could have married if she'd wanted. Certainly she could have pressed Simon to set a wedding date. Perhaps, if she'd shown a little more enthusiasm about the betrothal, Simon might have developed a tendresse for her, and even abandoned his rakehell ways for her. All men, she knew, had to sow their wild oats, even if Simon's oats had been wilder than most. Perhaps she could have changed him—though she'd never heard of a wife who'd ever succeeded in changing a husband.

But she wasn't certain she could have loved him. Granted, she knew that love was a secondary consideration in marriage. She'd witnessed no affinity between her own parents, or Archie and Harriet. But Serena couldn't help feeling that love ought to be just as important as money and position. If it were, then perhaps her mother would never have gone astray, and Papa wouldn't have died in that duel. Perhaps Archie and Harriet would be more tolerant of their daughter's love for Hamish Dunbar, if only they themselves had love for each other.

TRUE PRETENSES

But love, Serena knew, could not be forced. It happened whether one desired it or not. After all, she'd never made up her mind to love Gibson. She would never have consciously done that, because of the differences in their status. Viscounts' daughters did not marry men from the servant class, period. But it was painfully obvious that there was nothing to stop those daughters from falling in love with such men.

She wasn't likely to ever marry now, nor would she ever see Gibson again. And she had no one to blame but herself on both counts. Why, if she'd known a mere kiss would have resulted in all this trouble, she might have allowed Gibson to go even further last night, if only to make the ensuing heartache more worthwhile.

She reached the cottage and opened the door.

She nearly fainted as she saw Gibson sitting at the kitchen table with Felice.

Chapter Twelve

"Good morning, Miss Langley," Kit said cheerfully.

"Good morning, Miss Langley," Felice echoed, but more flatly.

Serena stood frozen in the doorway, gaping at them. Kit quickly rose to his feet. "I'm sorry, Miss Langley, I know I don't belong here, but—"

"But I invited him over for tea," said Miriam. "I didn't expect you out here for some time yet."

"I thought you were gone," Serena told Kit.

"You will never be rid of me, Miss Langley." He flashed a conspiratorial grin at Miriam.

"But Lady Paxton—"

"Had no authority to give me notice. As soon as I brought you ladies home last night, I returned to the Maxwells' as I still had an obligation to His Lordship, who was none too pleased to have been abandoned by Her Ladyship. He insists he needs a coachman, and since they're rather scarce these days, I remain at your service."

GET THREE FREE* BOOKS!

SIGN UP TODAY TO LOCK IN OUR LOWEST PRICES EVER!

A $19.97 value!

Every month, you will receive three of the newest historical romance titles for the low price of $13.50,* up to **$6.50 in savings!**

As a book club member, not only do you save **32% off the retail price**, you will receive the following special benefits:

- **30% off** all orders through our website and telecenter (plus, you still get 1 book FREE for every 5 books you buy!)

- Exclusive access to dollar sales, special discounts, and offers you won't be able to find anywhere else.

- Information about contests, author signings, and more!

- Convenient home delivery of your favorite books every month.

- A 10-day examination period. If you aren't satisfied, just return any books you don't want to keep.

There is no minimum number of books to buy, and you may cancel membership at any time.

*Please include $2.00 for shipping and handling.

NAME: _____

ADDRESS: _____

_____

_____

TELEPHONE: _____

E-MAIL: _____

____ I want to pay by credit card.

__ Visa   __ MasterCard   __ Discover

Account Number: _____

Expiration date: _____

SIGNATURE: _____

Send this form, along with $2.00 shipping and handling for your FREE books, to:

Historical Romance Book Club
20 Academy Street
Norwalk, CT 06850-4032

*Or fax (must include credit card information!) to: 610.995.9274.
You can also sign up on the Web at <u>www.dorchesterpub.com</u>.*

Offer open to residents of the U.S. and Canada only. Canadian residents, please call 1.800.481.9191 for pricing information.

If under 18, a parent or guardian must sign. Terms, prices and conditions subject to change. Subscription subject to acceptance. Dorchester Publishing reserves the right to reject any order or cancel any subscription.

"Have some tea," said Miriam, setting out another cup and saucer.

Serena sat at the table across from her sister. "Well, Gibson, it might interest you to know that because of last night, I'm no longer marrying Fairborough. Do sit down again."

He returned to his seat next to Felice. "That does interest me, but how does he know what happened?"

"He doesn't know yet, but he will. Lady Paxton is writing him a letter. She wants him to marry my cousin Jemma instead."

Splendid. Kit could hardly wait to read the harridan's account of what she thought she saw in the carriage last night. "But didn't you want to escape marriage to him, Miss Langley?"

"Yes, but so does Jemma. I see you've met my sister."

He glanced at Felice, who was busily copying a picture from an illuminated page in the book that lay open on the table.

"Is this why you were removing books from the library when I arrived this last week, Miss Langley?"

"Yes, she enjoys copying the pictures."

"She reminds me of a butterfly."

Serena smiled. "Why, I've never heard anyone describe her thus. That's beautiful, Gibson."

"I'm surprised no one else has ever noticed the similarity. She doesn't walk or glide about the cottage, she flutters—just like a butterfly. Is that not correct, Miss Felice?"

Without even looking up, she said, "I'm not a Miss Felice, I'm a Felice."

"But you are still a butterfly, are you not?"

Still she did not look up from her drawing. "I'm not a butterfly, I'm a Felice."

Kit chuckled and took a sip of tea, smiling broadly at Serena. "Her Christian name is quite fitting."

"She's blissfully unaware of the world's heartaches," Serena said with a sigh. "Her world consists of her art."

"Yes, and I'm amazed by it. I'm sure the pages in this book were painstakingly created by the monks five hundred years ago, but she can copy a complete page within minutes, using the very same colors and details—and the details, especially around the edges of the page, are very intricate."

"But perfectly proportioned," Serena said. "The monks' original and her copy are flawlessly matched—just like the paintings from Fairborough Castle."

"Where have you studied, Felice?" inquired Kit, but she didn't seem to hear him. "Have you been to Florence?"

"Florence?" she said, as if the city were hidden somewhere in Abyssinia.

"Yes, I thought all great artists studied there. And you're obviously a great artist."

"I'm not a great artist, I'm a Felice."

"Well, there's no doubt in my mind about that anymore."

"She's never studied anywhere," said Serena. "She's only nineteen. This all came naturally to her when she was about five years old. Yet everyone thinks she's mad and a monster, but she's not!"

"I don't think she's mad or a monster," said Kit. "I think she's the most gifted human being I've ever seen in my life, and I've traveled quite a bit."

"Of course, Gibson, you're a coachman," Miriam put in.

He quickly took a sip of tea as if doing so might cover up his near blunder. Kit Woodard had indeed visited Italy and even Greece before going to India, but Alfred Gibson's travels should have been confined to southern England.

"How could anyone call her mad?" he wondered aloud.

"When she was very small, it was thought she might be deaf and dumb, like our aunt Leah—only Leah could hear but not speak," Serena explained. "Felice, on the other hand, didn't seem to hear anything anyone said to her, nor did she ever say anything. She started at noises, but never seemed to notice voices. Then when she was about five, Papa called her an idiot to her face. And that was when she spoke for the first time, and told him she wasn't an idiot, she was a Felice. Papa was so astonished, he never spoke to her again."

"But I should think at that point he'd start talking to her constantly," said Kit.

Serena shook her head. "He'd long since decided she was mad, and best ignored. As far as Papa was concerned, he only had one daughter. But that's still better than my mother, who as far as she was concerned didn't have any."

Kit couldn't help wondering if Felice was really Marcus Langley's daughter. She resembled her sister, only Felice had a smaller nose and was much thinner.

Her passion for drawing was quite evident, judging from all the watercolors and charcoals that covered the walls of the cottage from floor to ceiling. Apparently Felice only dabbled in oils when copying paintings from the Fairborough collection. Her fingers, hands, and forearms were stained with blots of ink, splotches of paint, and smudges of charcoal.

"Not long after she spoke her first words, she started drawing," Serena said. "She drew on the walls of the nursery and raided Papa's stationery. Our butler kindly obtained the materials she needed to draw, since Papa refused to do so. It seems the butler had had a brother who reminded him of Felice."

Kit shook his head in disgust at Serena's father. Why would he not want his younger daughter to draw pictures if she showed such a talent for it?

"If only your father had made an effort to understand her," he finally said.

Serena took a sip of tea. "He was too busy running the farm. Besides, it's not as if he was ever as cruel to her as Fairborough might have been had I married him. Why, just last night in the conservatory, he told his stepmother that Felice couldn't possibly have painted those pictures from his ancestral home, that no one like her could have done such work."

Kit wanted to explode in rage. He had said no such thing!

He tightened his fingers around the handle of his teacup. "What precisely did he say, Miss Langley?"

She gazed back at him earnestly. "What I just told you. I vow I shall never forget his exact words: 'No idiot or monster could do that sort of work.' He sounded just like my father. Thank heavens I shall never have to marry him now. Poor Jemma! Incidentally, did any of you hear about Lord Dunbar?"

Right now Kit didn't give a tinker's damn about Dunbar. He slammed his teacup into the saucer with an angry clink.

"Don't do that," Felice chided. "Sip your tea like a lady."

He rose to his feet. "My apologies. But I'm not a lady, I'm a—a—" A Kit? A coachman? A duke? The obvious response was *gentleman*, but that was the last thing in the world he felt like at this moment.

Serena laughed lightly, seemingly oblivious of his simmering ire. "She's only telling you what Mrs. Kaye has told her a hundred times."

Kit had assumed as much, nodding as he pushed his chair into the table. "I'm sorry, but I'm wondering if perhaps you ladies won't excuse me? Miss Felice, it was a joy to meet you."

He sketched a bow, but she only ignored him.

He wanted to roar in rage at Serena. Why did she persist in her mistaken belief that he was nothing but a scoundrel who was utterly beyond redemption? So deeply ingrained was that belief, that now she was twisting things she'd overheard him say to make him look as dastardly as he surely felt at this moment. He had to leave for fear he'd snap and prove her assumptions correct.

He stormed out of the cottage. No sooner did he close the door—it took every ounce of self-control he possessed not to slam it—than it flew open again.

"Gibson!"

At the sound of that familiar contralto call, he spun around and grunted as Serena flew right into him.

"I was afraid I'd never see you again!" she cried, wrapping her arms around him. "I'm so glad you're going to stay!"

But he was so infuriated with her, he couldn't even bring himself to embrace her in return. He stepped back from her. "Miss Langley, what you're doing is very improper."

"What do you mean?"

"You're betrothed to another man."

"Not since last night. Have you forgotten last night?"

"No, but you know as well as I do that it was wrong."

She widened her eyes. "Why are you suddenly behaving this way? Is it because of Felice? Does she so disgust you that—"

"For pity's sake, woman, did I look or act disgusted just now when I sat next to her at the table?" Kit didn't care if his behavior was unbecoming of a servant. Thanks to Lord Paxton, his position was now quite secure.

"Well, no, but I thought perhaps you were concealing your true feelings, or maybe you were just being polite. But you're certainly not being polite now—in fact, you're behaving exactly like—like—"

"Like Fairborough? Why can't you give him the benefit of the doubt?"

She knit her brow. "What are you talking about?"

"Why do you assume the worst about him? You don't even know him."

"I met him last night. Remember, I told you all about it in the carriage."

"You overheard a conversation between him and his stepmother. How well did you think you knew *her* before you learned how she'd betrayed not only you, but Felice?"

Serena threw her arms outward. "What does any of this have to do with anything?"

Exasperated, Kit decided to cut to the chase. "Who told you about what Fairborough allegedly did to your aunt?"

Her arms dropped limply to her sides. "How do you know about that? Oh, don't tell me. Servants' gossip. I heard about it from an equally reliable source—his stepmother. Why would she spread lies about her own stepson?"

"That's a very good question," said Kit. "But I've heard another version of the incident. Some say your aunt's assailant was actually the previous Viscount Winslow—your father. It seems he may have mistaken his sister-in-law for his wife."

He watched the blood drain from Serena's already pallid face.

He continued, "It was Christopher Woodard who discovered your father with your aunt, and came to her aid."

"I've never heard that version," Serena said icily.

"No, I doubt that you would have," Kit replied. "It wouldn't have done for a young girl to know her own father was a . . ." He saw no need to complete the sentence.

She clenched her fists as if to steady herself. "Why are you telling me such a thing?"

"To make you understand that Fairborough is not the monster his stepmother would have you believe."

"I heard the things he said in the conservatory—"

"And it seems you misunderstood much of what he said."

"How do you know? You weren't even there."

Oh, yes, I was! Kit longed to bark. "Very well, then tell me some of the things he said that make you believe he's nothing but the devil's man-of-affairs."

She cast her eyes around wildly, obviously searching her memory for examples.

"For instance, you told me in the carriage last night that he'd been dallying with the Maxwells' maidservants," Kit said. "Did you actually see him doing so?"

"Well, no, but—"

"Then let's assume he didn't."

"Very well, but he did suggest to his stepmother that there could be nothing in her past worse than in his."

Kit bit his lip as he pondered that. Serena donned a smile more smug than pleasant.

"There, you see?" she said loftily. "He practically admitted it."

"Perhaps he was only going by what people have been saying about him for so many years."

Her smirk faded, and her eyes narrowed. "What do you mean?"

"What if his past consists of false accusations against him, perpetrated by the same people who thought he was dallying with maidservants? Has it ever occurred to you that others could think falsely of you, with the result that your reputation is staked on those falsehoods?"

She nodded, lowering her eyes. "Lady Paxton believes I'm as bad as my mother because of what happened last night."

Kit felt a frisson of satisfaction. "So let's assume for argument's sake that everyone believes her. And your reputation will be based on her accusation, till even you believe it—but as it happens, you believe it already. After we kissed, you said you didn't want to be like your mother. You scarcely needed the ton's gossip to plant that notion in your head."

Serena said nothing, but only stood there trembling.

"I'm reminded of something else you said a short while ago," he went on. "About your conviction that Fairborough believes Felice incapable of doing what I saw her doing."

"Well, he does believe it," said Serena. "He said, 'No idiot or monster could do that sort of work.'"

Kit nodded. "Does that mean he thinks Felice is a monster? Did he actually tell his stepmother that *Felice*, specifically, could not have done those paintings?"

She shifted her eyes from his as she contemplated that, and said, "No."

"No. Only that no idiot or monster could have done them. Yes?"

"Yes. What is your point, Gibson?"

"My point is that obviously Fairborough believes your sister did the paintings, *but*—he doesn't consider her an idiot or a monster. Ponder that! Unlike you, Miss Langley, the present Duke of Fairborough doesn't judge people he's never met, and he certainly doesn't do so based on the prejudices of others."

She crossed her arms over her chest, her silvery blue eyes flashing with anger. "You have some nerve, coachman. That's absolutely not true! That is, it might not be true of Fairborough, but it's not true of me, either. I never give credence to idle gossip."

Kit arched a brow and fought a smile. "You don't, eh? Then what does it mean when someone makes a general reference to an idiot or a monster, and you instantly think of your sister—or you assume that other person is referring to her? You've heard so many such references, perhaps you believe them—just as Fairborough has heard so often he has a scandalous past, he no doubt concludes he may as well accept it, since no one wants to believe otherwise. Deep in your heart, maybe you suspect Felice of being what others say about her."

A shrill cry of outrage shot out of her. "That's nonsense! I only believe what I've seen for myself."

"Yet you willingly believe every horrid little thing you've heard about Fairborough. I'll wager you don't even want to hear anything favorable about him. Not even of how he tried to save a lady in distress, a lady who couldn't even scream for help. No, you'd rather believe the rumors his vindictive stepmother has kept alive for so many years."

"My father would never have done such a thing to my aunt!"

"Oh, no, of course not," Kit said flippantly. "He was such a paragon that he called your sister an idiot because she never spoke. When she did, he was such a saint that he ignored her. He was so proud of her artistic talent that he forbade her the supplies she required to pursue it, and it was up to the butler to be her champion. You saw all of this with your own eyes, Miss Langley, and you justify it by blithely stating that he was too busy running his farm to understand her. Yet you eagerly condemn Fairborough sight unseen, and you base your judgment on nothing more than idle gossip."

"How dare you speak that way about my father!" she raged. "You never knew him, and you certainly can't know Fairborough!"

Kit roared with laughter.

"How dare you act and speak to me like this! And to think I thought I cared about you! I wish cousin Archie *had* discharged you. It's because of you I can't marry Fairborough now!"

"Oh, as if you've been pining for him all this time!" Kit bellowed, as she turned and fled back into the cottage.

Miriam appeared in the doorway a moment later. "What did you say? Did you tell her who you really are?"

He grunted scornfully. "As if that's the worst thing she'll ever hear. No, the coachman was merely playing devil's advocate, and I needn't tell you who the devil is in this case."

"She ran upstairs in tears, as if her heart was breaking."

He tightened his jaw. "Unfortunately, the truth has a way of doing that. But she's scarcely alone. Have you any idea what it's like when people believe the worst lies about you, refusing to consider even a soupçon of truth? How it feels when one of them is the person to whom you long to give your heart?"

Miriam's eyes widened. "Are you falling in love with her?"

A raindrop splattered on his brow as he realized what he'd just said. "Perhaps I am."

"And all you knew a week ago was that you'd have to find some way of marrying her for that wretched trust fund."

"Amazing, is it not, how much a man can learn in one week? I've learned that I actually want her even without the trust fund. But what has *she* learned—

aside from the fact that coachmen are just as heartless as dukes she's never met and never will, because she'd rather believe the vicious rumors and innuendo she's been fed for so many years?"

"Why don't you come in and ask her?"

Kit crossed the threshold of the cottage and followed her upstairs. Felice still sat at the table, busily working on her picture, unaware of the comings and goings of people around her. Kit scarcely believed that was a trait worthy of banishment to Bedlam.

When did everything start to go wrong? Serena wondered despairingly, as she lay on her bed fighting back tears. She thought she'd wept enough last night—and in the coachman's arms, no less! Small wonder he despised her now, though she didn't know why she should care what he thought.

But heaven help her, she did care. She couldn't help but care. She only wished she knew why he'd suddenly turned on her.

Was it because of last night? Did he think less of her now because she, the granddaughter of an earl, had wept in the arms of a manservant and allowed him a liberty or two? But how could that be, when Gibson had been the manservant in question?

Did he despise her because of her sister? He'd seemed enchanted with Felice. But he was good at pretending to be a duke. Was he just as good at pretending to understand Felice?

And why was Gibson suddenly defending the duke so staunchly?

She thought of all he'd said. Perhaps he'd made some valid points about Fairborough.

For instance, she'd always known in the back of her mind that the mildest affliction, the slightest slip in proper behavior, even the idlest rumor could cast someone out of "good society" with all the vengeance of Adam and Eve's expulsion from Paradise.

Mild afflictions had banished Felice and Leah, while Serena's slight slip with Gibson last night was threatening to send her in the same direction. Was it an idle rumor that had sent Kit Woodard to India? A rumor so idle that everyone at the Maxwells' party last night seemed to have forgotten it after so many years?

A rumor that, if false, would shift the onus of blame to Serena's father.

An errant tear escaped from the corner of her eye, and she wiped it away.

"I'm sorry, Miss Langley."

She turned to see Gibson standing in the bedroom doorway next to Miriam, and she promptly sat up.

"I know it hurts to hear such things about your father," he said. "But you'll probably hear it again one day from someone else."

"If it's true, then why have I never heard it before?"

"I told you why. You were a young girl. He was your father. Something like that would have been kept from you intentionally, to protect you."

"He's right, dear," Miriam added. "Remember how old you were before you learned the truth about your mother?"

Not till after her father died and her mother had left England. "Miriam, have you heard that ghastly rumor that it was my father and not Christopher Woodard?"

"I've heard both versions. But unless your aunt is found, who knows which one to believe? Only she can impart the truth. And Gibson understands that, don't you, Gibson?"

He was expressionless. "The version I told Miss Langley is the version I know. That's all I can say at this point."

Serena rose to her feet. "If you've heard it, Gibson,

then surely the Duke of Colfax would have heard it—after all, you worked for him."

"Oh, he's heard it, too, but whether or not he subscribes to it is another matter."

"But where would he have heard it? From Fairborough, of course."

Gibson's face hardened. "And if it's from Fairborough, it's not to be believed, is it?"

Serena matched his piercing gaze. "Actually, I've been thinking of what you said. And while I might be persuaded of Fairborough's innocence, I will never be persuaded of my father's guilt—unless my aunt says otherwise, and no one knows where she is or if she even lives."

He glanced at Miriam, then back at Serena. "So you'll marry Fairborough?"

She shook her head. "It's too late. He's marrying my cousin now."

Gibson donned a cynical smile. "Oh, is he? Have you seen the announcement in the *Times*?"

Mrs. Kaye joined the servants crowding Serena's doorway. "Lady Jemma is here to see you."

Miriam shot a sharp glance at Gibson and whispered, "You'd best be silent and stay up here till Lady Jemma leaves."

Serena scurried downstairs to meet her cousin, who stood at the foot of the steps.

Without preamble, Jemma said, "I've decided to marry Fairborough."

Serena stared at her. "What about Dunbar?"

Jemma twisted the handkerchief she clutched in both hands. "What about him? He's gone, and he may never come back. But I met Fairborough last night, and found him very amiable and quite handsome. I know I don't love him now, but in time I think I will—

which is more than my own mother can say about my father. I'm actually very fortunate."

Serena sank down on the steps. "Has Fairborough agreed?"

"Mother says he'll have to, if he wants his sixty thousand pounds. She's already written him that letter about—you know, about what she saw in the carriage last night. And I won't cry off from the marriage. My mind is made up."

Serena couldn't help heaving a great sigh of relief.

"I know you never wanted to marry him, though after meeting him last night, I do believe the two of you would have suited," Jemma continued. "I also know you didn't want me to marry him, either, that you had hopes for me and Hamish, just as I did. But it wasn't to be."

Serena took Jemma's hand and squeezed it. "I only want you to be happy."

Jemma smiled tearfully. "I am happy, Serena, truly. I'm going to be a duchess, and we do need the money. Now I must go. Mother wants to take me into Town so we can start shopping for my trousseau, if only she can find the coachman. She's actually relieved now that he's still in our service."

Serena thought the better of telling Jemma the coachman was upstairs. "I'm sure he'll turn up. He's probably sound asleep after having to work all night. Enjoy the shopping," she added, feeling only a faint twinge of regret that she would never have a trousseau for herself.

She waited till after Jemma left, then rose to her feet and turned to look upstairs. "Gibson?" she called out.

"Gibson!" echoed Felice, who still sat at the table drawing and coloring. She'd been silent and seemingly oblivious during Jemma's brief visit.

TRUE PRETENSES

Gibson trudged down the stairs with Miriam and Mrs. Kaye behind him.

"I trust you overheard?" Serena said. "Heaven be thanked, there's no longer any point in us debating Fairborough's guilt or innocence. Jemma seems rather eager to take him on, in fact."

"She's only pretending, Miss Langley."

She knit her brow. "I thought she sounded sincere. Or at least resigned."

He widened his brown eyes, which she suddenly realized were dark-rimmed and bleary. "Keep descending, Miss Langley. You've gone from sincere to resigned in just one sentence—"

"Actually, it was two sentences," Miriam chimed in.

"—and from there it's just one more rung down to 'pretending,' " Gibson finished. "She's only pretending to appease her mother, or don't you know at all when someone is pretending?"

"What are you rambling about?" Serena asked in bewilderment. "I think exhaustion is addling your senses."

"They're looking for you, Gibson," Miriam said quickly.

"So I heard," he replied wearily.

Serena stepped in front of him. "You didn't sleep at all last night, did you?"

"No, but duty calls, Miss Langley."

"And I shan't let you answer." She grabbed his broad shoulders. "Go upstairs and rest."

"That wouldn't be proper. I should go back to the carriage house—"

"Where they'll find you and make you drive Lady Paxton and her daughter to Town. Now go upstairs, Gibson. I'll tell them later on that *I* needed you."

He appeared to be vacillating between going upstairs

and leaving the cottage. "But they'll see that all the carriages are there."

Serena hadn't thought of that. She glanced out the window, and to her relief, saw that it was pouring again.

"Thank heavens," she said with a sigh. "Lord Paxton won't allow you to take them out in this weather. He only consented to go out last night because of the party, but I know he won't allow them to go out if all Lady Paxton wants to do is spend money. They're so far below the hatches as it is." Or maybe they weren't, if her hunch about Archie blackmailing Daphne was correct. "Now go upstairs and rest."

"Go upstairs and rest," Felice echoed, as she finally looked up from her drawing, and to Serena's astonishment, she gazed directly at Gibson. Felice rarely if ever made eye contact with anyone.

"Very well, I'll go upstairs and rest," Gibson agreed. "But only because Miss Felice commands it."

Chapter Thirteen

In the days that followed, Kit kept constantly busy shuttling various Langleys to and from Town. When serving any of them save Serena, he always kept his head down and his hat pulled low, so that Harriet and Jemma, at least, would not recognize him as the same man they'd approached at Lucinda's betrothal party. It helped that they treated him and the rest of their servants as if they were nearly invisible, and for the first time Kit realized that he was guilty of doing the same with his own servants. Naturally his employers wouldn't expect to see the Duke of Fairborough in their coachman's livery.

In his spare moments, he visited the cottage. And he wasn't the only gentleman caller—Jennings, the tutor to Jemma's eleven-year-old brother, Philip, was frequently there to see Miriam and even work a bit with Felice, though he wasn't paid to do so. If Jennings found anything unusual about Gibson's friendship with Serena, he never gave any indication.

And it was only friendship. Kit's conscience would not permit anything else. Though he desperately longed to be alone with Serena so he could kiss her, and his arms ached to hold her, he could not do so with the knowledge that he continued to deceive her.

He wanted Serena to fall in love with the duke—or even the coachman—but at this point he was losing hope of ever achieving his goal.

The more Kit drove Jemma and her mother all over London on their daily shopping sprees, the more determined he was to win Serena. Jemma was sweet and meek, with nary a word to say for herself. Most men of his acquaintance would consider those very desirable traits in a wife, and until he met Serena, Kit might have, too. But as she was very much under her mother's thumb, any man who married her would not so much be wedding Jemma as Harriet.

He couldn't help thinking that Hamish Dunbar, wherever he was now, was actually a very lucky man, after all. Damn that Warren for taking him down to the docks! Nicholas had reassured Kit at Lucinda's engagement party that he'd spoken to Dunbar, and that everything was set for Hamish and Jemma's elopement to Scotland. So much for that!

And the Bow Street Runner Nicholas had hired was making no progress in finding Serena's aunt Leah.

Though it made Kit queasy to think of what Calvin might do with that trust fund, he still couldn't help feeling that he'd gladly forfeit every penny of it, if only he could marry Serena.

Then one afternoon, Harriet, minus her daughter, directed "Gibson" to Woodard House, where she paid a call on his stepmother. Kit stole to the kitchen, where Mrs. Bannen gave him the letter from Harriet apprising him of Serena's scandalous behavior with the coachman.

TRUE PRETENSES

He asked for ink and stationery embossed with the Fairborough crest. So supplied, he sat at the kitchen table and quickly penned a brief note to Harriet. Without committing himself to Jemma, he wrote only that he intended to comply with the terms of his father's will, but that he still expected Serena to attend the festivities his grandmother had planned at Fairborough. *Since she was betrothed to my late brother for so many years, she seems just as much a member of my family as yours, and therefore should be present,* he wrote. If he'd won Serena's heart by that time, she could persuade Jemma to step back, and Jemma, who he knew didn't really want to marry him, would cheerfully comply.

Harriet looked decidedly grim when he helped her into the carriage later on. Her visit to Daphne must not have been a pleasant one.

Maybe the note he'd just written and asked Mrs. Bannen to post for him would cheer her up.

Serena hadn't wanted to accompany her cousins to Devon. What was the point? She was no longer the bride. Harriet had shown her the note from Fairborough. Obviously Simon hadn't communicated with his brother any more frequently than he'd communicated with Serena, or Kit would realize that she was scarcely like a member of his family.

She had the worst seat in the cramped carriage, wedged between the slightly pudgy Jemma and even pudgier Harriet. All day she had to endure Warren's constant, lascivious leers as he slouched next to his portly father on the squabs across from her. No one else in the carriage seemed to notice. Archie snoozed, Jemma gazed out the window at the verdant scenery, and Harriet complained about everything from the bumps in the road to the lack of air in the coach, which she never thought to attribute to her constantly flapping tongue. Philip sat outside on the box with Gibson. Harriet had objected vociferously to this till Archie overruled her—after all, he stood to benefit by having one less person crowding him on the front seat of the carriage.

Serena wished it were she on the box next to Gibson.

He'd been strangely preoccupied lately. On the few occasions he'd found time to visit the cottage, he'd enjoyed keeping company with her and Felice, as well as with Miriam, Mr. Jennings, and Mrs. Kaye, but he hadn't tried to steal any more kisses from her. Serena couldn't understand why, since she was finally free of Fairborough.

They spent the night at an inn in Salisbury, and when they started out the next morning, Philip again wanted to sit on the box with Gibson, and again Harriet objected.

"But Gibson's teaching me how to drive," said Philip. "He let me hold the reins most of the way between Sutton Scotney and Stockbridge yesterday afternoon."

"There's no need for you to learn such a thing," Harriet admonished the boy. "You're the younger son of an earl. You'll not grow up to become a coachman."

"But I still need to know how to drive horses. I plan to have my own coach-and-four one day."

"Such fustian nonsense!" She glared at her husband. "My lord, say something!"

Archie did: "Up on the box, Philip, so we can get started. I want to make Fairborough by nightfall."

"But, my lord—"

"Silence!" he barked.

The wagons bearing their servants and baggage had already left. Miriam was aboard one of those wagons, along with Philip's tutor. Serena wished she could at least be with them, if not up on the box with Gibson.

TRUE PRETENSES

She couldn't bear another day crammed inside the suffocating carriage. Even sitting on the tiger's seat with the perpetually drunken groom would be preferable.

Jemma ducked inside the carriage, eager to resume the journey. Serena remained outside with Archie and Harriet, determined not to take her assigned seat until she absolutely had to. She tried to enjoy these few minutes in a standing position.

Harriet glanced around the inn yard. "My lord, where is Winslow?"

"Who?"

"Our firstborn."

"Haven't seen him since last night. But he'd better show up posthaste, or he'll have to walk the rest of the way to Fairborough."

"Coachman!" Harriet said. "Summon Lord Winslow and hurry."

"Yes, my lady." Gibson headed out of the inn yard.

She stamped her foot. "Where do you think you're going, you fool? I'm talking to you, coachman!" He stopped and turned. "Didn't I just tell you to summon Lord Winslow? He should be upstairs in his room. Where is his valet?"

Gibson lowered his head deferentially. "My lady, I know where to find him. He's not upstairs in his room, and his valet has already departed on the servants' wagon."

"What do you mean, he's not upstairs? My lord, say something!"

"The coachman knows what he's about, woman; now for the last time, hold your blasted tongue," Archie growled.

Serena watched Gibson striding purposefully from the inn yard, as if he knew exactly where to find Warren. What a dreadful pity. She wouldn't have minded leaving him behind.

Harriet rudely nudged her. "Into the carriage with you."

Serena stood her ground. "I'll wait until we actually leave, after which there should be ample time to get crushed."

"You'll get in now!" This time Harriet gave her a hard push. "I won't stand out here all day while that coachman wanders all over Salisbury!"

Silently fuming, Serena quickly boarded the carriage before Harriet had a chance to add *My lord, say something!*

Gibson reappeared a few minutes later with Warren slung over his shoulder.

"What happened?" Harriet cried. "Is he all right?"

"He's perfectly all right," Archie grumbled. "Just indulged a bit too much last night."

"But where did you find him, coachman?"

"Never mind, the important thing is he's here and we can leave," Archie said.

Warren moaned and cursed as Gibson eased him into the carriage. Serena shuddered at the foul stench emanating from her cousin. Apparently he was not only drunk, but had a very empty stomach.

But at least he didn't spend the day leering at her.

It was still a miserable journey. At least three times Warren leaned over to open the carriage door, so he could eject whatever still brewed in his stomach. At least three times Harriet insisted they should find a doctor in the next village. At least three times Archie overruled her, countering that their firstborn did not need a doctor, only another good thrashing like the one he'd gotten at the London docks last month. At least nine times Warren whined for everyone to stop talking, because the chatter was splitting his head open.

Serena longed to cover her ears as well as her nose.

The sun sagged low over the horizon when Archie banged on the trapdoor in the roof of the carriage. Warren groaned and clutched his head in agony at the noise. The trapdoor opened to reveal Philip, who peered down at his family.

"Ask Gibson how much farther to Fairborough," Archie said.

"We're on the very edge of the estate now, my lord," Gibson called back. "It should be just another hour."

"I do hope the servants are there by now," Harriet muttered, daubing her face with a handkerchief. "I don't want to have to wait to change into a clean gown. Philip, close that door!"

Philip obeyed, as the carriage rolled down a lush green slope and into dark woods. Though the sun hadn't yet set, the tall trees obliterated what little light remained of the day.

"My lord, tell the coachman to light the carriage lamps," Harriet said.

"I'll do no such thing," Archie replied. "You heard what he said. We'll be there in less than an hour."

"But I can't see a thing!"

"I'm sure we won't be in these woods for long."

"The coachman seems familiar with the area. Ask him how long we'll be driving through these woods."

"Certainly less than an hour."

"My lord—"

"*You* ask him!" Archie snarled, as the carriage suddenly halted. Serena might have pitched forward at the abrupt stop, except she was squeezed too tightly between Harriet and Jemma.

Warren whimpered like a desolate hound.

"Now what?" said Harriet.

Archie glowered at her. "Doubtless the coachman heard your harping, like me grew weary of it, and therefore has stopped to light the bloody carriage lamps."

But no lamps were lit. The door on Jemma's side swung open, and a strange voice called out, "Stand and deliver!"

Harriet and Jemma screamed. Warren moaned a blasphemy. Serena, for her part, was too tired and cramped to panic.

"Oh my God," Archie muttered, as the other door opened on his side.

The trapdoor flipped up, and Philip poked his head inside. "Mother, Father, Gibson says we should just do as they say."

"Out o' the coach wit' all o' ye!" boomed another voice.

Archie was the first to obey, followed by his querulously indignant wife and tearful daughter. Serena was almost grateful for this diversion as she emerged from the coach. At least she could stretch her legs and breathe some fresh, cold air!

One of the cutthroats, obviously the leader, carried a torch that burned just bright enough to reveal a partially masked face. A black cloth with eyeholes covered the man's face from his hairline to the tip of his nose. "Right, let's all line up on the port side o' the coach, now!"

Serena stood near the rear wheel of the coach between Jemma and the groom, who as usual reeked of spirits. He swayed for only a moment before crumpling to the ground. She couldn't even see Gibson. She counted seven silhouettes ominously circling the coach, like a school of sharks closing in on a raft of castaways. All of them brandished pistols.

TRUE PRETENSES

"What about Warren?" asked Philip. "He's still in the coach."

"Silence!" barked the torchbearer. "An' ooh's Warren?"

"He's Viscount Winslow to you," Harriet snapped.

"Oh, 'e's Viscount Winslow to me an' 'e's still in the coach, is 'e? Well, 'e can bloody well stay there for now. That's it, all line up. Ooh we got 'ere? Coachman, young lad, Yer Lordship, Yer Ladyship, an' wot 'ave we 'ere but two fine bits o' fresh muslin!" With his foot he nudged the drunken man on the ground. "Ooh's this at the end wot can't 'old 'is ale?"

"That would be the groom," Gibson said.

"Here's my purse," said Archie, tossing it to the cutthroats. "Ladies, give them your reticules."

"Oh, we don't want no blunt," said Torchbearer. "We jus' need yer coachman."

"No!" Serena blurted out.

Torchbearer nearly thrust his flame into her face, and she reared her head back, her heart racing as she caught the acrid smell of burning pitch. "Beggin' yer pardon, miss? Could it be ye don't mind 'andin' over yer ridicule, but ye do mind givin' up John Coachman?"

Serena dared not breathe for fear she might inhale the flickering flame that licked too close to her face. But Harriet, who could never hold her tongue for long in any situation, mumbled something, and Torchbearer promptly turned on her.

Maybe if they were all lucky, he'd burn Harriet's cursed tongue to a delightfully useless crisp.

" 'Ave ye somethin' o' great import to impart, yer ladyship?"

"Say nothing, Harriet," Archie warned.

"I decide ooh says an' ooh don't, Yer Lordship. Now,

Yer Ladyship, do share yer thoughts ere I burn 'em out o' ye."

"I said she would likely mind a great deal if you took the coachman," Harriet quavered.

Torchbearer grinned, revealing a jumble of chipped, yellowish brown teeth. "Would she now? Pray tell why, yer ladyship? Never say such a fine lass don't like toffs?"

"May'ap she fancies cutthroats, eh?" One of the others stepped up to Serena and grabbed her by the arm. She shrieked as he yanked her out of line.

"Let her go!" Gibson bellowed.

"Quiet, coachman. May'ap we could use 'er, too."

For *what?* thought Serena with a surge of panic. She forced herself to take a deep breath in a futile effort to stay calm.

"Wot's yer name, miss?" asked her captor, as he jabbed the barrel of his pistol into her ribs.

"Serena," she barely whispered. "Serena Langley."

He turned to his confederates. " 'Ow now, blokes? She calls 'erself Serena."

Torchbearer waved his flame toward her. "Then she'll do. Take 'er back, lads."

"Where?" Serena cried fearfully, as her heart rumbled up to her throat.

"Look, I'll do whatever you want, just leave her alone," Gibson said.

"Oh, don't ye fret, coachman, we won't 'urt 'er," said Torchbearer. "We jus' think she might want to keep ye company on the journey."

"What journey?" asked Serena, her voice hoarse and tremulous with mounting fear.

"To Plymouth," Torchbearer said matter-of-factly. "The Royal Navy needs sailors to serve king an' country, it does. Coachman is the only one 'ere fit for duty.

Can't take the viscount. Navy's notorious for keel-'aulin' viscounts, I'll 'ave ye know."

Jemma whimpered, obviously thinking of poor Hamish.

Torchbearer pointed to Philip and then the groom. "Lad's too young, groom can't even walk straight on land, let alone aboard ship, an' as for 'is Lordship—" He flicked his gaze over Archie's rotund figure. "We're lookin' to sink Boney's fleet, not our own, thank ye very much."

"But what do you want with me?" Serena cried. "I'm not a man."

Torchbearer flashed another grin, this time sweeping his gaze up and down her own figure, which, unfortunately, had to be more pleasing to his eye than Archie's. "Aye, that's obvious. An' ye can be sure it's obvious to yer coachman too, or if it ain't, 'twill by morn. 'Ere's yer chance to do yer own bit for Jolly Ol', miss—send a sailor to sea wit' a smile on 'is face, wot? Now step forward, coachman, there's a good bloke. 'Ands up, if ye please. Mick!" Torchbearer beckoned one of his subordinates, who stepped out of the shadows. "Mick, ye see the coachman 'as two arms 'ere. Make sure 'e don't 'ave a third 'idden somewhere."

Gibson stood silent and expressionless, his lips pressed firmly together and his arms in the air as Mick searched him, patting him down and thrusting his hands into whatever pockets he could find.

"Aye, 'e's got a third arm growin' out 'is arse, 'e does," Mick crowed, as he reached under Gibson's coattails and pulled out a pistol that gleamed in the faint torchlight.

"Where on earth did he get that?" Harriet cried. "It's not loaded, is it?"

Torchbearer took the pistol and studied it in the flickering firelight. "May'ap 'e got it from under 'is Lordship's pillow. 'Tis almost too fine for a coachman to be totin' about. An' aye, m'lady, 'tis loaded."

"My lord, the coachman must have stolen that from you!"

"Oh, for God's sake, Harriet, how can you fret over something like that at a time like this?"

"Quiet!" Torchbearer commanded. "Don't matter no more any'ow, since it now belongs to me. Lads, ye know where to take the coachman an' the lass. Let's go. Wilkins, Potter, Smitty—'old the rest 'ere till the moon shows over the trees, so we 'ave time to make a getaway."

Gibson nodded toward Serena. "I beg of you again to let that lady go."

Serena glanced at her four cousins, who cowered against the carriage. None of them would second the coachman's plea. Blood was thicker than water, indeed!

"What do you want to let her go?" Gibson persisted, as if he had something of great value to offer them, when in fact all he had was his life. Yet Serena's gratitude toward the coachman for thinking of her safety was smothered by her fear that his entreaties on her behalf would get him shot. She much preferred whatever murky fate the cutthroats had planned for her.

"We only want to take 'er to Plymouth, and then we'll cut 'er loose," replied Torchbearer. "Now let's go!"

"Don't worry, Gibson," said Philip. "Thanks to you, I can safely drive the carriage the rest of the way to Fairborough Castle as soon as they let us go."

"You'll do no such thing!" Harriet exclaimed.

"Silence, Harriet!" her husband said in vain.

Prodding them with pistols, the cutthroats took Gibson and Serena into the woods. Twigs snapped and branches rustled. Serena had to lift her skirt to her knees to keep it from catching on every little thing in the rapidly spreading dark.

First Hamish, now Gibson! They must have pressed everyone in Plymouth by now if they had to maraud this far inland looking for recruits.

Her teeth chattered, though she wasn't sure if it was because of the evening chill or her own growing fear.

Fear of what? They only wanted to take her to Plymouth, then let her go. But why were they even bringing her along in the first place? None of this made any sense.

Perhaps it was the fear of losing Gibson forever.

They finally emerged from the woods onto another road, where a coach waited with a driver huddled on the box. The carriage lamps were unlit, and Serena could not make out a crest on the door, though a nearly full moon glowed brightly enough in the sky that she could clearly see Gibson's face as he gazed at their surroundings.

"I know this road," he said. "Are you men aware that you're trespassing on private property?"

"Aye, an' we're aware that we're kidnappin' ye, too," Torchbearer retorted, as they all guffawed. "An' if ye don't do as ye're told, we'll be aware that we're committin' cold-bleedin' murder, won't we, lads?"

"You're on the property of the Duke of Fairborough. And I happen to be—"

"Oh, for goodness' sake, Gibson, don't be a fool!" Serena cried. "Don't you even realize they're threatening to kill you? I scarcely think that telling them you're Fairborough is going to get us out of this!"

"Was that wot ye was about to tell us, coachman? That ye're the bleedin' Duke o' Fairb'ro'? Aye, an' I'm the mad King George! Jus' for that, we'll 'ave to tie up yer 'ands, an' the lady's, too."

As they bound Serena's hands in front of her, she

had a sudden, very inconvenient urge to relieve herself. Her insides seemed to turn into water.

"Please," she chirped, "I'm afraid I—that is—well—our carriage made its last stop to change horses about three hours ago, you see, and—well—"

Torchbearer waved his flame in her face again. "Once we reach Plymouth, miss, ye can go all ye want. 'Ow's that sound?"

Serena's face grew hot, but not from that annoying flame. She was not going to embarrass herself further by asking how far it was to Plymouth.

The cutthroats pushed her and Gibson into the coach. Her seat assignment was the same as it had been in the other carriage. At least the persons on either side of her were thinner; unfortunately they smelled worse. Gibson sat directly across from her, crammed between two others.

The coach took off at breakneck speed. Serena knew the destination. She only wished she knew her destiny.

Chapter Fourteen

Kit had to admit that being pressed into the navy would certainly solve his marriage problems once and for all. He wondered how many men could boast of having served in both the army and navy.

He gazed across the bouncing carriage at Serena, who'd finally nodded off. He longed to sleep himself, but he was worried about their captors possibly taking advantage of her—not that he knew how to come to her aid when his hands were tied up in front of him. He couldn't even attempt to loosen his bonds with the four men looking on. The carriage was so cramped that the slightest move by anyone jolted everyone else. No one spoke.

He hoped that upon arriving at Fairborough today or tomorrow, Nicholas would hear about Serena having been abducted along with the Langleys' coachman. Since Nicholas knew the coachman was really Kit, something, though Kit knew not what, would certainly be done to cut short his naval career before it had a chance to set sail. But he also worried about Serena.

Fury at her relatives blazed within him. None of them seemed to care that she was being abducted to God knew what sort of fate. Certainly the torchbearing leader had promised to release her as soon as they reached Plymouth. But then what? How safe could an unchaperoned young woman be in a port town like Plymouth? Serena could just as easily be pressed into service—not to king and country, but in an Eastern harem. Kit had heard of it happening this far north.

But if they wanted sailors for the king and concubines for some faraway sultan, then why take only Kit and Serena? Why not Jemma, too? Why not the groom, who was practically a divinely ordained target for press gangs? He was at least ten years younger than Kit, who'd always thought such gangs preferred recruits young and so drunk they could barely stand up—in which case the groom, by now, should have served aboard every ship in His Majesty's fleet.

And why not Lord Winslow? What was all that nonsense the ringleader had spouted about the navy targeting viscounts for keelhauling? It was as if the gang purposely intended to pass over not only Winslow, but the groom. They'd wanted only the coachman—of that particular coach.

Kit's heart began racing as he recalled that a month ago, Winslow and Dunbar, both viscounts, had ventured to the London docks where Dunbar had fallen prey to a press gang, while Winslow had escaped. Here was another press gang—and again, they'd passed over the yellow-haired bastard as if he wore some sort of magic talisman to ward off such attacks.

Kit suspected that both incidents were setups somehow instigated by Winslow. He understood why the cad might want to get Dunbar out of the way—the

TRUE PRETENSES

Scotsman had been a serious impediment to Jemma becoming a duchess. But why would he want to get Kit—no, *Gibson*—out of the way? After Lord Paxton overruled his wife's attempt to discharge Gibson, did she persuade her eldest son to secretly carry out her wishes in his own way? Yet why bring Serena into it—unless Harriet still feared the Duke of Fairborough would insist on marrying Serena instead of Jemma?

Only the Duke of Fairborough wouldn't be present for his own wedding, regardless of the bride, unless the Duke of Colfax acted very, very fast.

That remained the only hope for Kit and Serena, unless he could devise an escape plan for the two of them once they reached Plymouth.

His eyes flew open as Serena shrieked.

"Wake up, coachman, we're 'ere," said a man's voice.

Good God, how could he have fallen asleep? If not for the pale gray dawn outside the carriage windows, he might have thought he'd nodded off for no more than a minute.

But he'd obviously been asleep for several hours. And what of Serena? She was nowhere in sight.

"Where is she?" he demanded.

"Right outside 'ere. Come out an' see for yerself."

Kit awkwardly emerged from the carriage. It wasn't easy with his hands bound in front of him; plus he was taller than average. He had no choice but to literally fall out of the carriage to the ground, which fortunately was not cobbled.

"Gibson, are you all right?" Serena cried.

The cutthroats laughed raucously. "Stand back, missy, 'e's a big boy. Let 'im get up on 'is own."

Kit rolled to his side, and using his elbow for leverage, sat up. From there he worked his way into a kneeling position, and finally stood up.

She leaped in front of him, her face creased with

worry. Her bonds had been removed. Why didn't she make a run for it?

"Gibson, are you all right?" she asked again.

"Yes, I'm fine." Except he now had a big knot on his left temple, his knee throbbed with pain, and his hands felt as if they'd been crushed. He flexed his fingers—they all seemed to be in working order—as he glanced at their surroundings.

This did not look anything like Plymouth. In fact, it looked as if they were in the middle of nowhere.

"Where are we?" he asked.

The ringleader brandished a knife. "Crossroads. Sign's on the other side o' the carriage."

"I don't understand, what's happening?" asked Serena. "Are you just going to leave us here?"

He grinned. "Ye mean ye'd rather go to Plymouth wit' us?"

"Where are we and what are we supposed to do now?" she persisted, as he deftly cut Kit's bonds with the knife.

"Coachman should know where ye are an' wot to do," said the leader, as he quickly climbed onto the driver's box while the other men scrambled inside the carriage. "Oh, an', coachman—ye'll probably be needin' this in case ye run afoul o' bloodier ruffians than us." He held up Kit's pistol and hurled it into the tall grass at the side of the road. "Cheerio!"

And with that, the carriage rumbled off, leaving Kit and Serena standing alone at a deserted crossroads.

He bent over to rub his bruised knee as she said, "Well, what do you make of this? Why did they just leave us here? What do you suppose this was all about?"

He stretched his cramped muscles. "I think I know what it's all about, and it's a long story. But the most important question right now is, did they hurt you in any way while I was asleep? I didn't mean to nod off, but—"

"Nor did I, but you needn't fret, Gibson. Once we boarded the carriage, they were perfect gentlemen, if that makes any sense. I just wish they'd left us somewhere more convenient."

Kit knew precisely what she meant, for he remembered her stammering plea to their abductors last night; plus he was suffering from a similar complaint. He swept his gaze at their surroundings, but there was nothing but tall grass. "Well, Miss Langley, why don't you go that way and do whatever you need to do, while I go this way to find the pistol and do whatever I have to do?"

He fully expected her to protest and he wouldn't have blamed her, but to his surprise, she promptly turned and scurried into the grass. "You must promise not to look, and let me know if anyone's coming."

"I promise," he said with a weary sigh, as he went in the opposite direction where their abductor had hurled his pistol.

He did what he needed to do, and then he recovered the pistol. He returned to the crossroads, but Serena was still hidden in the dewy grass. He'd learned from married officers in India that women could take forever with that particular thing. He studied the weathered, arrow-shaped signs posted at the crossing. Their captors had absconded to Plymouth, but Fairborough was in the opposite direction, about twenty miles away. The nearest village along the route was about three miles away, and because they were on the crest of a hill, he could just barely make out that village's church spire from here.

She finally popped into view, wading through the tall grass to where he stood. "Do you know where we are?"

"Yes. Fairborough is this way, and you can see the

nearest village from here. Do you think you can make the walk?"

She gave him a withering look. "Surely by now you know me better than that, Gibson. I'm not some milkwater miss. It looks mostly downhill. Let's go. And on the way you can tell me that long story."

As they began their journey, Kit told her of his suspicions about Winslow planning their abduction.

"But why leave us here?" asked Serena. "It seems they rather defeated their purpose, don't you think?"

"I don't know. I thought I had everything figured out till they abandoned us here."

"Otherwise, your theory makes sense. I've thought myself that my cousin must have had something to do with Lord Dunbar's disappearance. And none of them seemed to care last night what those ruffians did with me. I couldn't help feeling they all wanted to be rid of me for good. Even Philip and Jemma."

Kit felt a surge of empathy as she lowered her head in dejection, and he longed to take her hand, even put his arm around her. He knew how it felt to be betrayed by your own relatives. His own father hadn't believed his explanation about what had happened that long-ago night at Langley House.

"Not Philip and Jemma," he said. "They're still too young not to go along with everything their parents say and do—in particular their mother. I'm sure they don't do so because they want to, but because they fear for their skins."

Serena sighed. "How did someone so wise ever become a coachman? It must be because your father was a tutor."

"He was tutor to the present Duke of Colfax until he—that is, the duke—went off to Eton."

"While you stayed behind and became the coachman. What about your mother?"

He sighed. "I'm afraid she died when I was born. I don't even know what she looked like, since there was never a portrait of her, but my father always said I resembled her."

"So we both grew up without our mothers, though in different ways. Why didn't you become a tutor like your father?"

"I liked horses too much. He never objected to that."

She glanced down, her hands behind her back as they continued down the road. "I've always thought that was why you speak and carry yourself so well. 'Tis no wonder you're able to masquerade as the Duke of Fairborough when occasion demands, though you don't quite speak the way he does."

"And how is that?"

"Oh, you know—surely you've heard the way many members of the ton talk. The higher they are in the instep, the higher in the air their noses. When I eavesdropped on him and his stepmother in the conservatory, I heard him talk that way and just knew I could never spend the rest of my life with him."

"Simply because of his highly aristocratic speech?" Kit laughed as he made a mental note to abandon his patrician enunciation if he ever found himself fortunate enough to become Serena's husband. As it was, he much preferred his present, more bourgeois accent.

"That and the scandal concerning my aunt."

"But you believe him innocent now, don't you?"

"I never said that. I only said I could be *persuaded* of his innocence, if I could be persuaded of another's guilt. But you will never persuade me of my father's guilt, so you'll just have to find someone else."

"So you still won't consider marrying Fairborough?"

"Why should I, when it's quite out of the question by now? Why, he's probably sharing a cup of morning tea with cousin Jemma this very moment. And I do wish I hadn't said that, since it only reminds me of how hungry I am."

As if on cue, Kit felt a sudden rumble in his stomach. "All we have to do is reach the village. At this pace we should be there within an hour."

"Only what shall we do once we eat?"

"Perhaps there's a stage or mail coach to Fairborough."

Serena paused to dig around in her reticule. "I have a couple of crowns. That should be enough for food as well as a coach to Fairborough—if there is one."

Kit, for his part, had about five pounds hidden on his person, though he didn't know how a coachman, scraping by on wages of fifteen shillings a month—and he'd scarcely worked that long for the Langleys—could explain the possession of such a fortune. He'd have to think of a good story in case Serena found out and asked. He already had another one in the event she inquired about his fine Bennett & Lacy pistol, which his father had given him for his sixteenth birthday.

"When we reach the village we can say we were robbed," she said. "How else to explain why we're on foot, with nothing but the clothes on our backs? You don't even have your hat. Only how to account for my reticule?"

"You can say your blunt was pinned in the hem of your pelisse. Haven't you done that before?"

"Yes, whenever I drove my own phaeton to Town, until the wheel somehow broke the day after you came. Only how to explain why we're together without a chaperone?"

What a great opportunity to test the waters. He paused, and so did she. He donned his most earnest expression and said, "Perhaps we should pretend to be husband and wife."

Her silvery blue eyes widened with that flicker of

light that reminded him of opals. "That's an idea, but I have no ring."

The waters seemed fine, he thought. "Your ring, alas, wasn't pinned in the hem of your pelisse. It was on your finger, bold as brass—or perhaps I should say bold as gold—where the bandits could clearly see it."

"But I'm wearing gloves."

"Bandits always force their victims to remove their gloves for any rings."

"You sound as if you know what you're talking about. Has this sort of thing happened to you before?"

"Never. And that's quite surprising when I think of how much I've traveled." He suddenly smiled. "Suppose, when we reach the village, I tell them I'm the Duke of Fairborough?"

She burst into laughter. "You do enjoy being Fairborough, don't you?"

Kit arched his brows and widened his eyes. "Yes, I do. Wouldn't you enjoy being his duchess?"

Her voice quivered with mirth. "No! Why do you think I allowed Lady Paxton to catch us in the carriage that night?"

"Allow me to rephrase the question, Miss Langley. Perhaps you'd enjoy *pretending* to be his duchess while in the village?"

"But he doesn't have a duchess," she pointed out. "And I refuse to pose as your—as the duke's—"

"Say no more," Kit said with a sigh, realizing she had a very good point. "Besides, he doesn't have one of those, either. It was just a thought."

They continued walking. "I scarcely believe you tried to masquerade as Fairborough again last night. Heavens, Gibson, I was so deathly afraid they might kill you!"

"Well, I was afraid they might hurt you. I only wanted to do whatever I could to protect you."

Serena stopped again, gaping at him. He paused alongside her, and saw a look of bewildered pleasure on her face.

"You would have done anything to spare me from those cutthroats last night, wouldn't you, Gibson? Even lay down your life for me."

"Why should that amaze you so, Miss Langley?"

She lowered her eyes. "Because I didn't think you felt anything for me anymore."

Kit's jaw dropped. "Whatever gave you that notion?"

She continued walking. "Then why have you behaved so—so *properly* with me since that night when I let you behave so *im*-properly? It's precisely because of what happened that night that I'm no longer wedding Fairborough."

He swiftly caught up to her. "Is that any reason for me to continue behaving *im*-properly?"

"Why not? And speaking of improper behavior, where exactly did you find Lord Winslow yesterday morning?"

"In a place where men behave improperly." He'd only known Winslow had gone to the brothel because the groom had followed him, but returned to the inn for lack of sufficient blunt. "But just because I behaved improperly with you once, doesn't mean I should do it again. I'm not like Lord Winslow."

"Or Lady Paxton. She thinks I'm little better than a lightskirt now."

"Oh, hang what Lady Paxton thinks of you!" Kit exclaimed. "All that matters is what *you* think of yourself."

"Yet why else shall I never marry?"

"Who says you'll never marry?"

"At least I'll never marry anyone—anyone—" She faltered, glancing up at him from beneath the brim of her straw bonnet.

"Anyone from your own class?" he supplied, and she looked away. "Have you ever considered marrying a coachman?"

She scurried down the road, nearly running.

"Well, have you?" Kit didn't bother to run, only lengthened his stride.

"It seems I'll have to be married to one once we reach the village," she called back.

"Ah, but it won't be the same. For we'll only be pretending, won't we?"

She did not respond.

Serena didn't want to pretend. She wanted to be married to him for real. Heaven knows she'd never be able to marry anyone else. By now she was irretrievably compromised with Gibson, beyond all redemption short of marriage itself—to him.

But all Gibson wanted to do was pretend.

She supposed she should be flattered that he thought so highly of her that he didn't dare attempt any more liberties with her—or did he only think so highly of her because she was the daughter of a viscount, while he was a servant?

Or did he simply not want her, regardless of their differences in status? Surely if he truly felt about her the way she did about him, he'd want more than just a pretend marriage? Wouldn't he want a genuine marriage?

Was he content only to pretend? Didn't he reciprocate the feelings that set her heart hammering out of control?

Gibson finally caught up to her. "We're almost there, so perhaps we should devise a plausible explanation."

"It's simple. We're husband and wife—" She waited for him to say again that they'd only be pretending, or to ask if she'd ever consider a real marriage, but all he did was smile. Her heart melted.

"Go on," he said. "We're husband and wife . . ."

". . . And we were robbed. They took my wedding ring and all our coin, save for what I had in the hem of my pelisse—oh, and they also took our carriage and horses—and baggage."

"Well done! But the villagers will also want to know where we're from, and where we're going."

"We're from London, of course, and we're going to Fairborough Castle."

"Yes, but why would Mr. and Mrs. Alfred Gibson be invited to Fairborough Castle?"

Serena pondered, thinking of what Gibson had told her about his background a short while ago. "Hm, I suppose we could say that instead of your father having been a tutor to Colfax, he was tutor to Fairborough. You and the duke were childhood playmates till he went off to Eton, so you're invited to his ancestral home to celebrate his upcoming marriage. How's that story?"

"Tightly spun, in which case the cutthroats should have taken my coat as well, since it's too obviously a servant's livery." Gibson dug around in his pockets, removing handfuls of something Serena couldn't see, though she thought she heard the jingling of coins. He doffed the coat and flung it behind the shrubbery at the side of the road. "Now what to do with this?" From behind his back he brandished the pistol. "I should hate to part with it. The previous Duke of Colfax gave it to me."

"That was very generous of him. No wonder it seems too fine for a coachman. But without the coat you have no place to hide it, and it won't fit in my reticule. You don't suppose . . ." Her voice trailed off as she realized he was scrutinizing her from head to toe. For some odd reason she enjoyed that, though the torchbearer had done the same last night and she hadn't enjoyed it one bit.

But instead of admiring her feminine form, Gibson, alas, looked as if he was trying to figure out a hiding place for the pistol on her own person. She'd once heard of a countess who always traveled with a pistol strapped to her leg with her garter, but for Serena to do likewise would require her to hitch her skirt all the way up to her—

"I promise not to look," he said solemnly, as if he could read her thoughts, though his brown eyes twinkled.

She took the pistol and stepped behind the bush where he'd tossed his coat. She lifted her skirt and pinned it under her arm while she fumbled with her garter, trying to secure the pistol to her thigh. When she thought it was about as snugly in place as it ever would be, she smoothed down her skirt and returned to Gibson, who stood waiting in the middle of the road. With each step she took, the barrel of the pistol slapped uncomfortably against her leg. It felt as if it were dangling from the garter and might drop to the ground at any moment. Thankfully they were almost to the village.

The village bustled with the usual early morning activity, though not so much that people didn't stop to stare at Gibson and Serena. They found the inn, where the innkeeper began glaring suspiciously the moment they walked in. Serena couldn't help thinking he'd condemned them before he even heard their story and thus made up his mind not to believe a word of it.

"My wife and I are from London, and we were en route to Fairborough Castle last night when we were waylaid by highwaymen," Gibson explained. "They took everything—our carriage, our horses—"

"Even my wedding ring." Serena tore off her glove and held up her left hand as she stuck out her lower lip.

"When is the next mail coach to Fairborough?" Gibson inquired.

"Not till noon," the innkeeper said dryly.

"Then could we break our fast in the meantime?"

The innkeeper pressed one hand on the counter and planted the other on his hip. "How do you expect to pay?"

Gibson tossed some coins onto the counter, and Serena was amazed at the amount of silver glinting amongst them. How did he come by so much money?

The innkeeper narrowed his eyes. "I thought you were robbed."

"Of all but what my wife had stitched into the hem of her pelisse. Now will you bring us some food or won't you? There should also be enough here for a couple of rooms where we can rest till the mail."

With his fingertip the innkeeper pushed a few of the coins around. "Sorry, but this isn't enough. A couple of rooms will cost you ten extra shillings."

"I believe we've been robbed already," Gibson said sharply.

"Then we don't have a couple of rooms, we only have one."

"One it is," Gibson agreed, as Serena's heart began pounding, though she knew not why. He'd already made it clear that he had no intention of taking any further liberties with her. Pretense, that's all he wanted.

The innkeeper swept the money off the counter and disappeared into a back room.

"How did you come by so much coin, Gibson?"

212

He fixed his gaze on the doorway into the back room. "I've been saving it, Miss Langley."

"I've heard Colfax is very generous with severance, but let me use my crowns. Or we can stay in the parlor. Why are you suddenly laughing?"

"Because that parlor is little more than a taproom." He lowered his voice to a whisper. "Save your crowns for the mail coach, Miss Langley. I only want you to be comfortable—"

"Not with your coin," she hissed back.

"Don't worry about that. Think of it as Colfax's coin if you must. I can break my fast down here, but you need a room to rest and wash up."

"And so do you. Besides, the innkeeper will think it odd if you stay down here." She flashed him her most charming smile. "After all, we're supposed to be husband and wife—speaking of which, you mustn't call me Miss Langley anymore. I'm Mrs. Gibson—for now." She wanted to add forever.

The innkeeper returned. "Let me show you the room. My wife will bring breakfast."

Serena sighed in relief as Gibson followed her and the innkeeper upstairs to a small but comfortably furnished room. His wife soon appeared with a tray bearing a couple of rolls, a slab of cheese, and a tea service.

"Perhaps I could trouble you for a razor?" Gibson asked, as she set the tray on the small table next to the room's only chair. "I know I don't look at all respectable."

"Nor does your woman without a ring," she retorted, and she slammed the door.

Serena sat down and poured two cups of tea. "Maybe I shouldn't have removed my glove," she whispered.

Gibson picked up a roll and tore it apart. "Don't worry about it."

"But she obviously suspects we're not married."

"And I suspect she's a French spy. Who can prove anything? Only a few hours, and we'll be on the mail coach. After that, it won't matter whether or not they believe us."

After breakfast there was nothing to do but wait for soap and water to arrive. Gibson stood gazing out the window while Serena remained in the chair. She supposed he could wait downstairs while she washed up.

She settled her gaze on him as he leaned against the side of the window, his arms crossed over his chest as he continued looking outside, seemingly deep in thought. He was certainly pleasant to look at. Surely he wouldn't mind if she stayed here while he washed and shaved. After all, it wasn't as if she hadn't seen him without his shirt before. She smiled at the memory of his first morning in the carriage house, after she and Miriam had discovered the disabled phaeton.

As if he sensed her smiling scrutiny, he cast his brown eyes on her. "And what might you be pondering that is so amusing, Miss Langley?"

"Mrs. Gibson," she corrected him.

"Very well—Mrs. Gibson," he said, smiling back. "What—" A loud pounding at the door startled them both.

He straightened and uncrossed his arms as the door flew open to reveal not only the innkeeper and his wife, but a man who, by his garb, was clearly a member of the clergy.

Serena noticed all three glanced immediately at the bed, which wasn't even rumpled.

"May I help you?" Gibson said with exaggerated politeness.

"How do you do?" the clergyman said coldly. "I'm Clarence Andrews, the local vicar. And you are . . . ?"

"Alfred Gibson of London."

TRUE PRETENSES

The innkeeper's wife glowered at Serena. "You there, hold up your left hand for the vicar to see!"

Serena obeyed without hesitation. "The highwaymen stole my wedding ring last night," she said dolefully, rapidly blinking her eyes as if to hold back tears.

Mr. Andrews glanced from Serena to Gibson. "According to Mr. Sewell here, you were robbed last night, and they took everything—horses, carriage—"

"And my wedding ring," Serena put in.

"We had to walk all the way here," Gibson said. "We're only staying till the noon mail coach."

"Where precisely did this robbery take place?" inquired Mr. Andrews, with just a bit too much skepticism for Serena's comfort. As it was, she thought it rather peculiar that Mr. Sewell had summoned the vicar and not the constable.

Gibson waved his arm around vaguely. "Somewhere on a road southeast of here."

"And where were you going?"

"To Fairborough Castle." Gibson told them the story he and Serena had woven together.

The vicar nodded toward the innkeeper's wife. "Mrs. Sewell is worried that you've brought an innocent spinster to her inn, and that the young woman's family would not approve any more than Mrs. Sewell does."

Serena stood up. "Then marry us, Vicar."

She stole a glance at Gibson. He gaped back in astonishment.

Did he not like the idea of marrying her? Or had he just not expected her to say that?

Heavens, she was surprised she'd said it herself. But she couldn't risk losing him again. And why shouldn't they marry? No one else would have her now. After all, Gibson was the one who had compromised her.

And Gibson was the one she loved.

Mrs. Sewell broke the silence as if it were a block of ice. "Ha! So I was right. You're not the first to come to my inn without a wedding ring and claim you were robbed of it."

"Very well," said Mr. Andrews. "I can perform a wedding within the hour."

"What about a special license?" Gibson asked.

"I can provide that," Mr. Andrews replied.

"But I thought only the bishop could issue one. And they're rather costly."

More than the two crowns in Serena's reticule. Tears smarted her eyes, not because she didn't have enough money for a special license, but because Gibson was clawing for an excuse not to marry her.

The vicar scowled. "I don't need you to lecture me on canon law, young man—*I'm* the clergy. Now are you going to do right by this gel or not?"

Gibson threw up his hands. "I'll marry her."

"Then come with me for the license."

"Now?"

"Now."

But Serena had to know if Gibson really wanted this. "Wait! Shouldn't he propose to me first?"

"You mean he hasn't?" Mrs. Sewell said sharply. "What were you thinking when he brought you here?"

Not this, Serena thought. And it was obvious that Gibson hadn't been thinking it, either.

"He knows your answer is yes." The vicar glared at Gibson. "Now you come with me and let Mrs. Sewell tend to your bride."

Gibson followed the vicar, but at the door he turned and offered Serena a rueful glance. "This isn't how I planned it."

The vicar grabbed his arm and yanked him out the door.

TRUE PRETENSES

And then Serena burst into tears. Gibson had never wanted to marry her, not even now.

She should never have removed her glove for the innkeeper; she should never have suggested the vicar marry them. What had she done?

Chapter Fifteen

Mrs. Sewell escorted Serena to the vicar's house, where his wife drew a bath for the bride. That alone was more than she'd hoped for at the inn.

"And you needn't worry about wedding clothes," said Mrs. Andrews, as she bustled into the bedroom with a kettle of hot water. "You can wear the dress I made for my Mary so many years ago, when I hoped she would one day be a bride. Now I don't think she'll ever marry. She just turned three and thirty."

"Did she have a fiancé at one time?" asked Serena.

Mrs. Andrews sighed as she slowly poured the water into the tub. "No, but I always hoped. Fortunately she's about your size."

Unfortunately, she really wasn't. Mary was not only a few inches shorter, but a few inches smaller in certain measurements. The bodice of the gown stretched taut across Serena's bust, while the hemline hovered well above her ankles, displaying her dusty half-boots. She emerged from the warm, steamy room where she'd bathed and dressed, and followed the women outside to the nearby church. It was cool and breezy outdoors, and just as chilly in the church. Serena was mortified as the tips of her breasts hardened into prominent little points that poked defiantly through the wispy batiste of her chemise and the thin, taut muslin of the borrowed wedding gown.

The innkeeper met the little party in the vestibule of the ancient stone church. "Allow me to give the bride away," he said, offering his arm to Serena. "Miss Andrews, did you not say you had a ring that would serve?"

Serena glanced at the vicar's daughter, nonplussed. Surely she hadn't kept a ring all these years in addition to the wedding gown? Serena couldn't help thinking the poor woman—no thanks to her mother—had unwittingly condemned herself to eternal spinsterhood by tempting fate so imprudently.

Sure enough, Mary produced a ring from her reticule. " 'Tis only fool's gold, I'm afraid, since Papa won it for me at a country fair many years ago."

Mr. Sewell pocketed the ring before escorting Serena down the nave of the dim, drafty church.

Gibson already stood at the altar, wearing a borrowed coat that was far too short on him; the cuffs seemed closer to his elbows than his wrists. But at least he'd managed to shave. He gifted Serena with a reassuring smile that sent a surge of hope flowing through her.

Vicar Andrews opened his prayer book and began the rite. Serena's heart pounded so hard, she was sure everyone could hear it echoing throughout the nave, drowning out the vicar's voice as he enumerated the three causes for which matrimony was ordained, followed by the standard invitation to the congregation, such as it was, to make any objections they might have. There were none.

"I require and charge you both, as ye will answer at the dreadful day of judgment when the secrets of all hearts shall be disclosed, that if either of you know of any impediment, why ye may not be lawfully joined together in matrimony, ye do now confess it. For be ye well assured, that so many as are coupled together otherwise than God's word doth allow are not joined together by God, neither is their matrimony lawful."

"Uhh—" Gibson blurted.

The vicar glanced up sharply, as Serena, her heart ready to explode, looked at Gibson with wide eyes. He was suddenly pale, no longer the self-confident bridegroom who had smiled at her as she approached the altar. That surge of hope now ebbed.

"Is there an impediment?" the vicar inquired.

Gibson abruptly cleared his throat. "I'm afraid having been forced into the nocturnal air last night—" He slapped his chest a couple of times and gave a small cough before glancing at Serena, then back at the vicar. "I'm sorry. Go on."

Her heart still thundered as the exchange of vows continued, the ring was placed on her finger, and at long last they were pronounced man and wife.

The Honorable Serena Langley, once the betrothed of one of the richest dukes in England, had just married her coachman.

The noon mail had already left by the time they returned to the inn, where Kit requested a bath in their room. Serena had obviously enjoyed a bath before marrying him—Gibson, he corrected himself—but he hadn't been allowed to do anything more than wash his face and shave. Entering the room, he wriggled out of the coat he'd borrowed from the vicar.

"And what shall I do while you're bathing?" she inquired.

He closed the door. "Perhaps my wife wouldn't object to washing my back?"

"Of course not," she said timorously.

He turned to smile at her, his eyes roving downward to the gentle swell of her breasts in the snug-fitting dress. Though Serena didn't have very big breasts, the tight bodice seemed to exaggerate their size. But there was nothing exaggerated about the erect little buds piercing the thin fabric. They seemed to be straining for his touch, and indeed, his fingers itched to caress them. Lust for his bride warred with his conscience, which told him he shouldn't consummate the marriage without first telling her who he really was. But she'd probably laugh and tell him to stop pretending to be Fairborough already.

"And perhaps," he added in a whisper, "she wouldn't object if I behaved just a little improperly with her now?"

Obviously aware of his scrutiny, she self-consciously held her arms over her bosom. "Of course not. You're my husband, after all, and I—I have to—"

"I won't force you. I won't do anything you don't want me to do."

"But I can't think of anything I don't want you to do, except . . . I don't want any more pretense, no more charades."

For a moment Kit thought his heart would stop. Did she know he'd been masquerading as the coachman all this time? *How* did she know?

Feeling a justly deserved stab of guilt, he forced his gaze into her opalescent eyes. Thank God she didn't look angry, though she did seem very anxious, almost fearful. But maybe that was just bridal nerves.

"How did you know?" he asked in a strangled whisper.

"When it seemed you wanted to confess an impediment during the marriage ceremony. What did you almost say to the vicar?"

Surely she knew the answer to that! But no, she had to torture him. It was a wife's prerogative—and they'd scarcely been married an hour! Kit took a deep breath before surrendering himself to his doom. "I was going to tell him that I'm really Fairborough."

Tears glistened in her eyes. "Why?"

"Why?" he echoed incredulously. "Because, my dear, it just so happens that I—"

"No, never mind, I don't want to hear it!" She held up her hands as if to shield herself from the dreadful truth. "I already know. I knew when you were arguing with the vicar over the special license, and when you said this wasn't how you'd planned it. It's because you don't want to be married to me!"

"What?" Confusion rolled over Kit like a dense fog. "On the contrary, I want very much to be married to you. And not for the reasons you fear," he hastily added, thinking of the sixty thousand pounds. "It's because I truly love you. I never dreamed I might fall in love with you, but somehow, over the past month, I did."

She dropped her hands, looking suddenly hopeful. He, for his part, was feeling hopeful . . . until she asked, "Then why did you scare me like that in the church—and again just now?"

He furrowed his brow. "How did I scare you just now?"

"When I said I didn't want us to pretend anymore, Gibson, you looked as if you might faint."

Us! And she still called him "Gibson"! Kit's heart tumbled in his chest as he finally understood that Se-

TRUE PRETENSES

rena was ranting about one thing while he was raving about another! "Is *that* what you meant—that you didn't want us to pretend at being husband and wife anymore?"

"What did you think I meant?"

His voice cracking tremulously, Kit said, "I don't know what I think right now."

"Then why did you want to tell the vicar you were Fairborough? He never would have believed you any more than I would have."

At the time that same thought had occurred to Kit, which was why he'd not gone through with confessing the impediment. Still, he couldn't help asking, "Why not?"

"Oh, really, Gibson—a duke pretending to be a coachman? Indeed! I already settled that absurd argument with the Duke of Colfax. Now that we're married, please, *please* desist from pretending to be Fairborough. How could you even consider lying to the vicar—a man of God? Did you think perhaps *I* didn't want to be married to you?"

"Yes!"

"That's why you seemed to want to get out of the marriage?"

"Serena, my darling love, at no time was I trying to get out of it for any reason. I only questioned the vicar about the special license because I'd always thought one had to pay an exorbitant fee to get it from the bishop." Kit was still puzzled over how the vicar had issued him one for nothing. "And I told you this wasn't how I'd planned it because I think we—or at least you—should be married in better circumstances than this, with a ring made of real gold, a gown made just for you by a modiste in London, and the bishop officiating in a cathedral with music by Handel."

She softened as she stepped closer to him. "Poor

dear, I do want to be your wife . . . and I want to be your wife for real. No more pretense, Gibson. We're married now, and that's all that matters. I don't need Westminster Abbey or the bishop or Handel, I only need you. For real."

Much to his surprise, she threw herself against him, twining her arms over his shoulders as he wrapped his around her waist. She nearly took his breath away as she pressed her lips to his. He opened his mouth as if to search for air, but all he found was her tongue. He eagerly welcomed it as he grew rigid with desire for this wonderful woman, who seemed to want him just as avidly.

God Almighty! Kit couldn't tell her who he really was even if he wanted to. Though he ached to possess her, he didn't feel right doing it while pretending to be someone else. When the time came for him to be inside Serena, he wanted her to moan *his* name, Kit or even Christopher—but God help him, not the coachman's. He reluctantly broke the kiss. "Serena, I still won't do anything you don't want me to do."

She smiled. "Did I not promise to obey you? I have to do whatever you say. I *want* to do whatever you say. You do want me as your wife, don't you?"

He stroked her tawny brown hair. "Well, dear wife, I must have a bath first. As it is, I don't know how you can bear to let me hold you and kiss you."

She held his face between her hands. "I know how. It's because I love you, Gibson. I love you no matter how grimy you are, or how badly you might smell like a barnyard. I love you even though you're only a coachman—or perhaps because you're a coachman. I don't think it matters. All that matters is that I love you and I want you. . . ."

Lust finally overpowered Kit's conscience as she kissed him again, pressing her hips into his erection.

TRUE PRETENSES

He cupped his hand under her breast just as someone rapped on the door.

Serena leaped back from him as the door flew open, and in came the Sewells with kettles of water. Kit felt as if one of them had just been dumped over his head, as a certain part of himself went limp under Mrs. Sewell's withering glare.

Serena stood back as the innkeeper and his wife set up the tub, towels, soap, and water. After they left, closing the door behind them, she stepped over to the washstand and began removing the pins from her hair. But all the while she watched Gibson in the mirror. He removed his waistcoat and then his shirt, revealing the same muscular chest she'd seen the morning after he came to Langley House. He sat on the edge of the bed to remove his boots.

Ping, ping went the hairpins into the empty washbowl. *Thunk . . . thunk* went the boots. As he stood up to unfasten his breeches, she felt a strange heaviness between her thighs. She watched, enthralled, as he stepped out of his breeches, and she nearly gasped at what she saw.

She quickly looked down into the washbowl as he glanced her way. Some splashing, some sloshing, and she finally turned to see him curled up in the tub.

Heat suffused her cheeks. "I can put your clothes outside so they can launder them for you."

"I was just about to suggest that," he said, as he poured water over his head. "And please lock the door so our hosts don't come barging in again whenever it amuses them."

She gathered up everything but his boots and piled them outside, then closed the door and turned the key in the lock. It suddenly occurred to her: What was he going to put on once he got out of the tub?

For that matter, what was *she* supposed to wear to bed tonight? She couldn't very well sleep in her borrowed frock. As he busily soaped himself all over, she stood behind him, wondering what she should do. He glanced over his shoulder. "Oh, there you are. Would you care to wash my back?"

She picked up the dipper, looking for a place in the tub to scoop. The only available space was between his legs, which were as muscular as his chest and arms, and just as hirsute.

She brushed her fingertip over a livid bruise on his knee. "What's this?"

"I got it falling out of that carriage this morning. I think there's one on my forehead, too."

She glanced up at his face. There was indeed a small discolored knot just below his hairline, but it didn't look as bad as the knee. On an impulse she bent to kiss the small knot, and then she kissed the scraped bruise on his knee. "That should make them feel better," she said with a smile.

He smiled back. "Oh, I'm feeling much better already."

A thin layer of suds concealed the most intriguing part of him as she scooped some water and poured it down his back.

She knelt behind him and scrubbed his broad, muscular back with a soapy sponge, spreading lather over his wide shoulders and the nape of his neck.

She poured the dipper down his back, watching the sudsy water sluice over his skin. She had a sudden, strange desire to taste him. She dropped the dipper and pressed herself against his damp back, touching her lips to his neck.

"Ah, Serena, yes," he whispered.

She slid her arms around his slippery skin to his rock-hard chest, moving her hands all over him till she found the beating of his heart, pounding as hard as her own. She rested her chin on his shoulder as he lifted his arm to wrap it around the back of her head, bringing her cheek to his.

"I don't know what's making me do this," she whispered.

"The same thing that's making me do this." He turned to press his lips against her damp cheek.

She turned her head till her lips met his, and this time she thrust her tongue into his mouth before he even had the chance to offer his. Though she was warmer now than she'd been all day, she could still feel her nipples puckering through her taut, soaking bodice. He took one of her hands and slid it down his belly, beneath the water where it closed around that part of him that had made her gasp earlier. Was it her imagination, or was it much bigger than she'd initially thought? As if by instinct, she ran her hand down its hard length till she came across something which, by great contrast, was quite soft, and she likewise closed her hand around that and squeezed.

He tore away from her mouth with a loud groan, and a shudder of physical longing spiked through her core.

She glanced down to see the tip of his manhood thrusting out of the water, swollen and red. "Am I hurting you?"

He gasped on a laugh, a dazed expression on his face as he grasped the rim of the tub and levered himself up. "Quite the contrary. Hand me the towel, darling."

She rose to her feet, grabbing the towel and handing it to him as he stood up, dripping soapy water.

So she hadn't imagined things. It *was* much bigger than it had been when she'd glimpsed it in the mirror over the washstand. And instead of hanging down as it had before, it now stretched almost upright from the rest of him.

His gaze swept her from head to toe. "You're just as wet."

She glanced down. The flesh of her breasts glared through the thin, saturated fabric of her bodice, their rosy tips so visible that there was no point in keeping the dress on any longer. She turned away, and with her hand brushed her long hair over the front of her shoulder. She stepped over to the bed, awkwardly reaching behind to fumble with the laces on the back of her dress.

"Give me a moment to dry myself; then allow me," he said.

Struggling to steady her breath, Serena gazed at the counterpane as she pulled off her half-boots and nudged them under the bed. She lifted her skirt to untie her garters, thankful that she'd remembered to remove that pistol from her thigh before the Sewells had come knocking with the vicar in tow. She took off one stocking, and just when she'd rolled the other off her foot, she felt the warmth of her husband's body right behind hers. His fingers brushed the nape of her neck before nimbly unlacing her dress.

She held her breath as he parted the back of her dress, sliding it over her shoulders before following suit with the chemise. They might have slipped easily to her feet if only they weren't wet and plastered to the front of her body. He reached around to tug on the damp bodice, peeling it down over her hips. The sodden clothes finally dropped to the floor, leaving her as naked as he.

But as he embraced her from behind, the most bizarre memory flashed into her mind—that rainy night in the conservatory, when she'd confronted Daphne and Kit, and he'd grabbed her from behind and held her in a close embrace that had nearly reduced her to liquid in his hands. She had that same sensation now, and she fought to wipe the memory of Kit's fleeting embrace from her mind as she concentrated on Gibson's more languorous, sensual one, with his hard arousal pressed against her back.

He cupped her breasts in his hands, teasing the taut buds with his thumbs as he brushed his lips around her neck and over her ear, tasting her sensitive flesh with the very tip of his tongue. His left hand continued to fondle her left breast while his right one moved downward, lightly brushing the dark hair at the apex of her thighs. A throb of yearning pulsated between her legs, and she whimpered with longing for a more intimate touch as his hand slid around her hip to her derriere. He pushed gently on the back of her leg. "Put your foot up on the bed, darling."

She complied, then lifted her arm back and wrapped it around the nape of his neck, turning her head in search of his mouth. She traced her lips along his jawline till they found his own, and their tongues met again. She moaned into his mouth as he slid his hand down the cleft of her derriere.

She nearly collapsed with desire as he firmly cradled her from behind, possessively cupping her feminine mound in his hand as if claiming it for his own. She broke from his lips with a startled gasp as she felt the tip of his finger slip inside her and then slide out . . . then in again . . . and then out. With each thrust she made a little sobbing noise, squirming against him in such a way that his finger inadvertently plunged all the way inside her. She cried out in surprise, and he quickly removed it.

He chuckled as he planted a kiss on the curve between her neck and shoulder. "I don't think you meant to do that, but you liked it, didn't you, love?"

"I—I think so," she gasped, still trying to make sense

of what had just happened. It had been so surprising, so strange, and yet so wonderful.

He reached around her to pull back the counterpane on the bed. "Would you like to lie down?" he whispered, stroking his hand over her hair as if he were petting a cat.

Serena swallowed hard, wishing to heavens her heart would stop thumping so uncomfortably as she collapsed facedown on the bed, which seemed to sink as he knelt over her, the heat of his hard body covering her like a thick blanket.

He stroked her hair back from her face. "You're not too shy to turn over for me, are you, sweetheart?"

"I suppose it would be helpful if I did." It would certainly make it easier to embrace him and kiss him. Plus she wanted to feast her gaze on his body.

He brushed his lips against her cheek, his voice soft and warm. "Someday, if you like, we can try it like this. There are many different ways, but for now, for your first time, I think it would be nicer for you if you turned onto your back."

She rolled over as he sat up. She felt no shyness since he'd already seen through her soaked wedding dress.

"I do enjoy looking at your chest," she confessed, smiling as she studied his broad expanse of hard muscles lightly covered with hair.

He chuckled. "I enjoy looking at your chest, too. In fact, I enjoy looking at every part of you."

Serena loved the way his heated appraisal of her body seemed to burn into her bare skin, further inflaming her desire for him.

"You're lovely," he whispered, smiling appreciatively as he stroked his hands up her thighs and over her hips and belly till they covered her breasts.

"My nose is too big," she blurted.

"No, it's not." He straddled her and pressed his hard shaft against the juncture of her thighs as his hands slid up to her shoulders. "I love your nose. And I love your eyes, they remind me of opals—silvery blue, flaming with desire and passion. But I especially love your mouth." He lowered his lips to hers, parting them with his tongue as it delved deeply to caress her own.

She held him close, breathing in the fresh soapy smell of him as she thought of all the wonderful things he said. He'd once compared Felice to a butterfly; no one had ever done so before. And just now, he'd compared Serena's eyes to opals. Only briefly did she wonder what a coachman would know about opals, but then this coachman seemed to know a great deal, having grown up as the son of a tutor in a grand household.

She stroked his shoulders and muscled back, while he traced his lips down her throat and over her breasts, feathering her with light, loving kisses. He swirled his tongue around one of her distended nipples, then took it completely into his mouth, suckling and tugging on it. She whimpered longingly as waves of desire rippled downward to her groin. He lavished the same attention on her other nipple as he slid his hand into her most secret place, and gently parted the soft, moist petals of her sex to find the very spot where she throbbed the most.

Serena closed her eyes, crying out in delight as he stroked the swollen bud of her femininity in a tiny circular motion. Spirals of exquisite pleasure swirled through her, weaving themselves into a taut, quivering knot between her thighs as she writhed beneath him, only vaguely aware that she was moving her hips in rhythm with his kneading fingers.

Just when she thought that pulsating knot couldn't get any tighter, it slowly loosened, and then suddenly it started unraveling swiftly. She cried out in wild splendor as the tightly coiled spirals unfurled themselves into long, fiery ribbons of ecstasy that fluttered and rippled through every part of her being, till she felt herself go weak all over.

He cupped his hand over her engorged mound as she finally opened her eyes to look up at him. Not surprisingly, he was smiling.

"What did you just do?" she gasped, as he slid his hand over the inside of one of her thighs.

"I made you relax," he whispered hotly, as he knelt between her open legs and covered the length of her body with his, propping himself on his elbows. "And I think you liked it."

"Ah, yes." She raked her fingers through his damp chestnut hair, then clutched his broad shoulders as she eagerly embraced his legs with her own, yearning to become one with this man she loved and needed so much. "But it only makes me want you more."

"I know that feeling," he murmured, probing her with the tip of his hard arousal. She gasped at a sudden, sharp twinge, trembling as a previously unknown part of herself stretched to receive his swollen masculinity.

He soothed her with soft little hushes and kisses, till the pain and tremors ebbed away. She clung to his shoulders as she gazed into his velvety eyes, thinking she might burst with love for him.

"All right now?" he whispered with a tentative smile.

"Oh yes." She smiled back, aching only with need for him now. "I love you, please don't stop. . . ."

As he slowly buried his shaft all the way inside her, he closed his eyes with a moan that sent a lovely thrill rushing through her. "Ah, Serena, you feel so good. . . ."

With a surge of elation, she felt the very core of her

femininity embracing him tightly, unwilling to let him go—for she never wanted to let go of him. She didn't want him to escape her heart any more than she wanted his manhood to leave the place where it was now deeply imbedded.

But still he managed to slide out of her almost all the way. He opened his eyes, and then he slowly pushed into her again. This time, Serena was the one who moaned.

"Ah, I love to hear my wife moan when I'm inside her." He gazed down at her with a tender smile that caressed her heart. "How are you, my sweetheart?"

"I feel wonderful," she whispered, smiling back.

"That you definitely do." He partly pulled out of her again, whispered, "I love you," then plunged back into her as this time they moaned in unison.

Each masculine thrust thereafter ignited a burst of pleasure deep within her, and she repeatedly whimpered in delight as she looked up at him, reveling in the intensely euphoric expression on his face. He gradually increased the tempo and she matched his steady rhythm with her hips, lost in the intoxicating bliss of her husband's deeply intimate strokes.

"Ahh, Serena." He buried his face in her hair as his movements became more urgent, driving her into a frenzy of mindless passion till he finally burst inside her, with a deep baritone cry. She clutched him tightly as he abruptly went still, then seemed to go limp all over, nearly crushing her.

She lightly ran her hands over his back, now damp with perspiration, as he raised himself on his elbows to look down at her, breathing raggedly.

"I love you." Sliding her hand over the nape of his neck, she pulled his head down and kissed him with all the joy and adoration in her teeming heart.

As they broke the kiss, he whispered, "I love you, too."

He carefully withdrew from her, then flopped over next to her, sighing heavily. She rolled to her side, sliding her arm across the width of his chest.

He turned his head to study her, and for a long moment neither of them said a word, but only gazed at each other. As his smile faded, she couldn't help noticing a strange shimmer in his brown eyes. What was he thinking?

"Serena," he finally said, his voice barely above a whisper, "you do realize there's no going back now?"

Her heart skipped a beat. After all this, did he still have doubts about their marriage? "Whatever do you mean? I don't want to go back." And then it dawned on her. Of course! As her husband, he was expected to provide for her.

She idly fingered the dark tendrils on his chest. "I know you're probably worried about how you're going to support me."

He shifted his eyes to one side and then back to her. "Not really, no."

She knit her brow as she gazed at him. He looked pleasurably spent from their recent exertions, but also strangely anxious.

"Darling, what's bothering you?" she asked, as she felt an odd trembling in her heart. "You shouldn't worry about any scandal. So I married the coachman. I've never played a very big role in society, anyway. I was barely seventeen when my grandfather agreed that I would marry the Duke of Fairborough before he turned thirty. So I didn't have a 'season' like other young ladies. I was never presented at Court, and I've never even set foot in Almack's. Simon and I were betrothed, and after that there was nothing to do but wait while he sowed his wild oats."

"He sowed them to death," Gibson muttered, with an unusual amount of bitterness.

"You sound as if you resent the fact that he left me alone all those years."

"It's sad that he did, but if he hadn't, then I wouldn't have you now. I guess I'm just worried because—well, all of this seems too good to be true."

She smiled tenderly. "And you're afraid you might wake up tomorrow morning and discover it was all a dream?"

"Something like that."

Serena pressed her fingertip into the dimple in his chin. " 'Tis all quite real, my love. We're married now, for better or worse, for richer or poorer, till death do us part. I love you and I will always love you."

"No matter what?"

"No matter what." She kissed him on the lips. "I told you that earlier. If I love you even though you're only a coachman who makes fifteen shillings a month, then I'm sure I would love you even if you were—uhh—" She hesitated as she searched her mind for an equally unlikely prospect.

"How about the Duke of Fairborough?"

Serena laughed lightly as she playfully slapped him on the shoulder. What was it about him and Fairborough, anyway?

He furrowed his brow. "What's so amusing? Would you or wouldn't you?"

"You mean would I love you if you were Fairborough? Well, if he were you, or you were he, I do believe I would—because, my darling, I love *you*."

Was it her imagination, or were his eyes shimmering even more, as if they might be welling with tears? It was hard to tell in the waning, late afternoon sunlight that barely shone through the window.

He wrapped his arms around her, pulling her close

against him. "That's all I need to know to be even happier than I am already."

She eagerly embraced him in return, and they held each other tenderly as daylight faded, till they finally drifted to sleep in each other's arms.

Chapter Sixteen

An urgent pounding on the door jolted Kit from a deep slumber.

"What's that?" Serena chirped in the darkness, and it took a moment for him to remember that she was now his wife—or rather, Alfred Gibson's wife—and thus was sharing his bed.

He got up as he heard a woman's voice on the other side of the door, bidding him to open it. He stumbled through the dark and stubbed his toe on the tub.

Kit cursed.

"Mind the tub," Serena called out too late.

With one aching foot, he growled as he unlocked the door. He opened it just a crack to glare at Mrs. Sewell. She pushed her way into the room, holding up a candle, which he quickly blew out. The old cow didn't deserve to see him naked.

"You fool, why'd you do that?" she demanded. "I need the tub. We have a duke stayin' here and he wants a bath."

"Which duke?" asked Serena from the bed.

"I will gladly give you the tub, just let me empty it first." He dragged it over to the window and opened the shutters. With a grunt he heaved it onto the windowsill, then tipped it. The water whooshed out, splattering below amid a series of enraged expletives that echoed in the night.

"I think you just dumped it on someone," Mrs. Sewell said. "You'd better hope it wasn't the duke."

"Whoever he is, he should be thankful this wasn't the chamber pot," Kit replied.

"Which duke?" Serena sounded worried, and he hoped it wasn't because she feared it might be Fairborough.

"Who the bloody hell is up there?" demanded a man's voice from below. "Why don't you bloody watch what you're bloody doing?"

Kit's heart nearly stopped as he recognized the voice. *Colfax!*

"It's the duke," he said with a sigh. "And you needn't fear, Mrs. Sewell, I know him." To Serena, "It isn't Fairborough, dear, it's Colfax."

"But he can help us, Alfie."

Kit cringed as she called him that. "Mrs. Sewell, go ahead and tell His Grace that I'm the culprit."

"Bloomin' right I will," the woman grumbled. "Did you expect *me* to take the blame?"

"If I did, then I wouldn't have asked you to tell him it was me, would I? I'll gladly talk to him and see that you get into no trouble, if only you'll fetch my clothes for me."

"I think they're still dryin' but I'll see." She took the empty tub and left the room, slamming the door behind her as Kit closed the shutters, then locked the door. His big toe was throbbing; it already felt swollen.

"Darling, I don't think you should tell him about us,"

Serena said anxiously, as he returned to the bed. "I think I should do that."

"Maybe you won't have to tell him at all." Kit slid beneath the covers and took her into his arms, holding her wonderfully naked warmth against his.

"But his mother and sister are probably with him. And they're all going to know at the very least that I'm here unchaperoned, and that I've been compromised."

"*Very* compromised, I might add." Kit chuckled as he pressed his lips to her soft, yielding mouth. Already he felt himself hardening again as she explored him with her wandering hands, caressing his shoulders and then his chest, moving down his belly till her hand closed around his pulsating shaft. He quickly forgot his big toe.

She broke the kiss, though she continued stroking his erection. "What will you tell them?"

He closed his hand over her breast, tracing his thumb over her nipple. It quickly puckered into an unmistakable point.

"Perhaps I'll tell them how happy you've made me," he whispered, nuzzling her silken cheek. "In fact, you're making me very happy this minute."

He lowered his head to her breast and drew the nipple into his mouth, delighting in her whimper of pleasure.

"As happy as you're making me?" she gasped. "Oh, never mind, don't answer . . . don't stop . . ."

But he couldn't help chortling, and he lifted his head. "Maybe I'll tell them how much I love you and adore you." He slid his hand between her thighs, where she was already damp with desire for him. "Open up, darling Serena, and let me show you how much."

With a sigh she complied, still holding his erection as she shifted slightly on the bed, allowing him easier access to the most secret part of her. He found the swollen nub of flesh that he knew was responsible for her own climax, and he gently kneaded it with the pad of his thumb as her entire body tensed against his. Moments later she writhed as she pressed her mouth into his chest to muffle her cry of release.

Kit would have loved to hear again the moan Serena gave him this afternoon, when he brought her to her first orgasm, but for all they knew, Nick's mother or sister might be in the next room. It wouldn't do Lucinda any good to learn of something she'd probably never experience with that dullard Humphries, poor girl. Kit nearly sputtered with laughter at the thought.

"What's so amusing?" asked Serena, panting for breath as she slid her hands up to his shoulders.

He settled himself between her wide-open legs. "You trying to hide your orgasm from the other travelers."

"My what?"

"What you just felt, sweetheart." He slowly plunged his shaft into her and kissed her deeply, suppressing their cries of passion as she tightly sheathed his swollen masculinity in a hot, wet embrace. She wrapped her legs around him as they broke the kiss and she pressed her cheek to his, her lips grazing his ear.

"Oh, my darling, I love you," she whispered. Kit felt a surge of joy at her words as he thrust in and out of her heavenly slick heat, losing himself in all the pleasure Serena gave him—not just physically, but emotionally. The very knowledge that she was his in every sense of the word, and that she returned his love so wholeheartedly, nearly made him weep with happiness.

Somewhere, far, far in the back of his mind was the tiny, nagging thought, like a mote of dust in his eye, that it was really only Gibson she loved, but as they lay here with their naked bodies intimately entwined, undulating as one, all Kit thought was that Serena

TRUE PRETENSES

loved *him*, and whether he was the coachman or the duke at this moment mattered not one whit. Didn't she tell him earlier this afternoon that she would love him no matter who he was?

Serena loved *him*. Kit could scarcely hold back his deep groan of ecstasy as he spilled his seed into her, leaving him drained him of what little energy he'd had since Mrs. Sewell had awakened him . . . and his wife had aroused him. He'd slept very poorly the night before, walked quite a distance this morning, and spent the rest of himself this afternoon becoming Serena's husband completely.

Afterward they drifted back to sleep, till another rap at the door startled him awake.

He rolled out of bed and staggered to the door, opening it to reveal a man clad in Colfax livery, holding an armful of clothes, which he thrust into Kit's arms. "His Grace would like to see you in his quarters as soon as you dress."

He closed the door and began dressing, for some reason acutely aware of his big toe.

"What are you going to tell him?" Serena asked.

"I won't tell him anything unless he asks. Try and go back to sleep. Everything will be all right, I promise."

The shirt and breeches fit him so well that he was quite sure they were his own—that is, Fairborough's clothes and not the coachman's. Kit had left most of his own wardrobe at Nick's town house before seeking employment with the Langleys. He pecked Serena somewhere on her face before stealing barefooted out the door, into a hallway lit only by a lone candle flickering in a wall sconce. The waiting manservant led him to a room at the far end of the hallway, where he scratched on the door.

At Nick's muffled response, the manservant opened the door and ushered Kit inside.

Nicholas lounged on his bed, a brandy in one hand as he puffed on a cheroot with the other. "By God, it really was you who dumped all that water on me!"

"What brings you here of all places?" asked Kit, as the manservant stepped back outside, closing the door.

Nicholas sat up. "Why, haven't you heard? I've been invited to Fairborough to celebrate the marriage of the duke thereof—to the Honorable Serena Langley, or so I thought. After all, there's the little matter of that announcement in the *Times* stating otherwise . . ."

"What announcement?"

"You didn't see the *Times* about a fortnight ago?"

"I've been a coachman all this time, remember?"

"Lady Paxton placed an announcement of your forthcoming marriage to her daughter."

Stunned anger spiked through Kit. "Damn it, I wrote a letter to that woman and—"

"Don't shout or you'll wake everyone and Sewell will throw us out."

Kit lowered his voice and ground out, "I worded it in such a way that she should have been satisfied I would marry her daughter instead of Serena."

"And, by God, you succeeded. She's so satisfied she wants the whole world to know of her splendid coup, hence the announcement."

"Mothers!" Kit growled, as if the word were an expletive.

"They can be quite a curse, can't they?"

That blasted woman! Had she seen through the ambiguous wording of his letter? But if so, how could he condemn her for this latest duplicity in light of his own charade?

If only Jemma could have eloped with Dunbar! He thought of the scandal that would erupt if he tried to refute the announcement on the grounds that he was already married to Serena.

Only it wasn't Fairborough who was married to her, but Gibson. Serena had told him this afternoon that she loved him—the memory of her words wrapped his heart in joy—but would she love him enough to forgive him for his masquerade *and* his supposed treatment of Jemma?

He drew no comfort from the knowledge that he wasn't responsible for placing that damned announcement in the newspaper, and had not sanctioned Lady Paxton to do so on his behalf. Since it was usually the bridegroom's obligation to publish such an announcement, everyone—including Serena—would almost certainly blame him for the scandal.

"Christopher!" Nicholas shrieked in falsetto, and Kit snapped out of his reverie. "Ah, I'm glad to see that old trick still works. Thought your grandmother was in the room for a moment, didn't you? What happened to your big toe, did you catch it in a mousetrap?"

Kit glanced down at his bare feet, astonished at what he saw. Not only was his toe swollen, but a good portion of the nail was missing, leaving only a bed of sticky, half-congealed blood.

"I stubbed it earlier, but I expect to live," he said curtly. "Aren't you even interested in knowing why I'm here, when I should be at Fairborough either coaching for the Langleys or pretending to be the duke?"

Nicholas burst into laughter. "Have you any idea what you just said?"

Kit rubbed his temple, wincing as his fingers inadvertently pressed too hard against the bruise he'd acquired falling out of the carriage this morning—or was it yesterday morning?

"I can barely think right now," he mumbled. "I don't even know what time it is."

Nicholas dropped his cheroot into the chamber pot. " 'Tis well past midnight. And I'm not surprised you're so addlepated, what with your abduction and whatever you've been doing with Serena since then."

Those words splashed over Kit like the tepid bathwater he'd dumped out the window this evening, and he dropped his hand as he gaped at Nicholas. "How do you know about all of that?"

Nicholas grabbed a silver flask from the bedside table. "Care for a brandy?"

"No, I'd care to hear what you know about our abduction and whatever you think I've been doing with Serena since then."

Nicholas refilled his snifter. "I'm rather surprised—and even a little disappointed—that you didn't recognize my handiwork, old fellow. I thought it was perfect."

Realization finally dawned on Kit. All this time, he—and even Serena—had thought Winslow was the culprit behind the events of the past two days—or was it three days?—when in fact, "It was *you* who hired those bandits, wasn't it, Colfax?"

Nicholas took a gulp of brandy. He was going to need it to deaden the excruciating pain Kit was planning to make him suffer in just a few moments. "Who did you think it was? I did you a favor. I thought you might need some time alone with Serena before you broke the news of your true identity to her this weekend. I've bought you an extra day of time. Think of it as my wedding present to you and Serena."

"Damnation, Colfax! You obtained the special license and gave it to Vicar Andrews, didn't you?"

"Bless my soul! So you and Serena did get married?"

"Yes, and you should be working for Wellington. Napoleon would beg to surrender by sunset tomorrow."

"Then maybe that will be my next scheme, since I don't know how else to top this one."

"Don't tell me the vicar was in on this, too?"

"And Mr. and Mrs. Sewell. They were told to expect a man and woman who claimed to have been robbed several miles from here of everything but the clothes on their backs."

Kit slumped down on the edge of the bed, which creaked and sagged almost to the floor. "I do believe I will have that brandy, after all. Just hand me the flask."

Nicholas obliged. "I trust everything has turned out better than I hoped? I only obtained the wedding license on the off chance you were able to convince Serena to marry you. How is your blushing bride? Or should I say, 'Her Grace'?"

Kit took a huge gulp of brandy. "I'm afraid she's still only Mrs. Gibson. Believe me, I considered writing 'Christopher Woodard' on the special license, but I thought that would only lead to further complications with the vicar, with whom I'd already argued enough." Staring down at his ravaged toe, he took a deep breath, as if to cool the fire of the brandy as it burned down his throat. He hadn't imbibed in weeks. "But Serena did say she would love me no matter who I am."

Nicholas slapped him on the back. "So what are you worried about?"

"That bloody announcement, of course."

"So? You're not the first man to fall into the parson's mousetrap by way of a rogue announcement in the *Times*, and I daresay you won't be the last. Never think I don't tremble in fear."

"But I can't marry Jemma—"

"And you won't. You already have a wife, you can't take another. You're not in Baghdad or Damascus, where you can have as many wives as you want."

"And I know she doesn't want to marry me. She's only pretending to protect herself from her mother's wrath. She's a very prudent young woman, if nothing else."

"Kit, I already—"

"She still wants Dunbar." He tore his gaze from his toe to his friend. "Nick, you've got to do something. You must know someone at the Admiralty. I've only been in England for two months and I only know army people."

"Kit—"

"If we could only find out what ship he's on—it would have had to be a ship leaving London almost—"

"Christopher!"

"Well what, *Nicholas?* Did you know that your name and mine are both Greek?"

Nicholas sputtered. "You damned fool, you never could hold your liquor. Any member of the clergy could drink you under the table. Listen carefully, Kit: The same ruffians who left you and Serena at that crossroads are the same ones who 'pressed' Dunbar in London. He's been my guest at Colfax Park all this time, though he should have arrived at Fairborough Castle sometime today or yesterday. I should be the last guest to show up. Oh, and guess who passed me on the road earlier today? Your favorite cousin, come all the way from the West Indies. And you won't believe who was driving him."

"His name wouldn't be Alfred Gibson, would it?"

Nicholas nodded. "My former coachman. So that's what happened to him. I assume your cousin has come at your grandmother's invitation, and to protect his own interests in that trust fund. But since you're already married to Serena, I wouldn't worry about that."

TRUE PRETENSES

Though it wasn't helping, Kit took another swig of brandy.

"Henceforth, it's up to Dunbar to get Jemma to Scotland," Nicholas went on. "Serena's abigail, Evans, agreed to be a conspirator. The whole idea behind that so-called impressment was to gull the Langleys into thinking Dunbar would no longer be an impediment to their daughter becoming a duchess. I do regret the anguish it must have caused Jemma, however."

"And somehow, Dunbar got Winslow to go with him so he could be a reliable witness to the impressment," Kit surmised. "Why didn't you tell me you were going to do this?"

"You were the one who suggested arranging an elopement for them. But you've had enough on your mind as it is, trying to marry yourself to Serena, without fretting over how to marry Dunbar to Lady Jemma. Besides, it was more of a lark this way."

"You and your larks and pranks," Kit muttered, feeling slightly dizzy. But it wasn't just the brandy, he knew—it was exhaustion from the past couple of days, disbelief at Nick's latest prank, and most importantly, overindulgence in the delights of marriage to Serena. "Only how did you ever lure a man of God into doing the devil's work?"

"Vicar Andrews? You saw the inside of his church. The bell needs replacing, his chalice is green with black spots, and his Bible is so old it antedates King James. It's in Latin."

"His Book of Common Prayer seemed current," Kit remarked.

"Then he's reaping the spoils of my beneficence already." Nicholas tore the flask out of Kit's hand. "Now why don't you return to your charming bride, and tell her she needn't fret over how you'll support her on only fifteen shillings a month?"

"She's not fretting over that, believe me. I think you should take her to Fairborough, and I should follow."

"I think not. My mother is already there, and if Serena and I arrive together, without a chaperone, then *I'll* have to marry her."

Kit heaved himself from the sagging bed. "You can't, if she's already married to me. She can't be compromised now."

"Why won't you accompany her to Fairborough?"

"Because once I'm there, I'm finished being the coachman. I will be no one but the Duke of Fairborough, and Serena will have no choice but to accept that she's the duchess. And I believe she will," he added, the memory of her declaration that she loved him no matter who he was still resonating not only in his mind, but in his heart.

"Why don't you stop being the coachman now, and tell her who you really are?"

"I tried to this afternoon, after we were married and before we—because I didn't feel right about—well, you know, and stop grinning before I relieve you of your front teeth. But she refuses to believe me. As Gibson, I've 'pretended' to be Fairborough so many times that she won't even consider the possibility I'm really he." An idea suddenly hit him. "But if you came with me and vouched for my identity—"

"Oh no." Nicholas quickly stood up from the bed. "She'll kill me."

"And she'll probably kill me, too, but at least we'll be able to enjoy each other's company in hell," Kit retorted. "Nick, it's the only way. If I go back to that room and try to tell her again, there will be tears and—" He raised his voice to a falsetto. " 'How many times have I told you to stop playing the duke, you presumptuous oaf?' " He lowered his voice back to its normal baritone. "Someone else needs to stand next to me and say,

'Yes, this man is Christopher Woodard, Duke of Fairborough'."

"Then let it be someone else, but not me. She knows me as a notorious prankster, so she's not likely to take my word for it, either. But she'll certainly believe it if, say, your grandmother is present."

Kit thought of the festivities his grandmother had planned for this weekend.

As if reading his thoughts, Nicholas added, "I suppose if you tell her once she is at Fairborough castle she is more likely to believe you—and less likely to make a scene. In fact, if she truly loves you, she'll probably just laugh the whole charade off."

Kit sank back onto the edge of the bed. "Do I dare risk that?"

Nicholas gazed back at him, his expression surprisingly sober for all the brandy he'd drunk. "That, my friend, is the biggest question of all. And what will you be risking? Your heart, your future, and your reputation, all to find out which man has captured Serena's love—the coachman, the duke—or just Kit Woodard? You have to ask yourself if Serena is worth that risk."

"No, I don't, because I already know she is," Kit declared.

Nicholas pointed to a trunk in the corner. "The rest of your wardrobe is in there. I'm glad I thought to bring it. So how do you propose we get Serena to Fairborough without her husband, and you without your wife?"

"You seem to have a great gift for coming up with harebrained schemes. For some bloody reason, unless it's the brandy talking, I remain open to your . . . shall we say, *suggestions*, for lack of a better word? But I warn you, Colfax: One day you're going to stumble and hoist yourself by your own bloody petard."

Nicholas turned the flask upside down over his snifter, but nary a drop fell out. "And what is that supposed to mean?"

"You and your pranks. Someday one of them is going to explode right in your face and get you in trouble."

"How much trouble? The kind that will send me to India?"

Kit said nothing, but only glared at him.

"I'm sorry, Kit. I know there was nothing amusing about what happened to you. But you know, since you were the second son, you probably would have joined the military, anyway."

"And you're probably right," Kit agreed with a sigh. "I neither resent nor regret my military service. India's not such a bad place if you're a bachelor. I only resent and regret the circumstances that sent me in that direction much sooner than I might have gone otherwise."

"Very well, so one of my pranks will one day be my doom. I will simply have to be careful. Now let's come up with a plan to get Serena and then you to Fairborough. . . ."

Serena stood in front of the mirror the next morning, pinning up her hair as she tried to make sense of everything her husband was telling her.

He sat on the edge of the bed, wincing as he pulled his boot over the foot with the ravaged toenail. "It seems the Duke of Fairborough also spent the night at this inn, but his coachman has taken ill. So he asked me to drive him the rest of the way to his home."

She turned from the mirror. "But why is Colfax taking the mail coach? Why isn't he traveling in his own coach?"

"He was traveling with Fairborough. But it seems they had a quarrel last night, and as far as Fairborough is concerned, Colfax can jolly well walk the rest of the way."

"Dukes!" she sputtered, with a scornful roll of her eyes.

"They can be quite a curse, can't they? Rather like mothers. But you can either take the mail coach with Colfax, or you can travel in Fairborough's coach with Fairborough."

"I am *not* riding in Fairborough's coach with Fairborough!" she exclaimed.

"You wouldn't care to be alone with Fairborough in his coach?"

"Absolutely not."

"But you would love him if I were he, wouldn't you?"

She laughed softly and cupped his handsome face in her hands. "My darling, you are *you*, and that's all that matters to me. I love you."

She bent to kiss him as he wrapped his arms around her, pulling her onto his lap.

"I love you so much," he murmured into her adoring lips. "Just promise me you'll be at Fairborough when I get there tonight."

"Of course I'll be there." She brushed her fingers through his dark chestnut hair, which obviously hadn't been cut since he'd come to work for the Langleys; it curled over his ears and around his collar. "I only hope I'll be able to see you tonight."

"You will. We're leaving right after the mail coach."

She gazed at him lovingly. His liquid brown eyes glowed back at her, and she thought she would melt in his embrace, so weak was she with love and desire for him. His shirt was wide open at the neck, buttoned only halfway up his chest. With a wonderful shudder of longing, she remembered touching the sparse curls of hair on that chest with not only her hands, but her mouth as she experienced her second climax last night.

He smiled as if he could read her mind. A wave of heat flashed across her face and down her own chest, prickling the tips of her breasts as she recalled the wicked pleasure that smiling mouth had given her earlier. They'd made love a third time this morning, and again he'd made her explode with those heated waves that made her want to scream with unbearable rapture—only this time he'd done it with his tongue!

She sighed joyfully as she twined her arms around his neck and kissed him. "I adore you," she whispered, brushing her lips over his cheek, his ear, and then his neck as she rested her chin on his shoulder, gazing at the bedsheets. She saw two small bloodstains, one in the middle of the bed and the other toward the foot, that one obviously from his stubbed toe.

A rap at the door startled her out of his lap. "Miss Langley, His Grace awaits you downstairs," said the same manservant who had awakened Gibson last night. "The mail coach has arrived."

"I'm coming," she called out, then turned back to her husband. "You didn't tell Colfax, did you?"

"No, you said you wanted to do that. I told him what happened the other night—not the version we invented for the Sewells, but what truly happened. He only said that for your sake, he would be discreet and not ask any questions."

She picked up her bonnet and the marriage certificate from the bedside table. She rolled up the document and thrust it into the bodice of her pelisse. "I haven't decided when or how to announce our marriage. But I'll think of something."

He rose to his feet and opened the door for her. "I know you will. You're very bright, and that's one of the things I love about you."

As she smiled back, for the first time she noticed how

well his clothes fit him. In fact, they almost looked new.

"Those aren't your clothes."

He pinched his shirt and flashed her that smile that made her want to melt into a puddle at his feet. "They're what Colfax's manservant brought me to wear last night."

"They fit as if they were made for you," she said in wonder. "And they're so fine they look as if they could be the duke's, but I think you're a bit taller than he is, maybe a trifle wider in the shoulders. Oh well, you look splendid." She pecked him on the cheek, then donned her bonnet. "I love you, darling. I'll see you tonight."

She pulled on her gloves to conceal her wedding ring as she went downstairs.

Nicholas was waiting for her in the inn yard. "Are you all right, Serena?"

"I'm fine," she said, as he guided her to the waiting mail coach. "But I think it's just ghastly of Fairborough to treat you this way."

"Well, he's Fairborough," Nicholas said lamely, as if that explained everything.

The mail coach departed the village, leaving Serena's husband behind. She was silent and pensive throughout the journey, dwelling wistfully over the events of the past twenty-four hours, scarcely believing all that had happened. She only half listened to the banter of the other passengers.

One of them was a Colonel Logue, who'd been the Duke of Fairborough's commanding officer in Calcutta. Logue waxed lyrical about "Captain Woodard"; numerous times he berated himself for not remembering that the captain was now a duke. He had nothing but praise for Serena's erstwhile fiancé, but she had no regrets, especially after yesterday. By now she could not picture herself with any man other than the one she'd married.

According to the colonel, the new Duke of Fairborough had been an exemplary officer in the Royal Army. Unlike his decadent older brother, he never drank, never gambled, and regularly attended Anglican services at St. Anne's Church in Calcutta. Though he was rather quiet and tended to keep to himself, Captain Woodard, or rather the duke as he eventually became, enjoyed hunting and riding—he was an excellent shot, and Colonel Logue had never seen a man who handled horses as superbly as young Woodard, especially when driving them. As a matter of fact, Kit won every carriage race the British officers frequently staged for sport in Calcutta.

A graceful dancer, the former Captain Woodard was always charming and polite to the eligible daughters of army officers and East India Company officials. But he never dallied seriously with any of them, since they invariably returned to the old country to seek husbands there. Few of them wanted to marry only to remain in India.

Captain Woodard had been disconsolate two years ago upon learning of his father's death, said Colonel Logue, who surmised that there'd been an unresolved quarrel between the two men. Woodard had been offered the opportunity to return to England, but hadn't seen the point since his father had already been gone and buried for months. But when his brother died a year later, he'd had no choice.

"Though he was certainly looking forward to starting a family of his own," Logue said. "He's the only man I ever met who admitted wanting daughters as much as sons. 'Tis a lucky young lady who's marrying Captain Woodard—bless me, I mean the duke. Why, I knew the bride's mother years ago."

That got Serena's attention, and she finally spoke. "You knew the Countess of Paxton, Colonel?"

"Before she married Lord Gorham's estate manager, yes. We come from the same county up north. I actually courted her briefly, but she wouldn't have me because I wanted a military career. She was very ambitious for a vicar's daughter. Set her cap for Gorham's estate manager because she thought it was the closest she would ever get to marrying Gorham himself. And to think she became a countess, after all!"

It was late afternoon when they arrived at Fairborough. The castle, a sprawling hodgepodge of Norman, Tudor, Jacobean, and Georgian architecture, was situated among undulating hills of lush emerald green that were partially blanketed by dense woods, including the patch where the Langleys' coach had been ambushed two nights ago.

No Woodards were present to greet the newcomers; the duke's grandmother was napping while the duke's stepmother was stricken with a headache. Guests who had already arrived were amusing themselves throughout the extensive grounds of the estate. Nicholas seemed relieved, as if he'd been dreading the reunion with his mother and sister.

Once in her assigned quarters, Serena doffed her bonnet and was about to remove her gloves when Harriet came blustering in. "Thanks heavens you finally arrived!"

"Did you summon the authorities to look for me?"

Harriet wrung her hands distractedly. "Never mind that now—the important thing is that you're here." In other words, of course they hadn't summoned the authorities. "You're going to have to marry Fairborough, after all."

Serena's heart lurched. "What about Jemma?"

Harriet burst into tears. "The selfish little chit! She's

disappeared—along with that impertinent abigail of yours. I never did like that Evans woman, and now—"

"When—where?" Serena felt a tremor of apprehension as her heart began pounding. "Cousin Harriet, I can't marry Fairborough. I've been—"

"You must! We need that money!" So distraught was Harriet that she utterly forgot to ring the usual fine peal over Serena's head for not addressing her as *my lady*. "We found a note in Jemma's room. Sometime during the night, she and that Evans woman—and Philip's tutor—took one of the Fairborough carriages and absconded to Gretna Green!"

Serena wanted to shriek with laughter at the delightful notion of Miriam eloping with Mr. Jennings, but for Harriet's sake she managed to remain properly dismayed.

"We didn't even know till noon," Harriet went on. "Jemma should have been abed, as I was. No one found the note till someone from Fairborough village came here to report that the carriage with Jemma, the tutor, and that Evans woman stopped at the inn shortly after midnight, where they picked up none other than that—that—"

"Surely you don't mean Lord Dunbar?"

"That's exactly who I mean!" Harriet's voice climbed higher in pitch with each word, till it was so thin and reedy it finally broke into sobs. "We thought a press gang took him, that's what Warren said, now Archie insists Warren must have been wrong about what he saw that night because he was so foxed!"

Serena had no idea what to say at this point. On the one hand, she was relieved for Hamish and happy for Jemma, but on the other hand . . .

Harriet continued: "We found the note, and sure enough, Jemma's not only marrying that kilted

TRUE PRETENSES

bounder, but intends to remain in Scotland till she turns one and twenty, so her father can't annul the marriage! They have too far a head start for anyone to catch up to them, and even so, we don't know which road they're taking, or even if they're going by ship. The scandal, oh, the scandal she's causing! We're in debt to half the merchants in London, and Warren has accumulated an entire alphabet of vowels from his club. Don't you understand now why you must marry Fairborough?"

"But, cousin, you know I've been compromised. And after these past two days, I can assure you I've been even more compromised. Don't forget, I was abducted with the coachman. You wrote Fairborough that letter, and you showed me his response. If he refuses to marry me simply because I kissed the coachman, then what makes you think he'll marry me now?"

Harriet grabbed Serena's shoulders, nearly shaking her. "Have you forgotten the sixty thousand pounds, you little fool? It doesn't matter anymore what you've done with that coachman, and Fairborough doesn't have to know. You *must* marry him! There are all sorts of little things you can do on your wedding night to make him think he's your first and only. Surely his stepmother knows a trick or two, we'll ask her."

"My lady," chirped a maid from the doorway.

Harriet let go of Serena's shoulders, whirling around to scowl at the girl. "Not now, you silly wench!"

"But, my lady, you asked to be summoned when the Duke of Fairborough arrived. He's arriving this moment."

Harriet glared back at Serena as she bustled out of the room. "You're marrying him, even if we have to lock you up till the wedding!"

Serena glanced around the room and spotted a letter with her name on it lying on the bed. Recognizing Miriam's penmanship, she snatched it up and slit it open.

Miriam wrote only what Harriet had just told her, only less hysterically. It was the closing paragraph that baffled Serena the most.

I know you'll be married yourself by the time we return from Scotland. Believe me, dear girl, it won't matter if he's Gibson or Fairborough—the important thing is you WILL be happy, I promise you that!

Whatever gave Miriam the idea, after all this time, that Serena might be happy married to Fairborough? Especially when Miriam must have known when the Langleys arrived here the other night that Serena had been abducted with Gibson, and thus had been—as he so aptly put it—*very* compromised by him?

Not that it mattered now. Let Harriet lock her in this room, even chain her to the bed, but Serena would not be marrying the duke. She pressed a hand to her still thundering heart as if to calm it down, and as she did so, she heard and felt the crumpling of the marriage certificate she'd hidden in her bodice.

That certificate would be Serena's key to every lock Harriet was hoping to use.

Chapter Seventeen

Kit arrived at Fairborough just in time for tea.

The first person he met was his former commanding officer, and upon hearing that he was expected to take tea with his grandmother, stepmother, and the Earl and Countess of Paxton, he insisted that Colonel Logue join them. He led the colonel into the dining room, where only Lord and Lady Paxton were seated. As usual, Daphne and Eleanor, his grandmother, were running late; neither were sticklers for punctuality.

When first meeting the new Earl of Paxton, Kit had only vaguely wondered whether or not he might be acquainted with Colonel Logue, since they both came from the sparsely populated Northumberland. It turned out to be very sparsely populated indeed, for Logue and the Langleys recognized each other instantly. Thereafter the two older men practically ignored Kit, as they waxed nostalgic about the old times they'd shared as much younger bucks.

Kit was left having to suffocate under the layers of

apologies Harriet heaped upon him for her ungrateful daughter's scandalous behavior.

"If she's following her heart, Lady Paxton, then I'm happy for her," he said earnestly. "I have no doubt that Serena will suit me just as well, if not better." Certainly better, he added to himself.

Harriet leaned forward in her chair. "So Your Grace will marry her, after all?"

He shrugged. "I want that sixty thousand pounds. Besides, she only stole a kiss from the coachman. It's not as if she'd ever go so far as to share his bed."

He fought to suppress his laughter as she nearly spluttered her tea back into the cup.

The two dowager duchesses finally entered the dining room.

"There you are, Kit, I've been wondering what happened to you!" Eleanor said, as he rose to greet her.

"I'm sorry, Grandmama, but I had a great deal of business in London." He took her thin, gnarled hands into his as he kissed her on both cheeks. "My commanding officer from Calcutta is here, and I'd like you to meet him. . . ."

Kit made the introductions as his former commander sketched a bow to the old duchess. Logue turned to Daphne and froze, gaping at her as she gaped back, her face suddenly ashen.

For some odd reason, Kit was reminded of that day last month at Woodard House, when he'd stormed into the study dressed as the coachman and greeted Daphne, who had reacted in much the same way.

Eleanor lifted her quizzing glass to peer at the colonel and then Daphne. "I say, you two look as if you've met before!"

"Why, I scarcely believe it!" Colonel Logue exclaimed. "I must say, I was astonished enough to learn that dear old Harriet went on to become the Countess of Paxton, but I never dreamed that Amabel would go on to become a *duchess!*"

Amabel? thought Kit in bewilderment.

Eleanor nearly dropped the quizzing glass. "I beg your pardon, Colonel? My daughter-in-law's Christian name isn't Amabel, it's Daphne."

"Then I must be mistaken. My deepest apologies, Your Grace. Granted, I haven't seen Amabel since I joined the army twenty-three years ago, but I must say this lady looks very much like her. The only Daphne I knew of was Lord Gorham's only daughter, who was always in such frail health that she was never seen by anyone."

Tears sprang to Daphne's eyes. "And when she reached a marriageable age, she suddenly made a miraculous recovery. You're not mistaken, Colonel—I *am* Amabel. But it wasn't my idea, it was my father's, because I was only a few months younger than she!"

"What wasn't your idea?" Kit asked, feeling almost as confused as he had during those moments when he wasn't sure if he was supposed to be a duke or a coachman.

Daphne pointed to Harriet. "Ask her!"

Kit turned to Harriet, who was suddenly as ashen as Daphne. "What should I ask you, Lady Paxton?"

For once, Harriet was speechless.

Eleanor turned to her daughter-in-law. "Am I to believe that the late Lady Gorham is not your mother?"

"No!" She began sobbing. "But Lord Gorham was my father, and he made me take the place of the real Lady Daphne after she died."

"But what has this to do with Lady Paxton?" asked Kit.

"She's the one who's been blackmailing me!"

"She—" Kit gaped incredulously at Harriet. Good God, it hadn't even occurred to him that his stepmother's blackmailer might have been a woman.

"I dare you to try and kill me now," Daphne told Harriet.

"You're not worth it," Harriet sneered back. "What are you but the by-blow of Lord Gorham and his Scottish housekeeper? Fortunately for you, you look more like your father than your mother, which made it easier for you to take Lady Daphne's place when she died." She glanced around at everyone else, obviously relishing her appalled audience. "Gorham had scarcely a feather to fly with in those days, and he needed a daughter to marry a man of wealth and position. His legitimate one died shortly before turning sixteen. I only know because I was the local vicar's only child, and the earl swore my father to secrecy when Lady Daphne was laid to rest with a headstone that bore the name 'Amabel.' Well, my father couldn't keep it a secret from my mother and me. And how it rankled me to see her not only take Lady Daphne's place, but marry a duke!"

"Oh dear, oh my," said Colonel Logue, clearly flustered. "I certainly didn't mean for this to happen!"

Daphne dabbed her eyes with a handkerchief. "Never mind, I'll return to London at once, since I'm obviously far beyond the pale."

"You'll do no such thing!" Eleanor exclaimed. "Why, that would only cause a greater scandal, and think of Rosalind!"

"But how could you still want me here, now that you know the truth about me?" Daphne glanced at Kit as tears poured down her cheeks. "Certainly *you* don't want me here, do you?"

"Actually, I agree with Grandmama," said Kit. "If you leave now, the guests will speculate, and they might guess the truth."

"You have my word of honor, I shan't tell a soul," declared Colonel Logue.

Eleanor took her daughter-in-law's hand into her own. "As far as I'm concerned, you're still Daphne, and you'll always be Daphne. I knew what Gorham was up to twenty years ago when he dangled his daughter in front of my lonely widowed son. Lady Paxton is right about that, but so what? Who is she to pass judgment? Her husband has scarcely a feather to fly with himself, which is why she's so determined that Kit comply with that stipulation in my son's will."

"It just so happens that I have sufficient plumage with which to fly, Your Grace," Archie finally said. "Unfortunately, my wife is so zealous about her new position that she feels compelled to live beyond my means. I only hope you'll be able to overlook that zeal, but I will understand perfectly if you elect to bring blackmail charges against her."

Harriet opened her mouth to protest. "But, my lord—"

"But, my lord, nothing!" he fired back. "What would your father say if he were still alive? We don't need that sixty thousand pounds. If Fairborough still wants to marry Serena, that's his affair, but I'll have you know I'm quite content with Jemma's choice of husband."

Harriet's jaw dropped, and her eyes widened. "My lord, you can't mean—"

"I do! I would have much preferred to take her up north myself, then out here to the west. I'm as homesick for the north as Logue is. After this is over, I'm moving up to Paxton Hall in Yorkshire, to see if I can make a go of the estates there. If you prefer to remain at the house in Hampstead Heath, then that is entirely your affair."

"Where is Serena, incidentally?" Kit asked.

Harriet loudly blew her nose into a handkerchief.

"Upstairs resting for the ball tonight, Your Grace."

"Perhaps I'll go upstairs and start resting for it myself," Kit said. "I am rather weary from the long journey here."

He was even wearier from the catfight he'd just witnessed, enlightening though it was. Aside from the revelation that Lady, and not Lord, Paxton was Daphne's blackmailer, much of the conversation had only confirmed what he'd long suspected from servants' gossip. The only other surprise was the fact that his former commanding officer, of all people, was the person who'd unwittingly shed a bright, glaring light on the shadows cast by old family skeletons.

He headed for the dining room doorway, then paused and turned back, touching his stepmother on the arm. "Daphne?"

She looked up at him with tearful blue eyes.

"I want you and Rosalind to stay, and I want you both here for my wedding," he said. "You're still members of this family, and nothing is going to change that."

"Perhaps I should take my wife back to London," said Archie.

"No, because Serena should have her family here, too," Kit replied. "I would appreciate it if for the sake of the bride, at least, everyone here could wipe the blood dripping off their hatchets and bury them for all time."

He left the dining room and went upstairs to his quarters. His only worry was how this afternoon's revelation could affect his half sister's future. Certainly Lady Rosalind Woodard would be accepted by the ton for her family name as well as the twenty thousand pounds Kit's father had settled on her. But she would suffer if people found out she was the granddaughter of a mere servant. Unlike most people, he didn't think there was anything wrong with that any more than he thought there was anything wrong about the way Serena's sister behaved. Neither Rosalind nor Felice was a threat to anyone. It was women like Harriet and Daphne one had to be wary of.

His valet was already in his room, laying out his clothes for the evening. "Shall I draw a bath, Your Grace?"

"Yes, why not?" Kit thought of yesterday's bath and wished Serena were here now. If only there were some way he could go back to pretending he was the coachman just long enough to make love to her again, before tonight's party.

But with a little luck—and, in fact, Kit believed he was enjoying a great deal of luck finally—he and Serena would be together after the ball tonight. He felt a hot rush of desire in his loins as he gazed at the massive canopy bed in front of him, thinking of Serena lying nude upon it as he knelt over her, pleasuring her body with his hands, his lips, his tongue, and especially his hard, swollen sex as she moaned his name— *his* name, *Kit*—while she dissolved into a climax so intense that it triggered his own. Oh, the things he'd learned in India from the forbidden Kama Sutra!

"Are you all right, Your Grace?" inquired the valet.

He started. "What? Oh, yes, of course. Why wouldn't I be?"

The valet shrugged. "I thought I heard Your Grace groan as if in pain."

Kit quickly bent down to rub his knee. "I'm afraid I bruised my knee stumbling out of a carriage yesterday morning, and it still throbs. I hit my head, too." He brushed back his hair to show the valet the small discolored knot high on his forehead. "Incidentally, I'd like you to trim my hair, too. I should be able to tie it back in the old style ere long."

The valet clucked and shook his head. "Your Grace should be more careful alighting from carriages. Can't be easy, I know, being so tall."

"My height certainly didn't help," Kit agreed, turning to survey the portrait of his fiancée that was propped on an easel near the window.

"I'll see about the bath right away, Your Grace," said the valet as he left the room, but Kit only grunted in response.

On an impulse he went over to the easel and pulled the portrait forward to remove the back. The canvas slipped easily out of the frame, and he turned it over. There in the upper left-hand corner, written in charcoal, were the initials FCL.

As he placed the canvas back into the frame, he wondered which other paintings here at Fairborough—aside from that hunting scene and the pastoral—were actually the work of Serena's enormously talented sister. Not that it mattered. He had no intention of ever removing them. He was proud to own and display Felice's work, especially if no one else would.

Felice was going to be very happy here at Fairborough, he thought. As happy as he and Serena would be.

That evening, Serena dressed in her finest gown of violet blue silk. After donning her long gloves to conceal her wedding ring, she accompanied her cousins downstairs to Fairborough's cavernous great hall, with its high, ornate hammer-beam ceiling.

Archie and Harriet both looked thunderous, as if they'd had a terrible argument. No doubt they were distressed over their daughter's elopement.

They went straight to the dais where the two previous Fairborough duchesses were enthroned. The duke was not on the dais, nor did he seem to be anywhere in the great hall, as Serena glanced around in search of a man who, by all accounts, bore a rather striking resemblance to her new husband.

Clad in a deep burgundy gown, Daphne was festooned with diamonds, including a tiara that glittered atop her golden hair. Her face, however, seemed puffy, and her china-blue eyes were unmistakably bloodshot, as if she'd been crying recently. Serena knew that Daphne didn't like leaving London for the country, but surely it couldn't upset her *that* much.

Or maybe the duke had been causing more trouble for his stepmother; he seemed to make trouble wherever he went. Serena had no idea what he and Nicholas had quarreled about last night, but she didn't doubt that Fairborough probably started it. And then left Nicholas to find his own way to Fairborough Castle! Thank heavens she wouldn't have to marry Kit now. With the fingers of her right hand, she felt the wedding ring through the thin kid of her gloves. Not only was she married to someone else, but she might already be carrying Gibson's child. The next Duke of Fairborough could not be sired by a coachman.

Daphne's mother-in-law, Eleanor, was dressed more sedately in a gown of gray so pale it was almost silver. Ropes of pearls, looped not only around her bosom but entwined in her silvery white hair, were her only jewelry. She chatted with the bishop, who was supposed to officiate the duke's wedding.

Serena smiled at Daphne's sixteen-year-old daughter, Lady Rosalind Woodard, who wore a pristine white frock that only made her blazing red hair all the more fiery.

Harriet grabbed Serena and yanked her forward to be presented, as Archie introduced her.

Eleanor held up a quizzing glass. "So this is our next duchess? You look just like the portrait that graces Kit's room even as we speak. The artist captured your likeness perfectly."

Serena felt a warm frisson of pleasure and pride in Felice.

A male voice startled her from behind. "So this is the lady who means to deprive me of my uncle's trust fund? Won't you introduce us, Grandmama?"

"I've barely been introduced to her myself," replied Eleanor, as the man stepped between her and Serena. "Miss Langley, may I present my other grandson, Mr. Calvin Granger."

He had the worst skin and teeth Serena had ever seen. The harsh climate of the West Indies obviously disagreed with him. No wonder he'd returned to England. She dipped a slight curtsey, while he bowed with a flourish that matched his lavishly embroidered gold waistcoat.

"How do you do, Mr. Granger?" she murmured.

"Pleased to meet you, Miss Langley. So tell me once and for all—do you intend to break my heart or Kit's?"

She bristled. "I've always known that if I didn't marry the tenth Duke of Fairborough, then I'd have to marry the eleventh. But I had no idea that if I didn't wed the eleventh, then I would have to wed you instead, Mr. Granger."

He chuckled. "You misunderstand me, Miss Langley. If you don't marry Kit, then I collect his father's trust fund. But if you do, then I shall have to return to the West Indies a very poor man, indeed."

Serena smiled faintly and lowered her voice. "Perhaps not, Mr. Granger."

He bowed again. "In that case, I look forward to getting better acquainted with the lady who may prove to be my savior. Do pardon me, Miss Langley." And he disappeared into the crowd of guests.

"Speaking of Kit, where is he?" said Eleanor. "Everyone else seems to be here, including my dear goddaughter!" Her face lit up and she held out her arms as Lady Lucinda Maxwell fluttered over to kiss her on both cheeks. "Where's your betrothed, Lucy dear? I was so hoping to meet him and give him my approval."

"I'm afraid he was detained by business in London," Lucinda said ruefully.

"I must confess, there were times when I rather hoped you might wed one of my grandsons," Eleanor said with a sigh, her blue eyes twinkling as she cast them on Serena. "But as long as you girls are both happy. My dear Serena, I think you'll suit Kit perfectly—in fact, much better than you might have suited Simon, heaven rest his soul."

"There he is—he's just now coming into the great hall!" Rosalind exclaimed, jumping up to wave at him. "Hello, Kit!"

"For heaven's sake, Rosalind, behave like a lady!" Daphne admonished her.

"Surely you can't expect her to behave like something she's truly not," Harriet said darkly.

Daphne scowled at Harriet. "How would you know? After all, you haven't exactly behaved as the daughter of a clergyman."

"That's enough, you two!" Eleanor hissed. "Remember what Kit said earlier."

Serena only vaguely wondered what Kit might have said to Harriet and Daphne this afternoon. Obviously there was trouble afoot. And the usual source was somewhere behind her, making his entrance into the great hall.

Lucinda whirled around and sailed past Serena. "Here, Kitty, Kitty, Kitty, come meet your betrothed at long last!"

Serena almost turned to look, but couldn't bring herself to do so. Her heart pounded hard in her chest, and again she gripped her hidden wedding ring beneath her kid glove, as if touching it might give her the strength to confront the duke and everyone else with the shocking truth. If only Gibson were here right now!

He said he'd see her tonight, but she didn't know how. He must be out at the carriage house.

She started as she felt a warm touch on her bare upper arm. *Fairborough!* She almost stopped breathing, then blew out a heavy sigh as she realized it was only Nick.

"Ready to meet your fiancé?" he inquired.

"No," she barely whispered, her heart still hammering against her ribs.

"Oh, come now, his hooves really aren't cloven. Just give him a chance, Serena. Why, I've already settled my differences with him from last night. Don't you think it's time you settled yours?" He glanced over her shoulder with a wide grin on his face. "She's right here, Fairborough, and she's lovely."

That unbearably pompous baritone she'd heard in the dark conservatory a month ago, now only a few paces behind her: "I know she's lovely, I've seen her."

When? she wondered, then remembered that his grandmother had said that her portrait was in his room. Only how could he think of her as lovely when her nose was too big for her face, and her eyes, set too close together, were of an indiscriminate color—blue or gray? Gibson had likened them to opals. Gibson loved her just the way she was. Simon hadn't wanted her because she resembled a Roman statue and was probably just as cold and hard. How could Serena expect his younger brother to think otherwise?

She heard Lucinda's voice over her shoulder. "Now you wait and see, Kit, Serena will tell you herself. You really do look a great deal like her coachman!"

"Kit!" Rosalind cried, lunging forward to greet him, but her mother quickly grabbed her by the skirt and yanked her back.

"Remember you're a lady now!" Daphne hissed.

"Rosalind, is that you?" Kit exclaimed. "Heavens above, but how you've grown!"

"That's right, you haven't seen her since you went to India," said Lucinda.

Serena sensed someone tall and masculine standing only inches behind her. "Greetings, my dear," Fairborough murmured in her ear.

Well, at least he wasn't foolish enough to dare a kiss. She remained frozen in place, despite the warmth of his breath in her ear, threatening to melt her defenses. Warm fingers lightly brushed the nape of her neck, and she tensed as she recalled Gibson's fingers doing likewise yesterday afternoon, before he unlaced the back of her dress. How dare the duke make such an intimate gesture when they weren't even married yet—no, she corrected herself, when they weren't even going to marry at all!

Nicholas said, "Fairborough, if I may present your fiancée—"

"Let him greet his sister first," Serena said, resolutely facing away from Kit. She couldn't help feeling that once she finally laid eyes on him, she would be at the point of no return. It would be time to announce the scandal she'd wrought yesterday.

"That's very thoughtful of you, my dear," Kit purred. He stepped past her to embrace Rosalind, who leaped off the dais and threw her arms over his wide shoulders. For a brief, bizarre moment, Serena saw the back of the coachman in her mind's eye, his ill-fitting, dark green livery hanging over his very broad shoulders as he sat in front of her on the box of the open carriage, driving her and Miriam to Town. The shoulders before her now were just as broad and even more prominent than Gibson's, since unlike the coachman, Kit wore a black superfine coat tailored to fit only him and not some portly predecessor. His hair, she noted, was indeed the same color as her husband's, but shorter.

"Rosalind, how the deuce did you ever grow so tall?"

"I'm not *that* tall, Kit—certainly not as tall as you!"

"No, but you're obviously much taller than you were the last time I saw you. I dare not pick you up now."

Lucinda tugged on his sleeve. "Kit, do turn around so you and your fiancée can finally see each other." She glanced at Serena. "I'm telling you, Serena, when you see Kit's face, you're going to think you're looking at your coachman!"

"But he was your—that is, my coachman was your coachman before." She frowned at Nicholas. "I always meant to ask you about that, Nick, but—"

"You'll just have to see for yourself, Serena."

"Kit, why don't you greet your fiancée already?" Eleanor said. "I daresay she's dying to know what you look like."

The duke slowly turned to face Serena. "It seems you have the final word, Miss Langley. Do I or do I not resemble your coachman?"

Her heart nearly exploded out of her chest, and she felt all the breath whooshing out of her lungs as she beheld the eleventh Duke of Fairborough . . . who did indeed look exactly like her coachman, right down to the dimples in his chin and left cheek.

And when he spoke again, his arrogant, nasal accent was gone, and he no longer sounded like the duke—he sounded like Gibson.

"Oh my God," Serena whispered in disbelief.

"I knew it!" Daphne sprang to her feet and stood next to Kit, looking as if she'd just stumbled upon a huge diamond. "Remember your last visit to Woodard House, Serena? Your coachman crashed into the study and at first glance I thought he might be Kit, especially since I could have sworn he called me by my given name. But because I fainted immediately afterwards, I couldn't quite recall with any certainty, and I didn't think it was possible that Kit would do such a thing!"

Nor had Serena ever thought it was possible.

Daphne glanced wildly at Kit. "But you did it, didn't you?"

He didn't respond, but continued beaming at Serena.

Lucinda smiled brightly as she placed one gloved hand on Fairborough's left arm and the other on Serena's right. "Oh, the look on your face, Serena! It must be true! Where is your coachman, anyway? We should bring him in here so we can make comparisons."

"Lucy, as usual you're at least three steps behind everyone else," Nicholas said dryly, punching the duke's right arm. "Serena's coachman is right here."

"What's all this prattle about coachmen?" demanded Eleanor, who was still seated behind her grandson.

Serena glared at Nicholas, her voice coming out as a hoarse croak. "You knew about this all along?"

"Knew about it? It was his idea!" Kit exclaimed, taking her hand. "I know you must be quite stunned at the moment, darling, but—"

She tore her hand from his grasp. "Don't you dare call me that, and don't you dare touch me!"

His face darkened as his voice dropped to a low growl. "Have you forgotten you're my wife now—in *every* sense?"

Serena knew perfectly well what he meant by those last three words, and that very knowledge, coupled with her realization of the truth, slammed into her heart with the power of a sledgehammer. The memory of what this man—not Gibson—had done to her three times since yesterday afternoon only fueled the flames of rage, humiliation, betrayal—and heartbreak—that blazed deep within her.

"I'm not *your* wife, and you bloody well know it!" she hissed. "And I will *never* be your wife, you—" With all her strength, she smacked him across the face. "—you lying, deceitful *bastard!*"

Everything blurred and swam around her as she turned and dashed out of the great hall.

Chapter Eighteen

Serena felt sick and dizzy as she staggered into her room, locking the door behind her. Hot tears streamed down her cheeks as she leaned against the door and slid slowly to the floor, too weak from the shock to even make it to the bed. She curled into a tight ball as she heard heavy footsteps thundering up the hallway outside, coming closer and louder like an approaching summer storm.

The storm broke with a rumble of powerful knocks on the door, which trembled at her back. "Serena?" the duke called out, and the doorknob rattled. "Serena, open the door, please, and let me talk to you."

She bit her lip, determined not to say a word. Maybe he'd think she'd fled elsewhere. She dared to exhale only after his footsteps faded down the hall.

She was still reeling from what she'd just learned. How could she have been so blind? So *stupid*?

After all, it wasn't as if Kit hadn't tried to reveal his true identity before: that morning at Woodard House, when he'd entered the study and Daphne had fainted at the sight of him.

And that same day at Plumlee's, when he'd pretended—or at least claimed—to be Fairborough himself. No wonder his act had been so convincing. Because it was no act!

Lucinda's ongoing insistence that the Langleys' coachman resembled Fairborough; Nick's half-joking query: "What would you say, Serena, if Gibson really were Fairborough?" Her own doubts that a duke would deign to pose as a servant: "What duke in his right mind would leave the comforts of his position to pose as someone's coachman?"

"A duke who wants to meet you very badly, and can't seem to do so any other way," Nicholas had replied.

Well, the duke in question obviously didn't want to explain his deception to her that badly, since he'd given up so quickly on trying to gain entry into this room.

Gibson's staunch defense of Fairborough the day he'd met Felice: All along it was the duke defending himself, making outrageous accusations about her father, pretending to be protective of Felice, the way he'd pretended to be the coachman, pretended to love Serena, pretended, deceived, *lied* about everything!

The bridegroom faltering yesterday when Vicar Andrews asked about impediments: "What did you almost say to him?" she'd asked him afterward.

"I was going to tell him that I'm really Fairborough." And indeed, he'd almost told her why, but she hadn't wanted to hear the reason—because she'd mistakenly believed that he hadn't wanted to marry her.

"I know you're probably worried about how you're going to support me."

"Not really, no." Of course not. With the prospect of sixty thousand pounds in one lump sum, he was smugly confident they'd somehow manage to scrape by.

"How about the Duke of Fairborough?"

"You mean would I love you if you were Fairborough? Well, if he were you, or you were he, I do believe—"

No! She'd only been joking when she said that, hadn't she? She'd certainly thought *he'd* only been joking.

Either way, the joke was at her expense, but she was damned if she'd pay.

She started as she heard a scuffling noise in the far corner of the room, on the other side of the bed. Mice! She quickly rose to her feet, glancing around the dark room lit only by faint moonlight waning through the window. The scuffling turned into crackling, and her heart bobbed up to her throat as light suddenly flared from the corner.

But then her heart plunged as the duke, clutching a brace of candles, swept into the room from a hidden servants' passage.

She whirled back to the door and turned the key to the right, but it wouldn't open. She turned it to the left; it made a clicking noise and she tried twisting the doorknob, but it wouldn't budge. Surely she'd unlocked it! She heard Kit's heavy footsteps slowly, almost leisurely approaching her from behind, and she caught a whiff of beeswax as the candlelight steadily grew brighter against the door. If only she could open it before he reached her, he'd be the fool for not moving more swiftly to stop her.

In desperation she feverishly jiggled the key in the lock, as if that might make it cooperate, but it slipped out of the slot and clattered to the floor.

Kit slammed his foot on top of it before she could bend over to pick it up. "I'm afraid the locks in this house have always had a tendency to stick and be uncooperative, especially when one is in a hurry."

Serena rushed around to the other side of the bed, hoping to escape through the servants' passage, but he'd already closed that door and she couldn't even see where it was. With fresh tears in her eyes, she turned to watch Kit as he set the candelabrum on a piecrust table next to the chair in front of the fireplace. He sat down, holding up the key just long enough to let the candlelight flash against it before he slipped it into his pocket.

She fought back her tears as she watched the play of golden light flickering across his handsome features. Briefly she wondered if perhaps there was some mistake, that somehow the duke and Gibson were still two different people. But as she gazed at Fairborough in his elegant black frock coat, snowy white cravat, and neatly trimmed chestnut hair, and saw the same eyes of liquid brown that had burned into her naked skin yesterday afternoon, perusing the most intimate parts of her body, she realized that this man was in fact a highly polished version of her beloved coachman.

She felt her legs wobbling beneath her, though she wasn't sure whether it was from the shock of what had just transpired, or that mysterious power he seemed to wield over her—*now* she understood why the duke had had the same effect on her in the Maxwells' conservatory that Gibson had always had everywhere else. She closed her eyes as if to shut out the horrifying fact that her body and emotions could respond so inexorably to the one man she'd wanted most to avoid.

"I'm sorry," his whispered voice drifted to her. "I never meant to hurt you."

Her eyes flew open, and she glared at him through a burning mist. "You married me under false pretenses! Everything was a lie, a pretense, everything!"

"On the contrary, I married you under true pretenses," Kit replied. "Certainly I pretended to be your coachman, but there was no pretense about my desire to win your heart—that was for real. I love you, Serena. You must believe that even if you don't believe anything else."

"Why did you do it?"

"I didn't want to do it. But Nicholas managed to persuade me that it was the only way to meet you. You wouldn't answer my letters, you wouldn't receive me. Not even he could pass a letter from me to you. I saw that with my own eyes that very first night as the coachman. What was I to do?"

"What were you to do?" she fired back. "I'll tell you what you could have done—you could have just let me be and searched for a more willing bride elsewhere!"

"Don't think that never occurred to me," he said sharply. "But there were sixty thousand pounds at stake—"

"So you just wanted to marry me for that money! Yet you expect me to believe that you love me!"

"Initially that was the case," he conceded. "But, Serena, I've been in India for nine long years. I returned to England and learned from the family solicitor of that stipulation in my father's will. I decided since I didn't otherwise know any eligible young ladies in England, I might as well start my search for a bride with you. That I might fall in love with you, or that you might reciprocate my feelings, was more than I could have hoped for. But it happened, much to my delighted surprise and, I was hoping, yours."

"I thought I was reciprocating *Gibson's* feelings."

"Yes, and I'm Gibson. You reciprocated *my* feelings. And you told me yesterday you would always love me regardless of who I was."

"That was before I knew I was being deceived," she said acidly.

Kit frowned. "Then it seems we're both guilty of deceiving each other. For just as you believed that I was your coachman, I believed that you loved me."

She scowled. "But unlike you, I did not set out to intentionally deceive you."

"I won't dispute that. As I said before, I never wanted to deceive you, but it's not as if I didn't try to divulge the truth before things went so far."

She felt a painful squeeze in her heart to hear him voice what she'd thought only moments before he broke into this room. It dismayed her that his thoughts were so often the same as hers—as if the two of them were predestined by fate to be together, when in fact they were only meant to be together because of that wretched stipulation in his father's will.

"The fact remains that initially you only wanted me for that trust fund," she said. "Even without it, as Duke of Fairborough you're still one of the wealthiest men in England. What do you need another sixty thousand pounds for?"

"I don't need a penny of it. But my cousin doesn't need it, either. Not for what he intends to do with it. He owns the biggest plantation in the West Indies, worked by hundreds of African slaves—including women and children—who are beaten and starved and God knows what else in the cause of making him even wealthier. Think of how many more human beings he can buy with that money."

"I thought slave trading was against the law."

"So is blackmail, but Lady Paxton has been perpetrating it against my stepmother all this time. Daphne was selling those paintings to Plumlee so she could pay off your cousin, who knew the truth about Daphne's origins."

"Don't change the subject—"

"I'm not changing the subject. I'm only trying to give you examples of how all the laws in the world won't stop certain people such as your cousin and mine from doing whatever they please for their own personal gain, even if they have to destroy other people to do it."

"Well, there must be a law against fraud," Serena said grimly. "And like your cousin and mine, you broke it for your own personal gain—to collect that sixty thousand pounds—and you didn't care if you destroyed someone else in the process."

Kit shifted in the chair, crossing one leg over the other. "I take it you're referring to yourself? Pray tell, how have I destroyed you?"

She clenched her fists. "Don't you realize I'm ruined now? You compromised me and tricked me into marriage with a man I thought was Gibson!"

"Actually, I had nothing to do with the marriage. Believe it or not, Serena, it was not my intention to marry you yesterday. If memory serves, you were the one who stood up and told the vicar to marry us. That was not how I wanted it to happen."

She had to concede on that point. Nevertheless, "But it was still your intention to consummate the union!"

"I believe I told you I would not force you to do anything you didn't want to do."

She knew that was true, too, but she wasn't about to admit that she'd desired the duke physically, even if she'd thought all along he was someone else. Though she bristled at the time-honored edict, she said, "I thought I was supposed to submit to my husband."

"In theory, yes. But I must say, Serena, you certainly never behaved as if you were meekly obeying God's command to endure your wifely duty."

Too late she realized that her actions had already

spoken louder than her words—and adding insult to injury, *he* was the one to point it out!

She trembled, ready to explode with rage at the arch smile on his face. "Don't you dare try to turn this around on me, as if *I'm* to blame—"

"I'm not trying to turn things around, and I'm not blaming you for anything. I'm merely stating facts. Heavens, I wasn't accusing you of enjoying our marital relations. Until just a few minutes ago when you hit me in front of everyone, I foolishly considered myself a very lucky man. But everything that happened yesterday, beginning with the abduction, was part of another one of Nick's convoluted pranks. He's the one who got the special license."

"Well, thanks to you *and* him, I'm ruined now!" she wailed. "All the ton will believe I'm married to a manservant who doesn't even exist."

"Ah, but he does exist." Kit lifted his hands and moved them outward. "He's right here, darling. You're married to *me*."

"I'm married to Gibson!" she thundered, brushing the back of her hand across her misty eyes. "The license says 'Alfred Gibson.' I vowed to take Alfred Gibson, not Christopher Woodard, to be my wedded husband. You and I are *not* married, Your Grace. The bishop is downstairs this very minute, and once he hears of this, I can assure you he'll declare the marriage invalid."

"Very well. We'll just tear up the license and make a fresh start, remarry as Christopher Woodard and Serena Langley."

"We'll do no such thing!"

The duke widened his brown eyes and smiled, revealing that dimple in his left cheek. "Oh, but we must. After all, regardless of whether I'm Gibson or Woodard, the fact remains that I have compromised you in every way a lady can be compromised."

Serena's body betrayed her with a strange shudder of pleasure as she remembered all too vividly the many ways he'd done so. Good Lord, she thought in horror, just this morning, only hours ago, this man's tongue—*Kit's* tongue—had stroked and laved her most intimate flesh while she moaned lustfully and clutched his head to her throbbing wet mound, as if she'd feared he'd stop before she found her release.

Her cheeks flaming, she quickly turned away to face the window, though she still saw his ghostly reflection in the glass.

He leaned forward in the chair, as if to stand up. "The bishop, as you said, is downstairs, and I'll just get another special license from him."

"Not before the present marriage is annulled. And that could take a while."

Kit sat back, chuckling mirthlessly. "Indeed it could, since that marriage was consummated. No, my dear, I think the best thing to do is confess the truth about what happened, and tear up yesterday's license."

"I won't allow it. I will insist on an annulment." Serena felt a frisson of gratification now that she had the upper hand. With a little luck, her marriage to Gibson would not be annulled before early September, when Kit turned thirty—in which case he would have to forfeit the sixty thousand pounds, after which he'd no longer have any reason for wanting to marry her.

"But you admitted yourself only moments ago that you've been ruined," he argued.

She crossed her arms over her chest as she resolutely kept her back to him. "So I have. But it's not as if I've ever been very active in Society. So I won't be granted a voucher to Almack's. So Lucinda won't invite me to one of her elegant little routs once she marries

Humphries. I'll consider myself blessed. I'll just continue living the life I've been living all these years with Felice. We've managed quite nicely on the modest stipend my grandmother left me."

She enjoyed a long, lovely moment of silence, savoring her little victory, before Kit very bluntly said:

"Suppose you're pregnant?"

Serena's heart lurched as her fleeting victory crumbled into irrevocable defeat. Just this evening, as she'd entered the great hall downstairs, she'd considered the possibility that she might already be carrying a child.

But it was Gibson's child she'd been hoping for, and the duke's child she dreaded carrying.

She whirled around to glare at him. "What if I'm not?"

"Then you're not, but what if you are? When are you due to learn either way?"

Without a word she turned back to the window, feeling her cheeks flush crimson.

"Probably not soon enough to suit me," Kit surmised. "And unlike my brother and your grandfather, I am not a gambler."

"I beg to differ, Your Grace." She pivoted again to face him. "It seems you took quite a gamble on me already. The way I see it, you wagered if I fell in love with Gibson, then I'd gladly marry Fairborough once I found out they were the same person!"

"Ah, touché. And would you like to know with whom I made that wager?"

"Colfax, obviously."

Kit shook his head. "No. Your charming little abigail was on to me almost from the beginning."

Serena felt as if she'd been struck by lightning. "Are you telling me that Miriam was in on this, too?"

"No, I'm saying she was *on to* it almost from the start," Kit clarified. "Colfax was the one who came up with the idea, and Miriam was the first to figure it out. She herself believed that you would never form an attachment to me as Fairborough, but you would if I were Gibson. And she believed that once you learned who I really was, it would make no difference to you."

"If that's true—and I don't believe it is—then she was wrong! If she'd known who you were, she would have told me."

"If that's what you believe, then why did she allow you to risk your good name with a lowly manservant?"

"But *you* were that lowly manservant! And she knew you were really not only a duke, but my fiancé, so—so—" So *what?* Serena thought wildly, as she felt herself teetering along the jagged jaws of the trap.

"Ex-*act*-ly!" Fairborough declared, rising to his feet.

A fearsome sense of helplessness, as if she were drowning and had nothing to cling to, washed over Serena. "Oh, I just know you're lying about all of this! After lying to me about who you are, what makes you think I'll believe your lies about Miriam?"

"Because she'll only confirm them to you once she returns from Scotland with Jennings. In the meantime, consider this: Why did she encourage you to dally with coachman Gibson? And how would I know that she did?"

Serena only stared at him through a wavering blur of tears as she suddenly remembered Miriam's letter. Not only did the abigail's cryptic words finally make sense, but to Serena's chagrin, they corroborated everything the duke was saying.

He stepped slowly toward her. "Miriam exhorted me to take whatever liberties I felt were necessary with you, while encouraging you to—well, to encourage me. Quite frankly, I was shocked that she of all people—the person responsible for safeguarding your virtue—would dare to even suggest such behavior." He fur-

TRUE PRETENSES

rowed his brow and tilted his head to one side. "Were you shocked, too?"

Of course she'd been shocked, but Serena was too mortified to give Kit the satisfaction of knowing that once again, his thoughts and feelings uncannily echoed hers. She burst out sobbing as she staggered over to the bed, collapsing facedown across the mattress. She soaked the counterpane with a torrent of anguish over the knowledge that as smart as she prided herself on being, she'd been utterly ignorant for the past month. She liked to think of herself as too intelligent to consider that she hadn't seen the truth simply because she hadn't wanted to; even when presented with distinct possibilities to the contrary, she'd stubbornly believed it impossible that the duke would actually do all he'd done to win—no, *steal* her heart.

"Serena . . ." She felt the warmth of Fairborough's hands lightly sliding up her back to her trembling shoulders, and she quickly rolled away from him.

"Please don't," she moaned.

"I never, ever wanted to hurt you," he said again, his voice hovering just above a strangled whisper.

She lifted her head to stare at the damp splotch on the counterpane; she couldn't bring herself to look at him. "None of this would have happened if—oh God, if only my parents, my grandfather—why wouldn't they—" She scarcely knew what she meant to say any more than she could say it; she was heaving so violently with sobs, as years of dormant resentment toward her departed relatives finally erupted from her soul's deepest well.

She dropped her head back onto the counterpane as she heard Kit's footsteps moving to the other side of the bed. She felt the mattress sink ever so slightly near her head, but she dared not look up.

"I know, Serena, if your grandfather hadn't given

your father's farm to my brother, and if only your mother hadn't . . . been the way she was, then you and I probably wouldn't be where we are at this moment. I think you and your sister have suffered a great deal on their account. I can't change the way your mother was, and I can't bring her back any more than I can bring back my own. But I wish more than anything for the chance to make you happy and give you all that's been unfairly denied you and your sister . . . because I love you."

She finally stole a peek at him. Kit was kneeling on the other side of the bed as if saying his prayers, his arms resting on the mattress. He gazed at her intently. This close she could see the faint bruise on his forehead, just below his hairline. Yes, this was the coachman she thought she'd married yesterday. She glimpsed the signet ring on his hand. It was the same hand that had touched the most secret parts of her body, making her moan and writhe with pleasure. And it was the same ring she'd seen his father wearing years ago . . . the same ring that had helped to identify his brother's remains last year. Yes, this was the Duke of Fairborough who had been so passionately intimate with her on three separate occasions since yesterday afternoon.

"Ah, I love to hear my wife moan when I'm inside her. . . ."

She closed her eyes as the memory of those whispered words echoed in her head, prompting another shudder in her womb.

"Serena . . . ?" The same voice, whispering in the present.

She opened her eyes. Kit was expressionless as he knelt at her bedside, obviously waiting for her to say something.

"Why would you want to marry me when you must

know now, after the way I behaved with you—with the coachman—that I'm just like my mother?" she said tremulously. "How do you know I won't abandon our children like she did?"

Kit smiled. "But you're nothing like your mother, Serena. She committed adultery with your father's cousin. All you did was behave a little improperly with the man you later married. That he was a coachman is beside the point; you were following your heart. And how do I know you won't abandon our children? Because you've never abandoned your sister. You've devoted yourself to looking after her when no one else would, not even your own parents. You're willing to sacrifice marriage, motherhood, and the chance to be a duchess, simply to protect Felice, when there are women out there who would cheerfully sell their own kin to the devil just to suffer the burden my father and your grandfather dropped on your shoulders."

Serena felt herself faltering as she stared at him.

Grinning, he added in a teasing tone of voice, "Besides, I'll overlook your indiscretion with the coachman. You're the only one I want to be my wife and the mother of my children."

At those words, she stopped faltering. Fresh anger sizzled through her veins.

Kit lifted his hand as if to touch her tearstained cheek, and she quickly recoiled, sitting up and out of his reach.

"Don't you dare touch me again!" she sputtered. "I'm sacrificing marriage, motherhood, and the chance to be a duchess to protect Felice from *you!* Naturally I'm the only one you want—and not because you love me, but because you want that sixty thousand pounds!"

He buried his face in his hands as Serena burst into a fresh spate of tears. Something deep, deep within her, something primal, cried for him to take her into his arms and exorcise all the agony from her heart, for she realized from past experience that only *this man*, regardless of his true identity, had that power.

But her pride, already battered by his successful deceit, would not allow it.

"Ah, Serena," he said painfully, "for a moment I thought—"

"You lied to me and made a fool out of me, and yet you still expect me to feel for you what I only felt for Gibson!"

He dropped his hands. "It was never my intention to make a fool out of you. All I wanted was to meet you and learn why you didn't want to marry me, and perhaps change your mind about me."

"You know why I never wanted to marry you in the first place!"

"Yes, I do know." His voice broke as he added, "But damn it, Serena, *I didn't do it!*"

"Well, my father didn't do it, either! How do you expect to prove otherwise to me? Why else were you sent to India immediately afterward?"

Kit slowly rose to his feet. "Since I was the younger son, I probably would have gone into the military or even the clergy one day, anyway."

"But not as soon as you did. And if you were truly innocent, then you never would have had to resort to this outrageous charade just to get near me."

He rolled his eyes and threw up his hands. "How else was I to get near you? We've been over that already! You wouldn't give me a chance to prove my innocence—not that I know how to prove it, since no one seems to know the whereabouts of your aunt. You just have to trust me."

Another spasm of sobs racked her body. "And why should I trust you after all that's happened? Why should I trust a man who lied to me for a month about who he was?"

"Oh, Serena, Serena, circles, circles." Kit turned away, but not before she saw that he looked as if he wanted to cry. "I tried yesterday to tell you who I really was, but you didn't want to believe me."

"Are you trying to turn things around again? Are you going to blame *me* for all of this because I wouldn't believe you when you wanted me to?"

"God, no." He turned back to her, his handsome face masked with anguish. "But did I not tell you what I wanted to confess to the vicar when he asked for impediments?"

"Yes, but why didn't you tell him the truth?"

"You said it yourself. He wouldn't have believed me any more than you did. I wanted Kit Woodard to marry you, and I still do. If you only knew how much I wanted you to whisper *my* name, not the coachman's, each and every time I made love to you."

Her voice dripped with acid sarcasm. "How dreadful that must have been for you! Small wonder you got any pleasure out of me—or did you pretend that, too?"

"Please don't say that, Serena. You know that—"

"Why should I believe otherwise?"

He looked at her as if she were mad. "Do you honestly believe I was pretending *that*? Pretending the pleasure you gave me, pretending the love I gave you?"

Hot tears attacked her cheeks. "Why not? Everything else you've done for the past month has been a pretense."

"But not that."

"I don't believe you!"

"Oh God, Serena, for the love of Christ!" His voice cracked with exasperation. "And if I told you that yes, I pretended to enjoy all the pleasure I got from making love to you, would that make your claws retract? I doubt it. No matter what I say to you, even if it's the bloody truth, it will not be enough. In your eyes, I'm damned no matter what."

Rage flared within her. "Listen to yourself. You lie, you swear, you blaspheme. You take advantage of women who can't defend themselves, and as for those who can, you lie and pretend to be someone you aren't so you can take advantage of them, too. You falsely accuse people who are conveniently deceased and no longer able to defend themselves, you—"

"*Stop!*" he barked, so sharply she flinched. "You've made your point. I'm a reprobate utterly beyond all redemption. Fine. If you want to annul yesterday's marriage, by all means do so. For my part, I will not ask the bishop for a special license, nor will I have the banns called in church this Sunday."

An odd chill shuddered through her as she stared at him. "Why not?"

"Because I'm going to finally accept your refusal to marry me," he said, his voice breaking again. "I may as well bury the dead horse I've been flogging all this time, since I can't bear the stench of it any longer."

She pressed both hands to her queasy stomach. "But what if I'm—if there's a babe?"

Silence stretched between them for a long, ominous moment.

Agonized despair shimmered in his brown eyes. "I honestly don't know how to respond to that, Serena, since you'll find fault with whatever I say. We can only hope at this point that there is no babe."

"But the sixty thousand pounds . . ."

"Let Saint Calvin have it," he said bitterly. "I'm sure you'll consider him more worthy of it than I am. The poor man can't possibly be expected to tend his hundred thousand acres of sugarcane all by himself. I suppose there's nothing so egregious about trading in human flesh, as long as he's not pretending to be a coachman to lure all those innocent people into his bloody shackles."

He turned and headed for the door, thrusting his hand into his pocket and pulling out the key. He jammed it into the keyhole, turning it with a sharp click. He twisted the doorknob, but the door wouldn't budge. He slammed the side of his fist against the brass plate with an angry bang, and the key clattered to the floor. He tried the knob again, and the door opened.

He paused and glanced over his shoulder at her, as if he were going to say something else. Serena's heart nearly froze as he opened his mouth slightly, then clamped it shut as he turned and continued out the door, slamming it behind him.

She gazed at the door for a long moment, and saw that he'd left the key on the floor. She was free to lock out the world if she pleased—unless he returned through the servants' passage.

But Serena didn't think the duke would be doing that ever again.

That prospect—or the lack of it—smothered her with dread, forcing another attack of plaintive sobbing.

Where was her precious pride now, when she needed it so desperately to fill the void Kit had just left in her shattered heart?

Chapter Nineteen

Kit wasn't surprised to be summoned to his grandmother's rooms for breakfast the next morning. He was surprised, however, to find someone else taking tea with her.

"Kit, my good fellow, I never got the chance to greet you last night!" the stranger exclaimed, rising from the table where he sat with Eleanor. Kit knew that in his grandmother's day, it wouldn't have been unusual for her to receive gentlemen in her private rooms this early in the morning, even while at her toilette. But this particular admirer, if that's what he was, looked too young to be Eleanor's contemporary.

Kit narrowed his eyes. "And you are . . . ?"

The man reared his head back in surprise. "You mean you don't recognize me? But I recognized you, though you're much bigger than you were last time I saw you. Of course, it helped that Grandmama said you'd be here for breakfast. I'm Calvin Granger, your long-lost cousin."

TRUE PRETENSES

Unfortunately, he hadn't been lost long enough to suit Kit, who only stood with his fists clenched at his sides, unwilling to embrace or even shake hands with his loathsome cousin. Calvin stepped tentatively around him, circling Kit like a vulture closing in on a rotting carcass.

Kit's eyes moved even if the rest of him didn't, warily following Calvin's paces. He was mollified to see that since their last meeting, he'd grown much taller than his cousin. Calvin's own eyes, of pale blue shot with crimson, peered back under heavy lids and over equally heavy bags. His unfashionably long brown hair, pulled back into a queue, was prematurely streaked with gray, while his face was leathery from two decades spent mostly in the Caribbean sun. His nose, however, was red with the telltale broken veins of one who'd also spent a great deal of time drinking Caribbean rum. A garishly embroidered waistcoat only barely disguised Calvin's paunch. Kit thought the fabric better suited to the upholstery in a Calcutta brothel.

Calvin halted in front of Kit, grinning in a display of teeth mottled with brown and yellow stains. "At ease, cousin, you're not in the army anymore. Aren't you going to say anything?"

"Dropped anyone down a well lately?" Kit asked.

Calvin cackled, turning back to their grandmother. "I think we may assume, Grandmama, that Kit did not resolve matters with his betrothed last night. He seems in a rather churlish mood this morning."

"Sit down, Kit, and have some breakfast," Eleanor said. "And do tell us what that was all about last night. I'm sure our guests are talking of nothing else this morning."

"Yes, Kit, do tell," Calvin added.

As Kit sat at the table, he glanced at the fireplace

behind his grandmother, and saw the same pastoral painting that had hung there ever since he could remember.

Only it wasn't the very same, but another one of Felice's brilliant copies. The original, he recalled, was at present on sale in Mr. Plumlee's dingy little shop off Piccadilly.

He picked up the teapot before the hovering footman even had a chance. Not surprisingly, serving himself at the table had become second nature this past month.

He concentrated on pouring tea into his cup. He'd been prepared to explain everything to Eleanor, but not in front of others, and especially *not* in front of Calvin, who held out his own cup. Kit glared back at him.

"Since you're doing the honors," Calvin said with a shrug, practically thrusting his cup under Kit's nose.

He only set down the teapot and reached for the creamer.

"Kit, you've said less than a dozen words since coming in here," said Eleanor. "I hope you're saving your breath for the explanation—it's surely a lengthy one."

He added just enough cream to his tea to form a pale cloud in the cup. "It is, but Calvin doesn't need to hear it."

"You can speak freely in front of him. He's family, and just as much my grandson as you are. Remember what you told Daphne and that insufferable Lady Paxton yesterday afternoon. Now what happened?"

"They say you've been masquerading as a coachman for the past month," Calvin said, as the footman refilled his teacup.

"That's true," Kit replied, stirring his tea more than was probably necessary.

"Whatever for?" asked Eleanor.

Kit did not eat—he was still too upset from last night

TRUE PRETENSES

to have any sort of appetite—but he did sip his tea as he told his grandmother the whole ludicrous story. He made a point of looking only at Eleanor as he spoke, never at Calvin. He preferred to act as if Calvin weren't even there, despite his cousin's frequent guffaws and occasional commentary whenever Kit paused to take a breath or another sip of tea.

Eleanor peered at Kit with narrowed eyes. "You say the name of Serena's aunt is Leah, and that she's a mute?"

"Yes, Grandmama." Kit leaned forward in his chair. "Have you heard of her?"

"Of course she has," Calvin put in. "A Bow Street Runner came here shortly after I arrived day before yesterday, inquiring about a woman by that name."

"Why would he come all the way down here?" asked Kit.

"I'll tell you in a moment," said Eleanor. "But there's still one thing I don't quite understand about Serena. From what you've told us just now, it sounds as if she actually fell in love with you this past month."

Frustration gripped Kit. He wanted to talk about Leah now. With as much patience as he could muster, he said, "She fell in love with *Gibson,* Grandmama."

"Who?"

"The coachman. His name was Alfred Gibson. Now about Leah—"

"What was wrong with just plain 'John Coachman'?"

"I wanted a real name, and Colfax suggested the name of his former coachman who, I understand, now works for Calvin."

Calvin snorted. "I have no idea what my coachman's name is, nor do I care."

"Well, his name is Gibson," said Eleanor. "Perhaps you should address him thusly next time you meet him, and see if he gives you an odd look."

"But Kit's wife or fiancée or whoever is married to him?"

"She's married to *me*," Kit declared.

"But what's the name on the marriage license?"

"Alfred Gibson."

"Which, you say, is the name of my coachman?"

"Yes," Kit ground out, his patience wearing thin.

"So, on paper she's married to my coachman, while in every other sense she's married to you." Calvin brayed with laughter, spraying tea over his side of the table. "I probably shouldn't tell my coachman about this, or he might want to claim his husbandly rights—and with a lady so far above him, no less! But even if he doesn't get ideas, what's to stop Serena from getting them? From the little I've heard about her, it would seem she's far too clever and headstrong for her own good. Obviously takes after her mother in certain ways."

Kit finally glanced at his dissipated cousin. "What are you talking about?"

Calvin wiped his mouth with the edge of the tablecloth. "Suppose Serena, instead, got the idea to grant my coachman his marital rights?"

"Oh, don't be absurd, Calvin!" exclaimed Eleanor.

" 'Tis not so absurd, I assure you, Grandmama. After all, it's not as if she hasn't willingly compromised herself with a coachman already. She just didn't realize he was a duke." He leered back at Kit. "I daresay your beloved Serena prefers men of the lower class. If you ask me, it's obvious why she won't marry you. She doesn't want her own kind. She only cavorted with you because she thought you were a mere servant. I ask you, Kit, would you truly want such a woman for a duchess?"

Kit suddenly felt sick. He'd almost hurled similar words at Serena last night as he stormed out of her room, but he'd somehow managed to bite them back, knowing they were as puerile and damaging as the parting words he'd shot at Daphne nine years ago.

"Marry Serena Langley," said Calvin, "and the next Duke of Fairborough will likely be the offspring of the butler, the gardener, or even the footman here." He grinned at the hovering footman, who could not have avoided hearing every word. "How would you feel, young fellow, to be the sire of a genuine duke?"

A taut thread of rage snapped inside Kit as he seized the teapot and slammed it into Calvin's face. The footman leaped back as the lid flew across the room, while the little tea remaining in the pot splattered over Calvin's waistcoat, losing itself in the intricately gaudy pattern.

Kit bolted to his feet as Calvin sputtered in surprise. "What the—" He yelped as Kit bodily yanked him out of his chair, throwing him against the wall as if he were nothing more than a rotten head of lettuce.

"Christopher James Alexander—" But Kit didn't hear the rest of his grandmother's reprimand, as twenty-five long years of helpless outrage at his cousin's atrocities possessed him like a vengeful demon. All Kit heard were his own terrified screams from a quarter of a century ago, as he dangled upside down over that frightening abyss while Calvin held on to his ankles and laughed wickedly. All he heard were the pitiful howls of his father's beagles echoing from that same well. All he saw were the kittens he'd found in the stable before Calvin came along and scooped them up. To this day he still heard their shrill cries of terror as Calvin tormented them. The time had come to avenge the beagles, the kittens, and a four-year-old boy who'd been too small and powerless to stop his cousin's savagery.

"Come back here, you coward!" he roared, as Calvin

scrambled to his feet, nearly knocking a startled Eleanor out of her chair as he stumbled to the fireplace and grabbed the poker, brandishing it like a sword. Kit hesitated for only a moment as the tip hovered mere inches from his throat; then with a growl he wrested it from Calvin's grip. Calvin promptly turned and fled the room as Kit hurled the poker at him like a javelin. He barely missed Calvin's plump backside.

He staggered back to the table, out of breath. "I'm sorry, Grandmama, but it was either that or call him out, and I'm sure you wouldn't want me to shoot him."

Eleanor took a deep breath as the footman hastily cleaned up the mess. She was clearly shaken from what had just happened. "No, Kit, he shouldn't have baited you like that. I was just surprised because I'd never seen you behave like that before. Calvin, on the other hand, was acting like Calvin. Takes after his wastrel of a father, you know." Tears glistened in her blue eyes. "I didn't want to have breakfast with him, either, but I feared him too much to send him away, and I thought, since he used to bully you so much when you were children—well, it seems the tables have turned, and let's hope for the better."

Kit sank back into his chair. "What about that Bow Street Runner, and Serena's aunt Leah, Grandmama? You said you'd heard of her."

Eleanor dabbed her eyes with a lacy handkerchief. "A mute named Leah? Yes, I have, and well I should. She lives in the dower house."

His eyes widened as he gripped the edge of the table. "You mean *our* dower house? The one down by the—"

"Yes, that one. She's lived there since—oh, since after you went to India. Your father was appointed her protector or some such."

"You mean she's been here at Fairborough all this time, and no one ever told me?"

Eleanor gave a slight shrug as she nibbled daintily on her toast. "No one really knew about it except your father and me. I've scarcely seen you since you returned from India and—well, my dear boy, you never asked."

"But, Grandmama, don't you understand why I was sent to India in the first place?"

"Until today, I'd thought it was because you were your father's second son. I do recall thinking it odd that he'd bought you a commission before you'd even finished your studies at Oxford, but I never thought to question it."

Kit leaned his elbows on the table as he buried his face in his hands. If only he'd approached his grandmother about this *before* he agreed to Nick's idea of posing as the Langleys' coachman!

"I never knew why she was brought here," Eleanor went on. "I've visited her occasionally over the years, and she's likewise visited here, but our conversations, as you might expect, have always been one-sided. She writes notes when she has something important to say."

"Well, I need her to write something important for Serena. I want to go out and see her, Grandmama. Perhaps we could bring her back here and reunite her with Serena."

"Let me finish my breakfast and don the proper attire, and I'll go with you and introduce you."

Kit ordered the footman to have a carriage brought around for him and his grandmother. He restlessly paced the room as he waited for her to dress. At one point he removed the pastoral painting from over the fireplace to look for the initials FCL on the back. He was not disappointed.

"What on earth are you doing?" Eleanor asked, as she finally reappeared dressed and ready to go.

He fitted the canvas back into the frame. "Just wanted to check the name of the artist, since it's concealed by the frame."

"I believe the artist's name is Fragonard. Or is it François Boucher? I can't remember, except it starts with F."

"You're right," he said, reaching up to replace the picture over the fireplace.

He accompanied Eleanor downstairs and into the front courtyard, where several carriages, phaetons, and curricles stood waiting for the various guests who mingled among them.

As Kit helped his grandmother into the open carriage, Calvin suddenly appeared at his elbow.

"Grandmama, I just want to apologize for my behavior upstairs," he said.

"You're forgiven," she replied. "Though I daresay you'll think twice before you bait your cousin again. As you can see he's become a grown man since the last time you tormented him."

"Going for a drive?"

"No, we're going to the dower house to visit Miss Langley's aunt Leah. We're hoping she can persuade her niece to marry Kit, after all."

Kit climbed into the carriage next to his grandmother, and ordered the coachman to move. He didn't want to spend another moment in Calvin's company.

All he wanted now was to pursue this one last chance to win Serena once and for all.

A rap at the door. Since it was just past noon, Serena hoped it wasn't someone summoning her to luncheon. Her morning tea tray still sat untouched on the piecrust table. Though she'd somehow managed to get out of bed and get dressed this morning, her appetite seemed to have abandoned her.

"Who is it?" she called out.

"Calvin Granger, Miss Langley. May I have a word with you?"

She opened the door. "Yes, Mr. Granger?"

"My grandmother has asked me to take you to the dower house to meet your aunt."

She furrowed her brow. "My aunt?"

"Yes. She's in the dower house here at Fairborough. Kit and our grandmother have already left to see her. They're hoping she'll vouch for his innocence and persuade you to accept his offer of marriage."

Serena could scarcely believe her ears. Aunt Leah had been at Kit's ancestral home all these years? How could that be, after what he'd done to her? Or had he done it?

"How do you know she's here, Mr. Granger? Fairborough told me last night that he didn't know her whereabouts."

"Grandmama told him only this morning. Remember, he's been in India for the past nine years, and since returning has spent very little time at his ancestral pile. Would you allow me to escort you to the dower house? If you'll forgive me, Miss Langley, you do look as if the fresh air might do you good."

Was it that obvious she'd spent the morning in tears? She vacillated as she tried to figure out what didn't seem right about Mr. Granger's offer. If he wanted that trust fund, then why would he want to help reconcile her with Kit? She knew Kit didn't need the money, but why was Mr. Granger so willing to forfeit? "Why wouldn't Fairborough ask me to go with him and his grandmother?"

"He believes you want nothing to do with him now. But once you meet your aunt, and she confirms his innocence . . ." He shrugged. "Well, you'll recall what I said last night. I shall have to return to the West Indies with my pockets still to let."

"Only if she really is my aunt, and only if she can assure me that he never harmed her," Serena said firmly, as she finally made her decision. "In which case I'll have to come with you so I can see her for myself. Just give me a moment."

After swiftly donning her yellow spencer and bonnet, she grabbed the marriage certificate, thrusting it into her bodice.

"What's that?" Mr. Granger asked.

"My marriage certificate. I'm sure you've heard all about it. I'd rather not leave it here."

He smiled ruefully. "Afraid Kit will tear it up, eh?"

"Instead of tearing it up, I'd prefer to get the marriage properly annulled." But if Leah corroborated Kit's claims of innocence, Serena thought, then she might marry him yet, if only the swelling on her bruised pride receded enough to allow it.

She accompanied Mr. Granger downstairs and out the front door, where an enclosed carriage awaited them. Numerous people milled about in the courtyard, and as she boarded the carriage, she thought she heard more than one person muttering her name.

Her flight from the great hall last night must be quite the *on-dit* this morning, she thought.

"Take the west road, Gibson," said Mr. Granger. He stepped in behind Serena and a footman closed the door.

Her heart tripped as the carriage began moving. "Your coachman's name is Gibson?"

He sat on the squabs across from her. "Yes. He previously worked for the Duke of Colfax."

"His first name wouldn't be Alfred, would it?"

Granger shrugged. "Not that I pay much attention to my servants' names, but yes, I believe it is." He knit his brow. "I say, isn't that the name my dear cousin used during his masquerade as your coachman?"

"Yes. I'd been led to believe that our new coachman had previously worked for the Duke of Colfax."

"And you married my cousin the other day, thinking he was your coachman, Alfred Gibson? And the marriage certificate is tucked inside your bodice?"

"Yes, but I'm really married to Fairborough."

"No, my dear, I'm afraid you're really married to that man on the driver's box outside."

A dark cloud of foreboding shrouded her as she peered out the window. As the coachman turned onto a road leading away from the castle, she spotted a house through a copse of trees. She couldn't be certain, but she thought it might be the dower cottage. She glanced back at Granger. "I think we may have passed the dower house just now. Perhaps we should turn around, just to be certain."

Granger ignored Serena's suggestion and banged his fist on the window behind the driver's box. "Gibson, I want them galloping!"

Serena tensed at his ominous command, clutching the hand strap as the carriage suddenly picked up speed, rocking and jolting relentlessly down the road.

He flashed her a decidedly unpleasant smile. "Now, Miss Langley, perhaps you'd like to give me the marriage certificate, so I might destroy it for you."

"That's very kind of you, but I can do it myself," Serena said tremulously. "Mr. Granger, must we travel so fast?"

"Aye, because I don't want you to try and flee this carriage."

Her heart thundered as violently as the horses' hooves. "Why would I want to do that?" she asked, dreading his reply.

He narrowed his bloodshot eyes. "You would if I tried

to take your marriage certificate. I strongly suggest you give it to me now, Miss Langley."

She pressed her hand to her bodice, feeling the document through her spencer. "Why do you really want it, Mr. Granger? I don't think it's so you can destroy it for me."

She shrieked as he lunged forward to grab her, ripping her bonnet from her head. She hastily produced the document before he could rip anything else. She flinched as his hand squeezed her breast, and she fought a wave of queasy disgust as he slumped back on the opposite seat, clutching the document. She glanced out the window at the verdant terrain speeding by. He was right: The carriage was racing too fast for her to escape safely. She realized in a flash of panic that he had no intention of taking her to the dower house at all—in which case, where *was* he taking her?

She dared another glance at Granger as he slid the marriage certificate behind his garish waistcoat.

"You're more than welcome to try retrieving it now, Miss Langley," he sneered.

Fear clenched her heart in an icy grip. "What do you want?"

"I want the sixty thousand pounds, of course," he snapped. "And you're going to help me get it by sailing to America with your husband, Alfred Gibson." He jerked his thumb upward to indicate the coachman outside. "We're only a few miles from the sea, where my ship will meet us in a cove. I will accompany you and the coachman aboard, where I will have the pleasure of watching the two of you consummate your marriage before I return ashore to await my cousin's thirtieth birthday, after which I shall claim the trust fund. I need that money to buy another slave ship, since the damned navy seized the only one I had. Two hundred Africans I'd already paid for were aboard that ship. My accounts have been bleeding red ever since! I have a constant need for more slaves to work my plantation, since they invariably drop like flies. You'd think if they could thrive so hardily in a place as barbaric as Africa, they could at least adapt to the Caribbean. God knows I've had no trouble adapting."

God knows Mr. Granger wasn't subjected to beatings, starvation, and living conditions conducive to the spread of disease, Serena thought grimly, as the horror of what this man represented finally became brutally clear to her. She'd heard of slavery in the Americas, of course, but it was so far away from her own world that she'd never considered what it meant to those enslaved, any more than she'd thought about the desolation facing convicts banished to Australia.

"You're mad!" she cried. "Suppose the coachman doesn't agree to be my husband?"

Granger smiled menacingly as he shifted on the seat, reaching behind his back as if to scratch himself. "You underestimate your charms, Miss Langley. I feel certain Gibbons or whatever his name is will be only too eager to find himself leg-shackled to such a fine piece o' muslin." She gasped as he brandished a pistol from the back of his breeches. "And I'm sure you'll be just as willing to submit like a good wife."

"But surely you know after last night that I don't want to marry Fairborough."

"Ah, but women are fickle. And I can't allow you the opportunity to change your mind any more than I could have allowed my other cousin to reach his thirtieth birthday."

She felt the blood draining from her face as she went limp against the squabs. "What are you saying?"

"I'm saying I killed Simon, the tenth Duke of Fairborough, last summer," Granger said flatly. "As his cousin, it wasn't difficult for me to get an invitation to his rural sporting house in Kent. I believe it was once your childhood home. He had some very lavish orgies there with half the House of Lords in attendance, Whigs and Tories alike. Heartening to know they're not so fiercely partisan about everything. But on the night in question, it was just Simon and me and a delicious little morsel he'd managed to abduct from neighboring Colfax Park. Seems the little morsel had been engaged to the Colfax coachman. Well, no sooner did I dispatch dear cousin Simon—with this very pistol, I might add—than along came the coachman to rescue his ladylove. I couldn't very well leave any witnesses to the murder of one of England's wealthiest dukes. And since the coachman was so misguidedly grateful to me for killing the man who'd claimed his fiancée's honor, I decided not only to spare the two of them, but to retain them for as long as I found them useful. The coachman himself dropped the candelabrum next to Simon's body, thus reducing him to ashes and concealing the true cause of death."

The carriage finally rumbled to a halt, and Serena glanced out the window to see a gray, rocky beach embracing a small cove, near the mouth of which was moored a clipper. But even though the carriage was now still, she didn't dare try to escape, not with that pistol trained on her.

"I took the coachman and his wench back to my island," Granger went on. "The wench, however, did not survive the voyage. Women make very poor sailors, as I'm sure you'll find out in the days to come. Your mother wasn't a very good one, either."

A dreadful chill clutched at Serena's heart. "What do you mean by that? What do you know about my mother?"

"I know that she and your cousin Marcus came to my island after he killed your father in a duel. Your mother took very ill on the voyage across the Atlantic, and never recovered. And since I had no use for Marcus, I buried him next to her."

Tears stung her eyes as she gaped at him in horrified disbelief. For years she'd wondered what had become of the mother who'd never wanted her or Felice. Frequently it had crossed her mind that her mother might be dead, but to finally learn it was a fact struck a blow at her heart.

"At least the coachman survives," Granger said. "We returned only this last month to see to the next duke."

"So you were going to kill Kit, too?"

He shot her a scathing look. "What sort of fool do you take me for, Miss Langley? Two Dukes of Fairborough in a row, dying under suspicious circumstances, a year apart almost to the very day? I may as well march myself into Bow Street and save them the trouble of delivering me to the gallows themselves. No, instead I decided to make his fiancée disappear. I have numerous connections along the Barbary Coast. I could have sold you into a harem, and for a very high price, in view of your coloring. Or, depending on the extent of your beauty and the size of your breasts, I thought of keeping you for myself on my island. But as it happens, Simon was right—you're not all that beautiful, and your breasts aren't big enough to suit me. That we have a piece of paper declaring you the lawful wife of the coachman, who is now opening the door, provides a very neat solution to the problem of what to do with you." He glanced out the open door at the real Alfred Gibson. "I say, coachman, did you know this lady has a marriage certificate stating that she's married to a man with the same name as yours?"

The coachman, a short, thin man with a nondescript face, blinked in bewilderment. "You mean I'm not the only Alfred Gibson in the world?"

"For our purposes, you are now the only one. It's been a long time since you've had a woman, hasn't it? How long?"

"Not since Sadie, m'lord."

With the pistol, Granger gestured toward Serena. "When my ship arrives, they will send out a longboat for us. Once aboard ship, you can have her all you want."

"I couldn't do that, m'lord, a fine young lady such as—"

"You will, or you'll be shot!" Granger now aimed the gun at Gibson. "And I'm going to watch. And who knows, maybe I'll try her out myself when you're done."

Serena fought to suppress her fear as he prodded her out of the carriage. With the coachman in front of her and Calvin behind her, she stumbled down a steep, narrow path to the beach where Granger indicated a rock where she should sit.

She trembled as Granger leered at her, as if eagerly anticipating the fate awaiting her aboard ship.

He licked his lips. "Tell me, coachman, when we get to my cabin, would you like to undress her yourself?"

"I'll do whatever you say, m'lord."

"Trouble is, I can't make up my mind whether I want to grant you such a privilege, or do the honors myself." He aimed his pistol at her pounding heart. "Or maybe we'll force her to stand in front of us and strip for our own pleasure," he added thoughtfully, his bloodshot gaze burning so intensely into Serena, that she felt as if her clothes were disintegrating into ashes before his very eyes. Strange, she thought, how Kit's burning gaze two days ago had inflamed her desire for him, while Calvin's burning gaze only made her sick with revulsion, fear, and a shame so powerful that it toppled what little remained of her already crumbling pride.

TRUE PRETENSES

That was when Serena realized that she truly loved Fairborough, whether he was a coachman or a duke, despite her longstanding belief that he'd attacked her aunt Leah. Only how much truth was there in that belief? "You just have to trust me," he'd told her last night. That pathetic, albeit heartfelt entreaty had been his only defense against the accusation that had kept Serena so implacably set against him for so long.

And she did trust him. Too late she did.

Her desperate gaze swept the shore, searching for any sign of life that might rescue her from this smothering cold nightmare.

Alas, there wasn't a soul in sight. And how could anyone know where she was right now? Certainly people had seen her board the enclosed carriage with Granger. But for all they knew, he was only taking her for a ride around the Fairborough estate. Who would dream that he was abducting her aboard his ship?

It might be hours before someone noticed that she and Mr. Granger had not returned. Hours before the Duke of Fairborough would order the formation of search parties, by which time she and Granger could be far out to sea.

Or would Kit even bother, once he'd learned that she'd gone off with Granger? Dread squeezed her heart as she remembered his words from last night: "I'm going to finally accept your refusal to marry me," after which he'd said his cousin could have the sixty thousand pounds.

Dear God. Kit wouldn't bother to come after her at all. Why, oh, why had she allowed her wretched pride to push him away last night?

She burst into tears at the realization that her dire fate was now sealed. And by her own hand.

Chapter Twenty

A maid showed Kit and Eleanor into the cozy parlor of the dower house. "The Duke of Fairborough and the Dowager Duchess of Fairborough, ma'am."

As if he'd last seen her only yesterday, Kit instantly recognized the woman who stood up and curtsied. He saw a vague resemblance to Serena in her eyes and the shape of her mouth as she smiled.

"Miss Leah has been expecting Your Grace," the maid told Kit. "A Bow Street Runner came all the way from London the other day and told us that you were looking for her. She wrote you a letter in the meantime."

Kit glanced at Leah. "Perhaps I should explain why I've been searching for you—"

She flipped up a hand as she bustled over to the secretary and opened a drawer. She drew out a sealed letter and offered it to him.

"The Bow Street Runner said only that you needed Miss Leah to assure her niece of your innocence in a certain unfortunate incident many years ago," the maid explained. "He didn't know the specifics, but she knew precisely what he referred to."

Kit glanced down at the letter Leah had just handed him. It was addressed to Christopher Woodard, Duke of Fairborough.

"Perhaps we should sit and have some tea?" Eleanor suggested. "Kit, why not read the letter aloud?"

He remained standing as he broke the seal and unfolded the letter, which was very lengthy. As he quickly skimmed over the words Leah had written, he felt a burning mist in his eyes. He glanced up at Serena's aunt, who nodded and smiled at him, as if to reassure him that nothing in the letter would hurt him.

He sat down in an armchair adjacent to the fireplace, while Eleanor and Leah sat on the sofa.

"Kit . . . ?" his grandmother prodded.

He found his voice, and began reading.

" 'Your Grace, many years ago I wrote a letter similar to this one and gave it to your father. He had made it known to all concerned that you were sent into the Royal Army because your position as his younger son dictated a military career. However, because you had not yet completed your studies at Oxford, another rumor circulated that you were dispatched to India on my account, following a scandalous incident at Langley House on Hampstead Heath the night of May 21, 1804. You know of the incident as you were there; however, be assured that you are innocent of any wrongdoing. I have wondered for many years if because of what happened that night, you might not clearly remember all that transpired.'

" 'I was staying at Langley House as the guest of my sister, Viscountess Winslow. Because of my affliction, neither she nor her husband, nor her father-in-law, the Earl of Paxton, wished my presence at a dinner party they held for the Prince of Wales that night. The party was still in progress when I went to my sister's bedchamber in search of a posset to help me sleep. I found her husband's cousin, Mr. Marcus Langley, in her bed as if he was waiting for her to come to him.' "

Kit glanced up. "Now I don't recall seeing Marcus Langley at dinner that night. I can only assume, because of his scandalous relationship with Lady Winslow, that her husband did not wish to sit at the same table with him."

Leah nodded.

Kit continued: " 'Mr. Langley decided very quickly to take advantage of me. I was only in my night rail, while he was already completely undressed. I couldn't even cry for help, which he found most amusing. A door opened to admit what I hoped would be my salvation. You stood there for scarcely a heartbeat before begging our pardon. I think you mistakenly believed you had walked in on an assignation.' "

He chuckled and glanced up again. "I do remember that, and you're correct it was exactly what I thought—or at least I thought it was Serena's parents neglecting their guests."

He resumed reading. " 'I remember opening my mouth as wide as I could in a silent scream, imploring you with my eyes. You looked as if you were about to leave; then you paused as you saw me silently entreating you for help. You dashed over to us, tore Mr. Langley off of me, and planted a facer that sent him sprawling to the floor away from me.'

" 'You knelt next to me to ask if I was all right, but I couldn't answer. All too quickly, Mr. Langley regained his senses and came up behind you with a large candlestick in his hand. He smashed it over the back of your head and you fell over me, nearly crushing me. Mr. Langley rolled you to your side but did not roll you off of me. He undid your breeches and put the two of us in a compromising position. Before leaving, he took a decanter of brandy and splashed it all over you and me and the floor surrounding us, to make it look as if you'd passed out from too much drink. I remember him saying, "I've heard from others that young Woodard can't hold his liquor, which is why he refrains from strong drink—at least until this evening." ' "

Kit slapped the letter into his lap as he glanced from his grandmother to Leah, thinking of the day he'd first met Serena, when she'd splashed her cousin Warren with brandy to make his father think he'd merely overindulged. "I think I know now where Serena learned that little trick about splashing unconscious men with brandy. It must be an old Langley family secret."

"But you see, it wasn't her father who attacked Leah after all," said Eleanor. "It was his cousin, that bounder Marcus."

"Only how could I have mistaken him for Serena's father? They didn't look that much alike."

"No, but I recall they had the same color hair and the same build, and under the circumstances, Kit, I daresay it would have been all too easy for you to have mistaken one for the other."

He shook his head. "It all happened so suddenly and so quickly that I scarcely remember all the details. And when he knocked me unconscious, that only blurred what memories I do have of that night." He absently rubbed the back of his head as if, after all these years, he might still feel the bump where Marcus had struck him with the candlestick.

"Read on, Kit," his grandmother urged.

He did: " 'Mr. Langley left us. I tried with all my might to move you off of me, or at least wriggle out from beneath you, but I was too weak and you were too heavy. Nor could I get you to regain consciousness. I could scarcely breathe, and feared I would suffocate when my sister walked in. She screamed, and presently the entire party, to include His Royal Highness, gathered in the room. My sister seemed not to care that she was exposing my shame to her guests. Her husband lifted you from me and slapped you until you regained consciousness.'

" 'For the next year, my sister kept me locked in my room, denying me paper and ink with which to communicate. It was my little niece, Felice, who let me out long enough to find what I needed one evening when everyone else was at a party in Town. I wrote a letter to my brother-in-law, Lord Winslow, telling him what had really happened that night when you were found with me. I left the letter on the desk in his study, and the next morning Winslow, while my sister was still abed, took me into Town to see your father at Woodard House.'

" 'After apprising your father of your innocence, Winslow said he felt partly responsible for your having been sent into the army so prematurely. He said he should have demanded satisfaction from Mr. Langley years before. He stated his intention to do so before myself and the duke. Winslow asked that in the event he did not survive the duel, the duke look after me, as I had no other family aside from my sister, who wished to see me in Bedlam Hospital. Your father sent me to Fairborough that same day.'

" 'The duel took place days later. Mr. Langley killed Winslow and fled the country with my sister. Shortly thereafter, the duke informed me that he had met with Winslow's father, Lord Paxton, to discuss the future of his orphaned granddaughters.'

" 'Your father knew that your older brother, the Marquess of Linden, had taken Winslow's farm the previous year in exchange for Paxton's markers. The Duke of Fairborough agreed to keep Paxton solvent, provided he betrothed one of his granddaughters to Lord Linden. To make Linden agree, the duke established a trust fund of ten thousand pounds per annum, with the stipulation that it pass to his nephew, Mr. Calvin Granger, if a Langley daughter did not marry either the Marquess of Linden or Lord Christopher Woodard before their thirtieth birthdays. The duke believed that even if Lord Linden eschewed marriage to Miss Langley and thus forfeited the trust fund, that you, Lord Christopher, would endeavor to see that Mr. Granger did not collect the trust fund, forasmuch as you shared your father's enmity for his sister's son. His Grace said he had been chary of Mr. Granger ever since an incident years before, in which his nephew cast some of the Duke's best hunting dogs down a well.'

" 'Your father was always confident that Mr. Granger would never see whatever amount of money would be in the trust fund when His Grace finally breathed his last.'

" 'In closing, I must remember that I still owe you thanks for coming to my aid that evening.' "

Kit finally laid down the letter, gazing gratefully at Leah. "I also owe thanks to you, for writing this so I may put things right with Serena. She believed that I was truly your assailant, and that I must have attacked you because your affliction made you easy prey. Consequently, she believed I might attack her sister Felice for the same reason. I'm afraid Daphne is the one most responsible for turning Serena against me."

"Only why would she do such a thing?" Eleanor asked.

"Perhaps out of vengeance, since I childishly insulted her right before I departed for India," Kit surmised. "Or perhaps she feared her true origins would be made public, if she became so closely related by marriage to the daughter of her father's vicar. I don't think it matters now. I just wish my father might have written to me while I was in India, to apprise me of my vindication. You were the only one who ever bothered to correspond with me, Grandmama."

"But he did write to you, Kit."

"No, he didn't. I never heard a word from him after I left England."

"Well, he'd never been a very faithful correspondent—even when he was a young boy at Eton, he never wrote to me or your grandfather. But I do recall seeing a letter addressed to you on his desk, the day after he passed away. What with all the ensuing confusion in the household, I don't think anyone ever bothered to post it. I'm sure if you search his study, you'll find it."

"Unless Simon took it and—"

"Simon never came to Fairborough after he inherited," Eleanor said flatly. "The letter must be there, Kit."

He sighed, wondering what his father could have written to him after so many years of silence—and so shortly before his death.

The maid entered with the tea cart.

"Oh, no, I don't think we should stay for tea." Kit glanced at Leah. "I'd like to return to the castle so we can reunite you with your niece."

"But we just got here," said Eleanor. "And look, Kit, there's a plate of scones on the cart. You love scones, and you didn't eat a bite at breakfast this morning."

"I wasn't hungry and I'm still not hungry." He swore he couldn't eat another bite till he'd reconciled with Serena.

"Then you'll have to wait while I enjoy some tea, and no, you're not leaving without me. You spoiled the party last night, but you won't spoil this."

TRUE PRETENSES

For the next hour, Kit struggled not to squirm in his chair while the ladies had their impromptu tea party. Eleanor regaled Leah with the story Kit had told her this morning. He occasionally found himself chuckling at Eleanor's account of the more ludicrous aspects of his charade. Nicholas was right: Kit had enjoyed a wild lark as Serena's coachman.

If only it hadn't ended in disaster.

Another quarter hour while Eleanor used the necessary and Leah donned her bonnet and pelisse, and finally they went out to the open carriage, where the coachman had been patiently sitting on the box all this time.

Guilt jabbed Kit. Had he forgotten so quickly what it was like to be in that man's position? He should have sent the coachman to the kitchen for his share of tea and scones.

They journeyed back to the castle through wooded hills. Just as they emerged from the woods the ocean came briefly into view, and a ship could be seen just off the coast.

"That looks like Calvin's ship," Eleanor remarked.

"What's his ship doing here?" asked Kit, craning his neck to watch the vessel bobbing in the waves.

"He has a ship moored out in our cove. How else do you think he came to England?"

Kit turned around. "Then why did Colfax tell me that on his way from London the other day, Calvin passed him in a carriage driven by Gibson?"

"He brought his ship here, took the carriage to London, then came back to Devon. Nothing odd about that. Surely he wouldn't come all the way to England without visiting London?"

Kit planned to send Calvin sailing straight back to the West Indies as soon as possible. In a few moments, Serena would be reunited with Leah, Kit would be exonerated, and he'd have the upper hand once again. When Calvin found he couldn't collect that trust fund Kit was sure his cousin would return to the Caribbean almost immediately.

Upon entering the castle, he ran straight upstairs to Serena's room. He'd wager she hadn't emerged all day. He wouldn't have left his own bed this morning if his grandmother hadn't commanded his presence in her rooms.

He was out of breath as he finally reached her door and tapped lightly. "Serena? It's Kit."

No response, which was scarcely surprising. After last night, why would she want to let him in?

"Serena, I have a wonderful surprise for you. We've found your aunt Leah. Surely you'd like to come downstairs and meet her?" He waited for a reply. Nothing. "I don't blame you for not believing me, but what if I brought her up here?"

Silence. Maybe she was asleep. He tried the knob, and the door opened easily. He glanced all around, but no one was there.

He stepped over to the tea tray on the piecrust table, next to the candelabrum he'd left last night. The toast was untouched, the teacup still upside down. He picked up the teapot. It was full . . . and cold. Serena had less appetite than he.

He heard a familiar feminine voice calling his name from far down the hallway. That wasn't Daphne, was it? He rushed out of the room to meet her. As she scurried up to him, she looked even more frightened than she had that day when he'd surprised her in the coachman's persona.

"Daphne, are you all right? What is it?"

"Eleanor just told me you were looking for Serena, but she's not here—"

"So I've gathered."

TRUE PRETENSES

"No, Kit, you don't understand. Several people saw her get into an enclosed carriage with Calvin." Daphne looked concerned. "They weren't going for a pleasant drive through the countryside were they?"

"Oh my God," he muttered, as he gave his stepmother a quick reassuring squeeze on the arm. "It's all right, Daphne—I suspect I know where they went. Go back to Grandmama."

He broke into a run down the hall. He didn't stop till he reached his own room, where he grabbed his pistol, still loaded.

He nearly flew down the staircase, pausing just long enough to pull Leah's letter from his coat pocket. He gave it to his grandmother. "Hold this until I come back with Serena. I don't want anything to happen to it."

He dashed out to the courtyard. There were no saddled horses in sight, but he spotted a phaeton hitched up and waiting. Nicholas and Rosalind stood next to it.

He bounded over and nearly vaulted into the seat as his friend and half sister leaped back.

"What are you doing, Kit?" she cried. "Mama said Nicholas could take me for a drive."

"And I say he can't, end of argument," Kit said tersely, seizing the reins and urging the horses into a gallop.

"You talk just like Papa used to!"

The phaeton thundered down the narrow west road that stretched all the way to the sea. He hadn't driven at such breakneck speed since he was in India, where he'd entered many a carriage race in Calcutta.

He'd never lost a race, and by God, he wasn't about to now.

As he deftly steered the horses around a curve, he saw an enclosed carriage ahead, and beyond it a pale gray light framed by thick trees. He pulled back on the reins as he neared the carriage, its own horses tethered to a nearby tree.

He jumped down and rushed over to the enclosed vehicle. Just as he feared, there was no one inside, though he did see Serena's bonnet on the floor.

He sprinted to the edge of the woods, catching a whiff of brine and a powerful gust of cold air as he reached the top of the beach. There, at the mouth of the cove, was Calvin's ship.

And nearly halfway out was a longboat carrying four figures. He immediately recognized Serena's bright yellow spencer.

He tore down the steep, narrow footpath that twisted around large rocks and chunks of driftwood, till he reached the dark gray sand of the beach, where foamy waves crashed against the shore.

Kit stood at the edge of the surf, surveying the longboat. Serena sat between the oarsman and a lump who could only be Calvin. Was it just the angle, or did the boat look as if it might be listing at the stern, where Calvin sat?

All Kit needed to do was catch their attention. Just as he cupped his hands over his mouth to shout, Serena suddenly leaped up in the boat, screaming and waving to him.

Calvin yanked her down and the boat rocked precariously. Even though he knew they were out of range, Kit pulled out his pistol as his cousin turned to see who had excited Serena.

Kit made a great show of aiming his pistol at the boat. Calvin laughed raucously, waving his arms like a windmill.

"Go on, Kit, see if you can shoot me from this far away!" Calvin swayed from side to side, making the boat pitch.

"That's it, keep up the posturing, you arrogant bastard," Kit muttered. "Soon enough you'll want to stand up."

"How well can you hit a moving target?" Calvin brandished his own pistol. "Why, I have a better chance of hitting *you!*"

"No!" Serena screamed, as she lunged forward to grab Calvin. With his elbow he pushed her backward and she fell into the oarsman.

He stood up, holding his arms parallel with his waist to keep his balance. "You had your chance with her, Kit; now she and the sixty thousand pounds are mine! What are you going to do? Go ahead and shoot!"

Without warning, Serena sat up and grabbed Calvin's pistol. He yelled in protest and twisted around, struggling with her as she tried to wrest the weapon from his grasp.

The pistol suddenly fired amid a cacophony of screams, one of them Kit's own. Dear God, had she been shot?

Calvin tumbled into the water, nearly capsizing the boat.

"Hold on, Serena!" Kit shouted, as the boat tipped steeply. She threw herself onto the opposite side along with the others and with their combined weight, the boat righted itself.

Or could Calvin have been shot? The bastard was nowhere in sight. The oarsman slowly turned the boat and began rowing toward shore.

"Kit!" shouted a man's voice from behind him.

He spun around to see Nicholas and Daphne on matching roans, gingerly making their way down the narrow path from the woods to the beach.

"I knew you didn't seize that phaeton to protect Rosalind from a confirmed rake like me," said Nicholas. "Daphne told me what happened, so here we are."

Kit pocketed his pistol. "I can't be certain, but I think Serena just shot Calvin."

Nicholas dismounted. "We heard the shot and saw him fall into the water, but I don't think he was wounded. He was probably so startled by the report that he panicked and went for an impromptu dip. Serena looks all right."

"I hope he drowns," Daphne said.

"Ah, no such luck," Nicholas replied. "There's his head bobbing on the other side of the boat."

Calvin thrashed in the water, entreating somebody to save him.

"Start swimming, you bloody fool!" Kit bellowed. "I know you know how, you tried to drown me in these very waters twenty years ago!"

"Maybe the tide will wash him ashore," said Nicholas. "We summoned some of the estate workers to come down and help hold him until the proper authorities arrive."

Kit finally regarded his stepmother, perched sidesaddle on her roan mare. "And what brings you here?"

"When Nick said he was going out to help you, I insisted on coming along. I want to see Calvin get what he deserves, and I don't want to wait another minute to make peace with your bride and her sister. After the way I've treated them I owe them that, especially since they're joining the family."

Kit could not suppress a grateful smile.

Daphne smiled back. "You might want to dry your tears before Serena reaches the shore."

He lifted his hand to his face, and felt something wet on his cheekbone. He would have sworn it was a droplet blown in from the sea, but couldn't because it was unquestionably warm.

Nicholas slapped him on the back. "I didn't want to be the one to tell you."

"Bloody hell," Kit hissed under his breath. "I thought I'd lost her forever."

TRUE PRETENSES

Daphne started sliding down from her mare, and he quickly stepped forward to help her dismount. "Thank you, Kit. Serena's aunt wanted to come, too. I'm so glad she's been found—truly, I had no idea she was at Fairborough all this time, because I rarely come down from London. But she and Eleanor thought it best to return only as far as the dower house."

Thanks to the incoming tide, the longboat rapidly approached shore. Calvin was now chest deep in water, and appeared to be wading.

"Serena, are you all right?" Kit shouted, once the longboat was about thirty feet away.

"Yes, I'm fine," she called back, and she tossed Calvin's pistol into the water.

But Kit couldn't wait another minute for her to reach the safety of dry land. He quickly doffed his coat and tossed it to Nicholas, then splashed headlong into the surf, swiftly making his way toward the longboat.

"Oh, Kit, I can't believe you came!" she exclaimed. "I was so frightened to death you wouldn't. I should have trusted you!"

He reached the side of the longboat, the water up to his thighs as he held out his arms to her. "I insist on bringing you back to shore myself. Put your arms around my neck."

His heart soared as Serena, without hesitation, lunged forward, and threw her arms around his neck. She clutched him tightly as he lifted her from the boat and into his arms.

"Kit, you'll catch your—ohh!" She tensed as he nearly lost his balance, but he kept a firm grip on her as he steadily waded back to the shore. "As I was saying, I'm afraid you'll catch your death of cold from doing this."

"Only my legs, and I'm wearing boots." He smiled into her opalescent eyes as she pulled herself up, bringing her face closer to his. Her hair had fallen loose of its tortoiseshell combs.

"Still, I think I should do something to warm you up when we get home." She pressed her lips to his.

Kit came to a standstill in knee-deep water as the sweet taste of her tongue sought his, and her arms closed in tighter around his neck. She broke the kiss, gazing into his eyes with the same adoration he'd seen two days ago, when he'd entered her for the very first time. He felt his legs weakening, and he dipped just slightly, but Serena scarcely batted a lash as she clung confidently to him.

His eyes met her incredibly loving gaze. "I nearly dropped you that time."

"But I knew you wouldn't," Serena replied. "Because I do trust you, Kit, with all my heart."

He hoped that was another droplet from the sea he felt in his eye. "You said something about when we get home. Where is home?"

She smiled. "Right here at Fairborough, of course."

He strode over to where Nicholas and Daphne waited.

Several estate workers had arrived, and were already splashing into the water to get Calvin.

Kit retrieved his coat from Nicholas, and as he put it back on, Serena ran her fingers through her tangled hair, plucking out the loose combs. "Could you put these in your pocket for me, please? They're the only pair I have. Oh, Kit, I swear I'll never again go anywhere without you!"

He laughed as he tucked the combs into his coat pocket. "I'll buy you a hundred pairs. And didn't I once tell you that you needed me to keep you out of scrapes?"

"When I thought you were the coachman, yes." She gazed at him with tear-filled eyes. "Kit, Calvin killed not only your brother, but my cousin Marcus . . ."

Shock rippled through Kit. "What—"

"And my mother died on his island. I often feared she was dead, but still . . ." Serena began sobbing in earnest as she hid her face in her hands.

"Oh, sweetheart," he murmured, and wrapped his arms around her, holding her close against him. This time she did not put up the slightest struggle, but submitted willingly to his consoling embrace. "I know how dreadful it is. And I'm right here, I'm always here."

"And I'm sorry about what happened to Simon, too," she added, gasping on her sobs.

"It's all right, darling. I'm so sorry." Kit stroked her hair as he continued fighting back all those briny, mysteriously warm droplets that kept blowing in from the sea.

Still clutching his shoulders, she lifted her head from his chest. The breeze from the sea blew her hair in all directions; most of it across her face. "I'm sorry, too. For everything, but most especially for last night."

The longboat reached shore, and Nicholas strode forward to greet it. "Well, if it isn't my former coachman! How are you, Gibson?"

But as Gibson leaped out of the boat, he had eyes only for Kit. "Your Grace, I just want to tell you I never meant to set your brother's farm afire last year. I only wanted to get my Sadie back. Mr. Granger made me—"

"What do you know about that fire and Mr. Granger's involvement?" Kit demanded.

Gibson quickly explained. Kit slumped down on a large log of driftwood, feeling as if he were hearing about Simon's death for the first time. Serena stood behind him and slid her arms over his shoulders, folding her hands over his pounding heart. He covered her hands with his own as he absorbed Gibson's account in silence. If not for that sixty thousand pounds, Kit's brother would still be alive.

"But then you might not have Serena," Daphne pointed out when he voiced his thoughts aloud; her own eyes shone with tears. "Your father told me after you left for India that sometimes good things come out of even the worst situations. Simon was never happy, Kit, that's why he was the way he was. But where he is now, with your mother and father, you can be sure he's happy."

"Thank you, Daphne." Kit squeezed Serena's hands, then reluctantly broke from her embrace and stood up. "I think I must agree with you for once."

Serena looped her arms around him. "Calvin took our marriage certificate and hid it in his waistcoat. It's surely ruined now, but I don't care." A smile lit up her tearstained face, still partially covered by her long, windblown tresses. "Now we can pretend as if that marriage never happened, so I can marry you instead."

Kit brushed the curls from her face, holding her hair firmly in place with his hands on either side of her head. "Ah, you're so very beautiful. But I told you, my darling, regardless of whether I'm the coachman or the duke, you're already married to me . . . in *every* sense."

"I just want to be married to Christopher Woodard now," Serena whispered, bringing her lips back to his.

He released her silken hair to put his arms around her again, and her curls flew free, seeming to tickle every part of his face as he devoured her mouth with his own.

She abruptly broke away. "Oh, goodness, I almost forgot—we're not alone."

"I suppose Christopher Woodard and Serena Langley will have to get married now," came Nick's voice from behind Kit.

Serena rushed over to him and threw her arms around him. "Thank you, Nick, for everything."

He gave her a quick hug in return. " 'Tis nothing at all, Serena. Kit's a very lucky man . . . finally. Now why don't you two run along and get married again or something? I'll settle everything here."

"Thanks, Colfax," said Kit.

The estate workers dragged a dripping, sputtering Calvin ashore.

"Why didn't you let me drown?" he demanded, as they tied him up.

"Because you shouted for someone to save you," Nicholas replied. "We'll gladly throw you back in if you like, but you're going to stay tied up."

"Let's go," Kit murmured to Serena, as he took her hand into his and led her to the path that twisted up from the beach. "Daphne wants to make peace with you and Felice—but I think that can wait for later."

"I would never have gone with your cousin, Kit, except he said he was going to take me to see my aunt at the dower house. Is she really there?"

"Indeed she is." He squeezed her hand and smiled as they climbed the path. "I didn't know myself until this morning. We'll go see her now. My grandmother's with her."

Holding hands all the way, Kit and Serena made their way to the phaeton, where he helped her into the seat. He climbed up next to her, taking the reins as he turned to look at her. Her eyes and face were red and puffy, while her hair was wildly disheveled. But she was still the most beautiful sight he'd ever seen. Happiness filled his heart as she gifted him with a smile.

He beamed back. "Well, Miss Langley, for once you're riding next to me instead of somewhere behind me."

She wrapped both her arms around his left one, resting her head on his shoulder. "I think I like it better this way. You don't need this arm to drive, do you?"

"No, I only need it for you to hold." He flicked the reins and the horses broke into a brisk trot.

Eleanor and Leah were waiting on the front porch of the dower house when they arrived a short time later.

"Auntie!" Serena leaped from the phaeton the moment it stopped, and she ran up the front walk. She and her aunt shared a long, tight embrace, and were still clutching each other by the time Kit joined them.

They entered the cottage, where Kit and Serena raided the plate of scones on the table. Their appetites had clearly returned, Kit noted with amusement, as he divided the last scone between them.

"I take it from the way you two are standing so close together at that table that we're going to have a wedding after all?" said Eleanor.

"Yes, and that reminds me . . ." Kit glanced at Serena as he nibbled a final crumb off his fingertip. "Your aunt Leah gave me a letter I'd like you to read. . . ."

Leah pulled it out of her reticule and returned it to him.

"Here," he said, offering it to Serena. "This should—"

He broke off his words as she clasped her hands over his. She gazed intently into his eyes. "I don't need to read it, Kit. I told you, I trust you now with all my heart."

"But I was wrong about it being your father," he said softly. "It was actually your cousin Marcus."

She sighed. "I should have known."

He smiled ruefully. "Can you ever forgive me for falsely accusing your father?"

She smiled back. "Only if you can forgive *me* for falsely accusing *you*."

"Agreed," Kit said gladly, as the two of them embraced and kissed again.

TRUE PRETENSES

* * *

Kit still wanted to get a special license and marry immediately, as long as the bishop was at Fairborough, but Serena resisted, and not because she wanted the sort of wedding he'd described for her the other day at the inn. She wanted Felice present for her nuptials—in fact, she wanted Fairborough Castle to become Felice's new home.

She also wanted Miriam and Mr. Jennings present, and even Jemma and Hamish, if ever they dared to return from Scotland. Cousin Archie assured her that he approved of their marriage, and would happily welcome them back to England.

And to Serena's surprise, Harriet not only agreed with her husband, but announced her intention to join him at Paxton Hall in Yorkshire. Now that her only daughter was married, Harriet saw no reason to remain near London and its marriage mart.

But Kit had been adamant. He did not want the next Duke of Fairborough born less than nine months after their marriage. They debated the issue all the way from the dower house to the castle that afternoon, and continued over dinner.

"But everyone knows now that you were posing as my coachman," she argued.

"But not everyone knows that you married him and consummated the union," Kit countered.

"I want Felice and Miriam and Jemma to be here," she insisted.

"My dear, it could be weeks before Miriam and Jemma return from Scotland with their husbands."

They called a cease-fire during the dancing that followed. Since Serena hadn't spent a great deal of time in society, she didn't know much about dancing, but Kit patiently and cheerfully led her through all the various, intricate steps.

"I must have danced 'Mr. Beveridge's Maggot' a thousand times in Calcutta," he told her, as they twirled around each other. "I can do it with my eyes closed and not hit a single dancer out here."

Serena believed him. His movements were graceful and precise, and he looked so handsome in his black evening coat, white cravat, and waistcoat of palest silver.

How could she not wish to marry him this very minute, right in the middle of the parquet dance floor?

It was past midnight when everyone retired. Kit insisted Serena take her aunt's letter, so after she got ready for bed, she sat cross-legged on the mattress in her night rail, and pored over her aunt's written words. If only she'd known all these years of Leah's whereabouts! But she supposed the secrecy had been necessary to keep Leah from someplace worse—like Bedlam.

She folded the letter and placed it next to the candle on the nightstand. For a long while she gazed at the flame, thinking of all that had happened today.

At the behest of the authorities, Calvin was already on his way to London, where he would be tried for the murders of Simon, the tenth Duke of Fairborough, and Marcus Langley.

Serena and Daphne had settled their differences. And the real Alfred Gibson already had a new position—as the Langleys' coachman.

Now if only she could settle her differences with Kit about their nuptials.

She started as she heard another scuffling sound in the corner on the other side of the nightstand, and she stiffened on the bed, for she still couldn't help thinking there were mice. But she watched as a perfectly vertical crack appeared in the wall, and the candle flickered wildly as the crack widened into a gap, through which glowed another candlestick.

Kit, wearing a velvet robe, appeared in the opening.

"You know, this *is* your house," she reminded him. "You shouldn't have to skulk through the servants' passages—especially if you already insist on a special license."

He closed the secret door back into the wall. "Would you like me to go back and come in through the other door?"

"Certainly not, now that you're already here."

He set the candle down next to the one already burning on the nightstand. Noticing the letter, he glanced at her. "Did you read it?"

She nodded and smiled. "So I suppose I have no choice but to marry you now."

He smiled back. "Oh, such a ghastly fate."

She held out her arms to him. "On the contrary, I find it an utterly glorious fate."

He eagerly sat on the edge of the bed and gathered her close. As Serena twined her arms around his broad shoulders, she felt at once as if she was exactly where she belonged, safe and secure in his warm, loving embrace. She brushed her lips over his ear and across his cheek to his waiting mouth.

After a deep, passionate kiss, he reached into the pocket of his robe. "I have another letter for you. Actually, it's for me, from my father, but I'd like you to read it, too."

She took the letter he drew from his pocket and opened it. "Where did it come from?"

Kit explained his conversation with Eleanor earlier. "Just a few minutes ago I searched the study like she said, and sure enough, I found it at the bottom of a desk drawer. He wrote it the day before he died."

Serena unfolded the letter and began reading.

My dear Christopher,

I've been plagued with frequent pains in my chest of late, which would seem to warn me that I have little time left, and will certainly never see you again. So that I can join your dear mother with peace in my soul, I am writing now to reassure you that I know you are innocent of the terrible accusations that compelled me to purchase for you posthaste a commission abroad. I should have known you were incapable of such heinous behavior, and I pray you can forgive me.

My own foolish pride, coupled with a misplaced obligation to those deemed of greater consequence, prevented me from granting you the benefit of the doubt—indeed, even the Prince of Wales was said to have witnessed what I've since learned was only a false tableau arranged by the real culprit.

The lady whom you were falsely accused of assaulting has been living in our dower house for the past six years under my protection. Though she cannot speak, she managed to personally assure me of your complete innocence and explain how you, like she, became a victim of circumstance.

I humbly concede I should have written you sooner. But the many letters you wrote so faithfully to your grandmother, and which she always shared with us, assured me that you were so content with your situation in India, that you must have put the unfortunate incident behind you. Hence I thought it unnecessary to risk opening old wounds, but again, that was my pride blinding me: I could not bear the notion of confessing to my own child that I had wronged him, out of a baseless fear that that child would no longer respect me.

So I want you to know now, Kit, once and for all, that you have never given me any cause to be dis-

TRUE PRETENSES

appointed in you. I wish I could say as much about my firstborn. I fear he will soon follow me to the grave with his reckless pursuit of what he calls "the three Ds." I believe you will one day be Duke of Fairborough yourself, and that you will bring great honor and dignity to the title.

This must be a short letter as I am not feeling well. But always know, Kit, that I will forever take pride in having you for a son.

Your loving father

Tears welled in Serena's eyes as she glanced up at Kit. "You wept, too, when you read this," she whispered, noting that his eyes did look a little pinkish.

"It was something I'd needed to know for many years. And I do forgive him." He sighed as he gazed at the letter in her lap. "If only I'd thought to rifle through that old desk when I first returned from India, then I could have shown you this letter and I never would have had to play the coachman just to meet you." He favored her with a playful smile. "But you know something, Serena—somehow, I don't think I would have had it any other way."

She laughed softly as she folded the letter and placed it on the bedside table. "Nor would I, my darling."

He took her left hand. "The only thing I would change is this ring. I must get you one of genuine gold."

"This one suits me just as well."

"Wait till it turns your finger the loveliest shade of green, if it hasn't already." With a contented sigh, he took her into his arms again. "I love you so much," he whispered, and gave her a deep kiss.

"I love you, too." She pulled back and grabbed the hem of her night rail. "As a matter of fact, I adore you. And I also want you . . . Kit."

He let out a short breath of delight. "Ah, I love to hear you say my name."

She smiled as she pulled her night rail over her head. "Well, don't you want me, too?" she asked teasingly. "Kit . . . ?"

His eyes widened, and he smiled. Without a word he quickly doffed his robe as she lay back on the bed. He moved on top of her, kissing and caressing her all over as she repeatedly whispered his name.

"Ohh, Kit, yes," she moaned, as his fingers pleasured the very core of her desire for him, till she felt those now familiar waves of ecstasy dashing through her body.

She swept her hungry gaze over his well-built naked body as he knelt between her open thighs. He was about to slide into her when she said, "Wait."

He abruptly stopped, flicking his eyes from one side to the other before looking down at her. "Did I forget something?"

She laughed softly. "No. I was just wondering . . . You said the other day that there were many different ways to do this . . ."

"And you'd like to try one of those different ways?"

She smiled timorously. "Perhaps."

"Well," Kit said, as he slowly rolled over next to her, "we could start by changing places. . . ."

That sounded very interesting, and she awkwardly moved on top of him, her long hair dangling over his face.

"But you have to straddle me," he added helpfully, brushing her hair over her shoulders.

Serena knelt upright, splaying her hands over his muscled chest. "I suppose sidesaddle wouldn't do?"

"Not too easily," he said with a smile, reaching up to fondle her breasts as she slowly lowered herself onto him. She couldn't help the moan that escaped her throat as he filled her with his pulsating masculinity, and she looked down at the darkly thatched juncture where their most intimate parts joined. Seeing that his shaft had disappeared completely, she slowly raised herself to expose about half of it, then slid down again as this time she and Kit moaned in unison.

"Ah, yes, just like that," he gasped, clutching his hands over her breasts. "Just keep rocking like that, sweetling, it feels so da—da—dazzlingly good."

Serena rocked rhythmically on top of him, watching him intently. He gazed back at her, a marvelous expression of pure joy mixed with burgeoning rapture on his handsome face.

"Oh, Kit, I love you," she whispered, and he closed his eyes and began bucking wildly beneath her, nearly unseating her, so to speak, as he climaxed inside her with a long, loud groan.

"Ah, Serena," he gasped, as she collapsed on top of him. "Believe me when I say this is a dream come true. How I do love you, my darling."

She kissed him passionately as she slowly moved her hips upward, releasing his manhood from her tight, slick sheath.

As she rolled over next to him, he said, "I think I've come up with a compromise."

"You just did," she replied, sliding her hand across the hard planes of his chest. "In fact, that's the fourth time you've compromised me—unless you count that kiss in the carriage, and—"

"No, not that sort of compromise." He laughed as he covered her hand with his. "You've claimed that a cathedral and Handel and all that are not important to you, correct?"

"I told you, none of that matters as long as we're married, one way or another. All I want is for Felice and Miriam—"

"Right, so let's ask the bishop to marry us very quickly and quietly, without any fuss, and when Miriam and Jemma return from Scotland with their respective bridegrooms, we'll have a lavish ball to celebrate all three marriages."

She sat upright and flung her long hair over her shoulders, allowing him a clear view of her breasts. "Oh, Kit, I think that's a wonderful idea—especially since Jemma and Miriam aren't having traditional nuptials, either."

"It will be just like a great big wedding, only without the exchange of vows—or if you like, perhaps we could exchange them yet again, just for the sport of it."

She smiled and leaned down to kiss him. "I like that very much, indeed. And in our case, it would be our third time exchanging vows. 'Tis said the third time is always the charm."

"Just so we exchange the second set of vows before my birthday."

She idly teased the hair on his chest. "That's still two months away, so there's plenty of time. But your cousin shouldn't be able to collect that trust fund in his present situation, should he?"

"No, but I don't want to wait any longer to marry you properly." Kit gifted her with a weary smile. "I've never really wanted that money, Serena—I just didn't want Calvin to have it. I'm going to spread it among the servants and estate workers, to improve their living standards. One month as a coachman quite opened my eyes to how they live."

"I love that idea, too, in which case I'm only too happy to marry you before your birthday." She rested her head on his chest. "But we still need to bring Felice here as soon as possible."

"We'll do that at once. And she won't have to be hidden away in a cottage, nor will your aunt, if she doesn't want to. They'll be free to roam Fairborough to their hearts' content."

"But Felice will be most content just to draw pictures." Serena lifted her head and gazed into his warm brown eyes. "Kit, will you come with me to fetch her?"

He stroked his hand over her hair. "My dear, I wouldn't dream of letting you go back there without me. This time, you *will* ride in Fairborough's coach with Fairborough."

She smiled. "Not just this time, darling, but from this day forward, so long as we both shall live."

Kit gave Serena the most tender of kisses before adding, "But from now on, someone else will have to drive the coach."

Karen Lingefelt

The Duke and Duchess of Fairborough
request the honour of your presence
at a celebration of his thirtieth birthday
and the respective marriages
of
Christopher Woodard and Serena Langley
Hamish Dunbar and Jemma Langley
Edward Jennings and Miriam Evans

Friday, the tenth of September
Eighteen hundred and thirteen
at seven o'clock in the evening
Woodard House, Park Lane, London

R.S.V.P.

PERILS OF THE HEART
JENNIFER ASHLEY

Sent to seduce the captain of the merchantman *Aurora*, Evangeline Clemens trembles in her innocence. Her stepbrother's life—and the life of the rugged sailor she must tempt—depends on her success. She swears to surrender her body, her virtue... but she never expects to relinquish her heart.

Austin Blackwell suspects the timid temptress is a skilled spy ordered to sabotage his plans. She plays the part of an untried miss to perfection. But after sampling her sweetness, the commander vows to navigate any course to discover the truth. For his soul mutinies at the prospect of sailing into the future without the lady by his side.

Dorchester Publishing Co., Inc.
P.O. Box 6640   ____5133-8
Wayne, PA 19087-8640   **$5.99 US/$7.99 CAN**

Please add $2.50 for shipping and handling for the first book and $.75 for each book thereafter. NY and PA residents, please add appropriate sales tax. No cash, stamps, or C.O.D.s. Prices and availibility subject to change.

Canadian orders require $2.00 extra postage and must be paid in U.S. dollars through a U.S. banking facility.

Name _____
Address _____
City _____ State _____ Zip _____
E-mail _____
I have enclosed $_____ in payment for the checked book(s).
Payment <u>must</u> accompany all orders. ❑ Please send a free catalog.

CHECK OUT OUR WEBSITE! www.dorchesterpub.com

THE MAD MARQUIS
FIONA CARR

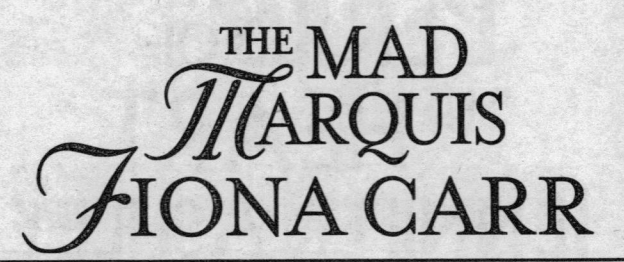

Julia Westfall is being forced into marriage—with her fiercest rival on the hunt field. True, Henry Pelham is her secret dream. But what the widowed marquis proposes is hardly suitable—a loveless union with no children. A woman who races her own stallions for the thrill and challenge of it can hardly be expected to rein in her passion.

Her new husband believes that madness runs in his family; that siring more offspring will be irresponsible. But Julia will show him that the craziest thing he can do is spurn her advances. For her most exciting and dashing competitor on horseback will soon be her most potent and powerful match in the bedroom.

Dorchester Publishing Co., Inc.
P.O. Box 6640 ___5186-9
Wayne, PA 19087-8640 $5.99 US/$7.99 CAN

Please add $2.50 for shipping and handling for the first book and $.75 for each book thereafter. NY and PA residents, please add appropriate sales tax. No cash, stamps, or C.O.D.s. Prices and availability subject to change.

Canadian orders require $2.00 extra postage and must be paid in U.S. dollars through a U.S. banking facility.

Name_____
Address_____
City_____ State_____ Zip_____
E-mail _____
I have enclosed $_____ in payment for the checked book(s).
Payment <u>must</u> accompany all orders. __Check here for a free catalog.

CHECK OUT OUR WEBSITE! www.dorchesterpub.com

NO PLACE FOR A LADY
KATHERINE GREYLE

The rookeries are slums, but an assassination is being planned there and Marcus Kane, Lord Chadwick, will not be able to navigate the labyrinthine underworld alone. His time spying in France is not experience enough; he will require a partner.

Fantine Delarive has survived the street for years and knows its every criminal. Though that makes her entirely unsuitable as one of his acquaintances, Miss Fanny fits in everywhere the investigation leads—even the crushes of the *ton*. Marcus thought his heart, like the rookeries, no place for a well-born lady, but Fantine is perfect in both. He vows to end with nothing less than her hand in marriage.

Dorchester Publishing Co., Inc.
P.O. Box 6640   __5202-4
Wayne, PA 19087-8640 $5.99 US/$7.99 CAN

Please add $2.50 for shipping and handling for the first book and $.75 for each book thereafter. NY and PA residents, please add appropriate sales tax. No cash, stamps, or C.O.D.s. Prices and availability subject to change. Canadian orders require $2.00 extra postage and must be paid in U.S. dollars through a U.S. banking facility.

Name _____
Address _____
City _____ State _____ Zip _____
E-mail _____
I have enclosed $_____ in payment for the checked book(s).
Payment <u>must</u> accompany all orders. ❑Check here for a free catalog.

CHECK OUT OUR WEBSITE! www.dorchesterpub.com

Major Wyclyff's Campaign
KATHERINE GREYLE

Pity, plain and simple, makes Sophia accept the offer of marriage from the dying Major Anthony Wyclyff. He is wildly handsome, but nothing will overcome her happiness at being "shelved." Then the blasted man recovers! Not that she wishes anyone ill, but Sophia expected to bury the earl's son along with all her childish hopes and dreams—not tumble with him in the dirt. He is resolved to claim his bride, though, and he forces her into a strategic retreat, to act in ways she never dreamed. His flanking attack brings him closer than ever—into her manor, her parlor, her bedroom—and the infuriating officer wagers he'll have terms of surrender within the month! Yet when his fiery kiss saps her defenses, Sophia swears the only terms she'll hear are those of love.

Dorchester Publishing Co., Inc.
P.O. Box 6640
Wayne, PA 19087-8640

__4920-1
$4.99 US/$5.99

Please add $2.50 for shipping and handling for the first book and $.75 for each additional book. NY and PA residents, add appropriate sales tax. No cash, stamps, or CODs. Canadian orders require $5.00 for shipping and handling and must be paid in U.S. dollars. Prices and availability subject to change. **Payment must accompany all orders.**

Name: _____

Address: _____

City: _____ State: _____ Zip: _____

E-mail: _____

I have enclosed $_____ in payment for the checked book(s).

For more information on these books, check out our website at www.dorchesterpub.com.
____ Please send me a free catalog.

Rules For A Lady
Katherine Greyle

A lady does not attempt to come out in London society disguised as her deceased half-sister. A lady does not become enamored of her guardian, even though his masterful kisses and whispered words of affection tempt her beyond all endurance. A lady may not climb barefoot from her bedroom on a rose trellis, nor engage in fisticuffs with riffraff in order to rescue street urchins. No matter how impossible the odds, a lady always gives her hand and her heart—though not necessarily in that order—to the one man who sees her as she truly is and loves her despite her flagrant disobedience of every one of the rules for a lady.

___4818-3 $4.99 US/$5.99 CAN

Dorchester Publishing Co., Inc.
P.O. Box 6640
Wayne, PA 19087-8640

Please add $2.50 for shipping and handling for the first book and $.75 for each book thereafter. NY, NYC, and PA residents, please add appropriate sales tax. No cash, stamps, or C.O.D.s. All orders shipped within 6 weeks via postal service book rate. Canadian orders require $2.00 extra postage and must be paid in U.S. dollars through a U.S. banking facility.

Name_____
Address_____
City_____ State_____ Zip_____
I have enclosed $ _____ in payment for the checked book(s).
Payment <u>must</u> accompany all orders.☐Please send a free catalog.
CHECK OUT OUR WEBSITE! www.dorchesterpub.com

ATTENTION
BOOK LOVERS!

Can't get enough of your favorite **ROMANCE**?

Call **1-800-481-9191** to:

✷ order books,

✷ receive a **FREE** catalog,

✷ join our book clubs to **SAVE 20%!**

Open Mon.-Fri. 10 AM-9 PM EST

Visit **www.dorchesterpub.com**
for special offers and inside
information on the authors you love.

We accept Visa, MasterCard or Discover®.

LEISURE BOOKS ♥ LOVE SPELL